CW00818715
RED
ROYAL
A PAS
DARLING
NOVEL
"Is it another one of those
trashy books?"
- Lola's Mom
USA TODAY BESTSELLING AUTHOR
LOLA ROCK

LOLA
ROCK

First published by Lola Rock in 2023

Ebook ISBN: 9781959927082
Paperback ISBN: 9781959927075

5764 N Orange Blossom Trl, PMB 68820
Orlando, FL 32810
thelolarock.com

This is an original work of fiction.

No artificial intelligence was used in the creation of this work or in its accompanying art.

VIBE CHECK

Redfang Royal is technically a standalone novel, but it follows the events and tone of the first Pack Darling books, featuring a mish-mash of heavier themes and humor.

This omegaverse is neither sweet and healing, nor gratuitously dark. It falls somewhere in the middle, depending on your taste.

For the updated list of tags and triggers, please visit Redfang Royal's book page on

thelolarock.com/shop

Please reach out to me or phone a friend if you have any other concerns about the content.

I only want you to read books that make you happy!

<3 Lola

IF NOT FOR the security cameras, I would've dropped out of the morning run the second my boots filled with blood.

But I'm always being watched, always being judged, so I jog twenty feet behind the other field agents, pretending I'm just like them—shiny toy soldiers who *want* to be made into walking weapons

"Speed up!" Our squad captain's voice whips back with the sour, sweaty pheromones of the "teammates" I despise as much as I hate doing cardio before dawn.

I'd kill for a blanket and a breakfast sandwich.

While the gamma squad picks up their pace in perfect sync, I drag my ass behind, not because I can't match the speed, but because even with the gap, their pheromones leave my scent glands prickling, ready to lash the hell out and shatter my good girl mask

Puffing, sweating, ignoring the squish of sock blood and the metal monitors scraping my ankles with each step, I force my head down and my pheromones down harder.

I'm in control.

I have to be in control.

We're miles into our loop and I'm wondering about ankle replacement surgery when the sun finally finds the base, peeking over the forest cliffs that hide the military bunkers and secret research labs where the Special Abilities Section makes its very classified home.

Five years after my forced enlistment, I still don't know what branch of the government claims the SAS.

Don't want to know.

They can keep their secrets.

I just want out.

But between fences tipped in razor wire, my electric ankle bangles, and four counts of semi-accidental murder that leadership can hold over me forever, my life options are prison-with-bars or prison-with-salutes. I have to play by their rules and prove I can pass as a civilian if I'm ever going to be discharged.

When I try to imagine where I'll go when I'm finally free, the first answer is *anywhere.*

The second is the broke-down baseball field that I'm not allowed to visit, even in my dreams.

I'll never belong running laps in camo and combat boots, but it's not like I've ever belonged.

The orphanage, foster care, the Omega Cultivation Center.

People sense when you don't fit in, even if they don't know why, and no matter where you are, leftovers get chucked.

I was four when my blood test results came back strange. The doctors thought I was a beta, but with an asterisk—maybe genetic defects

Nope. Wish I were a beta.

Or even a normal omega.

Try getting adopted when no one knows what you are.

The families shopping for daughters sneered and treated me like shit. I spent a few years crying in corners before I realized the girls who smiled widest were the ones who found forever homes

Never had much reason to smile, but I learned to fake it with the best.

Soon as I mastered swallowing the hurt, playing submissive and stupid, *bam.*

A family finally wanted me.

Yeah, my new home turned out worse than being orphaned,

but you have to believe in pushing forward when your past is a yawning suckhole.

That's why I keep faking.

That's why I keep running.

Just smile through the pain, lock down my freak powers, and wait to be cut loose, dropped into another gauntlet I'll have to fight to survive.

I don't expect a break 'til I'm dead.

Even then, I bet I have to run the same hamster wheel in hell and tell the assholes with the pitchforks how much I'm enjoying the steam.

I'm so focused on maintaining the distance between me and the others, maintaining the pace and the appearance of perfect compliance, I don't realize we're off course until I'm rocked by the invisible fence.

Lightning fries me from ankle to ass.

I swallow a frothy scream, cracking my tailbone on asphalt hard enough to hear color.

An angry, red buzz.

Leaking a groan, I roll away from the barrier I should never have let sneak up on me. My shins burn and my toes twist, every muscle shuddering with aftershocks.

Petty laughter echoes through my pain.

"Freak!" Elyse calls from the head of the column, sounding more like a tween mean girl than a twenty-something special operative

The insult doesn't sting as much as the atomic pins-and-needles

I shouldn't have let myself think about that baseball field, even for a misguided second—because then I think about *them* and the one time I *wanted* to be the real me, and the fire that I keep so carefully smothered refuses to stay banked.

I snarl.

The rolling sound is tipped in razors.

Between anger and electric shock, my control shatters.

My pheromones break their leash.

The squad senses the change—some shift in the air or my aura —and survival instincts leave alphas quaking in their tac gear.

Their laughter cuts.

The cowards scatter.

Because for the handful of seconds it takes me to pull my shit together, to reel in my scent and straighten my mask, the squad finally remembers why mine's the only special ability that needs to be muzzled.

It's quiet when their boot-falls fade. Just my ragged breath and the birds chirping beyond the fence.

Lucky I didn't pass out this time.

But the ultimate insult?

Now I need to recharge my manacles.

I consider rolling into the road and camping on the double-yellow line, but it's too early for traffic, and when I die, I'm dragging the base with me to hell.

Everyone but Gary—the beta who works the grill at the mess hall.

He's good people. Puts extra Swiss on my egg and cheese sammies

Knowing leadership is watching, I don't let myself wallow. I work from a crawl to a limp to a lopsided speed-walk, veering back to the main road to finish the circuit.

Nobody can claim I was slacking.

Weight room is next on the morning training schedule, but I hobble past the gym to the medical building. My ankles are shredded, and my legs are jellied. I want an ice pack for my ass before I fake my way through dead lift.

I reach for the door, but a body barrels through before I can brace or even blink.

Rocked by a mountain of military alpha, I go down, legs kicking out like a drunk baby donkey's.

Boosh.

I eat a second helping of sidewalk, head spinning 'til I see stars and stripes, and in a moment of pile-driven, post-electroshock stupidity, I slip up.

A microburst of toxic pheromones squeezes free. Then a ragged, awful retch warns that this guy's about to spray me in half-digested mess hall bacon.

Not again.

I spider-scramble out of his blast zone.

The alpha gags, eyes watering and bloodshot.

I force deep breaths, pulling my escaped scent back to pheromone zero. He only caught a whiff, but that's more than enough to screw months of work pretending I'm not a threat.

Shit. Damage control.

"Take off your shirt." I claw to my feet.

"Fucking freak." The guy hocks bile and starts to strip, ripping off body armor and holsters, whimpering and muttering. "Rotten eggs—" *Cough.* "Ugh. Fuckin'… Eggs and rotten horse meat."

I freeze, almost more concerned for him than me.

But only *almost.* "Why do you know what horse meat smells like?"

The guy ignores me, ripping off shirt, cargo pants, and then *what a wild Friday morning* because his tighty-whities go flying like I just did. He one-eighties into the building for an emergency shower with zero thought of apologizing—just a sausage salute and a flash of fuzzy ass.

I'd feel worse for pheromone-assaulting the guy, but now my tailbone is made of many small, powdery pieces of tailbone.

Plus, I've read the training materials that tell the SAS agents how to handle this kind of run-in with "Gamma 026."

I'm not at any point referred to as a person.

Avoid close contact with Subject Gamma 026, donning chemical masks and protective gear when in proximity. If contaminated in the subject's pheromone cloud, proceed immediately to decontamination and follow all grey alert protocols per hazmat regulations.

I'd rather be called a spicy omega.

But the SAS needs gamma to be a new sub-gender if they want

to collect that sweet government research funding. So, leadership finds, tests, and trains potential gammas like me—omegas with asterisks—keeping a chokehold on the elite few of us who actually awaken weird abilities.

Problem is, my ability came out a little *too* weird.

Too dangerous

I'm the freak among the freaks.

So much for this season of *Marisol-is-a-responsible-citizen* theater.

Now I'm tasting gastric juice cocktail.

We all know that collision was an honest accident.

Right?

That's a thing that we all know?

I brush my scraped palms, ready to scatter before the guys in plastic suits show up to spray the pathway with descenter.

Just keep moving forward.

I do move.

Almost one full step before karma has another cackle at my expense

Because Commander Bridget Fissure—beloved commander, perfect gamma, and the biological mother responsible for my pheromonal curse—marches into the toxic air of this godsforsook morning

Training uniform crisp. Posture ninety degrees. Scent as sweet and cloying as high-fructose corn syrup.

She struts out of the building like she's shooting a recruiting pamphlet. Meanwhile, I'm rumpled, bleeding, and rubbing my aching ass like a weird, guilty raccoon.

Bridget's regal gaze tilts, and a micro-flinch works her porcelain cheek, communicating shame, disgust, and loathing in a single stomach-stomping flicker.

Like she knows the depraved fanfics I have bookmarked, wishes I would stop appropriating government air, and disapproves of every facet of my existence from my disheveled blonde hair to the whacky fucking ability that spills the otherwise secret of my birth.

Hierarchy requires me to greet her, but I can't force a clipped "Commander" out of my choked throat.

She knows I'm her daughter.

I don't think she knows *I know*, because she's never acknowledged me, but some genetic data got left out during one of my sessions at the lab. That's how I connected the dots on why I was sent to an orphanage at birth.

Mom is the government's golden girl.

Dad runs a cartel.

She went into heat on an undercover mission, and *bam*.

Twenty-four years later, I'm still her biggest regret.

And that flinch.

Like I'm the one causing her the pain.

Like I *chose* to exist.

I didn't choose any of this, but here I am, pretending to be anyone but me, trying to live to bluff another day.

Still hurts like a foul ball to the throat.

But I don't need Bridget's love. Just her signature, clearing me to leave

Should be easy.

She's a pro at tossing me away.

"Twenty-Six," she barks, quick to regain composure, even though her candy-sweet scent sours every time she's forced to look my way. "You assaulted an agent."

"I—"

"No excuses," she snaps. "Report to the lab for control assessment."

Anger prickles my armpits, warning that my scent glands are ready to riot.

I must shift wrong, because Bridget reaches for the pocket where she carries my controller.

We both know she'll hit the button, and even without recharging, my manacles have more than enough juice for two more jolts.

Up to four, actually.

Don't ask how I know.

I clench my jaw and tighten my shoulders, forcing down the urge to challenge her authority. The first and only time I ever flexed on Bridget, her mates stomped me so hard they dislocated my shoulders.

Then I was treated to a six-month, all-inclusive vacation on the prison level.

Never again

The anger, the hate, the powerlessness and pain.

I shove them down to deal with later, someday far in the future, when I find a way to live that doesn't make me want to punch myself in the face.

Feels like sticking the pin back in the grenade.

Won't stop the explosion—just delay.

But it's the best I can do, and it's good enough when I find my fake smile, straightening my heels and throwing a perfect salute. "Yes, Commander."

Her lips thin.

I don't wait for more orders.

I run so fast, I'd smoke the squad. So pissed I can't feel a twinge of pain, even though I move like a fast zombie, fueled by spite

It's getting harder to fake being good.

Harder and harder to smile and walk away.

Stay in control.

I have to keep myself on the leash.

Because if they ever meet the real Marisol?

I'll never be free.

TWO
SOL

MY WAX SMILE strains when I'm buzzed into the lab. An alpha squad waits in the foyer, faces hidden behind hazmat gear, and the tips of their rifles lift to say hello.

If there weren't special agents crouched around the pillars and potted ferns, the place would look like your average office building on TV. But no employees dash past with coffee.

Leadership clears the floor when I'm summoned.

I don't mind.

The bad memories and red dots on my jacket are plenty of company

A shudder slips through my facade.

The lab is where I woke up in military custody after the worst night of my life. Covered in blood, coming down from the drugs that forced me into the only heat I'll ever have.

I was so confused.

Hurt.

And worst of all, realizing I'm not just broken—I was never whole from the start.

The past stays in the past. Keep moving forward.

Ignoring the guns and the guards' stress pheromones scraping my throat, I glide across the lobby like I'm here to ace my job interview.

But the elevator hits me with a retinal scan because I'm not heading to human resources.

I am human resources.

The ride takes me deep into bunker territory, where another waspy, off-putting buzz lets me through the blast door to the mad science lab.

Doctor Brandon Fissure meets me wearing a plexi-front gas mask that flashes blue eyes and lips twisted in disdain.

He's in his late forties, with grey wings in his dark hair. I'd say he was distinguished professor handsome if he treated me as anything other than a specimen he'd like to slice, dice, and store in a labeled jar.

All five of Bridget's mates are stupid hot silver foxes.

And her *real* kids are adorable.

"Go through decontamination." Brandon jerks his chin, directing me into the clean room.

Shitsticks.

I hate this part.

I step into the narrow sanitation chamber, close my eyes, and hold my breath. After the door suctions, the human car wash whirs, spraying me in a cloud of industrial de-scenter that vents into the filtration system like I'm patient zero for the zombie plague

My training clothes are soaked when the maelstrom cuts. Then the opposite door unsticks, and I wobble through, perching on my special stool so that Brandon's assistant, Thad, can plug in my ankle monitors and draw my blood.

I keep my arm steady while the beta trembles. He's stuck me hundreds of times, and I've never done shit to retaliate.

The lab techs are all skittish—they've seen me in action.

After Thad scurries away with a fresh-tapped vial, Brandon looms. His full-body biohazard gear blocks the worst of his scent, but a hit of piney alpha sneaks free.

Just enough to clench my throat.

I hate alphas' scents as much as they always hate mine.

"Elyse's mate may have permanently lost his sense of smell." Brandon folds his arms over his plastic suit in disappointment faker than my smiles. "I assume the attack was out of jealousy."

Jealousy?

Me?

Holy hand grenades do I deserve the best actress award if Brandon thinks I run on anything but egg and cheese and endgame revenge.

Besides. I didn't know the guy was Elyse's.

How could I?

The girl bonds new mates like she's popping mints, and to me, every alpha on base looks like an identical, wide-shouldered, soldier-Chad.

"So you can't explain yourself," Brandon says flatly.

"No!" I almost jump, but somehow I grip the stool and keep my boots on the ground. "I didn't attack. I ran into him. Neither of us was paying attention and—"

"Your control is flawless? If that were the case, how could your actions be anything but deliberate?"

"Check the CCTV," I grit. "It was not deliberate."

I grip the stool.

Deep breaths.

Can't give him proof I'm the monster he wants me to be.

"We'll run a full assessment," Brandon says. "No grounds access until you demonstrate that you're not a danger to our personnel. I know I'll have your full cooperation."

Acid surges from my stomach, possibly dissolving a chunk of my tongue. Doctor Brandon watches me through the plastic protection of his gas mask.

He doesn't have to say a thing.

He knows I don't have a choice.

Can't escape.

Can't say no.

I grip my high collar, forever loyal to the lies that are the only way I'll ever escape this shithole. "I'll cooperate."

"I'll prepare the test subjects. Change and get ready for testing." Brandon swishes away, leaving me with a guard detail of alpha enforcers armed for a rabid were-bear. Thad drops a pile of dry clothes like he's tossing beef shanks into the raptor cage.

Welcome to lab rat life.

I'm back to full-time observation, fun times with my besties, the military prisoners, and daily pin-cushioning with Brandon's experimental drugs.

The treatment isn't because I bumped into the wrong guy and accidentally dented his central nervous system.

It's because Brandon dives on any flimsy excuse to drag me back under his microscope.

I'll beat his test.

I'll beat all his tests and prove I'm ready to be free.

But I want to groan over the bundled tracksuit.

In a lot of ways, I'm not an omega.

The instincts don't ride me the way they should, and I haven't smelled an alpha who didn't make me itch, cringe, or want to hurl since I was fifteen.

I tried to be an omega.

I wanted it so hard during the OCC years. Four years of being bullied and learning to fight back, and they were the best of my life because I finally had hope.

I had a vision board with the pack and the nest and four names doodled with pink hearts.

That was a few lifetimes and upheavals ago—a version of myself who feels so distant, I think that Sol was some other girl.

One who had cute little dreams.

Now my dreams are pure practicality.

I want skin for my ankles, my own washing machine, and a job working with kids. Maybe run my own daycare. Be a teacher or a softball coach.

What I don't want?

Alphas.

Because there's no attraction.

No spark

All I've got is a killer scent that puts them on the ground.

I'll never have real mates, another heat, or my dream pack, and I've mostly buried my basic omega fantasies.

But even now, a teeny bit of not-so-gamma instinct survives.

Changing in front of an audience is pure omega torture, making me feel all kinds of raw and vulnerable.

I've mastered the rapid-change, stripping off de-scenter-soaked clothes and swapping them without flashing more than an inch of skin, but even that leaves me shuddering.

I zip the track jacket to my chin.

I hate being uncovered more than I hate cardio.

When I swap socks, I hiss.

The ankle monitors are strappy metal and way too tight. Always scabbing, rubbing, and oozing blood. But the faster I get through this gauntlet, the faster I can take the weight off my feet, hide under a sheet, and turn off my hyper-vigilant control long enough to take a full breath.

When I'm changed, the guard squad herds me down the hall, keeping their distance even though they're masked for an outbreak and outweigh me by a collective ton.

I walk like an innocent omega, all scrunched and submissive, pretending to be intimidated, but I've been through these bolted doors a hundred times before. I'm not usually the one who ends up on the floor.

Brandon's dispassionate voice sounds through the speaker system. "Proceed to the first interrogation room."

Breathing in through my nose and out through my mouth, I force myself into calm control mode.

Scent assessment is cake when I'm not freshly electrocuted.

The first door buzzes unlocked.

The SAS doesn't hold prisoners like the cop shows, where they sit a guy at a card table and offer him coffee in a paper cup.

The interrogation room is a cement square with a bolted-down chair and an alpha waiting for me in a jumpsuit and chains

He shifts, clanking metal. Unwashed and unshaven, he pumps

out stress pheromones in a gag-inducing mix of anger, despair, and steaming bat guano.

Blech

Have to get this over with so I can shower.

"Begin," Brandon commands through the speakers.

I take a step, carefully loosening the full-body tension that I'm always maintaining to keep my pheromones on lock. The one good thing about my ability is that I *can* control it—not like a factory-issue omega, helplessly pumping out scent with every emotion

I can push and pull my perfume—if you can call it that—at will.

But it's a muscle I have to train.

The trick is to never fully let go, unless I want to up my body count

I release the pressure hand-over-hand, like I'm slowly lowering a heavy rope, never letting the momentum build to a crash

My pheromones bleed into the air.

"The fu—" the prisoner gags.

I jump back with superhuman vomit-dodging reflexes.

He spits on the floor, shooting me a familiar red-eyed glare that's *so* unwarranted when I'm working so hard to keep him breathing that I can time my pulse by the throb of the vein at my temple

Brandon's clinical voice joins the party. "Describe the scent you're experiencing."

"You fucking kidding me?" Tears run down the chained alpha's cheeks.

Experience has me retreating to the wall, clear of loogie-hawking distance "If you need another hit—"

"No." A hard flinch rattles his chains. "Fuck, no."

"Then describe the scent so we can both get out of here." I bite back my pheromones, already dreading hearing how my scent reminds him of the worst moment of his life.

"Moth balls." The prisoner goes glaze-eyed. "Dust. Nan's sweaters. The blood. Fuck. They killed her. I hid and they—"

I tune out his trauma until Brandon gives the all-clear. "Next subject."

I bolt from the room, skin clammy.

The prisoner behind door number two says I smell like diesel and ash

Number three says unwashed pubes.

Just what every girl wants to hear.

That's why I can never see my dream pack again.

Never, ever, ever, and never even then.

I wouldn't survive them gagging, saying I smell like dead fish or grave dirt, or whatever terrible trauma my scent unearths.

Watching the boys I've always loved give me the same wrinkled nose, *who-let-in-the-freak* glare that everyone's shot me since the orphanage?

Nope.

We will not be doing that.

My chances of being with them were bad enough before my perfume came in—when I was a weird, stinky kid with a shaved head and no friends.

Freaking pheromones.

One whiff can change your life.

Like, meet your meant-to-be mate and *boom*. New worldview, new priorities, and rabid new instincts to bite and claim, to protect and love.

Bridget can manipulate her pheromones to smell like anyone's fated mate, so she's instantly adored wherever she descends

I'm the opposite.

Pure poison, hated everywhere.

Which makes sense. I smell like your personal nightmare and my side effects make me sound like one of those sketchy drug commercials

WARNING: Marisol may cause stinging pain, paralysis, heartburn, hallucinations, projectile vomit, foaming saliva, permanent loss of erection, and EVEN DEATH.

I'm basically a cobra with airborne venom, and the only reason I'm not permanently caged is that Team Fissure doesn't know how easily I can kill.

They think I have to work to use my ability.

In reality, I'm working twenty-four seven to keep myself leashed

They're alive, so I'm clearly doing gangbusters, but I'm not a machine

By the seventh test subject, my neck aches from the strain of keeping control. My jaw and shoulders go tight as cold rubber.

I'm stupidly relieved when Brandon summons me back to the lab. Then I spot his syringe cart, and the air roars between my ears

This is going to suck.

Knowing the drill way too well, I fake-obediently climb onto the exam table, trying to ignore the sound of clinking vials. "What are you testing now?"

Brandon makes a *don't-distract-me* hum. His blunt fingernail pings glass, and I fight to hide my flinch.

"Unzip," he orders.

I dry heave.

With shaking fingers, I tug my zipper and shrug the track jacket around my shoulders, feeling sick when my throat's exposed to raw air.

Brandon swipes alcohol over my scars.

I grip the table while he prods my scent glands through the red, ragged skin of what used to be my neck.

The marks tunnel down my throat to the base of my left shoulder

They're not from teeth.

They're from my nails.

From when I clawed out the bites.

I clawed out the bond and the scabs, bleeding and digging for weeks to erase the marks of the dead alphas who thought they could make me theirs.

"Lie flat." Brandon's woodsy scent is hidden under his hazmat suit, but my leftover instincts don't ever want another alpha in my space.

Don't want anyone seeing, touching, or *thinking about* my throat.

But if I don't want to be caged again, all I can do is comply and keep hiding my truth. I lie face-down, controlling my pheromones by a fraying thread.

"Hold still." He braces the back of my head and hits the plunger.

The needle stings, fire in my tender skin, but the heat only lasts a flash before it flares to ice.

Three seconds, and I'm shaking.

My neck goes numb and starbursts of frost form snowflakes in my veins.

"Hold still," he barks, pressing until my nose flattens against the hard-padded tabletop.

My flesh crawls—fire ants gnaw my neck and swim the six-legged breaststroke in my blood.

I can't hold still when he's touching me, when all I want to do is throw him off and teach him who the hell he's messing with, but one wrong move and I won't just be strapped to the table

I'll spend the rest of my life captive, a weapon that won't get to decide when or how to pull my own trigger.

I breathe through my flattened nose.

I've faked it this long.

Don't lose your shit now.

My teeth are chattering when he finally lets me free.

"Any effects?" Brandon steps away, quick to put distance between us

"C-c-cold." I wrench my zipper up my throat.

"To be expected." He makes a note. "Anything else?"

"Dizzy." I grab my temple, not sure if the spin is vertigo or shiver shakes.

While the room rotates, I sniff myself, trying to figure out what Brandon shot me with. Sometimes he pumps me with familiar pheromones—the gammas, omegas, or even alphas I've scented around base—so I can practice emitting different flavors.

Sometimes they're my mother's pheromones.

Gag.

But whatever chemical has my teeth chattering doesn't reek of Bridget's chemical sugar.

I smell neutral. After a car wash in de-scenter, I'm all clean skin and industrial dryer sheets.

"Dizziness noted." Brandon gestures to the bunker door of his private underground prison. "Let's see how you do in cell three. I want the subjects incapacitated as quickly as possible. Understand?"

"I understand."

After the door clangs, I brace against the wall, shaking. The freezing teeth fade, leaving behind a full-body prickle and a spinning hyper-awareness that something's deeply wrong and getting wronger.

Past the chill, there's a weird foreboding. Like my blood's been switched for slushy rocket fuel.

My heartbeat taps faster and faster and faster.

The muscles I've spent years training go limp.

My scent flares before I can react.

Through grit and clenched muscles, I force the pheromones down, but the rope I've clutched so tightly for so long is slicked in grease.

My neck crawls.

Another blast of scent slips, and my muscles don't respond to commands.

I stumble, horrified.

I don't know if the formula is a muscle relaxer or some weird ability super-booster.

All I know is I'm screwed worse than whoever's in that cell.
Stay in control.
Have to stay in control.
I'll bite through my tongue before I drop my act.
I won't surrender.
No matter how hard leadership sets me up to fail.

THREE
SOL

"ACCELERANT TEST PROCEED," Brandon's voice crackles.

I move robotically. Rigid, clenching like I'm holding in a devastating fart. But if I let my pheromones rip, I'll get worse than dirty looks.

Shitbricks.

Last time I visited the prison cells, I was shot up with some omega's french toast pheromones and delivered like a continental breakfast to twenty alphas who lunged for my throat.

But Brandon doesn't want me dead.

He wants me desperate.

Desperate enough to snap.

Then he can justify keeping me forever.

We've been playing this game for years—him pushing, me fighting—and today is not the day I lose.

"Enter."

The door buzzes.

I tighten every muscle. Jaw. Neck. Both sets of cheeks.

Need to stay tight. Need to fight but not kill—even if I have to eat an ass-kicking to win.

"Enter," Brandon repeats. This time, my ankle monitors chirp, warning me to stop stalling.

Motherfuck.

Before Brandon can make me sizzle, I slip inside the cell. I try to prop the door, but it sucks back into the frame with that evil buzz

Four alphas unfold from the corner.

Not cuffed or bound.

Pulse in my ears, I keep my back to the wall, adjusting to the dimness of the cell and desperately biting back the superpowered pheromones that want to erase years of my perfect lies.

No ventilation here.

The cell is so stained with old fear, I can't pick up their scents until the biggest guy steps forward.

He smells like black licorice, spiked with alpha anger, and his trash-can-lid hands are webbed in prison tats.

"Who the fuck are you?" The packleader puffs out his chest. "Omega?"

He takes another step, heavy with threat.

Keeping him alive is like trying to stop a rocket with the unraveling cord of my control.

You have to be a special kind of evil to end up in the SAS prison, but I don't care what these guys did.

I'm not playing executioner.

Control.

Shit on a biscuit.

Reel it in, Sol.

I'd give anything to go back in time, to be back at the OCC where my brawls were with omegas afraid to chip their nails, and my go-to weapon was a softball bat.

Where at least one person always had my back.

Now instead of proving you shouldn't mess with my textbooks, I have to prove I'm not a killer.

Only, I *am* a killer.

The alphas' nostrils flare, and an ominous growl rumbles. I shift my feet, ready to take this hand-to-hand.

They can try to break me all they want.

I'll never break my act.

"Wait." A goateed alpha yanks the packleader's arm. "Isn't she.."

They freeze.

Not pause*freeze* and suddenly I'm not the only one clenching cheeks.

"*Princess?* The tatted packleader's voice lifts three octaves from his snarl. "They caught you too?"

I'm no princess.

What I am is on my own with four big dudes bad enough to get ganked by special forces.

I'll say what I have to say to survive. "Bastard fucking Brandon brought me in."

I never realized there's a difference when an alpha snarls at you and for you, but their rumbles hit different when they're in my defense. The prickle at my neck fades, and if I weren't afraid of frying their brain stems, my shoulders might even droop.

So weird

These guys are full-on mafia soldiers.

Enforcer height, tattoos, and the threatening kind of movement that warns they know how to use their bulk for max damage

Guys like my half-brothers—Dominik, Erik, and the whole rest of the gangland side of my fam.

Speaking of family…

Now my skin prickle has nothing to do with pheromones.

"Boss'll go apeshit." The guy in the corner rolls the sleeves of his prison jumpsuit.

Red snake scales coil his forearm. His sleeve tattoo covers his bicep, but my bubbling gut knows the pattern tapers into a crimson, snarling cobra.

Redfangs.

Shit on a blackened biscuit with a schmear of anal jelly.

"Princess. Are you thirsty? Do you want to sit?" The alpha with arms wider than my head pulls a steamy, suspect bottle of water from his waistband.

I'm plastered to the back wall, reeling.

I have dozens of half-brothers because my father is both a kingpin and a slut, but far as I know, I only have one sister.

We've never met, and hopefully never will, because she already ruined my life.

We look alike.

Like scary, twinsy, fool-my-father's-goons alike.

She's why I was kidnapped from the OCC.

She's why I was gift-wrapped to an alpha pack—the store brand version of the cartel princess they could never hope to mate

So she's why I was drugged—forced into the heat that awakened my freak pheromones and obliterated my heart-ringed dreams

Suddenly, I'm hot.

No more ice, but flames.

All heat and blood and smoke.

That night.

That *fucking night.*

I can barely see the cell.

I'm lost

Shaking.

Sweating.

Sick.

Remembering the pain and the fire.

Snapping teeth and heat, fury and fear.

All my sister's fucking fault.

"Yo." The one with the water bottle squints. "That's not the princess"

Their growls shift.

Their gazes harden

"Her hair's wrong. And the eyes."

"Tits are too big." The smallest slurps his lips.

The schnasty sound brings me back to the darkness and their spiking scents, a whiff of bitter smoke lingering in my nose.

"Marisol Darling." The speakers click. "Five minutes have elapsed. You have five minutes to subdue the prisoners."

Brandon's announcement destroys my flimsy cover, tossing me under the rubber of this speeding prison bus.

"Fucking tricks," the packleader spits.

The pack fans out, wordlessly herding me to the corner.

Not their first time ganging up on an omega.

My arms shake.

My jaw trembles.

They read my strain as fear and slip feral smiles.

The only thing I'm afraid of is four more counts of murder—this time, caught on camera.

And once Brandon has proof of what I can do?

Goodbye, freedom.

They creep closer while I fight the chemicals begging me to let loose. To shatter their toothy smiles.

I won't give in.

But I never give up.

"Come here, Darling," the packleader barks, whipping out the dominance omegas can only obey.

Good thing I'm broken.

I don't have to do shit.

To me, an alpha's bark is just noise.

"What are you going to do to me?" I ask, dead-voiced.

"They sound the same," one mutters.

"It's not her," the goatee whispers.

"Tell me." I want to hear them say it.

Alphas like this, they all want the same thing.

"Make you take this knot." He grabs the front of his pants. "Then we're gonna take turns mauling that smooth fucking throa—"

I whip my scent the way he tried to whip me with his bark. "Don't think about my throat."

The big one swallows his tongue.

One, two, three, four, they drop to their knees.

Control, control, control, I chant.

But rage steamrolls the tinny voice of my conscience.

Redfang bastards

Between the drug and years of frustration, of always holding back, I'm *thiiiiiiis close* to finally saying screw it and dishing the punishment these assholes deserve.

"Good, good. Push your limits," Brandon's satisfied speaker voice is the ice bucket that yoinks me from the brink.

With superhuman willpower, I swallow the rage.

I'll never give him what he wants.

But these ass-wipes don't get to walk away that easy. I still have to subdue them to pass Brandon's contrived little test.

So, I kick the packleader in the chest.

He topples, skull bouncing off concrete. I crouch to grip his neck, pinching his scent glands and overloading him with just enough pheromone to make his nose drip blood.

He whines—the high, pained sound so out of place on that big alpha body

Bet the last omega he cornered made the same noise.

Men like him—men like them—they never stop.

They have to *be* stopped before they go after some innocent omega who'll be handcuffed by their bark.

I shouldn't push my luck.

Shouldn't hint I'm anything but perfectly behaved.

But I was running before dawn, knocked on my ass, electrocuted, and sneered at by my hateful birth-giver.

Plus, I never got my goddamned egg and cheese sandwich.

Good Sol can't come to the phone.

I choke the alphas until their lips foam.

They won't die.

Just pass out a little.

And if I blew their senses just right, then they'll never be tempted by another omega's pheromones, ever again.

I'm practically a hero.

When they're glazed and drooling, totally down and out, I wipe my hands on my pants and smile extra polite for the cams.

See, doc? Perfect control.

"Next cell," Brandon grumbles.

Leaving the alphas on the ground, I move to the next room.

And the next.

And the next.

The more the drug fades, the better my act.

Alphas go down and my secret smirk grows.

Hope my message is loud enough to hear at headquarters.

I'm not a tool.

I will not be used.

γ

THE BETTER MY ACT, the harder Brandon pushes my limits

After a week of daily tests, weird drugs, and melee fights, I'm flipping exhausted.

But I can't sleep.

The rattling *RRRRRRRRRRRR* of the ventilation system keeps me up all night. Plus, chemical dry mouth, the jitters, and other random side-effects of Brandon's pheromone steroids.

Not that I ever really rest.

I'm too paranoid I'll leak night pheromones, because you know Brandon has scent monitors hidden in the cell where I'm grounded

I survive on catnaps and enough paper-cup coffee to turn a normal omega into a permanent jackhammer.

It's freaking miserable.

But I will not crack.

Swallowing my powers and pride is good practice for being a free citizen.

I haven't tasted freedom since before my perfume.

Maybe ever.

The closest I came to following my heart was when I was still living with the foster-monsters—those rare days I could sneak out of the house and shadow the guys I planned to follow forever.

I'm trying not to get sucked into the past when my phone

chirps an alert. My data is monitored as closely as I am, so I mostly keep my browsing to the weather and weird fanfics, but I've always treated myself with baseball score notifications.

The settings must've gotten confused when my team made the playoffs

This time, the pop-up links to a video.

Cannot watch

I've spent years not chasing my ghosts.

I don't want the SAS tracking down my past any more than I want to keep fantasizing about a future I can't have.

But watched by cams, plugged into the wall to charge my ankle monitors, and with a headache hammering thanks to the drug-of-the-day, freedom feels farther and farther away.

My willpower's iron when it comes to the SAS.

But for my guys?

Weak as wet tissue.

Before I can think, I click.

No prep, no foreplay, I'm rammed with a bearded, boy-next-door dream in a white jersey, who tosses his curveball using the same form he taught me.

My heart flutters out of control, and I pat my chest to remind her*we can't have him*

Reese is number nine, with PARKER plastered across his tall, straight back.

I can't decide if I should be heartbroken or thrilled that he's still using his placeholder last name.

The guys haven't finalized their pack.

They haven't taken a mate.

That has nothing to do with me, except that it feeds the frantic gut-butterflies who never learn their lesson.

The pitch replay ends, cutting to a live-action of Reese and the guy replacing him on the mound.

His deep brown eyes pinch with strain.

Filling his uniform to aching perfection, the grown-up man

with the bushy playoff beard still reminds me of the scrawny orphan kid who was the first to ever pick me for his team.

Those summer days, when I slipped the bickering adults and screaming babies for batting practice with a sweet-grinning Reese.

My naive little heart throbs, gushing now that I picked the scab

Not just Reese.

SuJin

Bishop.

Dutch.

No matter how broken I am, no matter how small and shattered my pieces, I'll always wish they could be mine.

Turn me to dust, and every little fleck of me will fight to scatter on their skin.

I tilt the phone so I won't catch my pining reflection on screen.

Reese fist-bumps his replacement, and the camera follows him to the dugout. His teammates clap his back, but he retreats to the far corner, putting a towel over his head and tucking his face between his knees in defeat that sneaks under my lungs and makes me twitch to give a comfort hug.

It's not until they pan away that I realize I forgot to hit the volume

I could hear the ballpark in my memories. The crack of the bat and Reese's gentle voice that's probably dropped deep enough to resurrect my dead hormones with a single purr.

The game commentator isn't as dreamy as my fantasies.

"—worst performance of the year. Hope Yagami can turn things around for the Cryptids on the mound."

"I'll be shocked if Yagami isn't pulled up to the majors. But with that injury acting up, Parker'll be lucky to finish the season."

I press my chest, trying to stop its outraged thump.

His arm's still hurting?

Shit. I need to check the news instead of just the scores.

But why would the team let him go? Are they fucking morons?

Reese was born to—

No.

I power down and shove my phone under my pillow.

I can't be trusted.

Can't think about Reese.

Don't think about the boy who taught you how to play.

Don't think about the boys who gave you a place to belong.

The guys knew me better than anyone, but I made sure they never caught a peek of the real me. I'm just some kid they forgot.

I hoped that after I awakened, we could—

NO.

I roll deep into the sheet, tugging the fabric over my head.

It's too late.

It's too late, and I'm too broken.

FOUR
BISHOP

THE OMEGA on the other side of my desk looks perfect on paper.

Her name's Capri.

She has three degrees, a crocodile bag that costs more than a condo, and lashes faker than my father's charity foundation.

The girl showed up to her interview in a braless jumpsuit so tight that her nipples are answering the questions.

Dress for the job you want, right?

Maybe the secretary position got her into my office, but she flashes teeth like her heart's set on CEO.

Choking on mint chocolate perfume, all I want to do is boot her ass and bleach her chair.

Fucking despise mint.

I smooth my buttons to keep calm.

Capri's daddies own half my hotel's board seats, and I need their votes of confidence even more than I'm going to need some *deep* fucking head to bleed out her ice cream pheromones.

Dutch growls, low and threatening.

Playing bodyguard, he stands behind my chair, popping a reluctant tent in a suit tailored for enforcer bulk. Blond, smelling like maple butter bacon—so much tastier than fucking *mint*—he curls his juicy lips.

As soon as I gracefully toss this omega, my throbbing cock will be *his* problem.

"You have an MBA. Why would you want to be my secretary?" I push away her resume, fighting the urge to pump a hit of hand sanitizer. My fingers are *soaked* in toothpastey omega juice.

"Hotel management is my passion." Capri's coy smile sharpens. "Besides. My fathers said I'd learn the most by working at your side. And my grandfather? Marcus Bloom—"

"You're hired."

Fuck me.

Fuck the Blooms and fuck my fucking father for scamming three generations of their pack with his Ponzi schemes.

White collar criminals deserve the fucking guillotine.

Two years after my father's sentencing, I'm still holding the bag, trying to keep the family business from crumbling like artisanal sheep's milk feta. But I'd rather drink my bleach than hand an outsider my weakness.

That's the one thing I learned from Bishop Barrington Senior.

Well, besides how to bullshit and cook books.

It doesn't matter if you're drowning.

Never let them see you squirm.

The Barrington Hotel is mine, mess and all.

I take care of my own.

So I smile and offer a handshake. Let Capri try to spy. Whether she wants to steal intel or make a play for our empty mate slot, I'm not giving her anything but contempt and polished professionalism. "See HR. We'll onboard you right away."

"Pleasure. Can't wait to get started." She returns the shake and struts from my office.

I'll worry about schemes later.

First, I pump a glob of sanitizer to scrub off her touch. Then, I swivel in my chair, pointing to the bulge in my on-trend, in-season, designer pants. "Fix it."

Mint chocolate is even more putrid than corporate espionage, but my dick doesn't give a fuck.

"Bish..." Dutch's thick lower lip juts. His bodyguard persona, the tough guy act, just fucking melts when we're alone, turning him back into his real self—the puppy dog linebacker. He cups his junk. "What about me?"

"Get on your knees if you want me to fuck your ass over this desk. Otherwise you're not coming 'til your birthday."

Serious threat.

My boy is a leap year baby.

He clenches his teeth, puffing out a wave of ruffled dominance. I let it pass, refusing to submit.

Instead, I spread my legs and wait.

Dutch is miles more dominant than me.

He could snap me in half and bark the shit out of me if that were his kink.

But we have an agreement.

He insists we stay true to the sweet beta we lost and are never going to fucking find.

I insist he prove his loyalty with his mouth.

Fair trade, no?

Dutch has the poker face of a cherub.

A jacked, Viking angel baby.

He stares at my bulge, licking his lips. "You'll fuck me? Not just tease me again?"

"Not if you keep me waiting."

Dutch drops to his knees, muttering even though his ears are pink. "Asshole"

"Lick it if you're interested."

He pops my button and grabs my zipper, but before he can go all in, I yank his sun-kissed tips. His hair's just long enough to grab a tight fistful. "Use your mouth."

Defiant, Dutch takes the metal zipper between his teeth. He drags it down slow, holding my gaze with sex-starved baby blues.

I shiver.

My favorite vice.

I don't get off because Dutch is bigger, more dominant, and more powerful than me, and it's kinky as fuck putting him on his knees

Well. Obviously, I get off on that.

But the shit that truly pumps my knot is the slow way he savors my body. Gently pulling out my cock with those big palms. Thumbing my leaking slit and sliding hot, broad fingers up and down my shaft. His blackening pupils eating up the blue of his eyes. Body-builder ass bobbing up and down.

Eager for a taste.

Dutch drags my head between cashmere lips and moans.

"That's my boy." I yank his hair, dragging his lush mouth deeper, sinking into his heat until I have to brace against his hair to hide the shake in my knees.

He makes pleasure noises. Strangled grunts and muffled groans, enjoying every lick as his throat muscles work my cock.

"You love that dick in your mouth." I rake his scalp, encouraging. "A good boy like you can take it even deeper."

I drag him until he's nuzzling my knot.

Dutch groans and arches his spine, popping that thick ass high

Biggest alpha you've ever seen and my boy acts like an omega, so fucking desperate to be railed.

Fuuuuuuck he's good

Soft mouth taking me like a champ while his rough hands roam my thighs, clamp my knot, and stroke my balls.

The rougher I yank, using his fucking face to get myself off, the sweeter he moans around my cock.

Dutch gives *full-service* head, throwing in a deep, rumbling purr that vibrates until I'm clawing his throat, knot heavy with the tingling pressure about to explode.

Thighs shaking, I clamp him where I want him.

Fuck me. "Swallow good ."

I spill down his waiting throat.

Dutch drinks me until my toes curl, draining my balls and purging the last of the bullshit omega pheromones.

I sink back in my chair, stroking Dutch's head while he gives my still-twitching shaft the ice cream cone treatment, licking it clean

So. Good. "That's my boy."

When he releases my head with a pop and a sex-glazed smile, a shining thread stretches from the corner of his thick lips.

Sexy as hell until it dribbles on my pants.

I hiss and knock Dutch away, duck-walking to grab soda water from the bar of thousand-dollar bottles refilled with water and food coloring

Dabbing the stain with a damp cocktail napkin, I glare. "These are bespoke."

He climbs to his feet, wobbly around his strained bulge. Dragging his thumb around his mouth to capture the stray jizz, he gives the finger a hard suck. "Pants don't talk."

I make a disgusted noise.

You can tell *he* never got whipped with a riding crop for wearing sweats in public. "My image is all I have."

"Your image *and* your sweet personality." Dutch steals the soda water, looming to grind his bulge into my hip. "Can you stop with the housekeeping? So hard I'm gonna die."

I cup the front of his slacks, stroking his thick length through the stretched-out fabric. He's hard and so fucking warm, all maple and musky with lust underneath the lingering stain of my peaches and champagne.

"Yes." Dutch's forehead drops to my shoulder. He breathes against my neck, trembling like a hummingbird. Fully under my control. "Please, Bish. Need it."

Fucking putty. "Omega got you all stirred up?"

"No. Yes. Shit. Pheromones aren't fair. Unfair-amones. Huh. Ha."

My ball-squeeze flips his laugh to a sucked-in wheeze.

"Maybe it's time we find our own." Some loaded socialite who checks all the boxes.

A pedigree, a fortune, and just enough power to keep Jin's

father from taking out a hit. Now is our best mate-finding window.

With his favorite son comatose and*~~fingers crossed~~*—permanently damaged, Kairo Moon is fatally distracted. "If Jericho gifts us a funeral, then Jin inherits the Triad and we become the Moon pack. We'll probably have to mate some yakuza omega to seal the deal."

"Never." Dutch's thick fingers bite hard enough to snap my collarbone. "Won't cheat. I'll wait until we find him."

"How long?" I grip his cock until he's forced onto his toes, panting and twitching. "How long are we supposed to wait for someone who doesn't exist?"

"He exists. And we'll wait for fucking ever. That's what you do for your mate."

Sneering, I drop his cock. "We don't have a mate."

I'm done waiting.

I just want to fuck something other than Dutch's juicy ass before the Triad buries us in cement.

"You'll see. The law of attraction—"

"Manifest me some omega pussy or stop reading that bullshit."

"It's not bullshit. What's bullshit is you giving up." Dutch shoves me, done playing submissive. "He's out there, Bish. He's out there and he's probably alone, waiting for us."

Ignoring the old ache in my chest and the wet spot on my pants, I zip away my dick.

Our so-called beta popped out of the streets one summer and started playing ball. Sweet kid. He had big, brown eyes that saw too much and pierced too deep.

We let him tail us for years, planning to make him ours forever, but we lost our window after Reese's assault limited our life choices. Kairo already had us on the ropes, threatening Dutch's family.

If he'd found out we had a prospective mate?

Game. Set. Murder.

We had to go dark to keep Solomon safe.

Just a few weeks.

By the time I tried make contact again, *poof.*

He was a Meadows kid with no resources. After all these years, tracking dead-end leads, I'd bet my building that someone made him disappear.

And if our sidekick did survive?

I wouldn't bring a French bulldog into our current mess.

We're well-trained, ultra-disposable package boys, and short of pulling an escape more flawless than my smooth, white ass, the Triad will always have us by our unfulfilled balls.

Solomon deserved better.

I pump sanitizer and scrub until my palms burn. "The kid's gone"

Dutch collapses on my office sofa. "Well, I'm not hard anymore. Bastard."

"I wish." Unfortunately, I *am* my father's legal son.

I return to the inbox full of bullshit that needs raking thanks to the trash fire of his legacy. The only thing he ever did right was make sure my trust was ironclad. No one can take my hotel shares to pay his debts.

But after years of his mismanagement, running schemes instead of the business, The Barrington is still bleeding cash. I feel like the kid living in an empty hotel room—when I had to tighten my tie, smile, and lie that *everything is fine.*

Dutch, a true friend even when cockblocked, bleach-cleans the chair that Capri contaminated.

I'm politely telling the contractors to fuck off over their estimates on our roof replacement when my door busts open.

Finally home from his playoff game, our boy Reese is ragged in his traveling suit, and I can't get past the woodland fucking creature clinging to his cheeks. "The beard needs to die."

"Least I can shave now that we lost." He slumps on the couch and wrinkles his nose. "The hell? Did you have an ice cream party before the sex, or is that an omega?"

I scoff. "My new secretary. Probably sent to heat-trap us. Definitely a corporate spy."

"Shit." Reese itches his chipmunk.

"Gross, right?" Dutch drops next to him on the couch, pressing close to wipe Reese's frown with his golden retriever impression. "Ignore the pheromones. Tell us about your game."

"Does it matter?"

"Yes," Dutch and I snap, in-sync.

One of us needs an achievable dream.

Being tangled with the Triad regularly ruins our plans, but Reese always gets done the dirtiest.

He had a full ride to a baseball school with pro scouts on speed dial. Then Jericho Moon dragged him on a drug run that ended in a shattered shoulder and a coma.

After the surgeons turned Reese half cyborg, reconstructing his pitching arm, the scholarship evaporated and Kairo tightened our leash

Reese could only join us for a higher education in black-ops and rehab his ass off for the chance to keep playing. Now he misses games and strains his muscles every time Kairo forces us to take a job

I refuse to be seen in a mini-van, but I'll drag his ass to practice like a helicopter parent if he tries to walk away now.

"What's to tell? We lost. I got pulled and Coach ripped me a few new assholes." Reese fishes a paper-bagged bottle from his duffel. "When's Jin coming home? I need to get shitfaced."

"Maybe he has good news," Dutch says. "Jericho could be dead'

I snort. "That fucker won't die."

I'd put money on Jericho Moon surviving a plane crash, let alone a sabotaged drag race. He'll probably pop up from his traumatic brain injury with superpowers.

I text Jin for confirmation.

Too soon to send funeral flowers?

JIN

He's still alive

"Fuck." Reese pops a message into our pack chat.

REESE

I'll save you a bottle

JIN

Only if it's champagne. Things are changing.

While Dutch types out a big-fingered, and probably enthusiastic reply, Reese and I trade looks.

Him and I could get out clean—neither of us ever had blood family to give a fuck about.

Dutch's mom and little sister have always been our weak point. We can't risk moving them until we're ready to take our escape plans nuclear.

So, as much as I want to detour to the hospital, hand Reese a silk pillow, and watch him deliver poetic, smothering justice, now is not the time to break the status quo.

I can only control what I can control.

I rub out another pump of sanitizer and straighten my tie, ready to play cool as fuck for any corporate moles, Triad spies, or hotel rubberneckers who think today is the day they're going to catch me lacking.

I'm Bishop Augustus Barrington the fourth, and if you come at my pack, you can fuck all the way off.

On a long enough timeline, I swear we'll survive to see the Triad brass decapitated and skull-fucked.

In the meantime, we drink.

"Hotel bar?" I offer Reese a hand up from the couch. "Top shelf's on me."

"Screw top shelf. I'd drink fucking liniment." Reese lets me pull him up, then rubs his shoulder with a wince. "Which I have in my bag. *Ugh.*"

"Come on." I pluck his shirt. "We'll toast to Jericho's suffering"

Dutch jumps to Reese's other side, skipping through the office suite on the way to our private elevator. "You get me drunk, you're either fucking me or letting me fuck you."

"I'm a pitcher, Dutch Baby." Reese's laugh would be sweeter if he didn't chase it with paper bag vodka, but it's an improvement from his defeated slump. "You're gonna have to catch."

"Don't. That's what *he* calls me." Dutch scrunches his shoulders, hunching comically small.

They bicker and laugh. I keep my shit professional, nodding to the shift manager and the housekeepers.

Whether it's the guys or the familiarity of our routine—drinks and wings after a game—the itch to sanitize and scrub my skin drops to manageable.

My boys. My family. My hotel.

I've got a fake watch, maxed-out credit, and a car lease pushing me ever closer to turning tricks, but no matter how fake I am, *this*.

This is real.

No matter who comes at us, no matter if Jericho, Kairo, or Senior himself tries to break our stride, they won't so much as wrinkle my slacks.

I'll protect our pack with every plastic fiber of my heart.

SOL

I'M HUNKERED in my cell, watching pasta-making videos under the faux privacy of my threadbare sheet when an emergency text blares

> URGENT MISSION
>
> MUSTER AT 20:00

No way

I'm on the subterranean level of the SAS phone tree, only summoned as a last resort, and I've been full-time grounded since the run-in that cost Elyse's mate the ability to taste any flavor weaker than ghost pepper.

So why now

Fishy as fuck, but it's already 19:45, so I don't have time to figure out why leadership is tossing me the rotten cod.

Commander Fissure will remote-fry my ass if I'm late.

I rapid-change into all-black gear, with a turtleneck to hide my scars. Door after door buzzes open like a chain of dominos, and the sound is sweet as a personal massager when it leads me straight to freedom and the fresh air I haven't tasted in days.

Cutting across the fenced no-man's-land around the lab, I let out the high-pressured pheromones I've been keeping down just as long

My scent bleeds into open air.

Loosening my throat gives the relief of a *looooooong* stretch. I slip a blissy moan before my ankle-scraping sprint takes me across the lawn where I have to bottle my truths.

No matter how ridiculous the mission, I won't ask questions, flog alphas with my scent, or do anything but smile, bob my head, and drone, *Yes, Sir.*

I'm just an extra, killing time.

The real A-team waits at the loading dock.

Commander Fissure, all her mates except Brandon, and twenty top SAS operatives stand in a circle of SUVs. There are only four gammas—maybe the only four in the world—and I'm the only one who inherited my abilities.

Bridget and the others are first-generation misfits.

Elyse looks almost military, decked in tac gear and holsters with her dark hair slicked into a bun, but her smokey eye makeup is more fit for a photoshoot than a mission. Five of her latest mates surround her like sentinels, lapping up her lip-plumped smiles.

Her piña colada pheromones can warp your brain until you believe almost anything she wants.

But *she* doesn't have to wear ankle monitors.

Then there's Dara.

Her ability has nothing to do with pheromones; she's an honest-to-blob telekinetic who can open doors, make mental shields, and flatten alphas with nothing but a squint and her brain

Never seen *her* on probation.

Because Dara smells like fresh cherries instead of horse-flesh.

Physiologically, we all seem to function more or less as omegas, so we're all test subjects as the SAS science squad studies the special sauce that gives us that gamma asterisk.

But only one of us is guinea-pigging Brandon's formulas.

Hello, double standard.

Everyone will pinch their noses and edge away if I move too close, so I don't breach the circle of trust. Instead, I slink between black cars, aspiring to be an unproblematic NPC at the back of the crowd with my scent leashed.

With her sixth sense for my unwanted presence, Commander Fissure gives her teams the nod. "You know your roles. We've got a long ride to the mission site, so stay alert and be ready to hit the ground at full sprint. Everyone on board?"

The agents shout, "Yes, Commander," in perfect unison.

I bite my cheek.

No one told me my role.

But I know my place well enough to head to the tech van and wait to be called—after the shit hits the fan so hard it splatters the clouds

Simon, a chubby-cheeked beta who smells like a walking potato chip, scowls when he meets me at the door. "Don't touch anything"

"When have I ever touched anything?"

"Just don't." He climbs behind the wheel.

Ignoring him, I jump in back. The potato-starched space is clogged with monitors, weapon racks, and gear I'd love to poach. But I'm not allowed a hand weapon, so I play docile, popping a squat in the corner next to the spare tire.

While we're on the road, I scour the internet for news of any event dire enough to need me off the bench.

Nothing important is scheduled except for an APOCALIPS concert.

I'd black market my best organs for tickets, but I don't think tonight's going to drop me in a boy band's lap.

Which is for the best.

I can't see where we're going with no windows at the back of the van, but after a couple hours, we brake through stop-and-go traffic. Soon enough, we're parking. Simon climbs back from the cab, scowling when he remembers I'm still here, hands obediently wrapped around my knees.

He straps on his hazmat mask before climbing into his chair.

I dig my nails into my legs.

After all my recent lockdown "training" with Brandon's prisoners, my control is the best it's ever been. I can't hold back forever, but haven't leaked a single particle into Simon's precious van

He's just a salty asshole.

But Simon is efficient, flicking on monitors and checking comms. The first images appear from shaky body cams. A few agents in plainclothes merge into a well-dressed crowd.

Then more cams fire online from dark alleys—the strike team in their gear, armed to kill an insurrection.

Hope they save the day and forget I exist.

Simon taps his mic. "Status check?"

I can't make out the answers without moving closer. *So not happening* Simon's personality is as foul as the stale-fart undertones in his potato chip scent

"All green," he announces.

The cam views flicker.

I follow the strike team. They're the ones who always need my help

Led by Bridget and her action-hero mates, agents slip along corridors lit night-vision green. When the view opens on a too-familiar scene, my heart kicks against a strobe of memories.

An empty stage.

An underground auditorium.

An auction

I don't know if I'm seeing the present or the past

I blink to clear the shadows.

The crowds, the chains, the shouted bids.

I clench to keep my pheromones from giving Simon nerve damage, trying to breathe through the nightmare anxiety that vibrates my lungs.

On the screen, the seats are empty.

The past stays in the past.

I'm not the one headed for the stage.

I wish I could be on the front line, using my ability for good and stopping anyone else from living my same trauma.

But right there is our problem.

If the SAS were *good*, my ankles wouldn't be oozing pus.

I have to get my own shit in order before I can help anyone else

Scooting back, determined to keep my head down, I accidentally jostle the van's hatch.

"Don't!" Simon mad-grabs the controller on his lanyard. "I'll put you down."

"Simon. Relax," I soothe, trying to channel omega.

He's a beta. Unmated.

Mr. Potato Ass should mash himself if I blink.

But my pheromones are never normal.

Have to mash him myself.

I'm really, *really* tempted when Simon slides his thumb toward the red button. "Move away from the door."

I scoot forward and grab my knees, bracing for a jolt. "I'm not going anywhere."

"And you'd better not try." Fondling the remote, Simon turns back to his monitors, pretending to be some slick secret agent.

Meanwhile, his neck hair prickles horizontal.

His instincts know he's not my match.

I could lay Simon out before he hit the juice. Bet I could even sprint a few blocks and duck the SAS satellites long enough to find a chop shop and hack away my cuffs.

But I can't outrun four counts of pack murder.

The SAS will call in cops, bounty hunters, and all the other feds to hunt me down, and if they don't find me fast enough, the Orlov pack's allies won't leave me time—or body parts—to worry about facing justice.

Rance, Tommy, Forbes, and Ilya Orlov.

They're dead.

I should never have to think their names, let alone feel their ghostly teeth in my throat, but their hooks never seem to fade.

Their touch reaches beyond the grave.

A flesh-crawling shudder rocks my ruined neck so hard I almost ventilate Simon's nervous system.

Past stays in the past in the past in the past.

I'm betting the only thing worse than being an omega with an asterisk is being an omega with an asterisk in federal prison.

So I don't run and I don't complain.

I wait for my chance to escape, putting my hands in my pockets and clinging to the moral high ground, watching the mystery mission unfold on screen like the good girl I'm not.

Incognito agents infiltrate a swanky reception hall, joining a cocktail party raging under gaudy chandeliers while they wait for the auction to start.

The alphas who came to bid are tatted in gang colors from their knuckles to their tree-trunk necks, and there's not one female in sight.

Tells you who's for sale.

My stomach roils.

Backstage, the strike team rushes to shut the shitshow down before it starts.

The gammas are machines.

Bridget and Elyse charm and manipulate the auction guards, freezing them under a dual-pheromone assault. While black-clothed agents zip-tie hostiles, Dara blows open the next door.

It's all perfectly coordinated, because while I'm training my mental muscles alone, getting shot up with Brandon's original torture recipes, they're drilling together as a unit.

I never get picked for the team, whether it's baseball or black-ops, but lately I'm happy being the outcast. I could never keep my distance or my act if anyone expected me to be part of the group.

Eventually, Dara bulls through the barred door to the night-mare scene I knew was coming.

Women in cages.

Their long, white gowns glow eerily green in night-vision. When the team moves into the cell block, a throat pang sets my scars on fire.

The prisoners aren't women.

They're girls.

Thirteen, maybe fourteen years old.

The scream that shakes Simon's earpiece punches through my shields to stab the last soft spot in my heart.

That first scream breaks the seal on their silence.

Suddenly dozens of girls are screaming, crying so hysterically that Simon rips off his headset with a yelp. The agents shush the girls' cries, Elyse and the commander do their pheromonal gamma thing, but their abilities work better on solo targets. And when Dara rips open their cages, all it does is fuel their panic.

My heartbeat thwaps like chopper blades.

That's the sound of the shit about to spray.

Simon grabs his mic. "Hostiles incoming."

Gunshots patter in the green-tinged darkness, and a heavily armed guard squad falls into formation in the corridors around the cells.

"Send the B team!" Bridget shouts too loudly to pretend I didn't hear.

Simon tosses me a phone. "Follow the signal."

Shit on a show-tune-singing shingle.

I can't sit on my thumbs while baby omegas are in danger.

Even if thumb-sitting is my favorite occupation.

I rocket from the van.

Simon parked us in a public garage. Rescue team of one, I sprint, only slowing to check the tracker app and steer toward the flashing dot that marks the dungeon.

I duck down a dodgy alley and find the auditorium's back door. Then I'm racing darkness, passing open doors and hopping unconscious guards while my heart chugs with leaded gasoline.

Gunshots boom.

I pick up my pace.

When I hit the last area I saw on camera, I finally catch up with the guy the A-team left as rear guard.

The barrel of his gun swings to my forehead.

Pure gun-to-the-face reaction, I whip my scent to the max.

He goes down.

Shit.

I hop the body

Maybe he won't remember it was me?

When I reach the war zone, I check around the corner with my phone cam. The SAS agents keep cover behind doorways and the shimmer of Dara's mental shield.

Returning fire, hostiles duck in and out of the open.

Easy pickings.

"Masks!" I scream over the bullets.

Not waiting to see if the team follows instructions, I let loose.

The enemies stand far out of my normal range, but the hall's so tight, my scent can do distance. I push for staying power—a lingering knock-out cloud instead of a one-off whip.

Retching replaces the gunfire.

When I peek out, Dara's busy air-snatching the enemies' guns, her team whipping out zip ties and taking down the bad guys one-by-one.

Too easy

I activate drama mode, messing my hair and drooping against the wall like I just came in last place in an all-day ruck. When I ooze into the cell room, drooping with fake exhaustion, Bridget gives a curt nod.

That's all the thanks I'll get for saving her team's unappreciative asses.

Muffled sobs cut through the echo of bullets, still ringing in my ears.

"I won't hurt you," Elyse says in a baby voice. Her tropical scent can't erase the cage room's mildew. All she does is mask it with toasted coconut and pineapple persuasion. "You can trust me"

Elyse crouches by a white-gowned girl in a wire cage so tiny, it pins her on her knees. The door is ripped off its hinges, but Elyse's words are nothing but wind to the trembling girl with white knuckles and a dirt-streaked cheek.

She's too terrified to crawl free.

Meanwhile, Elyse has the cell block smelling like a piña colada bar at prison camp.

On any other mission, I'd play dead and try not to get caught smirking while the A-Team fails.

I should stick out my thumb and squat firmly in place, but the girls' haunted faces have me opening my stupid mouth. "Let me talk to them."

"Twenty-Six," Bridget barks, alpha-sharp. "Assist with cleanup."

The girl she's trying to charm flinches.

Bridget's mate-magic pheromones don't work for shit before puberty

I keep my scent locked down, but I refuse to yield. "You need me here."

Bridget's narrow shoulders push back, puffing out her bullet-proof vest as she warms up for some verbal hit that I'd usually just shut up and take.

Not today.

"You're scaring them." Besides. Between me and my so-called mother?

I have way more experience raising kids.

Something like common sense circulates behind her brown eyes—maybe she finally remembers there are more important things than cutting me down.

"Elyse, with me," she says stiffly.

Shooting venom through a dry cough, Elyse follows the commander, both of them masking up to enter the lingering pheromone cloud.

They leave me alone with zero sense of victory in a room of caged girls.

I wish I didn't know what they're going through.

Just hope they only have to live this once.

Controlling my scent at zero, I crouch next to the girl Elyse couldn't sweet-talk. Her dark hair falls out of its ponytail, and her eyes scrunch while she clings to the rusted wire cage.

"Everyone's gone," I say softly. "I won't touch you."

She doesn't open her eyes, but some of the whiteness fades from the joints of her clenched fingers.

I wasn't caged for long.

Mostly chained and hung from the ceiling by my wrists.

Thought I'd never be able to use my hands again.

Trying not to flash back, I lift my voice so all the girls can hear. "I was nineteen when they took me."

The girl's lashes flutter.

I catch her peeking.

Oh man

I do *not* want to trudge through the memory suckhole, but I don't have siren pheromones to save my ass.

Have to bank on shared trauma.

"My brothers sold me. Half-brothers." I focus on the girl, watching her reactions so I don't have to hear the spill of words. "They put me on the stage. After I was sold—"

I choke

A+ bravado, Sol.

The girl watches my toes through glistening lashes. "Alphas took you'

"Uh huh. That's not the future we want for you." I offer my hand. "You want to get out of here?"

She drags in a breath, hesitantly reaching for help. Just before she touches skin, she finally lifts her head.

Hard-won calm flashes to horror.

"You—you—you—" She scrabbles away, jamming herself deeper into the cage.

Another girl shrieks.

When I whip to find out why, she crouches, tucking her head under shaking arms.

I check behind my shoulder.

No one else is here.

Which means she's terrified of me.

What the hell?

The girls shake, refusing to look at me. One clutches her knees, the hem of a white gown pooling around her bare toes, but the bars and the circumstances can't put out the bright spark burning behind the shadows in her eyes.

Brave girl.

"What's wrong?" I ask, soft and slow.

"We didn't try to escape." She ducks. "That pineapple lady tried to make us leave. But none of us went. We kept our promise"

"I'm those people. We came to bring you home."

She shakes her lowered head, so submissive I ache to drag her to her feet. "You said we wouldn't get hurt if we listened. I listened. I swear, I listened."

She rocks back and forth while I scrape the roof of my mouth with my tongue, trying to work spit down my bone-dry throat.

I'm nothing like Bridget, tiny and brunette. All I inherited from her were brown eyes and my curse.

I look like my father.

Tall and blonde with resting bitch face.

So there's only one person she could be mistaking me for.

The Redfang Princess.

Shitsticks.

My *sister* is in on this auction?

So much for shared trauma.

With this face, I *am* their trauma, and there's no way to escape being cast as the villain.

I do the only thing I can to make the girls comfortable. I crawl into the dry spot in the corner, lie down, and wait for the A-team to come back and peel my useless ass off the floor.

Full-on, thumb-sitting corpse mode.

Not a threat to anyone.

That's where the mission should end, but my birth has clearly pissed off the people who run the show upstairs.

The floor vibrates.

An earthquake would be the best possible way to end this day, but I'm not that lucky.

I've been planking on a trap door.

"Cover your noses and mouths," I whisper-shout. "The bad guys are back"

One mutters, "you're the bad guy," but I don't have time to argue

Pheromones cocked, I roll into a crouch.

A grunt echoes, then the lid pops.

A blonde ponytail rises through the floor, and the familiar face that follows freezes my blood.

Our eyes connect like destiny.

Hers are green with the same glint-edge gaze I have to see in the mirror every morning.

The same cursed genes I inherited from Nikolaj.

Serafina life-ruining motherfucking Redfang.

Her lemon-vodka pheromones spike in alarm as sharp and acid as the primal scream eating up my throat.

Act?

What act?

Send down the curtain.

The girl I've always wanted to murder is about to take her bow.

SOL

CHOKING, losing her grip, Serafina Redfang falls into the same dank hole she just crawled out of.

I follow more athletically, dropping into the secret passage cushioned by a raging pheromone cloud that turns my sister into a twitching bundle of leather-wrapped legs.

Some sane, still-functioning part of me begs me not to kill.

I'm not supposed to be a threat.

But when Serafina defiantly peels herself from the floor, frothing pink at the lips?

I love being a monster.

"Another bastard." Serafina coughs. "Thought we killed you all."

"Missed one." I strip her knives, keeping my pheromones just strong enough to make her suffer without passing out.

"I don't have time for this." Serafina swats my boot like I'm keeping her from her manicure, which is already perfect—black coffin-tip nails decked in diamonds. "Kill me or fuck off."

"What's the rush?" I bite back the urge to make it happen.

"You—" She chokes.

My sister is sheathed in leather from her thigh-high boots to the corset bustier that bares her unmarked throat.

Awful fancy for a dungeon. "Were you supposed to be the MC?"

"You have no idea what you—" She hacks until it clicks, and then she shoots me *the look.*

The same wrinkled-nose, *what-the-fuck* glare everyone gives when they realize I'm the source of the stench. "What is that?"

"You tell me"

"Cigars and newsprint." Serafina shudders so hard her pupils shake. "You smell like part of the fucking family."

I shelve that for later, reeling back my scent so she can speak without swallowing her tongue. "Are you running the auction?"

"I was running away. You'll want to take notes for when Daddy hunts you down."

"Daddy?" My eyebrows lift to my hairline and possibly outer space. Before I can ask what kind of *daddy* we're talking about, a gas-masked face appears in the door hole.

Elyse curses. "Reel it in, Stinkbug."

Shit shit shit.

I yank myself from the edge, but my scent lingers, snitching what I've done.

I'm floored when Serafina doesn't do the same.

Instead of ratting me out, instead of doing anything I expect, my sister shoots Elyse a look of pure, Redfang venom. "Who's the bitch?"

Do I despise my sister more than pre-dawn cardio?

Yes.

Do I cackle?

Also yes.

Elyse splutters before remembering she's a secret agent. Then she blasts us in toasted coconut and a pheromone-spiked request that isn't a request. *Put down your weapons and get your asses up here."*

Her words can't force me any more than her pheromones, but when Serafina goes puppet mode, I'm happy to follow on the same strings.

Piña colada obliterates the evidence that I stepped out of line and almost made a tragic mistake.

Not the murder part.

Just the getting caught.

I keep my head down and my mouth shut, quietly following to the closest black site where the SAS can secure their Very Important Prisoner.

Unlike the agents, Bridget doesn't do a double-take when she sees me and Serafina all twinsy, but she carries a weird tension when she orders me to follow instead of banishing me to the potato-mobile where I belong.

Leaning against the wall of an interrogation cell, I try to make it look like I'm so exhausted I can't stand, but I'm so keyed up, I'm clawing concrete.

How stupid can I be?

I should've insta-killed Serafina or let her go free.

Now I'm so looped in, I'm going to have to earn a golden statue to escape this tangled mess.

Commander Fissure steps up to the plate as soon as Serafina's secured to the bolted-down chair. Her gamma perfume puffs out in a candy-sweet cloud.

It smells like the store brand to me.

Sucralose or dextrose or one of those other -osey plastic sugars that rot your brain and give you liquid shits.

I've never caught a whiff of fated mate from her manipulative scent.

Not that I would.

I'm too broken for mates. My only romantic fate has twelve speeds, realistic thrusting action, and a suction cup base.

The alphas aren't as immune.

Their pupils yawn, and they shield the fronts of their bulging cargo pants, proving my mother's poisonous charm.

Instead of worrying about their alphas being charmed, Dara and Elyse are busy ping-ponging looks.

They flick to Serafina, then to me, staring back and forth with silent comparisons that make me want to ooze down the drain in the center of the floor.

"Serafina Redfang." Bridget thickens her throat-clogging syrup. "We were expecting your father. Where is he?"

Serafina locks her jaw.

Her pupils are blown, but minus the bedroom eyes and the hard nipples punching through her bustier, the girl could be kicked back at a coffee shop.

Unshakeable.

Can't say the same of Bridget. A quaver vibrates her military-sharp tone when she's forced to speak my father's name. "Where is Nikolaj?"

I claw the wall.

Some fucking mission.

I bet Bridget only let me out to use as bait.

Bet she knew Serafina was on site and didn't give me so much as a heads-up about my evil twin.

I'd feel betrayed if I'd trusted Bridget to begin with, but I've been side-eying her since the SAS plucked me out of an active murder scene like they'd been waiting in the wings for me to fuck up

"He must be in town for your brother's funeral. Tell me where to find him, and we'll cut you a deal on these human trafficking charges"

Serafina tilts her head—a butcher sizing up a bleeding cut of meat, seeking the softest spot to slice.

Being dragged to a black site hasn't smudged her acid pink lipstick. Even hammered with the full force of Bridget's loathing, drowning in pheromones that put her face-to-face with the ghosts of her fated mates, Serafina doesn't flinch.

It's clear that my sister is evil.

You don't *accidentally* traffic a bunch of little girls, if that was what she was doing tonight.

But shit.

Serafina's a badass.

I want to switch teams.

"I only speak with my lawyer. Or with my sister." Her head tilt finds me, throwing me under the spotlight when I'm trying to play dead.

Freaking seriously?

Cancel the trade.

I hate my family.

Every single member, on both sides of the twisted tree.

"Marisol." It's the first time my mother's ever spoken my name, and I wrench so hard the back of my skull kisses cinder blocks. "Show us what you can do."

Commander Fissure stands aside. Her mates embrace her, whispering consolations.

As if giving me the most logical command is a strain.

I swallow acid-reflux rage and shuffle in front of Serafina, letting out a half-hearted blast of pheromone just strong enough to make her nose run. "Sorry, Commander. I'm tapped for the day."

Serafina laughs, weirdly bubbly. "Oh, I like you."

"It's not mutual." She has no idea what I've been through because of her.

Or does she?

I doubt I'll get another chance to ask my questions.

Instead of slumping to my corner, downcast and keeping the status quo, I lean into her shoulder, positioning the glands in my wrist so I can target my stink without smoking the room. "Did you know I existed?"

She shrugs awkwardly, hands zip-tied to the chair. "Daddy has whelped more than a few bastards. Your name was never on his radar."

A long-held fear relaxes.

Ever since I learned my origin story, Nikolaj was one more bogeyman to escape.

Lucky I wasn't worth calling home about.

My brothers must've been too busy cashing checks and favors from the Orlovs.

"Why do you play along with this pig show?" Serafina flips the spotlight. "Get me out and we'll both be free. My jet's fueled. We can go anywhere. World. Oyster. Us."

Tempting, if true

Too bad I like seeing my sister in chains. "What are you running from?"

"My soon-to-be-deceased fiancé taught me an expression. *Bàn zhū chī lǎohǔ.*"

My lip curls.

At what point was I supposed to learn Chinese?

At the orphanage?

After the third set of twins was born?

Maybe when the fosters yanked me from middle school so I could raise their kids full-time?

"Playing the pig to eat the tiger." Serafina matter-of-factly tosses her ponytail over her chains. "It means pretending to be less than you are to win a fight. Oink too long and you'll forget you have claws."

I bunch my fists so tight, my nails slice my palms.

"Look what you can do," Serafina presses. "Break me free. We'll start a new family business. No parents. No brothers. Omega pussy power or whatever the hell you are. I don't give a fuck as long as you get me out of town tonight."

Commander Fissure clears her throat. "This girl is loyal to our organization."

"*This girl?*" Serafina's laughter trills. "You're so fucked when she snaps. Come on, Stinkbug—"

My pheromones stab my jugular. "You don't get to call me that."

"And…they…do?" Serafina chokes, suffocating in my blown-out scent. "Have…some…fucking…pride."

Pride is for socialites coddled by their daddies.

Not for girls like me—the ones they abandoned.

All I have left are my claws.

I have no problem finding the pointy ends when I wrap my hands around her throat. "Where is Nikolaj?"

Red-eyed and barely breathing, Serafina huffs a laugh. "What…waste—"

"Where?" I push and push, but Serafina doesn't surrender.

Her jaw crunches tighter and tighter, her knuckles going whiter and whiter while foam slips through her mocking smile.

Makes me crazy

I want to stand on her throat.

Force her to submit.

Make her pay for the audacity of asking me for favors, when I've lost everything because of her.

Before she passes out, her green eyes flash with something more complicated than hate.

Panting, I reel back my scent.

I almost cracked a rib and still got squat.

Serafina won't break.

But it's not me. It can't be.

I practice on three-hundred-pound alphas with prison tats.

Serafina's an omega. She should be naturally sensitive to pheromones

What the hell has she been through to give her carbon fiber nerves and no reaction to my nightmare scent?

When I turn, every agent has their back to the wall, wearing plastic gas masks that don't shield me from their looks of horror.

Now Serafina owes me even more.

Shit on a broken chip.

My sister's a freak too.

"Did we secure any other leads?" Commander Fissure asks, happy to go back to the status quo where she ignores me and I try not to get caught staring lasers at her throat.

"This was in the car we found on site." An agent offers a plastic keycard, and my stomach coils just as tight as the elegant script font spelling out The Barrington Hotel.

I purge all thoughts of Bishop Barrington from my brain before his smirking ghost can spirit me away.

"We're running out of time. As soon as Nikolaj realizes his daughter is missing he'll—" Bridget's brows pinch. She turns to me with a weirdly assessing expression. Like she's suddenly seeing me as a *person*. "Twenty-Six?"

Nope. Still a number.

But this is new. She never looks at me by choice—I prefer it that way. "Commander?"

"You bear a remarkable resemblance to this girl."

No shit. "We're related."

"If you posed as—"

"NO," I cut her off way too loudly. Her lips do that thinning, *you're-a-disgrace* thing, but this is not the time to back down. "I mean, respectfully, I'm not fit for the assignment."

Can't think of a worse idea.

"True." Commander Fissure nods. "Your control isn't up to mission standard. It was a mistake to bring you off base."

What? No! "My control is perfect."

"Then what's the problem? We have an urgent mission need that you can easily fulfill." Commander Fissure folds her arms. Her mates echo the motion—Silas on the left, Holder on the right, each big enough to bench a tank. When they flex, my shoulders throb in phantom remembrance.

They're waiting for another chance to rag doll me, and that's not the only problem keeping me from volunteering.

Problems two and three are my chewed-up ankles, followed by problem number four, which is *fuck you, not happening*

"It's just that I'm never going to be an official field agent. Someone about to be discharged shouldn't take point on such an important job."

Right?

That sounds more reasonable than *hellllll no, I'm not sticking my neck out for your bullshit.*

"There would be incentives."

After a hanging pause, my mouth can't help opening. "What kind of incentives?"

"If you have the skill to infiltrate the Redfangs and help us apprehend Nikolaj, it would remove the doubts regarding your readiness to return to society."

I want to go all Braveheart.

Flip my kilt and scream *FREEEEEEEEEEE-DOOOOOOOOOOOM.*

But I'm wearing pants, and even though Bridget knows my weakness, I know better than to show her what I want.

I rub my palms on my thighs. "You'd discharge me?"

"If you're able to fill this role? Certainly."

That's a big IF.

Huge.

But…

It's an opportunity, and those never come around twice. "How long would I have to be disguised?"

"Ten minutes, in and out of the hotel. We'll make you over. You grab Serafina's effects, case the room, and get us a lead on Nikolaj's location."

My heart chugs. "I'm dead if the Redfangs find out I'm fake."

"That's a risk," Bridget agrees. "But isn't it worth the risk to put a man like him behind bars?"

Is she offering an olive branch or the fat end of a grenade?

As sweet as it would be to topple my father and his drug empire, I know what happens when you fall into Redfang hands.

The SAS won't come blazing to my rescue. They'll watch from a distance, hoping I crack and hit a power level where they can justify keeping me in electric cuffs forever.

Ten minutes, ten seconds, or ten years—I'll be on my own while they gleefully wait for me to fail.

"You can't do it?" Bridget is a head shorter than me, but I'm the one being looked down on when her judgey upper lip curls.

It's not so much her words.

That attitude pulls the cord in my chest until flames burn through my blood and spray out my steaming ears.

I know she's goading me.

I know she wants me to do this so she can bag her nemesis and finally land the promotion that'll get her whisked off somewhere she'll never have to share my air again.

But all this time, I've been backing down.

Playing the good girl and keeping the peace.

Before I escape, I want her to know how badly she fucked up by throwing me away.

I stand tall, pulling to my full height so I'm the one looking down on her. "I can do it."

"Good. We have to move." Bridget clicks into commander mode. "Dara, hoist the prisoner so we can swap their clothes. Elyse. Take your mates on a supply run. Makeup and green lenses. And Silas. Work the auctioneer until he tells us that routing number. I want money transferred before anyone realizes we killed the auction. Spread word that a private buyer purchased the lot. Everyone else, ready to roll within the hour."

The agents dart into motion now that we have a plan.

I'm silent in the storm, swallowing nerves while Dara levitates my sister to mentally unlace her stiletto boots.

My fingers shake from anticipation, from facing Bridget, and from finally being thrown an actual rope.

I never expected stripping my sister down to her designer lingerie would be on my Bingo card to freedom, but I also never expected to be handed *any* chance, so I'll take the free square.

Maybe it's the chance to prove myself or maybe it's the chance to run

But a chance is a chance, and pretending to be someone else is my bread, butter, and my raspberry jam.

So bring it on

I rub my hands, crack my knuckles, and get ready to brave The Barrington's five-star halls wearing my sister's rich girl mask.

SEVEN

JIN

LIKE EVERYTHING ELSE, the corner office belongs to my brother.

Jericho Moon, Director of Investment.

I don't get the fancy title, the perks of being born into a crime family, or credit for running the show.

Until now

Kicking my feet up on my brother's walnut desk, I watch the city skyline twinkle while my ass warms his leather chair.

I thought I was in for another decade of playing yes-man. Following my father's orders while gathering power to protect my real family.

Then Jericho shattered his spine and cracked his skull.

I owe a deep kiss to the angel who cut his brakes.

While my father hovers at Jericho's bedside, I'm finally making moves.

I'm not just standing in at the helm at our legal businesses—*I'm fucking taking over.* Starting with Jericho's inbox.

Our clients were spooked when my brother's racing accident hit the news cycle.

I couldn't let them panic. I had to step out of the shadows before they pulled their cash.

They were cautiously optimistic when they found out I've been managing their portfolios from the jump.

Jericho's been busy partying. Chasing omegas, snorting lines, and racing cars.

I've been covering his shit for fifteen years. Ever since I came first in final exams.

Some fathers pay their kids for good grades.

I never met the deadbeat until the middle school hearing where he accused me of cheating. Then I was rank-stripped, suspended, and put on notice.

The illegitimate son isn't allowed to outshine the rightful heir.

That's when Kairo started grooming me as my brother's pawn. He threatened Bishop, Dutch, and Reese, who were already so obviously my future pack.

Eleven years old, what was I supposed to do?

Fight the Triad with a water gun?

I failed my classes and aced Jericho's homework. Took his tests. Won his fights. The better I performed, the better Jericho looked

That's where Kairo fucked up.

He shouldn't have given me a chance.

Now, the investors know who to trust, and they don't give a fuck where I came from as long as I keep making them rich.

I'm not strong enough. Not yet.

But soon.

Soon I'll have the capital to protect what's mine.

I just need a little more insurance before we're safe to break away

I'm emailing investors, buttering them up for when I jump ship and poach their accounts. My cell vibrates on Jericho's cluttered desk.

KAIRO.

I kill my feral grin so he doesn't hear my smugness. "Father."

"Su-Jin. My office."

He kills the call before I can answer.

Typical power play

Used to be, I'd sprint, knowing he'd retaliate for being kept waiting

Petty shit like tailing Dutch's mom or paying thugs to make trouble at The Barrington.

Now he needs me or his firm will tank.

I'm not cocky enough to hit him yet, but I'm confident enough to take my time. I unfold from my chair, stretch, and stroll across the C-suite.

Kairo Moon is a figurehead CEO, laundering money and putting on a show. His real power comes from the Triad's dirty business. But he has a corner office and a door plate made of gold, just in case you forget who's in charge.

I knock with my knuckles to hide my Triad tattoos.

"Get in here," Kairo barks. "It's urgent."

"News about Jericho?" I shake his command, praying the devil told my brother the coke's stronger on the other side.

"Of course not. He'll make a full recovery."

Damn.

I take the chair across from Kairo's desk, disappointed but loving the view.

I've always looked like the younger version of my father, and it's a toss-up which of us hates that most.

Thirty years of crime family stress was giving him grey patches and hard lines around his dark eyes. A week after Jericho's accident, he looks like my grandfather.

His salaryman standard black hair is showing fresh white. Wrinkled suit. Crooked tie. His firm chin sags, deep new wrinkles carving the granite of his icy glare.

Weak.

Even his alpha pheromones taste stale.

Crushed black peppercorn used to drop my shoulders when he whipped me with his bark. Now, when Kairo hammers his dominance to enforce my position at the ass-end of the hierarchy, I battle the chest-rumbling urge to throw down.

Not yet.

I gag my growl and lower my head, but he must sense we're beyond the point he can force me to submit.

His pepper-cracked dominance clears my sinuses as he shoves an envelope across his desk. "We have a situation."

Instincts picking up a subtle vibe, I cautiously open the envelope. It holds a gold-embossed invitation that reeks of old money and older power.

Nikolaj Redfang presents his daughter,
Serafina
Friday at 9pm
Best offer welcomed to the family

Nothing says *auction* but the subtext leaves me smoothing another tooth-licking grin. "Nikolaj is selling Jericho's fiancé?"

Fucking beautiful.

Jericho destroyed Reese's shoulder, got our pack exiled to military college, and made us lose tabs on our perfect beta.

Now he's broken and about to lose his contract mate.

As much as I want to take revenge with my own hands, I have to give karma the W for that poetic justice.

My father's jaw grinds hard enough to count his fillings. "He's demanding we dissolve the engagement."

I've never met Serafina Redfang, but I've heard a hundred faded rants about Jericho's spoiled omega-to-be. "Maybe it's for the best. They hate each other."

"Their feelings aren't relevant," says the man who hated his mate enough to knock up his personal chef and bring me to life. "Nikolaj is blaming the Triad for the crash and Konstantín's death."

My brow-furrow deepens to a trench.

The Redfang Cartel's succession battle has been raging for months. I keep tabs because Konstantín has always been Jericho's fuckboy wingman, and the more I know about his business, the easier it is to mop up their mess.

Konstantín slaughtered his brothers to be crowned the

Redfang heir. Last I heard, he was the only surviving male. "So who inherits the cartel?"

"Serafina, in name. In reality? Her alphas."

Here it comes.

The part where Kairo orders me to wipe my brother's ass.

But before my pack is out of the country, I have to keep asking my father the only question he wants to hear. "What do you need me to do?"

"Sabotage the auction." Kairo's cheeks redden from popped blood vessels and entitled rage. "Use any means necessary to stop that girl from being marked. Jericho will bite her as soon as he wakes."

I wouldn't call his plan a *plan*, but even as an idea, it bleeds with holes.

Jericho could be unconscious for weeks.

Even if he woke tonight, he's not about to weather a mating heat with a broken spine.

That's already assuming we can get to Serafina, who Nikolaj keeps vaulted like the crown jewels.

Totally implausible.

That's why I love it, coast to coast.

There's no scenario where I help Jericho abduct and mate-rape an omega just so he can add a billion-dollar drug empire to his power base.

Might as well put a pistol in my mouth.

"If I do this, I want out. My pack and our family go free, and I get controlling shares in Crescent Entertainment." I clench the trident tattoos inked over my fingers. "You get the Redfang Cartel, Jericho gets the girl, and I get to leave. No strings."

The last time I tried to negotiate with Kairo, he had five soldiers beat the shit out of me and dump me at the dock where the Triad sinks their bodies.

You need power to trade favors.

For the first time, I have *his* ass over the barrel.

His jaw clench says he knows it. "It's not as simple as walking away. The businesses—"

"I'll do a proper handover. Get everything in line for Jericho to take the wheel." I fold my hands. "Better me handle the job than Fletcher and Dooley."

Jericho's zero-loyalty "packmates" are the heirs that round out the Song-Lin-Moon Triad. If Kairo sends them after Serafina, they'll either fuck up getting plastered before the job, or worse.

They'll mate her without Jericho and ice out the Moons entirely

If my father doesn't want to lose his kingpin slot, me and my guys are his only option.

Knowing the score, he pumps out peppercorn stress pheromones. "Intercept her before the auction. As soon as Jericho takes her throat, I'll sign your severance."

I offer my hand across the desk. "Our lawyer will prepare the contracts"

"Don't get greedy." Instead of a shake, he returns a bone-crushing grip, whipped dense with dominance. "The omega belongs to Jericho."

Fucking everything belongs to Jericho.

I never wanted shit from the Moons.

I just want to be strong enough to stop them from taking what's mine. "Consider it done."

I have a plan percolating by the time I'm in the garage, where my sedan is boring, but bulletproof. Before I click my belt, I clock two suspicious cars watching my moves.

Kairo and probably one of Jericho's deputies who has standing orders to tail my ass. I dial Bish and tear out.

Three cars follow my bumper.

I could lose them, but it's too soon to tilt my hand.

Let them circle.

Let them think I'm easy prey.

The ringing connects, and Bish's lazy tone bleeds through the speakers. "Jericho dead yet?"

"Not yet. But Konstantín Redfang is." The pause lasts so long I frown. "Bish?"

"Hold on." Glass clinks. "I saved a bottle of champagne for this"

I grin until my teeth cut my lips. "Kairo just handed us an assignment."

"You took another one of his bullshit jobs?" His voice sharpens with that subtle panic he could hide from anyone else. "But our plan—"

"New plan. *Better* plan." I flick my turn signal, taking the fast route across the city toward The Barrington. Kairo might need me for now, but Jericho's crew won't waste a chance to take a hit.

I stopped driving with music the first time his assassins T-boned me. "Get Dany and Lisa on a plane to the island."

"You're not serious," Bish says flatly. "We're months away from—"

"Doesn't matter if we're ready. We can't risk them on this job." Dutch's family is our family. Our only liability.

"What's so dire?"

"Need you to find out where Nikolaj Redfang stashed his daughter."

"Redfangs?" His sneer fills my speakers. "They booked my penthouse. Since when do we give a fuck about them?"

"Since we're kidnapping Jericho's fiancé." The line goes silent so long, I think I dropped the call. "Bish?"

"You're on the way home?"

I glance in the rearview. "Be there in ten if they don't ram me with an armored truck again."

He groans. "I'll double security. You can explain the master plan to the pack."

"Trust me"

"Against my better judgment."

My speakers click to silence.

I grip the steering wheel until my knuckles crack.

My instincts never lie, and the tension tightening my spine says the power's finally shifting.

Just one more job

Grab the omega. Smear the blame on the Triad. Then kick back and watch the gang war explode.

And when Kairo's at his weakest?

I'll finally knock the king off his throne.

EIGHT

SOL

SERAFINA'S LEATHER is so tight that I'm going to need to butter my boobs to wedge into her bustier, but a bucket of lube won't be enough to hide my other problem. "Her boots won't fit over my ankle monitors."

Even my loose-fitting uniform pants barely squeeze around the super-conspicuous shock boxes that'll make any other disguise pointless.

Commander Fissure purses prim lips.

I volley her glare. "The plan doesn't work if the Redfangs murder me in the lobby."

After enough scrutiny to leave me flop-sweating, Bridget reaches under her bulletproof vest, pulling out my remote.

Hers has a lot more buttons than Simon's.

Don't want to remember what those do.

My cuff beeps, then whirrs, the heavy-duty straps unspooling until there's enough slack to tear them off my feet.

"You'll stay in sight of your handler at all times," the commander warns.

"Sure." I wouldn't expect her to let me off my leash without a babysitter.

I'm too excited to complain, rubbing the raw skin I've barely seen in five years. Both ankles are red and oozy, but I feel a thousand pounds lighter without the extra weight.

I can't even remember what it's like to walk without clanking, without the constant fear of being zapped.

I wiggle my toes and promise.

Never again. That's the last time I let myself be chained.

When Elyse and her mates return with colored contacts and a bag of drug store makeup, I duck into a scary, black site bathroom with squidgy floor-stains that hint it doubles as an extra cell.

Jamming into Serafina's leather feels like stuffing a sausage. My skin pebbles in the raw air. As soon as the bustier's laced, I jam my black sweater overtop.

No way in hell am I flouncing around flashing my throat.

The scars would ruin my disguise.

After putting in contacts that scrape my eyelids with every blink, I copy my sister's hard-ass look using the long-lost beauty skills that were drilled into me at the OCC.

Deep liner shaped to emphasize the trademark Redfang glint. Thick mascara. Sharp, contoured cheeks. Then a blonde ponytail with a cheap extension, secured high on my head.

After a final hit of venom-pink lipstick, I size up my latest disguise

I've always worn a mask.

A girl sweet enough to be adopted.

Then a boy, helpful enough to be kept around.

At the OCC, I played a normal omega.

I would've had to play mate if my scent hadn't morphed into a special ability.

Instead, I was captured, forced to play a gamma soldier and the long game, patiently bluffing my way to freedom.

None of my masks have ever been me, but why be myself?

Everyone hates the real me.

For being a weird beta, for being an omega, for being the wrong type of omega, and even for being the wrong type of gamma

Whatever I am, everyone always wants me to be something else

That's why I love my masks.

Then it's not really me being rejected again and again and again

But this mask?

The face in the mirror shakes my heart.

In slinky black, with predator pink lips, I don't feel like Serafina. I look like the Sol I wish I could've been.

A girl who never dulls her edge.

Confident. Wanted. A genuine gangster princess.

I twist to check my ass in the painted-on pants.

Shit.

I look good.

But it's all a costume.

With stilettos half-a-size too small pinching my toes, and Serafina's acid lemon perfume wafting from her clothes, there's no forgetting who I am underneath.

The Sol who isn't wanted.

The one who survives anyway.

As long as I bluff the same as ever, no one will spot the subtle differences between me and the real thing.

Ten minutes.

In and out of the hotel, and if anything goes wrong, I whip out my pheromones and run.

The OCC made us train walking in heels, but the pumps I borrowed weren't five-inch stilettos sharp enough to pop a tire.

After a few baby-giraffe stumbles around the bathroom, I remember how to strut.

Ready with Serafina's boosted car, Commander Fissure and her team wait for me in the underground garage. I'm more confident with every click-clacking step, holding back a catty smile when the agents' jaws drop from my makeup magic.

Bridget leaves the mission command huddle, gliding over with a critical gaze. "Well done. If only you—"

"I'm ready." I cut her off.

No way is that a comparison I want to hear.

"Silas?" She summons the mate who must've drawn the stump straw and ended up my keeper.

In a dark suit with a gold chain ripped from an alpha captured at the auction, Silas should look Redfang as hell. But with a crew cut, no tattoos, and the posture of a flagpole, the guy screams narc

I don't offer my professional opinion.

Nobody cares.

"Stay on your earpiece," Bridget warns. "Ping us when you have Nikolaj or his whereabouts. We'll be on standby with reinforcements surrounding the hotel."

"Yes, Commander." Silas gives a crisp salute that jangles his chain, looking like a cadet in a mafia costume.

"Roll out," Bridget commands.

When I climb into Serafina's bulletproof sedan, Silas hops behind the wheel, already failing his role. It's fine if he wants to get himself killed, but I plan to survive the night. "Serafina's bodyguard would've opened the door for her."

"I'm not acting until we're on site." Silas hunches, maxing the distance between us in the limited space of the car. "And you listen to me, or I call the mission. You run, you pay. Got it?"

When he glares over his shoulder, I do a Serafina head tilt, trying to match my sister's deadly confidence. "Got it."

Silas flinches

I'm just not sure if I nailed her persona, or if he's traumatized because he couldn't pack his gas mask. My pheromones prickle, reminding me how easy it would be to take Silas down, but if half the SAS is surrounding the hotel, the other half is probably following our path to make sure I don't go rogue.

Serafina's razor-sharp lemon doesn't make it any easier to keep my scent on lock. Her perfume climbs from her clothes, punching through my turtleneck until I feel her manicured hands around my throat.

Desperately need a shower.

Ignoring the itch and the glares from the front seat, I practice

Serafina's posture while Silas drives across town. By the time we hit The Barrington's marquee, my scent is under supermax security, and I'm ready to order a martini, then berate the cocktail waitress

But the hotel sign sparks a quaver under my skin.

The Barrington's sky-high letters match the height of Bishop Barrington in my heart.

He played baseball in a bleach-white, collared shirt and never caught a speck of dirt. All he did was smirk.

On fight nights, he'd flick my baseball cap and peel a fifty from his billfold, sending me to fetch snacks and booze. But Bishop only needed a gofer the nights that bloody fights spilled out of the ring, and he always let me keep the change.

He said coins were filthy, and he was too rich to count pennies.

With foster parents who only wanted me for child labor, who yelled and backhanded and sniped at every little thing I did wrong when I was the one raising *their* crotch goblins, I've never had trouble spotting real kindness.

I wanted to get closer to him.

I wanted to help Bish, even if I was just the kid who carried his hand sanitizer.

But he and the guys are three or four years older, and they grew up first. I saw them less and less before I was kicked out of town, and what I wanted with them was never going to be more than a dream.

Even after I stumbled onto Reese's roster, I never looked up where the rest of the pack landed. One, because the SAS reads my internet history. And two, I don't have the balls.

Because, see?

Just Bishop's name rattles my game.

Get your shit together.

If I blow this op but somehow survive Redfang vengeance, I'll be locked in Brandon's dungeon and pin-cushioned with potions 'til I'm eighty.

Not that I'll live that long.

My heart pumps pre-emptive adrenaline when Silas parks under the covered entrance.

Showtime.

Silas finally hears the curtain call, opening my door before tossing the keys to a valet who submissively stares down the red carpet runner.

Channeling Serafina's badass vibes, I strut into a lobby so swanky, my fingers flatten to my thighs. Vivian's shrill warning echoes from the past. *Don't touch a thing or I'll beat your ungrateful butt!*

My foster mother. What a saint.

I resist the poor-girl instinct to shrink.

Serafina Redfang could take a bat to the grand chandelier and the manager would have to apologize for falling glass.

Silas herds me to the reception desk and slaps our keycard onto the mirror-polished wood. "Key stopped working."

The girl at the desk blanches—not at his gruff command, but at me, flinching when I toss my ponytail over my shoulder in fake impatience

Wow. Wonder what Serafina did to her?

"Right away, Miss Redfang. I'm so sorry for the trouble." Her fingers tap-dance across her keyboard, possibly sending an SOS. "Can we send a bottle of Bergerac to the penthouse to make up for the inconvenience? We have a thirty-year vintage in the cellar."

"Fine." I wave, pretending I always drink five-thousand-dollar booze

So good being the princess.

If I get to reincarnate, I'm choosing mobster's daughter for my next life.

Oh wait

Already tried that and it sucks.

Next time, I'll try being a normal omega. Mate sweet, stable alphas, roll my own pasta, and try to be born in a family that doesn't prefer me dead or caged.

This life's already effed.

Carrying fresh-minted keycards, we ride the elevator to the penthouse. Luckily, my so-called teammate sticks to his silent bodyguard persona.

I have no bandwidth for chit-chat.

With a quarter of my concentration keeping my pheromones under wraps, and another quarter wasted balancing in Serafina's stripper boots, the other fifty-percent of my brain goes goblin mode, populating images of a grown-up Bishop walking the halls in one of his tailored suits, dressed to maim, slaughter, and fucking kill.

To ground myself, I pat Serafina's weapon holsters. When I win my freedom, I'll treat myself to a one-time image search of my vision board mates.

But when the elevator opens on the penthouse level, I kiss my victory screen-lick goodbye.

Two guards flank Serafina's room.

In suits tented with hardware, they don't have to snap to attention. They're already glaring from the end of the hall.

My stomach somersaults, expecting the inevitable.

The shout. The chase. The instant realization that I'm nobody's princess

But the alphas don't draw their guns.

Yet.

"Give me the key," I mutter.

"You're not going anywhere alone," Silas answers with too much rumble.

He probably has permission to shoot me in the head, but he'd never put *himself* in danger. "You think you can pass as the guy you stole that chain from? The one with the face tattoo?"

Silas isn't stupid enough to argue. He jams the keycard in my hand. "You're dead if you run."

"Find my purse," I command, happy to shove him back into the elevator.

But when the doors slide shut, my heart checks into my throat for an extended stay.

Pushing my shoulders back with a confidence I can only fake, I catwalk to the penthouse.

Turns out I never needed a key.

"Princess. Where the hell were you?" A beefy guard whips out his card and practically shovels me into the room.

"Boss is pissed," the second guy adds with a toothy alpha grin that insta-corrects my stupid misconception, dropping a star-shaped ice cube down the tube of my throat

These aren't Serafina's guards.

They belong to Nikolaj.

"I'm back. Don't bother me."

"You sneak out again, we'll teach you a lesson." His grin widens, wolfish and off-putting, and I bite down to stop my scent from rising to the challenge. If he touches me with those grease-stained fingers, he's the one who'll *learn*.

"Stop." The first guard yanks his homie back. "The boss'll take care of her."

"Sounds fun." His scent rises, all sour pomegranate.

I slam the door and take a shuddering breath.

Halfway there.

Just can't kill any Redfangs and blow my cover.

Even if they *really* deserve a nervous-system smackdown.

The penthouse suite opens up like a magazine spread. Makes me paranoid I'll leave fingerprints as I tip-toe inside.

The only time I've ever felt at home was with the guys. Riding in the back of Jin's janky old truck while Bishop complained about fast food. Dutch and Reese took turns passing me nuggets and kicking his seat.

I grew up in loud, dirty, chaos, taking care of three sets of twin boys younger than ten, plus my older foster brothers, who were worse than babies.

Eight kids, five foster parents, and one weird little gamma girl in four bedrooms and two baths.

I'm at home with hand-me-downs and the day-old, half-price hot dogs you snag right before the bodega closes.

This place has an infinity pool off the living room.

Pin-drop silent and pristine.

The dining room table's set with glittering crystal, chocolate-dipped strawberries, and a chilled bottle of Bergerac that someone must've sprinted to the room.

I can pretend to be an heiress—I'll pop chocolate strawberries all day—but I feel more like a cockroach dropped in cream.

Get me out of here.

I hurry through room after ridiculous room until I find the only one being lived in. Serafina's jewelry box spills open on the cloud-white duvet of my dreams.

She owns more diamonds than a mine, all sparkling in the open, but nobody's stupid enough to bling ring a cartel heiress.

Some of those diamonds are stuck to knife hilts.

I snoop until I find her bag propped on an armchair in the sitting area that's bigger than my living cell.

Inside are her laptop, wallet, and phone.

Binga

Hugging the bag that's my ticket to freedom, I check the last room. With an empty walk-in closet and a luxe, unwrinkled bedspread, there's no sign that Nikolaj or anyone else has been in the suite.

And there's no way I'm busting my ass to dig deeper.

I need out.

I'm heading for the door, ready to lie or blast free, but there's already a body in my way.

"For you." The guard who offers me his cell phone isn't leering anymore. He's paste-pale, with shaking fingers and bloodless lips.

"Who?"

"The boss." He swallows.

Holy shit.

Nikolaj?

Play it cool, play it cool.

Giving an extra hard swallow of my own, I grab the phone

and prepare to hit my mark. I just have to be a spoiled princess. Ask him where he is, then pass the intel to command.

"Serafina." The poisonous drawl kills my schemes half-cocked, rubbing my flesh like a wire brush.

Danger.

"You've grown bold." Nikolaj's voice pricks like blood-tipped icicles

I'm no expert in what a loving parent sounds like, but apparently, neither is my sister.

I may have read her wrong. "I—"

"*Did I give you permission to speak?*" His bark snaps my teeth.

I think I read *everything* wrong.

"Your futile act of rebellion has compromised the hotel. I'll defer your punishment to your future packleader, but if you can't be an obedient daughter, you have more value to me as a whore. Do you understand?"

My lungs squeeze until I taste chalk. "I understand."

"Remember. Mouth shut, legs open. If you perform well tomorrow, you won't have to sneak outside, looking for alphas to fuck"

My father hangs up.

Vomit climbs my throat.

Like...what?

What?

I had zero expectations, but *that's* my father?

I'm still numbly holding the alpha's phone when boots stomp from the hall.

Five, ten, twenty alphas, then I lose count in the sea of Redfangs taking over the floor. Enforcers shove past me, securing windows and checking rooms.

A muffled scream yanks my attention.

My original door-guards kick the carpet, each trying to escape a chokehold, but it's too late for anyone to run.

Snap.

Crunch.

Ugh.

They stop struggling when their necks break. The fresh guards drags away their wide-eyed bodies.

"Room's clear," barks a super-dominant alpha with an earpiece. "Boss wants you to eat dinner, take a bath, and sleep early. Best follow the rules. I'm not losing any more of my guys because you're desperate for a knot."

"We'll take care of you ourselves," another alpha stage-whispers on his way out.

"We on the same page, Princess?" The big guy glances at the bag tucked under my arm.

Whether he's the packleader or the head of security, the guy reminds me of Bridget's mates—boy scouts who follow the rules until no one is watching, and breaking them is more fun.

I swallow sword-sharp pheromones and frustrated disgust. "Get out of my room."

"Stay in your room," he commands.

I slam the door in his face, then go to throw a bolt that doesn't exist.

There's no peep-hole, either, but I can guess how much Redfang muscle is swarming the property.

Now I understand why Serafina left without her phone.

She really was running.

I wish I could follow in her footsteps, but no matter how desperate I am to level the guards, I can't take down the cartel on my own. There's too many alphas, and if I drop my disguise, I have to drop one-hundred percent of their bodies.

Have to wait for the right moment to take the risk.

Retreating to the master bath, I run the water and text command

Redfangs know they're being watched. I'm locked down in the penthouse.

The response is instant and gut-punchingly predictable.

Where is Nikolaj?

I imagine Bridget hunched over a console, ready to sacrifice my ass

I reply anyway. She might not rescue me, but Serafina's incriminating computer?

That's the motherlode.

Nikolaj isn't here. Sounds like he'll be around tomorrow. I have Serafina's laptop and phone. When are you coming to get me?

Too much heat. Stay in place, and we'll send someone to collect in the morning.

Collect *me*?

Or just the gadgets?

I wait for more info that never comes.

I fill the bath in case these creeps check if I followed orders, but after a while, I drain it without touching the water.

Baths are for rich lady omegas who aren't worried about being caught without their contour makeup and sent to the auction block

A-freaking-gain.

I yank off Serafina's stilettos to return the circulation to my toes and be ready to run. Then I paw through her luggage so I can refresh the lemon pheromones slowly fading from my stolen clothes

I'm hoping for a big T-shirt or a gown, but Sera's nightwear is all black satin and crotchless panties.

Nope.

I'm not dabbing "share panties" off the Bingo card from Hades, crotched or un-crotched.

The best I can do is a pair of lemon-scented leggings long enough to hide my ankle grizzle and a yoga shirt that zips up the throat. For added disguise, I belt into a cushy hotel robe and stick a knife in my pocket before checking the main room.

The dining room table is spread with enough food for a family of five, and I hate that I didn't hear so much as a rustling take-out bag when the guards waltzed into my room.

Did I read the wrong script?

This can't be how you treat a princess.

But I'm stuck, starving, and I can't remember the last time I had a meal that wasn't served on a plastic tray, so I pounce, ready to enjoy me some rich girl food. Like prime filet, and caviar wrapped in bacon and gold.

Nope.

Sushi.

Plates and plates of dishes I can't name or recognize.

It's not that I won't try new things, but I'm in disguise, highly stressed, and the fanciest thing I've ever eaten is bow-tie pasta.

Can a girl get a cheeseburger?

But my empty stomach demands food, and dinner isn't the hill I'm going to die on. So, I paw until I find cold noodles with sliced cucumbers and a brown sauce that turns out to be spicy peanut.

Okay. Yum.

I scarf them down, then make a plate of sushi and mess up the spread so that the guards who clear the table think Serafina went to town on her faves.

Then I carry my plate to the bathroom and flush the evidence, returning the sliced fish to their home in the sea.

At least one of us can be free.

I can fake it through the night.

But if this mission lasts beyond tomorrow morning?

I'll be the one sliced, diced, and served to the Redfangs on a board

NINE
DUTCH

BEING ALONE BLOWS GOAT BALLS.

Our home-suite-home at The Barrington is soaked to the studs in my brothers' scents, but when I can't see them, hear them, *feel* them, and know they're not going to disappear, my insides are so empty my heart falls down my ribs.

We've always been a pack, but no matter how tight we're twined, we aren't bonded.

Not blood-official.

Jin says bonding isn't a priority when we're hustling to shake the Triad off our ass.

I say, *body-swap me and see how fast you crack.*

If the pack were bonded, I wouldn't be rolled into a burrito on the futon, deep-sniffing my packleader's blanket like a creeper with a fistful of broken-in panties.

Jin is working and Reese is grabbing pizza, but Bish isn't even *gone*, gone

Just locked me out of his bedroom so he could make calls in peace

Silence is the worst.

Reminds me of the funeral.

Watching Dad's casket sink in the earth, nothing but that numb, silent hum drilling my ears because he's lost and gone forever.

I need noise and touch and the guys' scents to fill the needy holes that warn I can lose them just how I lost Dad.

Just how I lost Solly

I fill the silence and my mouth-hole with barbecue chips, crunching away the seconds until Bish breaks me free of the torture

The second his door unlocks, I flying-squirrel-launch into a hug, clinging like a neglected string-bean omega instead of a quarter-ton alpha dominant enough to bark a cattle train off the rails

Why bark when you can hug?

Bish stiffens. "If there's chip dust on your fucking fingers—"

"Licked them clean." I love licking.

Fingers. Dicks. *Mmf.*

If it fits in my mouth?

Just stick that shit in.

Bish drops his head on my shoulder.

He'd never ask for a hug, but he needs me—needs the pack—maybe even more than I need him.

'Cept, usually, he only holds a few seconds before he's storming away or barking me onto my knees.

I stroke his neck, feeling the prickly pieces of his perfectly gelled brown hair. He vibrates my fingers when I drag him closer. Even his scent is tense. Sharp and fizzy. "What's up?"

Soon as I break the sound barrier, Bishop struggles free. "My cock if you don't stop clinging."

Always salty.

"That's not a problem." I lick my lips, but when he starts counting his buttons like he's hiding something, it's impossible to go full chub. *The fuck happened now?* "What was your call about?"

"Jin's on his way," Bish answers. "He'll tell you himself."

I squint, planning an attack, but before I can force another hug, I hear my favorite sound—the door beep.

Reese has a stack of pizzas, a case of beer, and our fearless leader at his side.

I rocket between them, hooking their shoulders and grinding

into the stormy scent of Jin's suit collar like the golden retriever they left caged all day with no treats.

"Dude. Pizza." Reese wriggles away, balancing his boxes, so I have both arms to go after Jin.

I'm not much less dominant than him, but there's alpha and there's *alpha* I'm man enough to admit that Jin's energy is everything I need.

'Sides. Our leader has enough juice to spare me an extra squeeze

"You've been working too much," I complain, rubbing his shirt.

Jin strokes my neck with a dark chuckle. "Hard work is about to pay off."

He doesn't push me out, all shy and shady like Bish. Even without an official bond, Jin knows what I crave.

Never letting go, he backs me to the futon and rubs his cheek against mine, giving me his scent before he drops me on my ass, sitting me between him and Reese.

I wish Bishop would pile in with us instead of sitting in his special armchair throne, but with the four of us around the coffee table, 'least my heart pumps blood instead of dust bunnies.

Thigh-to-thigh, shoulder-to-shoulder, skin-to-skin.

So warm.

So fucking good.

I never feel home unless they're here.

Wish we could be together alllllll the time.

"Tell them." Bish folds his arms over his starched shirt, deflating my high before I can hit the ceiling.

Right. The simmering under-problem.

The scent of pepperoni pizza hides the swirling pheromones, giving zero clues. I squint at our packleader. "What's going on?"

Jin whips out an envelope. "Kairo gave us a job."

"You took it?" Reese mirrors my squint—the one that says *you must be fucking kidding me* in the secret language of our pack.

Bish and Jin trade a bullshit look that tickles my bones and spells trouble.

"We have to stop an auction." Jin slaps a bougie gold invitation on top of the pizza box tower.

I blink

Did I forget how to read again? "That can't say Serafina Redfang"

It can't. Jin wouldn't get us tangled with the cartel.

Our plan has always been to get away from the Triad. To smuggle Mom and Dany out of the country, and do witness protection or, like, move to Sumatra if that's what it takes to disappear.

The plan is not to put my mom, sister, and pack brothers in the middle of a fucking gang war that'll rip away everything we've built.

The plan is *definitely fucking not* to sniff around gangster omegas when we have a perfectly perfect beta waiting for us to find him and reunite.

There's only one thing I can say. "What kinda chudfuckery is this?"

"Well said." Bishop nods.

"Uh huh." Reese plucks the card from my numb fingers. "And can I add? Are you fucking nuts?"

"I'm serious." Jin pushes out his packleader mojo, silencing my auto-rumble. For the first time in a long time, I fight his muzzle, but Jin sets his jaw and pushes, throttling my challenge before I can squeak out a real snarl.

With his dominance sinking my shoulders like a family of anvils, all I can do is X-ray his brain.

No dice.

So I ask again. "What the *fuck*, Jinnie?"

"Listen first," he insists. "It's an opportunity, not an order. But you have to let me explain."

"All ears." Bishop crosses his legs.

I'm an ice cube, whipped to a freeze and fighting to rebel.

This explanation better win awards.

"Kairo wants to claim the girl for Jericho. He needs us to grab her before she's auctioned." Jin presses a hand to my chest, silencing the horse pill of an objection in my throat. "I know. He won't honor the deal. He'll kill us this time. That's why I'm proposing we do the job. Only, we keep the girl instead of making the delivery, and force a Triad/Redfang war while Kairo is weak."

Reese whistles. "That's some bold-ass shit."

"Double-cross the double-cross." Bishop strokes his tie. "We've done it before."

"*Wait, wait, wait.*" I hold up one hand, then another. "Keep the girl? And do what with her?"

"Take her underground," Jin says. "I have a plan."

He always has a plan.

Bet it's super smart, but that does nothing to wash out the gnarly taste growing on my tongue. I look around for help. "You don't agree to this, right?"

Bishop drums long fingers against his armrest. "Not really, but if Kairo keeps pushing, we're going to run out of moves. I'd rather go out with a bang than a pissant whimper."

"We already know what happens when we don't play Kairo's games," Reese says bitterly. "I'm not sold, but I'm tired of hitmen in the parking garage."

We've all had beat-downs and close calls.

I'd do anything to keep my people safe.

But Serafina Redfang?

She's as safe as a loose grenade.

I can't breathe through the iced gravel clogging my chest. "No. If Kairo finds my family—"

"Dutch." Jin squeezes my shoulder, force-pumping air into my lungs. "They're *our* family. Kairo will never touch them."

The packleader's *I'll-take-care-of-everything* dominance almost quiets my anxious rumble. But not even he can snuff the chaos in my chest when I imagine losing my girls.

"I'll have them on a plane tonight," Bishop offers. "We'll make other arrangements for the omega."

Fuck.

I'd rather lick the North Pole than send my family away, but I'm not letting them stay in this city if the guys are *seriously* serious about kidnapping the gangster girl.

"Yeah. About that omega?" Reese's knee bounces. "Why would the Redfang Princess want to kick it with us? Like, do we drug her? I must've missed class for a game the day they taught Kidnapping 101."

Jin's jaw tightens. "We're a better option for her than an auction."

"You're making it too complicated." Bishop waves. "An omega isn't that difficult to handle."

"What would you know about handling omegas?" I speak through the lava in my throat.

"I'd like to know more."

"Solomon—"

"Is gone," Bish says softly.

Our beta is *not* gone.

Solomon's still out there and I don't know why I'm the only one who knows, but I can fucking feel it in my bones or my gut or wherever my body stores all the real deep intuition. Maybe my left ass cheek. *Doesn't matter.* "I'm not screwing around with a Redfang omega. And we're not mating anyone but our fated one."

"Whoa." Jin pushes my ass down before I can leap the table to lovingly strangle Bish. "Who mentioned mating? If anything, this is a rescue."

"But if she goes into heat..." Bishop shrugs off my glare. "What? A gentleman doesn't leave an omega to suffer."

"How can you be so..." My finger-claws form a circle the size of Bishop's throat. Need to remind him which of us is more dominant.

Shouldn't have given him all those hugs.

Next time, I'm fucking *him* over his desk.

I'm so pissed, I even shrug off Jin's grip. "I'm going to the safe house"

Bishop's phone chirps. "Wait."

"What?" I'm already headed to the door, already hating being away from the pack as much as I hate their stupid plan.

"Serafina just came through the lobby."

"She's staying *here?*"

"Penthouse suite." Bish scrolls his phone. "Should we say hello now, or in the morning?"

Fuck. *Thaaaut.* "I'm leaving."

"Dutch." Jin catches me at the door. "Bish will send you the flight info. Help the girls pack, but take the long way. At least three cars tracked me home."

"I'm not that stupid." I push past him and make it halfway down the hall before the silence slithers into my ears, and I swear I hear the *tump* of a wilting rose hitting a coffin lid.

Can't believe I have to say goodbye to Mom and Dany.

Not that keeping them cooped up at the safe house is the best life, but sending them away—where I won't know if they're okay —is ultra-worse.

Reese finds me blocking housekeeping carts and foot traffic without giving a single fuck.

"Go." He ruffles my hair, then forces two pizza boxes into my hands. "I'll keep the guys honest."

"You're going along with this bullshit?" I lean into his palm, banking warmth for the ride across town.

He rubs his bad arm. "It was always going to be us or Kairo in the end. I just want to be done with this shit and move on, you know? Even a crazy chance is a chance."

"That's the part I hate." I hug him one more time before braving the elevator.

I'm not afraid of many things.

Not violence, pain, fighting, or even fighting the Triad.

I'm just afraid of what the fighting costs.

I can't lose anyone else.

That thought would usually send me into a sick tailspin about cancer and Dad and the beta who got away, but before I can spiral, a bizarro scent invades my nose cave.

My skin shrink-wraps my skeleton.

Omega.

Spicy and sweet, but not too sweet.

Tangy-delish.

My cock doesn't just stiffen.

It *boi-oi-oings* to my waistband, blowing up my knot like I'm face-to-flesh with my mate in heat, ready and able—*but totally fucking unwilling*—to stay hard for days.

I muffle my bulge with the pizza boxes, trying to breathe out the vampire woodie sucking my blood.

But not even double meat cancels the mystery omega's crop-dusted super-pheromones.

Like, *brooooo.*

Save the salami for the mate who's waiting for us.

Don't whip out the thiccness for some elevator ghost.

Too late.

I'm probably already piercing cardboard.

Looking like a fucking perv with a free-samples sausage fest in my sweats, I waddle to the bus stop, praying this sweaty lap heat is from the oven and not from a rogue pepperoni hugging the tip of my swollen hog like a jaunty nitrate bonnet.

But four route switches and almost two hours later, I waddle off the bus in the Meadows just as raging hard as when I boarded.

What in the Neapolitan *fuck* was that scent?

A bag lady whistles. "Need me to take care of that knot, big boy?"

I speed-walk, trying to ignore the weight swinging between my thighs. "It belongs to my mate!"

Yeah, Bishop takes my ass all the time, but that's different. It's not like we kiss. I don't even let him blow me—not that he would.

Can't risk jizz on his button-down.

Point is, this dick is pristine.

Swollen knot untouched.

Saved myself for my beta—my fated mate.

Not some rando elevator omega.

But not even a stroll through the slums softens my grundle.

I cut through alleys littered with bullet casings and sky-high trash bags, wishing I had to go farther before the buildings opened up to the neighborhood where Mom and Dany have been crashing

I want to move them somewhere with a fence and a security system, but Kairo can hack cameras.

Jin says they're safer in the slums.

Anonymous.

But what good is keeping them safe from Kairo if they get car-jacked or home-invaded?

'Least no one will be able to hurt them once they're on the plane

"Mom?" I announce my arrival while I unlock the first set of bars. "It's me."

"Baby?" Bolts and chains rattle. "What's going on? Bishop sent an itinerary." When the barred door swings open, she bundles me into a hug.

Mom's red hair has badass grey wings, and her beta scent is as warm as her hug—crusty, yeasty bread. I chuck the pizza boxes to squeeze her.

She's the reason for my hug gene, but she pulls away real fast. "You seem…agitated'

Nooooooooooo

Fuck you, elevator omega.

I dodge behind the threadbare sofa. "It's nothing."

"Doesn't look like nothing." Her blue eyes flick downward. "Do we need to have another talk about the birds and the bees? Or the birds and the birds?"

"Mom. No." My neck sweats, but even judged and mashed into the sofa, my cock won't go soft.

What do the commercials say?

If it stays up more than three hours, I'm either going to urgent care or Bish has to take one for the team. "Please just pack."

Dany peeks out of her room, her strawberry blonde hair tied in two poofy, frazzled buns. "How much luggage can we bring? And how long are we going away? I need a bunch of notebooks for... projects"

"Take whatever you need. I don't know how long. Things are kind of a mess right now."

"Everything's always a mess." Dany drifts into the living room. "Ooh. Pizza?"

"Wait!" I dash and grab the top box, shoving it into her hands before confiscating the bottom one.

Hope that wet spot is pizza grease.

"Why?" She holds the box, her sisterly intuition making me sweat.

"Just... Don't."

"Dandelion. Finish packing." Mom shoos her. "I'll run the inquisition"

"Get good answers." My sister takes a slice for the road, then Mom drags me into the micro-kitchen.

She folds her arms over her cardigan. "Talk."

"Didn't Bish explain?" I run my fingers through my hair.

How do I tell her what's up without mentioning the guys are planning to kidnap an omega?

She'll murder me, and I didn't even agree to this bullshit plan.

"Don't stall."

I wince. "Triad power struggle. Just need you to be safe for a few days."

"But you won't be safe?"

"No. I'll be safe too. Promise. Everything will blow over soon."

While they pack, I scarf smegma slices. Even though the girls bustle around the tiny-ass house, my ears are already starting to echo with silence.

Everything would be fine if I could hug my beta.

But Solly is gone.

Soon, Mom and Dany will be gone.

And *fuck*.

I don't care if you're alpha, omega, triad, or cartel.

If you're not my family and you're not my pack, then leave me the fuck alone.

I don't give a liquid shit if Serafina Redfang is having a rough life

My caring card ran out of space when I was fourteen, and I'm fresh out of fucks to give for anyone new.

All I care about is protecting my own.

To set my intention, I sneak into the bathroom and jerk my frustrations into a washcloth.

Fast. Dry. Angry.

I cum so hard I bellow in wingdings:

(Forget you, elevator omega!)

This load belongs to Solomon.

TEN

SOL

I SPEND the night staring at my phone, waiting for an update and sleeplessly researching how to craft a parachute from sheets if I have to emergency-bail the penthouse.

When the sun rises through spotless, floor-to-ceiling windows with zillion-dollar views, I have to face the *womp womp* music that says I'm getting screwed.

I'm a good actress.

But good enough to fool Nikolaj Redfang longer than it takes to microwave a hot dog?

Not betting my life.

Instead of obsessing over thread counts and wind resistance, I cave and take a shower, releasing the tension in my neck by freeing my tightly leashed pheromones. The detachable shower head washes my stink without ruining what's left of last night's makeup mask.

It's nine a.m. and I'm pacing, playing with the throat of Serafina's only high-neck top when someone finally knocks.

"Yeah?"

"Your dresses, Miss Redfang," a familiar female voice answers. "Could you have your guards let me in?"

"Let her in." I rush to the door.

In a pantsuit and red lipstick, with her hair flowing in fat curls, Elyse pulls a garment rack into the foyer. I catch a hint of piña colada and the moonstruck guards before she slams the door, jamming her rack in front as a barricade.

"You are so fucked." That plastic smile melts, her voice fraying to a hiss. "Every Redfang in the city is camping the hotel." She tosses her hair and sticks out a manicured hand. "Give me the laptop."

"And then what?" If the SAS is seriously going to abandon me, I'll chuck it off the balcony without a sheet-chute.

"Stay undercover." Elyse unzips the rack, revealing a row of terrifying white gowns. "Serafina's guards cracked. Tonight's some kind of party for her. Nikolaj will be there in person to escort his baby girl. Commander needs you to fake it until then."

"No. Even if I can pass off her mannerisms, her scent—"

When Elyse yanks out a zippered case, my stomach drops to The Barrington's wine cellar.

"Serafina made a visit to Doctor Brandon's lab. He synthesized her perfume for you."

"Please tell me that's lotion."

"Syringes. Doctor says you'll need to inject every two to three hours to maintain the scent." Her eyes sparkle. "Want me to give you the first jab?"

"If I do this—"

"You don't have a choice. We have no way of getting you out without starting a war, and—Well, you already know."

Commander Fissure wouldn't start a war for me.

Commander Fissure wouldn't *cross the street* for me.

I take the case

"Give me her laptop and phone." Elyse makes a grabby motion. "Simon geared me up to unlock everything. Then shoot up while we jailbreak, because we've got maybe twenty minutes before my pheromones wear off and your guards realize I'm not your party planner."

Wet-swallowing, I head to the bathroom.

The case passes as a clutch or oversized phone wallet. It's black and semi-rigid, with a length of heavy-duty elastic that can be looped for a discreet wristlet look, or wound through inserts for a more covert, thigh-holster, classy drug-smuggler vibe.

Unzipped, it looks like a girl's on-the-go makeup kit, holding eyeliner, concealer, gloss, and a pouch of green contacts.

It could pass a search until I unstick the false back.

A pen-shaped cartridge, spare needles, and dozens of vials the size of pencil erasers are hidden beneath. Each glass shimmers with a few concentrated drops of piss-yellow pheromones.

Popping a vial into the slot is no harder than filling a candy dispenser, but instead of giving me a treat, twisting the cartridge reveals the stabby end of the finger-length needle spring-loaded inside

Finding scent glands is easy. Just rub until you hit the sensitive spot on either side of your neck, right beside the pulse.

All I have to do is aim and tap the plunger.

Easy as clicking a pen.

Only, my numb thumb refuses to finish the job.

Icy fingers tingling, I stare down the green-eyed girl in the mirror

I bet Serafina could sacrifice a whole hand without a flinch.

If I'm playing her, I have to steal her juice.

Without giving myself time for dread, for a countdown, or even a deep breath, I stab myself in the neck.

Pain blanks my vision. The needle-cartridge clatters to the tile.

Head whirling like I'm hostage on the playground spinner, I reflux hard enough to taste flushed sushi. Then my lips pucker and my throat closes and all I can do is retch on vodka-lemon pheromones that taste like a flaming shot of kitchen floor cleaner

When I stop sweating, shaking, and spitting bile into the sink, I'm pumping out Serafina's hard lemonade like it's my original recipe

My real pheromones are pushed down but in reach when I stretch past the sour itch in my veins and a little to the left

The fact that I can still protect myself keeps me from a full-on freak-out, but if I have to drop my act, I'm already screwed.

My pheromones have distance limits.

I'm not Dara who can block Redfang bullets with my brain—unless you count the literal way that turns me into a bloodstain.

The only way I'll survive is by playing a perfect pitcher of gangster lemonade

I shake off the fear and the sour candy aftertaste of the shot that leaves my neck itching.

I can do this.

Not because I want to, but because I need to prove I can.

The risk increases the reward.

Also, there's the part where I have no choice.

But every second I survive, I'm showing what a good girl I can pretend to be.

That I'm safe to be free.

When I leave the bathroom, sweat mopped and mouth wiped, wearing the case as a wristlet, Elyse has Serafina's laptop and phone hooked to wires on the dining room table.

She gives a cautious sniff. "Perfect. I can't tell the difference. Now find a dress that fits."

"Is there one with a neck?"

"One. But it shows more skin than fabric." She yanks the contender from the rack.

It's a poof of a princess skirt with a high neck and long sleeves that would be demure if they weren't made of see-through, rose-patterned lace

I swallow. "Will that cover my nipples?"

"Not really." Elyse shrugs. "I guess Serafina wants to mate fast? She's old to be unmarked."

Right.

I checked Serafina's ID.

She's an ancient twenty-three, a whole year younger than me.

Flicking through the rack, my only options are V-necks, halters, and tube tops.

"I'll try the lace." I reluctantly drag the flouncy bundle into the bathroom. It zips with complaints in the boob area, but I'm more worried about the neck.

Delicate lace climbs to my chin, and even though the fabric is sheer, it masks my scars. The pattern gets denser below the knee, where there's a hint of lining, and the hem falls low enough to keep my janky ankles under wraps.

I cup my throat.

I want to throw on a fur shawl or a gaiter or a freaking fleece vest, because just having the outline of my neck on display makes me feel worse than naked.

My skin crawls until I'm back in yoga gear with the hotel robe closed tight to my chin.

Resigned, I re-hang the dress. "It'll have to work."

But I'm crossing nibbled fingers that the SAS nails Nikolaj before I have to show my face at the clown cotillion.

"These should match." Elyse hands me a pair of pearl-studded heels that are absolutely going to blister. "Take her phone, too. It's unlocked, but add your face so you can get in again."

I tap through Serafina's settings and after a few front and side scans, I'm officially my sister.

With zero time to spare.

A guard knocks. "You about done?"

"Shit." Elyse jams cords and gear into hidden pockets at the small of her back. "Commander will give you the signal tonight. Don't do anything without her orders. And if you try to run—"

"I'll wait." I bunch my fists.

I bet the SAS has thirty contingency plans to handle me going rogue and zero in place for if I get caught.

Is it too late to steal my sister's jet?

Elyse's smile flips its switch, and she pours pineapple sugar into my waiting guards' ears. "Thank you so much, Miss Redfang. I'll be back to escort you tonight. Enjoy your spa day."

I start to scowl.

I *plan* to scowl—but then Elyse goes glaze-eyed for the men she's passing, and my face can't make a single twitch.

I freeze like I just did an ice bucket challenge with liquid nitrogen. Like my strings are cut and my heart stopped beating and I cease to exist, because all the light and air in the universe just got stolen by *them*.

Bishop Barrington.

Su-Jin Moon.

A thousand years stretch between their footsteps, and I absorb every detail as they move through stilted time.

Bishop wears a vamp-red suit with a purple tie, pulling off the cut and color like no one ever could. He's taller than he is in my fantasies, but his neatly styled brown hair hasn't changed. There's something newly dangerous in the easy grace of his stride, but his smirk hasn't budged and neither has the sarcastic twinkle sparkling in his hazel, thick-lashed eyes.

Then SuJin

Jin.

My Jinnie.

Ink black hair hangs to his forehead, artfully messy.

Black tux

Black eyes.

Black soul.

But sweet for me.

Or he used to be.

Now he moves like a panther or some big cat, his dominance so intoxicating, I tremble before I'm absorbed into his orbit.

Just by being, Jin claws out my deepest truth.

It's impossible to see him and not remember he's the only boy I've ever kissed.

Just by existing, he owns me.

But that's not the truth I've been dreading.

Not the truth that chokes my airways and leaves me puffing stolen lemon pheromones with all the softness of zested disinfectant.

They take one more slow-motion step before my world collapses

Because then I'm hit with their scents.

Bishop tastes like peach juice dribbling down my chin and fresh champagne so crisp that phantom bubbles tease my skin.

Jin is lightning. Ozone, salt, and magic after a wild summer storm.

I shiver, I shake.

They're so edible my mouth floods, but there's no signs of life from my dead, gamma soul.

No pull to jump them or beg for their knots and bites and bonds. Any butterflies that could've survived are pulped by the black hole pit that obliterates my gut.

My scars throb.

They're not meant to be mine.

My throat itches, my eyes prick with tears, and I'm already mourning my teenage dreams when Bishop chokes.

"No fucking way." He grabs his collar. "You're—"

Jin's nostrils flare, and I thought his eyes were black before—now they yawn, spinning abyss.

Lemon rises like Serafina's ghost wants a piece of her own, and when their scents rage to match, Jin makes the sound that shatters my heart.

He *purrs.* "You're the one."

But he's not purring for me.

He's purring for the lemon pheromones I shot into my throat.

He's purring for *her.*

The men I've always loved?

The only ones I ever wanted to be mine?

Serafina Redfang is their fated mate.

ELEVEN

JIN

LEMON BUTTERMILK CAKE.

Serafina Redfang smells like my favorite dessert, drizzled in glaze

I want to lick her throat

Need to

A rumble stakes my chest, and the fact that I don't believe in fate is fucking irrelevant when my future mate parts her lips.

She tugs a hotel robe across her chest like she's tightening her armor. She's sharp all over—cut cheekbones, tight ponytail, bladed eyeliner.

But when I'm drowning in cake batter, soft and sweet and made to drive me fucking insane, Serafina's hard edges don't mean shit

She's all fluff, trembling for me the same way my veins are roaring for her.

Fuck the long-term plan.

Fuck Jericho, Kairo, and everything Triad.

Serafina is mine

Bishop yanks his tie, loosening the knot

I've watched him bury a body in a buttoned vest. His pretentious ass only steps out of formalwear to shower.

Now his Adam's apple bobs, throat working so hard, he pulls apart his collar, breaking his own rules for the heiress who just delivered our pack a double-tap to the chest

Bang. Bang. Done.

She's ours.

And fuck are we gonna have to fight to keep her.

"Mate," I growl, so deep and darkly possessive, Serafina's guards pull semi-automatics

I forgot they were here.

Serafina flinches.

She should be diving into my arms, letting me rub her in my scent and mark her for our pack's protection.

Instead, she tucks her neck.

She's thrown.

I get it.

Me fucking too.

I soften my tone, not wanting to scare my omega. "Serafina."

She flinches, hands creeping to shield her throat. "Don't call me that."

The defensive reaction makes no sense, unless the hallway grew a headwind that's blocking her from tasting our scent.

We already belong to her.

She has to know. Has to sense gravity rearranging, dragging us to spin around her and no one else.

"*Princess*," Bishop rasps, choking on his straining tie. "You feeling this?"

Ten guards with trigger fingers cocked are the only reason she's not already in my arms.

"No," her ragged whisper tears my chest.

Before I can ask or purr or figure out what's wrong, she slams the door.

The *thunk* echoes in sudden, empty silence.

Her stormy exit wafts one last breath of cake and lemon that yanks my heart and stirs my knot.

My teeth ache and my blood froths. "That's our mate."

The reaction's too wild to be anything else.

"Yeah? Why's she not think the same?" Bishop pierces the door with eyes as joy-crazed as the day Senior landed twenty to life. But the expression breaks with his voice. "Fuck. Did she just...?"

"Reject us." I haven't felt this helpless since Kairo's enforcers pinned me down to tat my hands.

"Can she do that?"

We didn't give her a reason to say yes, but we didn't give her a reason to say no.

Unless she recognized us.

The bastard brother of the fiancé she despises, and the heir of the fallen hotel magnate.

"Not for long." I swallow bitterness and a growl.

I've given everything to Jericho.

Blood, sweat, and *years* of my life.

He can't have my meant-to-be-mate.

Jericho doesn't want *her* He wants Serafina's stake in the Redfang Cartel.

If not for private security—and the invisible cord binding me to the girl behind that door—I'd already be on the way to make his coma permanent

While Bish and I try to reel back our souls, Serafina's guards close ranks, blocking the path to our future.

"You wanna walk away, or you wanna take the shortcut down the laundry chute?" The head guard growls with paper dominance

Before I can waste the asshole, Bishop recovers, straightening his tie. "Gentlemen. I came to extend greetings to a treasured guest of my hotel. This is my associate, Mr. Moon."

My father's last name is the magic word.

These toy soldiers won't play with the Triad.

The leader holsters his shit and finally speaks with some respect. "Make an appointment with the boss. Our princess doesn't meet with unapproved alphas."

"Of course. We'll give Old Nik a ring. Have a wonderful stay." Bishop drags my elbow.

A rubber band stretches, painful tension forcing out a growl so deep it shakes the building.

Wrong way. Need to go back. To her.

But I let Bish take the lead.

I'm not thinking clear-headed.

Maybe never will again.

When we turn the corner, Bishop flashes his master key, yanking me into a vacant nesting suite.

Past the foyer is the windowless den where I can already picture her spread between our bodies on a mattress big enough for five.

Rubbed in our scents.

Taking our bites.

Finally patching the ragged hole left by the beta we lost.

"Fucking disaster." Bishop touches his buttons one-by-one, rubbing up and down the row on his suit jacket. "Need a shower. No. *Fuck.* Shower in vodka."

"You need *her.*"

"Yeah? She's not interested." Bish goes rigid, no way to let loose when he can't wrinkle his clothes without triggering a flashback

"She will be." I palm his skull and rub, destroying his style until he squawks.

"Ass." He yanks a comb from his pocket, shouldering past me to the bathroom mirror. As soon as he has something to make neat, the logic I need from him clicks back online. "We're not going to lose her."

"Exactly. We're going to win."

Serafina Redfang has to be ours.

Not because she's the prize, but because it's written in the stars

See? She already has me simping like Dutch.

Before we can bring her home, I have to make her safe.

"We're advancing our bug-out plan." My temples throb at our exploding list of enemies. The Triad. The Redfangs. *Every alpha who ever looked at our mate crooked.* "Call Dutch and Reese. We need the whole team if we're going to get her out before the auction."

Bishop grabs his phone. "Everything just got so much more fucking complicated."

I lick my lips, tasting lemon dust that adds a buzz to the utter fucking terror of the truth.

I've never come out on top against the Triad.

But cheat, steal, kill—*whatever it takes.*

Our pack is done playing dead.

We're going to fight.

We're going to *win.*

And we're going to fucking pray that Serafina Redfang can look beyond our shitty families and imagine the pack we'll build together after we bulldoze all this gang bullshit.

TWELVE

SOL

I HYPERVENTILATE.

Rasping, I claw at my throat.

Itchy. Aching. Swallowing globs of red-hot lead.

I sprint to the shower, wanting to scrub off the nightmare lemon that just forced me to say good night to my last sweet dream. But when I stagger into the bathroom, the straps of the syringe case chafe between my thighs.

If I wash off Serafina's scent, I'll have to stick my neck again.

Unless I want to be caught. Then killed.

I don't want that, even after the crater to my ribcage.

Needing to be somewhere small and dark, I crawl under the bathroom vanity and hug my knees.

Bishop and Jin are beautiful.

They're powerful, dominant, and still so hypnotizing.

Of course they don't want me.

I'd cry, but all my sockets do is sting.

No tears. This is old news.

The Serafina part is a forced-update that leaves my stomach digesting my exposed-to-air lungs, but I've known I was broken forever.

I was fifteen when I kissed Jin.

Scrawny, wearing Kayden or Jayden's old cargo shorts with a shoelace for a belt. Vivian kept me in buzzcuts—said my hair clogged her drains—and I always wore a baseball hat.

The guys thought I was a boy, and I made sure they kept

thinking that, terrified they'd kick a leftover little girl out of their crew.

Jin was a little older, his alpha pheromones just starting to spark. Being in the same room as him made my skin crackle.

I'd been avoiding him and the others for weeks, afraid they'd see through my lies. With them growing up and hitting their pre-awakening before me, I couldn't figure out which smile I could wear that could possibly convince them not to leave me behind.

Bishop always ran fights.

Then, suddenly he was running them every night.

I overheard my foster brothers gossiping. *'Reese Parker took a gang hit. Fucked up his whole arm. Barrington is scraping for cash."*

Late at night, I sprinted to the warehouse alone, hopping needles and risking getting shot.

Jin was in the cage. Blood-spattered, taking out his rage on some kid's face. Dutch had to drag him out of the ring.

I never found out what happened, but I could *feel* Jin shouldering the blame.

Lost, angry.

His grief sliced like razors.

I followed him to the changing room.

His chest was heaving, his knuckles split, and there was so much blood and pain, all I wanted to do was take it away.

So I kissed Jin.

It was fast.

A press of lips, a butterfly landing on a stem.

He tasted like electricity.

Numbed my tongue.

Then my toes curled and my belly cramped in the scariest new way, and I *knew*. I couldn't keep pretending to be friends.

I ran before I had to hear Jin say he didn't feel the same, but I figured I had my answer when the pack disappeared.

Afterward, I heard Reese lost his baseball scholarship. One rumor said their pack got in trouble with the Triad and had to run from Jin's dad. Another said Bishop's father shipped them to college in Italy to make mafia contacts and let Reese recover by the sea

Maybe they came back, maybe they tried to contact me, but I never found out because I had to disappear too.

Jin's kiss rocked me into pre-awakening.

My toxic gamma stink didn't come until my traumatic full awakening, but within a few days of tasting Jin's lips, my strange, sour, omega-with-an-asterisk pheromones peeked out. Before I knew what was happening, my foster "fathers" started looking at me a way that no grown man should ever look at a fourteen-year-old girl.

Vivian flipped, but not because she mated a pack of trash bastards

She was jealous. Full-on, ragey-territorial.

Remembering makes me dry heave.

Luckily, my second-worst mother figure was so desperate to boot me fast and far away that she accidentally made a good decision. She banished me to the Omega Cultivation Center.

So, I was blindsided yet again, finding out I was an omega* the same way I'm always blindsided by shocking new revelations about who and what I am.

I've lived through some bombs.

But that kiss was the one that rearranged my foundation.

For almost four years at the OCC, every day, every time I thought of Jin, Bishop, Dutch, or Reese—*my dream pack*—my belly gave that same shivery twist.

I had no reason to think they'd accept me, even if I hunted them down

But I *hoped*.

I hoped and dreamed and fantasized about five-way heats.

Then my Redfang brothers recognized this store-brand princess face, stole me from my bed, and ran a sale on a fake heiress

I clutch my stomach, but it forgot how to flutter the night the men who bought me bit my throat.

I didn't bite back. Didn't complete the bond. But they forced a partial mating, just deep enough to ruin my hope.

An omega can survive a broken bond, especially one that's already weak or fraying, but it's a hell of a different ride when your mates die and their bites are bloody fresh.

Also, when you're their murderer.

Now, I'm basically a bond widow.

Hormones MIA.

I never had a second heat after they drugged me into the first.

And fuck a fluffy duck.

I didn't know what I was doing. My ability popped out of nowhere when I was terrified and bleeding, barely aware of anything beyond the blood and smoke. I couldn't feel my body, let alone control the brand-new gamma whammy.

If it were now?

I'd make them suffer.

So. Much. *More.*

Being freakish and halfway widowed never stopped my obsession with the guys. As much as I dreaded ever seeing them again, I clung to that last, desperate hope that we'd find each other and my body would magically heal.

I'd be perfect and whole, for them.

Now even the dream I couldn't admit to myself is dead.

I have other reasons to survive.

Like my burning desire to grind Bridget Fissure's face in gravel.

To escape the SAS and figure out who I want to be when I'm not hiding behind a mask to survive.

I want to travel, learn to make every kind of pasta, and live long enough to read the final chapter in my favorite APOCALIPS smut fic

But I feel hollow.

The point of pretending to be someone else was to *stop* the hurt.

I should've known Serafina Redfang couldn't be a shield.

She's a diamond-encrusted knife to the heart.

Eventually, I climb out of the hole and shake off the shadow of my past.

After I wipe my face, I call room service for a vat of coffee and a breakfast sandwich, extra greasy.

Fuck family, first loves, and freaky special abilities.

Cheese and caffeine are the only things keeping me going.

γ

SERAFINA WAS SCHEDULED for a mud wrap and a six-hand massage with three betas who want to touch my skin and rub gunk on my scars.

Hell no

I shut it down, only grudgingly letting the spa staff give me a manicure and some lighter blonde highlights to perfect my costume. I need to be more-than-perfect if I'm going to fool Nikolaj.

Between treatments, I duck into the changing room to re-up my lemon.

The nausea passes, but the itch deepens, crawling beneath another layer of skin.

I breathe through the ick.

Only a few more hours.

With black, coffin-tipped gel nails decked in real diamonds—that at this point I'm assuming are from the Redfang blood mine—I hole up in the penthouse linen closet with a towel around my throat and the syringe clutch strapped under my robe.

If I can't be comfortable in my skin, I at least need to be comfortable in my role. Desperate for a distraction, I snoop through Serafina's phone.

My sister has a running text with HOUSEKEEPER, who I assume brings whatever she vomits into the chat, whether she wants snacks or whole people.

honey mustard pretzels

thongs (not the itchy ones)

shotgun shells

Colton and Jack but tell Xander it's a threesome and he's not invited until he's man enough to eat ass

coconut water

no, the other coconut water, the one with the fucking green coconut on the label you utter walnut cunt

tarp

Her contacts are labeled by titles instead of names. My scent glands strangle when I hit *Fuckboi Fiancé.*

Internet-translating the multiple languages in their chat doesn't make it clear if my sister's accusing this guy of fucking hedgehogs or telling him to sit on the sharp end of a quill, but, "you'll never touch me with that diseased dick," is clear enough English

I remember to breathe.

I can't fake a relationship with someone who genuinely *likes* my sister. But the more I dig, the more I realize nobody belongs in that bucket.

When I find Nikolaj's texts, I need to add brain bleach to her list.

<3 DADDY <3

Your trainer reports you've been slacking. Have you gained weight?

No, Daddy

<3 DADDY <3

Be dressed and smiling at 8. I trust you've learned the proper way to treat my suppliers?

Yikes on electric trikes.

I thought *I* was putting on a show of obedience.

The peek behind the curtain clears my doubts about my acting chops

I've done the rehearsals. I've practiced the lines and the smiles until my cheeks burn and my anger's all stuffed down.

Serafina's role is even easier than my day-to-day, bad gamma schtick. All I have to do is act docile for Nikolaj.

I can call everyone else cunts and cashews without getting fried for insubordination.

I'm pacing, ready for anything when a guard finally calls. "Marie's here!"

"Send her in."

When the door cracks, I glance away.

Bishop and Jin wouldn't be waiting, but it took me all day to restart my heart, and I can't risk another spiritual earth-shake. I'm busy not getting recognized, ripped apart, and slowly murdered.

"Miss Redfang." The party planner, Marie, is a forty-something beta with long wavy hair, wearing the same pantsuit Elyse must've charmed her out of to fool the guards.

Her gaze is slightly glazed, but she tosses her hair, quickly regaining the rapid-fire pace that must be her original speed. "The venue is divine. Everything has been decorated according to your father's specifications. Oh. But didn't we rule out this dress?" She lifts the high-necked gown I left hanging. "Your father wants—"

"Is there a fucking problem?" My voice whip-cracks, sharp as my killer pheromones.

Marie ducks, instantly submissive. "No! That's not what I— It's lovely. Truly, truly lovely. No problem at all. Anything you want, Miss Redfang."

Bitch mode is the best. "Walk me through the final itinerary."

"My team will do your hair and makeup while your guests enjoy craft cocktails in the smoking lounge. You'll be announced promptly at nine, when your father escorts you inside. The prospective packs will inspect you and present their offers, followed by your...*ah*..individual meeting with the victors in the en suite nest."

"*My what?*" Years of practice pay off when I squash the panic in my voice, but I can't pretend I'm not feeling the dread bomb shredding my intestines. "Give me the guest list."

"Your father—"

"Fucking give me the list," I snap.

Biting her lipstick until it stains her teeth, Marie grudgingly offers her phone. "Just a peek. Please don't tell him I let you see."

"I'll take it to the grave." *Probably a few hours from now.*

The list is short. Only four packs, but they're a *who's who* of gangland alphas Bridget would cream herself to apprehend.

Scanning their names and photos, I already need paper-bag oxygen

Then I catch the heading I skipped.

Confirmed Guest List
Redfang Heiress Auction

No way

Noshitfuckingway.

I try to swallow the panic, but my soul squeaks out of my body with the ominous whine of a soon-to-explode airship.

I was told tonight was a party.

No one mentioned I was the favor.

While I silently spin out, Marie snatches her phone. "Your limo is waiting. I'll tell you more about the alphas on the way."

Following her from the penthouse at the head of a column of way too many Redfang soldiers to take down in a single swoop, I fumble under my robe, desperately shooting a no-look text to mission control.

When's the intercept?

I climb in the limo, waiting for my phone to buzz.

I ride to the venue, waiting for my phone to buzz.

I listen to Marie gush over the rich underworld alphas who're dying to "adore" me, trying not to pass out and forever waiting for my phone to buzz.

Silence.

The only buzz is the one in my brain, screaming that I'm up shit creek with a paper straw for a paddle.

I'll die before I let myself feel the heat of another alpha's sewer-scented breath.

No.

Even better.

They'll die.

Screw earning my freedom.

I'm gonna run for it.

FOUR CARS ESCORT us to an uptown mansion where the gardens say historical drama, the security says mob thriller, and the scream buried behind my collarbone says raunchy teen horror flick

Guess who's playing the virgin sacrifice?

Maybe I can escape on a technicality.

Tell Nikolaj some alphas named Jack and Colton have been dicking me down, knotting me up, and munching my ass in circles

Redfang alphas in suits and earpieces stop the limo at the gatehouse, using a long-poled mirror to check underneath for bombs.

That's just the titty-tip of this shit-berg.

I'm used to cameras, electric fences, and armed guards.

Stun a few dudes and hop the wrought-iron fence?

Cake.

But I count twenty cartel soldiers on my side of the lawn. That's way more than I can smack down with my firepower weakened in the open air.

Then there are the dogs, led by teams of enforcers.

I couldn't fake past them in a dress lined with tenderloin.

Animals loathe my pheromones.

Cats. Squirrels. Birds.

Once, on a training hike, a pissed-off prairie dog tried to gnaw through my boot

I'm the opposite of one of those fairy-tale princesses.

As the limo coasts down the long drive, every leashed killer perks its ears like my shoved-down pheromones are sounding the dinner whistle.

Knew I was due for a new leading role.

Next up: chew toy

"Is something wrong?" Marie cuts into my doom stare.

I recover with a hair flip. "What's with the security?"

"The guests are...distinguished." She suppresses a shudder. "And you, of course. You're Master Redfang's precious heiress, and you've never made a public social appearance. Everyone's dying to meet you."

Sure. There'll be lots of dying.

Marie's pep strains as tight as my nerves.

The limo stops at the mansion's back door. As soon as we climb out, armed Redfangs flood the steps, pulling Marie for a pat-down.

I'm prepared to princess-shriek, "IT'S TAMPONS!" if the grizzly alphas come anywhere near the syringe case strapped high on my thigh.

But either my innocent face is on point or Serafina Redfang is allowed to smuggle weapons. The alphas let me inside without a rub-down.

Marie escorts me upstairs, then instantly bails. "I'm off to receive the packs. The beauty team will get you settled."

With door guards eyeing me, all I can do is enter. The fussy parlor overflows with doilies and the floral scents of four ultra-submissive betas waiting to serve me with their heads bowed.

"Leave," I snap before they can twitch. "I'll do it myself."

"Yes, Princess." They bow out, freeing me from their pheromones and the need to be touched by strangers.

I pry apart the curtains.

A door leads to an outside balcony, but it's no good as an escape route. With the sunlight long gone, the thorn-lined gardens are well-lit and just as well patrolled.

No place to hide.

I duck into the bathroom, run the faucet to drown out any surveillance, then dial mission control. My pulse beats in my fingertips as the line rings.

When no one answers, my neck prickles.

The SAS is cruel, but they're not stupid.

There's no way Team Fissure hasn't gotten the memo I'm about to be broken and sold.

Holy shit. She expects me to go through with it.

I mean, I expected to be screwed, but not *this* hard.

I dial again.

Again.

A few more times.

After twenty or thirty calls, the line finally connects.

"Simon here. What can I do you for?" he trills like he's taking pizza orders.

Meanwhile, I'm undercover in a cartel, alone, and about to be auctioned*a-fucking-gain*—without a whiff of a plan to reassure me this is a mission and not a set-up.

"*What the hell?* I hiss. "Elyse said you'd give me a signal. When are you moving to grab Nikolaj?"

"Oh. It's you."

"Simon!"

"Yeah, yeah. So, here's the thing. Serafina's talking and the commander wants to keep her talking. We need you to stall."

"For how long?" I grit my teeth until I taste powdered jaw bone

"A few days. She—"

"Put Bridget on the phone."

"Commander Fissure said—"

"I will fry your potato chip ass. Put her on. *Now*."

Simon grumbles, but eventually the line clicks.

"Twenty-Six. The situation has evolved." My heart squeezes when Bridget speaks, military crisp—like I'm not about to be sacrificed and everything is going perfectly to plan.

Oh, right.

It is.

The plan where I fuck up and have to show my hand to save my throat.

"Evolved how?" I ask lightly, so disgustingly used to swallowing my fury.

Has Bridget ever once thought of me as her kid?

Don't answer that question.

"Serafina is willing to testify against her father, but it takes time to prepare warrants and a case. We need you to keep Nikolaj distracted. Buy us twenty-four hours and then we can discuss your freedom."

Twenty-four hours?

I'm *minutes* from being bought and bitten.

But that's never happening again.

Never.

Again.

So, more like I'm seconds from snapping and showing the Redfangs, the SAS, and every shady gangster pack in the building that they picked the wrong fucking girl.

Discuss my freedom?

Let's be honest.

The SAS never wanted me free.

But I'm not stupid either.

My words come out so flat and smooth, Bridget can't possibly imagine the magma churning through my heart. "If you want time, I'll have to make a scene. You know it's an auction?"

"Yes. Use your discretion. The primary goal is keeping the target from fleeing."

Sure.

My *discretion* notices that my safety and sanity were never a factor, and we've stopped pretending this hell night is anything but my funeral party.

Now all I care about is front-loading the idea that I'm going to cause trouble. Then I'll have a few more seconds of pre-planned chaos before leadership realizes I'm already gone. "Yes, Commander. I scouted a fire alarm I can trigger. There's no way the Redfangs can continue if emergency services invades the property"

"Good. Contact Simon with concerns. Fissure out."

The disconnected line roars. Or maybe that's the smoke bleeding off my brain.

I would say I can't believe this, but of course I can.

Bridget's the one who made the mistake.

She never should've taken off my cuffs.

Officially in escape mode, I move.

Yanking my collar and tightening my robe, I head for the balcony. All I need is an escape lane. A dark corner with no dogs. Even a medium-dim corner with a slightly smaller dog.

I step out and taste fresh air.

Then the balcony guard whips a handgun to my forehead.

Ignoring a *shit-he-almost-shot-me* heart stutter, I lift my nose and go full-on heiress. "Are you fucking insane?"

"Princess." The alpha drops his weapon, wide-eyed. "You can't be out here. It's—"

"Says fucking who?" I'm throwing too many F-bombs, but one per sentence keeps the Serafina edge slicing-sharp.

"Says the boss." The alpha ducks his shaved head, submitting more to Nikolaj's authority than my trophy princess status, but he's alone, and I have to roll the dice.

"Make it up to me?" I ask more sweetly.

I catch a face-full of nauseating lust pheromones—like loamy, misfit potatoes that got dug up and were promised a fuck.

It's official.

Potato-scented people are the worst.

My robe and the darkness team up to hide my shudder. "Bring me a drink? I heard there were craft cocktails."

"Can't leave my post." His eyes dart to the steps.

So do mine.

Careful as tugging a spiderweb, tightening my abs for max control, I tease out fake lemon pheromones. *Real* omega pheromones—not my nightmare-inducing gamma stench.

"I'm thirsty." I'm almost desperate enough to lick my lips.

He licks his before I have to sink another level. "I'll call. Have them send someone up."

"Fine." I lean on the rail. "But ask for a pretty server. It's my last night as a lone omega."

Preferably a tall-ish blonde I can knock out, strip, and replace.

I'll play a waitress.

I'll play any role that saves me from being marked.

"Uh. I'll ask. For a pretty one. But you need to get back inside. Boss's orders."

Bet he's more worried about his thick neck than my safety.

I risk another squeeze of lemon. "Maybe we—"

"Boss's orders." He sets his bodybuilder jaw, and I'm happier than I should be when his lust fizzles, knocked out by a brick wall of starchy dominance that I have to pretend to obey. "*Go inside, Princess*."

Some royalty

Even security gets to alpha-whip the heiress.

I go back to the stuffy dressing room and the drawing board.

As much as reality makes me want to hug a trash can, my options will be better later in the night. When alphas are drunk and power-tripping, pheromones are high, and my father signs me away to be someone else's problem.

Redfang security will be on my ass until the ink's dry.

Whether I flash scars and ruin my disguise or snap and melt alphas' brains until I run out of steam, tonight's my curtain call.

For better and more likely worse, I can finally stop pretending that I'm fine, that I'm strong, that I'm...whatever I am.

Whoever I'm supposed to be.

I miss Lilah.

She's the only one I never had to pretend for. Not because I didn't try, but because it's impossible to hide your real self when you're fighting rich girl omegas ten against two.

We had this unspoken deal where I didn't pry into her secrets, she didn't ask about mine, and we could just *be*—hanging in her closet room at the OCC, streaming bad TV and munching stolen chips

The only thing we pretended was that we'd both get to have the futures of our dreams.

I promise I'll figure out how to contact her as soon as I'm free.

Wherever she landed, I'm betting she found herself some crazy forest hideout with a bunker and steel blast doors.

No place I'd rather flee.

Stuck playing Serafina, I sit at the makeup table and slather on war paint until I'm gangster glam.

Fake lashes and thick eyeliner emphasize my green-eyed glint. I take down Serafina's trademark pony and tease my hair into neck-hiding curls.

Although, if we're at the point where my neck's on display, I'll be showing throat as a corpse.

Before squeezing into the lacy party dress, I slather foundation from shoulder to hairline, adding an extra layer of cover to my pheromones and scars.

I'm turning back and forth in the mirror, making sure every secret is zipped, locked, and painted over, when a soft knock sounds

"Who is it?"

"Your drink." The voice is muffled and male.

Definitely not Nikolaj.

It's too velvet smooth.

Too warm.

My blood surges, instincts pinging a different flavor of danger.

The guy must be *really* pretty if his pheromones cut through hardwood

But it's not like I'll be attracted.

Alpha, beta, omega.

Not counting childhood crushes, my body's never once been moved

Hoping for a target I can rope into an escape plan, I tense my real and fake pheromones and unlock the door.

I'd rather face a dozen drug kingpins than the lean, bearded alpha who dances from my fantasies into my dressing room.

My blood crystallizes, the entire world going slow and sluggish

I tug the rope of my control, cutting off my scent before he responds to the stench.

Or worse.

Responds to Serafina's lemon.

But I'm leashing my body so hard, I forget to stop my mouth. "Reese?"

Not in a jersey but a fitted suit.

Long, athletic lines.

Brown eyes, brown hair.

His nostrils work. Pupils widen. "You know my name?"

My shrinking ribs claw at my heart, tearing the ragged seams in my soul already ripped raw by Bishop and Jin.

I open my mouth to lie, to protect myself.

Too late.

His scent slides down my throat.

A thick, gooey hit of chocolate hazelnut, warm and rich, with a hint of buttered bread.

All my favorite flavors.

Boy-next-door on toast.

I wish I could disintegrate, but that would be too easy.

No.

I have to face him and pretend.

I have to face him, smile, and then give him away.

My scent glands bite, real pheromones rising like they're begging me to tell the truth.

I fumble through a thousand practiced lies, a million ways to make him leave, but when I check my script, the lines are as blank as the numb hum muffling my head.

Past, present, even wearing my sister's face.

Every role I've played.

Every me I've ever faked.

I *always* want Reese

FOURTEEN

REESE

EARLIER...

I NEED to be on a date with the ice bath, resting my arm so I can convince Coach I'm not a total fuck-up waste of roster space.

Instead, I'm flat on the roof across from The Barrington, counting Redfangs through the sight of the sniper rifle that's starting to feel more natural than my favorite glove.

Getting in game shape isn't rocket sorcery.

All I have to do is sleep, stretch, stay in my lane, and stop running jobs for the mob.

But none of us has a choice with Kairo on our ass, so I always end up doing the dumbest possible shit for my janky Franken-shoulder.

My body is more like a stash house than a temple.

"How many?" Jin asks through my earpiece.

"Too many to do shit." We were supposed to grab the omega *before* her auction. Then Redfangs fucking quintupled their security

Now cartel soldiers choke the lobby like a concert crowd, wearing gangbanger suits instead of band merch.

I have zero beef with the Redfangs.

Least, I didn't until this morning, when Bish and Jin dropped acid, claiming Serafina Redfang is our scent-matched mate.

"She's moving," Bishop's voice goes stiffer than his starched pants

I quit praying in grade school, after the fifth or fiftieth time I walked in on my parents hitting fent. The dude upstairs either doesn't exist or he wants to fuck me up in particular.

Been fixing my own problems ever since.

But when my pack brothers broke their news with that *look*?

Shell-shocked. Feral. Half terrified and half horny.

Jin stared at his hand for ten minutes and Bishop's tie was crooked

Now I'm praying with the rifle between my palms.

Praying they made a mistake.

Serafina Redfang can't be our fated mate.

All I wanna do is escape what I came from. Become more than the junkies' kid who everyone said would never amount to jack shit

Make it to the majors. Make a home for my pack and my family

Do *something* with my useless fucking life.

But now we're supposed to bond some gangster princess?

Not just mate the girl, but full-on kidnap her and wade our asses deep in cartel business?

I mean, *goddamn.*

Jericho's dying.

I thought we were finally gonna graduate our gangbanger phase. Not upgrade to elite.

On the move, Redfangs slither outside. Squinting through my scope, I catch a flash of blonde.

Tall girl in a bathrobe. She ducks into a limo, and I feel…

Fucking nothing

Just the everyday agony in my robo-shoulder and roof pebbles poking my abs

She can't be ours.

I'd know from across the ocean, let alone the street.

But I keep my head on straight and my mouth shut. The limo stops at the corner light, and civilians flood the crosswalk.

I take my shot. Even silenced, it pops like a muffled firecracker.

But in this city?

No one flinches.

Not even the businessman whose ass I almost clip to glue a tracker to the limo's bumper. "Got 'em."

"Nice shot. Now get down here." Jin's pinched urgency has me skipping steps, but shutting my mouth doesn't stop my racing thoughts

This girl already rejected our pedigreed rich boys.

Penthouse door slammed straight in their faces.

If she doesn't like them, what the fuck's she gonna think of *me*?

Still haven't shaved. Even if I were clean and shiny, wearing a fancy suit fresh from Bishop's tailor?

Got nothing to offer a girl like her.

Calves burning by the time I hit the street, I jump into Jin's car. He hits the gas when I'm half inside. I grab the handle, off-balance without another big body to slow my lean in the back seat. "No dice on Dutch?"

Bish snorts, glued to his phone. "He hung up. Said to call back when we weren't day-drinking."

Yeeeaaah…

I would've said the same if I couldn't *feel* my brothers' wild vibes. They're more like street alphas than the slick sons of bitches who taught me how to smoke cigars and earn respect.

Dutch is always pining for our little buddy.

So am I, but we've been looking for the kid for years.

Solomon was too much like me.

All bones, running alone in a neighborhood with clockwork gunfire. Never mentioned parents. Hated anyone coming too close

Dutch and his mom adopted me after my parents died or disappeared who-the-fuck-cares where.

I tried to adopt Solly, but he was skittish. Always tucked under his hat, hovering at the edges of the group we knew was gonna be our pack someday.

When we got railroaded into military college, we were dumb-ass kids. Even though we had no idea how to take care of ourselves, it eats me every day that we didn't take better care of *him*.

Now Solomon's disappeared.

I can't fucking fathom what twisted, still-on-the-clock god thought it would be fun to swap our sweetheart for a pedigreed gangster.

A spoiled princess doesn't fit our pack.

Bishop always runs his own game, and Jin can hang with anyone, but we need someone *real*. An omega who'll call the hustlers on their bullshit, snuggle Dutch when he goes cling-mode, and sit through double-headers wearing my jersey.

Serafina's not the type.

I'd call bullshit out loud, but Jin is driving it like a fucking go-kart, white knuckled with the need to get his girl.

We'll see if she's my girl.

I have a tenner and my heart set on this entire mission being a bad trip

We turn hard, and a garment bag slides off the back seat. The penguin suit that falls out puckers my ass. "What's the plan?"

"You're undercover," Jin answers.

I finger the frilly-ass waistcoat. "As a butler?"

"Cocktail waiter."

I hate taking orders from rich pricks.

Especially fucking gangsters who make bank flooding the Meadows with cut drugs.

But it has to be me.

Dutch can't lie or blend for shit. Bish and Jin are too recogniz-able on the dirty rich kid circuit, and they already paraded their criminally smooth faces in front of a whole squad of Redfang soldiers

Least I'm good for something. "We have a guest list?"

"It's bad." Bad enough that Jin spares a glance from the road, conscience screaming in his dark eyes.

"Which packs?" I'm already whipping off my pants, sliding commando into the penguin suit. Anything to distract from the pheromones. Car smells like rotten peach and scorched salt, making my neck hair dance a fucking disco, wanting to help or soothe or some fucking thing to put my brothers back to normal.

"Kitagawa, Al Sharin, Salerno, and Bourg."

"Bourg?" I jerk, almost zipping the tip of my dick. "The same ones your brother keeps paying to hit us?"

"Them." Jin's shoulders shake. "I should be the one going in."

"How 'bout no?" I safely button my fly and swallow a gut full of nerves. "I trained for this."

"You weren't supposed to," he says sadly.

I smack his headrest. "Yeah, well, maybe after this, I switch careers. I'm better at spy shit than pitching."

Forget playoffs lost and what could've been if Jericho Moon weren't a life-ruining psychopath, and I'd been born to love, money, and promise instead of fetal alcohol and baby food ramen.

My pack brothers are the guys who put my name on the try-out list when I never believed I'd make the cut

They're the ones who worked their asses off to pay for my rehab. Made me do the work when my arm was toothpaste, and all I wanted to do was quit

I've had their back as many times as they've had mine.

Bishop. Dutch. Jin.

Who needs dreams?

It's enough if I can be what they need.

γ

JIN PULLS AROUND the corner from the kind of mansion where he'd be invited for crumpets and polo, and I'd be working the stables shoveling shit.

I adjust my earpiece, adrenaline pumping.

"You good?" Bish asks, voice in stereo when the sound clicks.

"Good." I know the plan. I know the stakes.

Find the girl.

Don't get caught if I want to keep my fingers or my pulse.

Jin yanks my arm before I can roll out.

"You'll feel it when you meet her." His eyes swirl, so crazy intense that my gut kickflips. *He's fucking serious* "Just don't get hurt."

"We're behind you the second anything goes sideways." Bish grips his tie. "Tag her location inside. We'll do the rest."

"On it." I stretch out my fist.

After a three-way fist-bump that we hold too long, I go ghost and hop the fence.

My brain flips into the zone where everything numbs out and my view tilts, almost going third person.

I used to think everyone could focus like this.

When I'm pitching, I *feel* when the guy on second twitches, even thinking about stealing. I see the lady in the stands rubbing nacho cheese off her kid's jersey. I taste the wind and read every micro-expression on the guy stepping up to bat.

My Little League coach said I was born to play.

Few years later, my hand-to-hand combat instructor said I was a scary motherfucker.

I see *everything*

The guards' patrol patterns.

Which dogs are sluggish.

Hiding spots between bushes.

And also?

This McMansion is a fucking McVault.

I'm not gonna luck into an unlocked window.

Have to bluff instead.

I strip my weapons and stash them in rosebush. Then I time bleeding out of the shadows, and bold-ass take the footpath to the back door.

"State your business."

I lift my hands, flashing a business card, courtesy of Bish. "Sorry, I'm late. Waiter called out last minute. But between you and me? If you want to turn me away, I'd rather be on a date with a beer and my beta."

"Wouldn't we all." The guard alpha jerks his rifle toward the back steps. "Talk to Gustav."

I salute and jam my hands in my pockets, walking real casual.

I'm only half faking.

Feels a lot more natural walking toward the servant's entrance than the main gate.

"Gustav?" I eye the big guy manning the back steps.

I've got ten pounds of muscle on him, but he reeks of sardines and angry rage.

My knuckles twitch.

I trade the urge to challenge him for a weak-ass smile, reining in my dominance and flashing him the card. Bish phoned in a favor. He always comes in clutch, digging dirt on every pack in town. "I'm here for—"

"Hands in the air," Gustav barks, all alpha, no manners.

I surrender.

While his buddies watch the show with rifles cocked, Gustav rubs his knuckles. "Spread your legs."

All I can do is kick my legs apart and hope I don't have to snap his neck and screw my cover.

Doesn't come to that.

Gustav pats me down until I feel like I should shove a sweaty ten-spot in his rifle band.

Too fucking thorough to be all business.

When he finds nothing hidden in my deepest nooks and crannies, Gustav finally clears me through. "Twenty says he doesn't last the night."

The guards cackle.

I step into the servant's entrance on highest-alert.

A metallic scent sets the tone for how tonight's about to go.

From the middle of a sludgy blood puddle, a beta in a waistcoat just like mine stares dead-eyed at the crown molding.

His dress shirt rocks a red flower, centered by the hilt of the hunting knife buried between his ribs.

"Go on." Gustav nudges me with the barrel of his rifle. "Unless you wanna be the second body dropped tonight."

I've got a better place for him to stick that weapon, but I'm not green enough to blow my cover this soon. I step over the dead dude's limp arm, focused on the mission.

Find the girl.

And hey. There's something we must have in common.

Being completely fucking numb to casual violence.

"What's the situation?" Bishop asks in my ear.

I cluck for silence.

Not a good time.

Redfangs are posted every few steps, even in the servant corridors. They follow my steps, fucking *waiting* for me to make a mistake

Bish and Jin have tragically underestimated enemy numbers at this fucked-up party, but the danger fuels my focus.

I can do this thing.

I pass the last pair of throat-tatted guardsmen, stepping into a kitchen that's weirdly quiet for such an important night.

Nobody's cooking

Three penguins hunker at the service station, rock-paper-scissoring for who has to carry out the next tray.

The waiters whip to me, wide eyes suddenly glowing.

"New guy." The one with the crooked bow-tie shoves a case of cigars into my hands. "You're on smoke duty. No arguing."

"Fine." I take the case as a chance to scope out the packs—maybe even glimpse their guest of honor.

One step out, wall-to-wall cigar smoke and alpha pheromones have my feet dragging like my loafers are already sunk in cement.

Street alphas smell earthy. Uncomplicated.

These packs smell fucking *expensive.*

Pheromones like top-shelf liquor, glass-bottle cologne, and blood money.

The air pulls tight and close, either because the lounge is dim as a nesting cave, or most of these guys are already five lines deep in the fancy dishes of coke at their tables.

I muzzle a rumble.

After years of wiping Jericho's ass, I know how to keep my head down and my nose clean of rich boy business.

Just wish it didn't feel so natural playing the help.

A pack owns each corner of the lounge. Four or five alphas with a packleader, each running their cluster of leather sofas like it's their own avenue back home.

There's a bar set up on one side, with a corpse-stiff beta tending the liquor and two conspicuously empty seats placed at the center of the action.

When the alphas aren't snarling at their competition, they're licking their lips, glancing at the empty spaces and waiting for the show.

Waiting for *her.*

I drop my shoulders even lower, full-on submissive before I approach. Bish and Jin breathe sharply in my ears.

The first pack speaks Japanese.

All business, in suits fancier than my catering disguise. Stone sober, they haven't touched their powdery party favors.

A bougie place card gives their name.

Kitagawa Pack.

They ignore me and my cigar box, so I suck my teeth and continue my lap as smoke bitch.

The Al Sharins cluster their packleader's laptop. I spot banking screens and keep moving before they notice my eyes wandering.

My sixth sense rattles when I cross into Bourg Pack's territory.

The Bourg crew should be too low-level for an invite to a party with big dogs like the Redfangs.

They're back-alley hitmen.

Dime a dozen or a dollar for the whole crew—Jericho must get bulk pricing.

But the assholes have glowed up.

Whether Rod Bourg sucked the right dick or straight-up killed his competition, he can't wait to flex his newfound power on my unlucky ass.

He summons me with a finger-flick.

I'm tall enough that I have to duck to offer the cigars.

In no rush to pick the perfect stogie, he rolls one between his fingers, keeping me bent in half. "You seen the omega?"

"No, Sir," I answer, beta-soft.

"You smell her?" He drags along the cigar like he's working that nose hair up the girl's inner thigh.

"No, Sir." My beard hides the blood vessels popping off in my cheeks

I don't go around sniffing omegas like some sick fuck.

"Rod Bourg," Jin growls, adding the name to our pack's kill list.

Reminded this isn't about me, I put my anger on ice.

"Bet that pussy smells so fucking lush." Rod licks the cigar.

Bishop snarls.

I zip my disgust, but no omega deserves that skeevy bullshit.

Seen all I need of these packs.

I'm about to back away when the air shifts.

Instincts wilding, I dodge just fast enough to keep my fingers from being pinned to the bookshelves by a flying blade.

Half an inch from losing a chunk of ear, Rod knocks back his sofa. "You want to start some shit, Salerno?"

I hug the wall before they start trading fire.

Big thanks to the crazy asshole who tossed knives at my ass during training

The Bourgs snarl, low and dirty, but Tobias Salerno is too cultured to set down his bourbon.

"Don't put our future mate's pussy in your mouth." Tobias's dead-eyed smile triggers my gag reflex. "Unless you're paying for a lick."

Rod strokes a row of knuckle rings, but sits his ass down after a glance at the empty chairs. "Auction hasn't started. Wait and see who gets a lick and who takes the whole pie."

"Cigar," Tobias barks.

I could take him in a fight, but the crazy buried in his authority kills my instinct to challenge.

When I offer his smoke, I clock the blood spatter on his collar.

Tobias keeps me hunched, making me watch him finger the cigs, but he's not flexing power like Rod.

If he's waiting for me to clap back, he picked the wrong guy.

My ego died when I was shitting in a bedpan, nurses wiping my battered ass, and Jericho's smug cackles ringing in my punctured eardrums.

I'm not good at much, but I'm *patient as fuck.*

I know when to hit and when to run, and that sure as smog rises, rich pricks have the attention spans of mayflies.

When I don't react, don't dance like a clown, the alphas forget I exist.

After Tobias lights up, I back away, my calm steps not showing how fast my gears are cranking.

Have to get the girl.

One, before these assholes touch her, and two, before Bish and Jin rush the place to stop them talking shit.

I'm scoping my next move when the bartender signals. I set down the cigars, and he yanks me close enough to catch a buzz from his tequila fumes.

"Run this upstairs. Just don't look at anyone, touch anything, or breathe too much." He slides me a pink martini, then pops open a secret door in the wood paneling behind the bar.

It leads up a shady staircase.

Unless Nikolaj Redfang called down for the baby doll special, I just scored the omega's location.

"On it," I whisper-nod.

My shoulders barely fit turned sideways in the secret passage, but narrow means no guards.

Important to know.

"She's close," I warn the guys.

"Hurry," Bishop urges.

Must be him and Jin pounding in my chest.

Can't be me, this nervous.

Halfway up, a scent lassos my throat ball.

That perfume.

Sharp, but subtly sweet.

A tickle torques my abs like I'm about to toss the pitch of my life

It's worse upstairs.

Worse with every step down the hall, because my feet start to move like I'm one of those dumb birds on a track around a clock, helplessly pulled toward the only possible ending.

Toward *her.*

Now that I've caught her scent, I'd find her across a continent.

Lemon donut.

Sugary and undeniable.

Horror grows with the gut-punch of recognition.

Because if she's really mine…

There's a lot of hardware between us and the exit.

Lot of shady fucking alphas who need to be choked out.

Breathing through waves, I debate wasting the alphas manning the door, but I can't stop, can't slow. I duck and knock the wood

"Who is it?" A satin voice stun-darts my ass—not exactly sweet, but so fucking *rich.*

Lemon, sprinkled in gold leaf.

Way above my pay grade.

"Your drink," I answer, trying to swallow an unholy

purr/growl/snarl of rage. Because she's my mate. Because I can't let her *breathe* near those alphas downstairs.

And because *fuck.*

I'll be lucky if she doesn't slam the door in my face and reject me the same way she rejected the better half of my pack.

My panting gets caught on audio.

"See?" Bish whispers.

I see, Sherlock

My fucking soul is vibrating, like my heart snagged on an out-of-control kite, and I don't know if I'm gonna soar to heaven or crash in a dumpster of spent needles.

The girl who whips open the door has me soaring and burning

Flying and falling and fucking *terrified* how close I am to dropping to my knees and begging for a chance to earn my spot at her side

A blonde in a bathrobe.

Did I say I feel nothing?

Yeah.

Nothing but her.

Her green eyes widen, sweet lips part, and a car bomb goes off in my gut

"Reese?"

One taste of my name on her lips and black-manicured claws lock down my heart

I clench my fist, crush glass, and barely feel the slicing shards. Pink liquor and blood drip through my fingers. "You know my name?"

Bish snickers.

Jin sighs

Bracing for rejection, I scream the only word that comes to mind

Fuuuuuuuuuuuuuuuuuuuuuuuuuuuuuuuuck.

FIFTEEN

SOL

HIS GAME VIDEO was already a war crime.

Real-life Reese waterboards me in hazelnut butter.

I suck shallow breaths, trying not to devour the silken cocoa scent that's ten times as deadly as I dreamed. "Why are you here?"

"For you," he rasps, rough and raw.

My heart quits, giving a pathetic, stuttering thump before I remember his words aren't meant for me.

They're for Serafina.

Reese is for Serafina.

I need to rally.

Shove down my real self and go all-in as the gangster princess, because I'll lose what's left of my light if I'm rejected as myself.

It helps that my instincts don't react.

No mate response. *As if I needed that confirmed.*

No rejection either.

When Reese moves into the room, I step back, ready for the clockwork flush of revulsion that leaves me shuddering every time an alpha comes too close.

But there's no disgust.

No fear.

Because it's *Reese.*

The boy who taught me how to throw.

Grown-up Reese with fire in his eyes, and a heart-ripping smile hidden behind his beard.

He'd never hurt his mate.

My door guard snarls, "Back the fuck up, cocktail boy."

Terror and rage and twisty hormones tempt me to take down the threat.

No one hurts Reese while I'm here.

Instead of punting my baseball dream-boy away like I should to spare my heart, I yank his sleeve, drag him in, and lift my chin like the queen bitch. "Don't be fucking walnuts. Daddy said I could have company."

"No. That's not what the boss—"

"You're already dead if he finds out you let an alpha through my door."

They freeze. They know I'm right.

After a long second, the other guard growls. "Five minutes."

"No clock, or I tell him you disobeyed." I slam the door before they can argue.

My heart speeds until my fingertips numb, but not because of the close call.

Reese eats the distance between us.

He's so much taller than I remember. His voice is deeper. Rougher. Rumbling dangerously close to a purr. "Need to get you out of here."

"*You* need to get out." I dodge his advance, catching a lung-full of nutty cocoa butter.

I don't get it.

Why does my mouth flood when my body's dead?

I'm like a freaking vegan salivating over steak.

If Reese isn't mine, then his scent should turn my stomach, just like every other alpha's always has.

I'd worry *why* he's the exception, but my basic brokenness explains it all.

Freak

"Nikolaj is on the way," I choke through his chocolate-scented head-trip. "If he finds out you're—"

"Your mate?" Reese finishes the death sentence.

"I'm not..." I'm not Serafina.

Not his mate.

I'm not anything to Reese—not anymore.

He sets his shoulders like he's bracing for a haymaker to the face. His comforting, perfect cocoa sharpens until it's so bitter, his ache curdles my blood.

Spacy vertigo yanks me back from the cliff.

I can't reject Reese when my fake scent is promising I'm *the one*.

I'd rather grind my heart to dust than taste one more lick of the hurt he's never deserved.

I'm the liar.

Have to see my own bullshit through to the end.

"Nikolaj doesn't care if we're fated." I dance around the truth, half happy and half shattered when life returns to Reese's eyes—chocolate brown. They sparkle as his scent sloughs off its bitterness, mellowing with hope.

I need him gone before his sugar rush rots my brain and makes me forget I'm acting. "I'm a trophy, okay? You can't come in here, screw up his sale, and expect to walk—"

"Fuck the auction," Reese's saw-blade snarl strokes my insides. "We're getting you out."

Don't crack.

Don't crack now.

I shiver, voice small. "This isn't your fight."

"No? Already drew blood." Reese flashes a gory palm, dripping glass shards, blood, and cherry juice.

I hiss.

Idiot.

"Sit." Pretending I don't feel the flex of shoulder muscles, I man-handle him onto the vanity stool, forcing him to sit while I grab the first aid kit I found when I was snooping under the sink.

I should've researched chemical bombs instead of penthouse parachutes

I'm going to have to blast my way out of this nightmare.

Reese doesn't budge.

All those major-league muscles still while he perches obediently on the pink velvet pouf, following my every move with a subtle, hopeful sparkle. I have to keep reminding myself.

None of that belongs to me.

But, his real mate would take care of him.

Right?

I dry swallow.

Have to keep up the act.

Kneeling with a pair of tweezers, I spread his sticky fingers, biting my lip and gently plucking glass slivers from the mess of his skin.

It was always like this.

Reese would hit until his hands bled. I'd pull him into the dugout to disinfect and bandage popped blisters, but the next day, he'd be bleeding again. Now he has thick calluses after years of practice, but under the fresh cuts, even those are red and peeling.

I click my tongue, wishing he'd learned to take better care of himself. "You've been working too hard."

His fingers twitch. "You..."

Shit.

I'm the idiot who can't keep her roles straight.

I'm supposed to be Reese's mate, not his trainer.

"What?" I toss my hair, channeling Serafina's rich-bitch confidence. "I looked up the pack after you tried to invade my penthouse"

I clean his cuts as fast as I can without hurting him, sponging off the spilled liquor, dabbing on ointment, and wrapping his broad, hot palm while I resist the stupid urge to pet his fingers.

Hell, the urge to rest my head on his thigh.

To wrap around him like a cobra, clinging to the soft warmth I've always craved.

I balance on the tightrope.

Just enough concern to play his mate.

Just enough held back that I can still walk away.

I hope.

Reese's scent doesn't give a shit about my boundaries.

Hazelnut curls around me in a melting, chocolate hug, and his voice hits with the same silken roughness as the warm lips behind the beard I'm desperate to stroke. "You're not what I expected."

Because I'm not your girl.

I harden my voice and hopefully my will. "You need to leave."

"Yeah. With you. Don't worry, we have a plan. Jin says—" Reese tenses, a finger to his ear. "Shit. Cars on the way up the drive."

"Nikolaj." I swallow a plastic bubble.

Those thirty seconds of stupid hope were a trip, but I've always known better. Falling back to reality, I tie off Reese's gauze. "It's too late to run."

For me, at least.

Not for him.

"Wait." Reese cups his earpiece. Bishop and Jin scheme, but all I catch are tempting whispers.

I don't need to hear the words.

I know the guys.

The way they cared for Reese when he was in the hospital, fought side-by-side against Bishop and Jin's messed-up families, and stood with Dutch and his mom through their loss. Even the way they watched out for little baby Sol, trying to walk me home and kicking the shit out of my wannabe bullies.

They may have left behind a weird little tagalong beta, but they'd never ditch their real mate.

They're ride-or-die.

So, I'm strapped in until they realize I'm just a placeholder for their real princess.

Now I have to conjure a believable reason to kick Reese's stubborn, muscled ass out of this snake's nest so I can get to work. "How much backup did you bring?"

Reese scratches his beard. "Just Bishop and Jin."

Their names punch my lungs like a straw.

We need a freaking *army* of disposable soldiers, not three of the only four alphas on the planet that I can't risk frying.

"We're enough," Reese insists, gripping his bandaged hand. "I'll pick off the inside soldiers while the guys thin the perimeter."

They're not enough.

Not even if I go nuclear and smoke the mansion.

But all I care about is tricking Reese out of my blast zone. "Fine, but not until later. Security will be on point until the deal is signed. Let me handle Nikolaj. Wait for my signal to make your move"

Ripped that one right out of the Fissure playbook.

Wait for the signal.

You know the one?

The one that never comes and probably never existed.

I was always going to have to solve my problems myself, and no way in hell am I letting the guys witness the monster under my mask.

They argue in Reese's ear.

Bishop's voice is sharp and sexy, like an expensive custom knife

Jin's is more of a black hole.

Dominant.

Everywhere.

Let's not even talk about Reese, whose building, possessive rumble will melt me to lemon-scented goop the second I lower my guard

If Dutch were here, I'd—

My stomach sours.

Don't go there.

"We don't have time." If my father sees through my disguise, so be it, but Nikolaj can never be in the same room as Reese.

Never.

"I'm not leaving you." Reese pushes off the stool, standing with the coiled, ready stillness of the SAS' top brass. Perfectly balanced to take or give a hit, with a steady gaze that says neither would be his first.

He's trained?

How? Where?

Reese could always brawl with the best, but you don't get a posture like that from street fighting.

If we worked together, maybe—

Nope.

I don't care if Reese has his own action figures.

I mean, I'll buy a whole shelf and pose them with their muscles flexed.

That changes nothing.

I'm stronger alone, with my gamma freak off its leash.

If Reese gets in my way, I'll be handcuffed, and not in the fun way

I use my height and the weird genes that let me stand up to alphas, pressing forward with confidence I don't have to fake. "Do I look like the kind of girl who'd let myself be sold? I have my own plans. Wait for my signal."

Reese's lips part to argue.

I cross my own line, covering his mouth.

Holy shit.

The beard.

Ignoring the silky scratch against my throbbing palm, I spill the hidden yearning that dips my words in desperate truth. "Trust me, Reese. I'm not leaving this party with anyone but you."

"*Princess.*" Reese's purr vibrates, rabbit fur and razors.

So impossibly soft.

So destructively cutting.

I can't tell if I'm shivering, shuddering, or leaking shoved-down pheromones when Reese's broad, bandaged hand finds my waist.

I'm expecting the cringe—the full-body, *get-the-fuck-away-from-me-and-my-throat* clench that's been the go-to since my forced awakening

Surprise.

The curse is broken.

Or possibly just starting.

Reese's hands are warm and familiar and everything I feared, sparking longing, sweet memories, and not a single twinge of fated mate

I want to hug him so deep, I melt into his purr.

I want to throw my arms around his shoulders and let him carry me somewhere safe.

What I don't want?

Reese's bite.

He smooths up my spine. Rough gauze tickles through my lace as his head dips. He reaches higher and higher. Fingers caressing toward my neck, Reese draws me in for a kiss I can't afford

There's the panic.

A high-pitched alarm blares from my brain stem to my still-bruised tailbone.

I wrench out of Reese's killer arms before he hits the ridge of scar tissue hidden at my throat. Before I feel his heat and *really* freak

"Hurry." Decisive and a little bit deranged, I shove him away. "Nikolaj can't find you here."

"Yeah." Reese's eyes drop from my lips, and he awkwardly lowers the bandaged hand that hovers where my neck used to be.

I breathe through the bitterness of burnt chocolate.

Failing to act like Serafina, Marisol, or any sane girl alone with the childhood crush I'd die to mate, I shove Reese into the hall and shrill my voice. "Bring me a new drink."

Make it a whole bottle.

He hesitates, dropping his chin like a bull about to charge.

The guards tense.

I frantically flick my eyes. *Don't be stubborn. Please, Reese.*

He must hear my pleading.

Reese finally turns down the hall, leaving my pulse roaring

with a weird mix of adrenaline, regret, and misplaced appreciation for his ass in that suit.

When he's out of sight and hopefully out of danger, I brush off the guards' scowls and slam the door. Fingers shaking, heart in hummingbird mode, I hide the evidence that I'm anything but the trophy daughter Nikolaj is expecting.

Using a prissy throw pillow, I sweep shattered glass under a curio cabinet. Then I tidy my hair, spritz on pheromone-boosting perfume, and slosh a little extra on the rug to cancel out the spilled liquor and anything left of the cocoa shellacked to the roof of my mouth.

When I'm done, my disguise is perfect, and there's not a whiff of Reese.

So why am I drooling?

Oh, right.

Because I sucked his breath like he was giving me CPR.

I duck into the bathroom, praying Reese follows orders and stays hidden, but back in real life, after a gargle of mouthwash breaks his chokehold, I'm the one about to be revealed.

My real pheromones claw my scent glands from the inside, raging to be free. After I grit them down, there's nothing left.

Serafina's lemon either burned off or got snake-charmed and stolen away by Reese.

I wasn't planning on taking another hit of my sister's poison, but I also wasn't planning on him and his beard taking a swing at a kiss, leaving me freaking *ragged* when I need to be on point.

It takes too long to slide the case off my thigh. I drop a vial twice before it plugs into the needle cartridge.

Palms sweating, I finally shoot up, riding the roar of lemon while the mirror strobes and citric acid reflux eats the lining of my throat.

The vials are teeny—only a few concentrated drops per dose. Brandon jammed in enough liquid Serafina to last me for weeks.

But this had better be my last hit.

I can't keep this up.

Drunk-stumbling to the couch, I wrench on my heels, then smooth the lace of my dress to make sure all the bumps and secrets stay under wraps.

With my mask game on and a whole lemon wedged down my throat, I fold my hands in my lap, obediently waiting for the boss to arrive

One minute.

Five minutes.

Fifteen minutes

A clock ticks, and every so often, alpha chatter buzzes through the floor.

I guess Nikolaj prioritizes pre-gaming with the bidders over saying goodbye

If he sees the daughter he raised as furniture, I don't want to fuck around and find out how he'll treat the secret baby from his tryst with an undercover fed.

I'm box-breathing when the lock clicks. Then I choke on a corner.

Nikolaj Redfang doesn't enter a room.

He takes it over.

Dense pheromones sink my shoulders, the taste of ash and cigar smoke stopping my lungs.

Nikolaj has neat, silver hair and blue eyes so sharp, his cutting once-over turns me into a wax figure. When his eyes pinch, his wrinkles bunch

He's older than I expected.

Seventies, if not eighties.

But age only hones his dominance.

I barely feel the enforcers filling the room behind him. If I passed those alphas on the street, I'd slip my keys between my knuckles. Next to my father, they're ghosts.

Tight as a spring, I contort my fingers in my skirts.

I remember my lesson from the phone.

Don't speak unless you're spoken to.

"*Marie*," he barks.

The beta I forgot existed darts to obey. She dips a bow that would be a curtsy if not for her pantsuit, and levels her gaze low enough to submit to an emperor. "Master."

"This isn't the dress I chose." My father's voice is flat—almost no intonation—but it's backed with so much dominance, even *I'm* tempted to kneel.

Lacking rule-breaking gamma genes, Marie can only tremble. "It's my mistake. I thought the lace was more tantalizing than bare skin."

I've done this lady zero favors, but even though her knees quake, she doesn't rat me out.

Nikolaj reaches under his jacket.

"Daddy!" I jump to my feet. I'm not watching Marie get executed over a stupid gown.

Nikolaj turns slowly, tilting his head just like Serafina.

Only, Nikolaj doesn't have to plan how to rip me apart—a lifelong butcher knows exactly where to cut.

I'm waiting for the frown or flinch or furrowed brow when he sees through my flaws.

But if he pulls his gun and demands his real daughter back, I'll be the one forcing *him* to kneel.

Besides. I am his daughter.

Nikolaj doesn't frown. His wrinkles freeze in a solid, icy mask that makes it clear I'm being weighed and measured.

Ignoring the skeletal fingertips fretting down my spine, I flash him the good-girl smile I've been feeding authority figures for freaking *years*.

The smile I practiced in the mirror for the parents at the orphanage, my foster monsters, and the trainers at the OCC. The smile I still shoot Doctor Brandon every day I convince myself not to end his breathing.

A bright-eyed, empty smile, so cotton-soft it could blunt a cannon ball.

Not a threat.

Not even a challenge.

A smile that ticks all the vapid boxes while I bide my time to strike

I know I pass the test when Nikolaj focuses on my neckline instead of pulling his gun. "How prude."

I bite my cheek through the tinkling clatter of another shattered fantasy—the one where I had a father who ever wanted me.

It doesn't sting like it should.

Biological family is so overrated.

Ignoring the army of leering guards, I beam and twirl my skirt like a music box ballerina. "I wanted to look elegant for my future pack. Do you like it?"

Nikolaj buttons his coat. Kicking Marie out of his way, he crosses the carpet. "They'll have you out of it soon enough."

My pheromones froth.

I ache to kill the act.

Screw Bridget's case and the whole SAS for stranding me in this mess.

But while my heart screams *do it,* my brain screams *do the math*.

Eight guards in the room.

I can floor eight in an enclosed space, but more bodies are waiting in the halls, and too many alphas to count are out patrolling the grounds.

Whether Bishop, Jin, and Reese thin the herd, or I stall until I'm alone with the pack that thinks I'm letting them claim me, I have to wait.

I chain down the pheromones rattling their cage, but I must slip a flash of inner fire.

Nikolaj's dominance *thwacks* behind my kneecaps. "Do you need another reminder of your role?"

"No, Daddy." I bite my lip.

I've tolerated worse than this.

"Do what you were born for. The next time you're insubordinate, your mates will be the ones teaching you to obey."

I swallow a blob of hot glass, but silence isn't what he wants from me

He wants *submission*.

"Understood?" Nikolaj jerks my chin.

"Yes, Daddy." My shudder is real, and it's exactly what he was waiting for.

"Let's not keep your alphas waiting." He drags my hand to the arm of his suit, and the Redfang foot soldiers split into files, forming a path for their leader.

My smile hardens to plastic, but Nikolaj can't spot my colored contacts, let alone my wild discomfort.

"Be grateful for the chance to mate. If your brother were here as he was meant to be, you would've lived and died a Triad whore."

I trip on the words and my skirt.

Now I get why Serafina was running.

I'm not going to run.

I'm going to *wait*.

I'm going to lie and smile and disarm my so-called father and every evil alpha in his shady operation.

And when they think they have me helpless?

The monster shakes her cage.

Soon.

They'll find out what happens when she's unleashed.

THE OCC MADE us practice fancy etiquette, so I know exactly how to be escorted. How to glide in heels and place my fingers just so on an alpha's arm, like the kind of girl who spends her time at cotillions and not convenience stores.

There's no glide with Nikolaj Redfang—just drag.

His grip is too tight, his walk is too fast, and his sickly sweet cigar smoke sears so deep, my skin may never scrub clean.

Shouldn't have worried I couldn't pass as a rich girl.

A cow could fill this role.

I just have to trot on my leash and ignore the ashy nastiness taking over my arm like a quick-spreading zombie bite.

Every time I cringe, my pheromones pulse.

All I want to do is shut this auction down, but I haven't come this far to spin out of control.

I won't kill my father.

I won't kill my father.

I mean, I'm *definitely* going to kill my father, but I can't pull the trigger until the math makes sense

I let myself be dragged through guard-lined corridors, counting bodies and waiting for the perfect time to let loose.

I won't kill my father.

I won't kill the enforcers staring at my throat.

I won't even kill the door guard with the mullet who sneakily brushes my ass as Nikolaj herds me past.

Yeah. No. Definitely killing that guy.

My stomach bubbles when we reach the stage.

The SAS prison cells smell freshly laundered compared to the smoky leather lounge where cigars and aggressive pheromones massage my sinuses with sandpaper.

Nasty

Alphas spiked with lust and greed and violence.

Liquor and toothpaste.

Diesel and corn chips.

Toilet water and mushrooms, and a dozen shittier and shittier scents leave me shuddering on a hair-trigger fight-response that begs me to go for their necks before they come after mine.

The alphas' up-and-down gazes rake my throat, tugging at the flimsy layer of lace holding back my lies. Their old-boys-club is walled in bookshelves and wild-eyed alphas pumping lust like their dress slacks are already unzipped.

Nikolaj tosses me to the sofa at stage center, taking the armchair/throne and giving me the second I need to holster my shit.

I let out a tainted breath and hold off on taking another, trying to ignore my vibrating throat.

When I try to think of sweeter things, I slide into Reese's cocoa like I'm slipping into a cozy bath. Jin's crackling storm clears my head, and Bishop's sweet champagne bubbles through the gross cigars

Dutch probably smells like a muffin.

Something big, soft, and huggable.

Even though I've never tasted his scent, the idea of him—of *them*—is all the reset I need.

Mates or not, the guys are my people, and with them hovering somewhere nearby, not even my A-game is enough.

I have to be perfect.

Four gangster packs stare with enough dominance to decapitate. I'd heard their names over the years at the SAS before I memorized their faces from Marie's cheat-sheet.

Kitagawa. Al Sharin. Bourg. Salerno.

I tuck my neck to hide from their laser-beam attention.

I'm not giving in, just shifting to bottle the urge to hit back.

But no matter how rich and dominant, underworld alphas are *alphas* and they see what I want them to see—a shy gesture of submission

Testosterone-soaked chuckles bleed through the smoke.

Laugh now

You'll never guess what comes next.

"Meet my precious Serafina," Nikolaj says with zero sincerity. "She's been trained to serve and obey. The pack with the most generous offer can bite her tonight."

"What if we don't wish to mate?" the Kitagawa packleader asks. His expensive suit sleeves are rolled high enough to flaunt his yakuza tattoos.

"Is your sincerity so shallow? If you want the cartel, take her throat. After that..." My father's cold, *help-yourself* wave hooks behind my belly button.

When my brothers put me up for auction, I wanted to die of shame

This lounge is nothing like that stage—with a few elite alphas instead of an arena of bottom-feeders—but it's the same old shit squeezed into fancier casing.

What's different is, I'm not ashamed.

I'm freaking *pissed*.

My muscles scream. *Let go of the rope!*

When I grip my dress, shaking from holding back, the alphas see what they expect.

A helpless little girl, trembling.

"Give us a taste, Omega." The greasy Bourg packleader with the ten-o'clock shadow pats his thighs to summon me.

I don't move.

I *count*.

Seventeen bidding alphas.

Twenty enforcers standing guard.

One smug kingpin who lights a cigar and leans back to watch

the fireworks, plus one poor beta in a pantsuit who took a job planning the wrong party.

That's thirty-nine bodies.

One-on-one, I'm lethal.

A handful of alphas are easy as ice cream cake.

After ten guys, physics put me to work. Bullets can fly faster than my pheromones, and in smoke this thick, I may as well be attacking underwater.

When I let go, it can only be for the killing blow.

Ten is the magic number. Fifteen if I'm absolutely desperate.

I swallow hard, holstering the rolling boil of rage.

Nikolaj waves permission. *As if I asked*. "Show the Bourgs how well you're trained."

My mask strains, teeth and control cracking.

I do not sit in laps.

Neither would Serafina.

I fold my arms, tightening my core and death-gripping my scent. "I'm not a pass-around omega."

"We're talking about playing for keeps." The Bourg packleader dishes out dominance, trying to put me in my place.

I lift my nose like the queen bee at her own tea party. *Never mind the bubbles in my throat.* "Talk to me after you win."

"What if we already have you in the bag?" Red flags wave when his lips slide across his teeth in a dark smile that says the bag is black vinyl, and I'll leave his den in damp, shrink-wrapped pieces if I don't obey right now.

My scent glands burn, desperate to prove I'm not prey.

"We'll be the ones who take the pie." The packleader in the opposite corner unfolds. A dark-suited, chain-wearing mafia clone who's grey-haired and old money rich.

Salerno Pack.

They're much too old to be my mates. But, good news:

Older means easier to kill.

"The girl is unimportant," the Al Sharin packleader announces over his laptop screen. "Let us make our offer before we discuss rewards"

"Very well. Straight to business." Nikolaj swills his drink, clinking ice and oh-so-casually selling off his blood.

Hope I'm worth more than a cow.

The packleaders came prepared with leather folios. Marie collects the offers, then delivers them to Nikolaj with a ninety-degree bow

While he skims, ice cubes clink and my throat throbs.

During my first sale, packs called out their bids.

Now, the business is more complicated—properties, assets, and favors—and I'm glad the extra admin keeps me in my seat, far away from sticky alpha hands.

"Pack Al Sharin." Nikolaj shuts the folio, and the room tenses for the king's decree. "I appreciate your sincerity, but you aren't the best match for my precious child. We'll discuss the remainder of your proposal on another occasion."

"It's our honor." The packleader shuts his laptop, and five alphas nod before Nikolaj waves them out.

Four guards lead away the pack that must've negotiated a side deal.

I don't care if they negotiated to take away my firstborn.

Their bail-out drops the body count to thirty.

Halfway there.

"Kitagawa Pack." Nikolaj *thwaps* their folio on the coffee table. "Insulting"

"You reject our offer?" The packleader's snarl shoves the room energy harder into the red.

I stay still. He's not snarling at me.

"You thought I wouldn't notice Kairo's fingerprints?" Nikolaj huffs. "The Triad is finished, and so is any organization that aids the traitors"

"Then we've wasted our time." The Kitagawas rise in scary unison

I cross my fingers he'll start a gang war and save me some

strain, but Nikolaj finger-flicks before he can escalate. "Follow them out of my city."

Four guards haunt the Kitagawas out of the room, dropping my enemies to twenty-two.

I sit prim and pretty, hoping the high collar hides the strain in my jaw.

No threat here.

Totally not going to blow out your brain-stems, grab your cash, and burn the evidence.

I'm just a dumb heiress, head filled with blood diamonds and coconut water.

Not that I need to think pretty, sparkly things to fake my smile. Nothing's a happier thought than setting this place on fire.

Soon.

Just hold on a little longer.

My father sets the final folios side-by-side, then steeples his fingers over the mahogany table. "Rod. Tobias. How unexpected."

The Bourg and Salerno packleaders flash matching cat-stole-the-caviar smiles that bottlebrush-puff my non-existent tail.

"Why be enemies?" Rod Bourg licks his lips. "Plenty of pie to share around."

"Is our joint proposal acceptable?" Tobias Salerno smirks.

"Indeed." Nikolaj inks both contracts with a flourish. My heartbeat kicks when he passes them to Marie. "Prepare copies and the heat drugs. We'll finalize the hand-over in the nest."

Tobias and Rod unite to shake my father's hand. Then they hug it out like long-lost brothers instead of enemies who fooled me into thinking I could end this night in control.

"Welcome to Salerno Pack." Tobias pats Rod's shoulders. Their alphas mingle, all handshakes, fist-bumps, and leering gazes that tell exactly who's on the agenda for their first full-group activity. Tobias lifts a high-ball glass. "Here's to being bonded in blood. To the cartel. And to our lucky mate."

"Dibs on second bite." Rod licks his lips again, proving that my gag reflex is as ready as ever.

"It's yours." Tobias nods. "You're my second-in-command."

"Bring on the heat." A Salerno alpha rubs his palms.

"*Go*" Nikolaj whip-crack barks the beta I thought was already gone

Marie catches my gaze as she bows out of the lounge, a guard on her ass and watery eyes overflowing with silent apologies.

I slip out-of-body, drifting up into the smoke and watching my nightmare unfold from the cloud while echoing words hammer my nervous system.

Heat. Drugs. Nest.

Heat. Drugs. Nest.

Heat.

Drugs.

Nest.

Bite?

Never.

It's time.

I'm done with good girl smiles that turn my lips to wax.

I smile *flames*. "Why wait? Show me to my nest."

"You've trained her well," Tobias says to my father.

"She'll be a good girl for you," Nikolaj replies.

I'm strung too tight to shudder.

So close to letting go.

"Good? How? She's making demands before I even get my taste." Rod's pheromones punch through the smoke. He smells like diesel splashed on asphalt.

Sharp and lingering, just like his eyes cutting my neckline as he creeps into my space.

Rod lifts my arm, so close to blowing my fuse.

Still blissfully distant, I watch the alphas surround the poor, little lamb. Rod sniffs my wrist and drags his nose to my elbow like he's doing a line off my lace. "Vodka lemon. Daddy likes."

Crawling doesn't cover the waves rolling underneath my skin.

Buckets of tarantulas would be a joy compared to Rod's dog-shit touch.

My skin roils like my blood's determined to boil off the ick.

His hands beeline to my ass.

One hard pull, and I'm flush to his sweaty, motor-oil body. "Give us a kiss, Omega."

I'm too far gone to panic.

With a lemon-sugar smile, I sidestep, not resisting, but gently encouraging Rod onto the couch.

Oblivious, he drops, yanking me over his lap with a satisfied growl.

When my thighs spread, I linger in the cold, numb haven I've visited too many times before.

I don't feel his hands.

I don't feel anything but licking flames as I lean into his body, letting my hair fall forward to hide my toxic kiss.

"Good night, Rod." I blow poisoned air between his lips.

For a fraction of a second, his eyes pinch.

Too late, he realizes he's not the hunter.

Nineteen to go

I clamp his mouth and muffle his croak with a porn-star moan. "More. *Alphas.*"

The air's so heavy with lust and smoke, no one scents the subtle whiff of death.

All feral growls and cocky expectations, the Salernos crowd to steal the taste they think they're owed.

Hands paw my skin, rip at my skirt

The roiling, blood-boiling ick spins through my veins, but I focus on using the tangle of bodies as a screen.

The alpha who nips my wrist gets whipped with killer pheromones before his teeth rip skin. Easy as snapping fingers, he sags

Before he hits the ground, I'm already dodging another attempted kiss, blowing toxin into a Bourg's tear-drop tatted face.

Alphas grab for me, and the more they tangle, the easier it is to hide the truth. I keep my pheromones low, taking them out with a breath, a press of my wrist, a quickly covered mouth.

Their groans make it sound like they're having fun.

Tobias Salerno is the last man standing.

White nose-hairs wave when he trembles. His eyes flash with sweet realization just before my pheromones rip, close-range.

I hide behind his body until it drops.

Then, wide-eyed, clutching my ripped gown, I catch my father's gaze—just a poor, innocent omega, shocked by my alphas' sudden eight-way stroke. "Daddy? Why would you drug them?"

Twelve to go

I shake, fighting the torrent now that I've loosened my seal.

Nikolaj's shoulders tighten.

My father has ruled the underworld too long to buy my bullshit, but this time, I won by being born.

I'm a girl.

The daughter he thinks is a soft omega.

I can flash all the claws and teeth I want, and he'll *never* believe I'm a threat he can't beat down.

Waving soldiers to surround me, Nikolaj moves in.

I see myself in the set of his eyes and the angle of his cheekbones, but that's where the familiarity ends.

He doesn't give a single whiff of kinship.

Of family or love.

All he gives is sociopath, ready to watch his enforcers bleed me dry the same indifferent way he would've watched the Salernos strip me bare and take my throat.

My mother has one thing right.

The world will be a better place without Nikolaj Redfang.

He and his men feed themselves into my trap.

No more waiting.

No more faking.

No more pretending.

I unleash.

Not just minutes of holding back but fucking *years*.

Finally.

Finally.

The pin pops, and all the bullshit I've swallowed sprays loose in a glorious grenade-blast of nightmare pheromones that knocks the alphas on their asses.

Want to know the truth?

I *really love* being a monster.

My satisfied sigh bleeds out with my scent.

Alphas wheeze and whine, dripping snot.

I push to paralyze, but I don't rush the kill.

The ghosts of oily paws burn my body everywhere the alphas looked or touched.

It's their turn to suffer.

Nikolaj lands on his knees, one hand clutching his chest.

My mask isn't the only facade that's snapped.

His growl flies straight out of hell, lips twisting in a feral snarl that betrays the persona of a straight-faced cartel king.

Who's in control now?

"What are you?" he chokes through foaming lips.

I bump up my scent another notch, grinding my pearly stiletto into the twitching palm of the downed enforcer with the mullet.

That's for grabbing my ass.

The blast robs the last of my father's air. "Whatever I am, I got it from you."

Wind screams past my ears while his blood vessels pop. The super-familiar feeling of falling off a cliff is supposed to remind me to stop.

I *would've* stopped if Commander Fissure hadn't screwed me over.

I would've refused every scrap of credit and let her drag my father to her favorite black site before helping her celebrate her inevitable promotion.

Then I would've testified, smiled, followed orders, and lied my way to freedom.

But here we are.

I finally feel like myself when I'm standing over the bodies.

The Sol I hide behind smiles and lies.

The Sol who kills assholes that need killing with zero remorse

The Sol who doesn't take shit and never pretends to be anyone she's not.

This is the darkest, truest me, the one that no one else can ever see

Because even if I love being the monster?

No one ever loves the monster back.

Now that she's out, there's no such thing as STOP.

Pheromones pulsing, I cover my father's mouth to watch him die

The scent of cigars fizzles.

He snaps to bite my fingers, but he's too late.

Too weak

I'm in control.

When Nikolaj Redfang falls, everything is silent.

My heart should be pounding, but it's scary even, considering the body count.

I'm relaxed

My pheromones are happy off their leash, all my lies unraveled

I don't know what comes next, but I've spent so long dreaming of freedom, I know exactly how to take my next steps.

First, I ditch the phones that belong to Serafina and the SAS, popping out their SIM cards and smashing their hardware to kill any chance of being tracked.

Then, I turn out the dead alphas' pockets.

Mobsters never expect to get mugged, so I score a few thousand toward my next life. My father doesn't have a wallet, let alone loose bills.

All the king of the cartel left behind is a fountain pen, a handkerchief, and a heavy, gold-plated lighter, decorated with a line of rubies that snakes around an embossed letter R.

We'll consider this my inheritance.

I hop bodies to the bar stocked with every flavor of old, brown booze

I promised Bridget a distraction.

I owe myself a freaking *bonfire* to burn this mansion off the face of the earth.

Nikolaj gives me one last gift; his handkerchief makes the perfect starter for a Molotov cocktail.

I dunk it in vodka and cleanse myself with the lighter's sweet *click*

Who needs therapy?

It's free to set the bad guys on fire.

I light the fuse and hurl my bomb.

Bang.

Whoooosh.

The crash is glorious.

I love the sounds.

The *pop* of flames, eating booze-soaked glass.

The *hiss* of fire, flowing through wood and cloth.

I'm drenching bodies in vodka when I catch the sound I hate the most.

Running footsteps.

"Serafina!" A roaring yell knocks me out of psychopath mode so fast I almost pass out.

The name isn't mine, but I *dream* of that voice.

Soft roughness, like a textured tongue-stroke.

Even on the run, his tone curls with absolute command.

Jin.

Those emotions I ignored when I offed a pack of predators?

They snap home.

Adrenaline bursts between my eyes and seethes outward from the crash-point, the kick-started mess of emotions leaving me shaking, twitching, *gasping* with ghostly, groping touches flaring on my skin in time with the pulse of the glowing flames.

"We're here!" Reese bangs the door, turning my blood to slush.

They can't see me like this.

A hot mess of a murderer, standing over the bodies in a ripped dress, stained with a dozen alphas' scents.

I clutch my throat, digging into the sweat-soaked lace.

I don't want them seeing me at all.

"Smoke," Bishop hisses. "Do you hear anything inside?"

"Nothing," Jin mumbles.

"*Princess,*" Reese croons. "Let us in."

I miss enough breaths to forget the blooming smoke.

"You were supposed to wait for my signal," I finally answer, voice as dry as my hopes of getting out unseen.

"The signal fire?" The door creaks as Jin shoulders the wood. "Are you hurt? Are you alone?"

Oh, I'm alone.

I'd like to stay that way.

So I do what I do best.

Lie.

"Wait. I can get free." I'm already heading for the side door.

"They tied you up?" Reese's rich, protective snarl plucks my spine and leaves me stumbling.

Running out of time.

I unlock the side door that used to be guarded, but instead of a way out, I find a windowless nightmare cave. It holds a single piece of furniture. A bed covered with a plastic sheet.

My eyes water from the reek of stale sex and lung-rotting pheromones

The nest.

That's how close I was.

My pupils shrink, body pulling rigid, but the *whoosh* isn't only in my head.

New air feeds the growing flames.

I nope my ass in a circle, slam the door, and try the kitchen instead

It's locked from the inside. The staff must've fled.

"I'm picking the lock. One more minute," Bishop promises.

While the door rattles, my head spins.

The flames take care of my rogue pheromones, but they need more time to toast the dead alphas.

I cough, eyes stinging.

Metal clicks. Bishop curses.

I have to glue together the exploded fragments of my mask.

If only I could fake a personality where I'm not a dishrag for these men. Then I could move forward, unbothered by their horrified disgust

Good luck with that.

Coughing more and more, I grab a coffee table that hasn't caught fire and flip it over the biggest pile of bodies. I do the same with the sofas and armchairs, but the enforcers are too big to hide.

I need refrigerator boxes to do the job right

"Almost," Bishop grits.

Biting the bullet feels more like sticking my fingers in a chainsaw, but my choices are burn to death or embrace the revolving blades

Before the click that steals my last initiative, I throw open the lock

Bishop jumps, dropping his pick. Between surprise and the billow of smoke that follows, I don't give them a chance to peep beyond the crack

I shut them out and hold back my scent

Before I remember who I'm meant to be, Jin yanks me to his chest

Then I can't think.

"You're okay." He hugs me to his rapid-beating heart

One of us trembles.

Not sure who

His rainstorm clears my senses, blitzing away the smoke and panic and leftover alpha filth.

Jin tastes like salt and soul-cleansing storms.

He feels like coming home.

My skin crackles like the old days—lightning and despair.

When Jin drags a ragged breath at my hair, I close my eyes and sink into his arms, stealing the moment before the warning sirens blare

For one deep breath, I let myself pretend that Su-Jin Moon is mine

That I'm not an outcast, a freak, or a full-on murderer.

I'm not Serafina, Solomon, or even Gamma Twenty-Six.

For exactly one breath, I'm a blank slate.

I only exist where our bodies touch, lapping Jin's rock-steady dominance and letting him shield me from all things bad, trusting that the eye of the storm will hold me down forever.

Then I exhale and get face-smacked with the truth and the ticking clock

For a monster like me?

There's no such thing as home.

SEVENTEEN

JIN

WAIT FOR THE SIGNAL, she said.

The only signal I needed was Reese's heartbeat, roaring over comms

We hit the property like we've planned this mission for *months,* finally grateful for the training we never wanted.

Drop. Choke. Kill.

I lost track of how many Redfangs we took down.

Lost track of everything after Reese's ragged whisper.

"They have her in the room."

Now my knuckles are slicked with blood and my memory's fuzzy on what went down before I snatched my mate into my arms

I thought awakening was intense—hormone rushes and a week-long hard-on after a two-second kiss.

Serafina didn't just hot-wire my instincts.

She stole both sets of keys.

I fixate on her surging pulse. The piece of golden hair clinging to the sweat on her forehead. The maddening rips in her princess skirt.

And her *scent*—

Her cakey lemon perfume is hidden under smoke and the greasy lust of other fucking alphas.

I'd tear through the wall, but her firm softness leaves me helpless to move. The *snap* in my soul says I'm finally where I'm meant to be.

Doesn't matter what the Triad schemes.

All I have to do is be strong enough to protect her.

"You're okay." I don't know if I'm asking a question or making a promise.

Serafina doesn't respond.

Lemon butter, she melts. I tuck my chin above her crown.

I need to erase the scents. Make her feel protected. Let her know she's in good hands, strong enough to keep her safe.

She fits so perfectly. Feels so soft.

How could she belong to anyone else?

I stroke her spine. She sinks into me until all I can think about is sinking into *her*—teeth and cock, knot and soul.

My fingers slip beneath her ash-streaked golden hair. Nothing's more natural than drawing her close, until I brush the back of her neck.

Serafina jumps like I jammed a pin into her throat.

Dodging me, Bishop, and even Reese, she bolts.

The sudden distance opens a pit between my ribs, and Kairo's poison seeps from the abyss.

She belongs to Jericho.

I crush the thought.

I have to crush my weakness harder than ever. Doubts are a waste of fucking time when my mate's still in danger. "Let's get out of here before the fire spreads."

"Yeah. Let's." Serafina whirls in her stilettos, but freezes when her turn leaves her facing a carpet of corpses. "You…"

Bish and Reese fall in at my sides, forcing themselves to keep the distance she clearly wants.

I want to close the space, but not if moving pushes her farther away

"We took care of the guards," I reassure her. "The mansion's clear."

"Even the dogs?"

"Sedated," I quickly explain.

I want my mate to know we're strong enough to keep her safe.

Not think we're fucking animal abusers.

"Fantastic." She lets out a breath of relief that lights my chest.

Barely a blip of approval and my heart launches.

When she jogs away, we follow like lost boys.

My instincts chitter not to let her run ahead. We smoked every Redfang snake on the property, but I don't like her running point.

Not because she can't handle herself.

Her athletic stride and the way she checks her angles tells me that she can.

She's hot as fuck, hopping bodies in heels and lace as tight as leather. Her silhouette makes my canines ache, and I'd empty my accounts for the chance to watch her fight.

Serafina motions for us to wait while she checks a corner, naturally throwing a military hand signal. When she waves the all clear, her nod hits like a head pat.

I crave her approval to the point that I'd be fucking *delighted* to stand between her and a forward-rolling tank.

But Serafina wants none of my protection.

She skips ahead whenever we close within three steps, pumping my lungs with lead.

Bish and Reese trail with me, none of us daring to approach.

Can't give her a reason to pull farther away. "We hid our car near the back entrance. Surveillance is down, but we didn't spot Nikolaj leaving the property."

"He didn't leave," she says flatly.

"You killed him? By yourself?" Reese sucks a hard breath before Bishop elbows him quiet.

Our mate rubs her arms, but her voice is iron. "He was evil."

"More than you know." Bishop flicks dust off his pristine sleeve. "Reese *meant to say* that with us here, there was no need to dirty your hands."

"There was need." Her voice is so small, her shiver kicks me over the edge.

I lunge before I can spot her flinch, her toes shifting to take a hit.

Then the blow hits me instead.

Every time she draws a line, it cuts across my throat.

I rock back on my heels. *Respect her space. Prove yourself later.* "That's one less enemy to handle."

As long as Kairo doesn't find out the cartel's throne is empty.

When that news hits, Redfang assets will be free to snatch. The street-level gangs are about to go ape, fighting for freed territory.

But generational criminals like Kairo and the Triad kings only move for legitimate power. With Nikolaj on ice, mating Serafina is the fastest path to the crown.

I'm all about cementing my base, but even if we wanted to switch careers, our pack doesn't have the manpower to hold the reins of an international cartel.

Already riding the same train of thought, Bishop gives a *slow-your-roll* head-shake. "Safe house first."

And schemes later. I nod. "Let's go."

"Wait." The word from her lips glues my feet to the tile.

"What do you need us to do?" Reese asks eagerly.

Serafina clicks a golden lighter, flames dancing in her eyes. "Let me finish my fire."

My cock jumps as Serafina torches the curtains.

Reese lets out a strangled groan. "How is *that* our omega?"

"Beautiful," Bishop murmurs, face bathed in the flames spreading from her fingertips.

Serafina's gown is made of long-sleeved, high-necked lace. The rose pattern hints at skin, but my imagination doesn't need the assist.

Already memorized her curves.

I want to help, but I *need* to watch.

My mate moves businesslike, from curtain to curtain. The security systems are down. No alarms can stop her. And I can't work my mouth to say we're in a rush.

Kairo can wait.

When flames lick the ceiling on all four sides, she tucks the lighter into her corset. "We can go now."

"Fuck," Reese whispers.

Our mate glides from the mansion she just torched.

My throat corkscrews with the sway of her ass.

Did I say we'd have to work to keep her?

Hell.

We have to work to prove we're worth her time.

EIGHTEEN

SOL

I IGNORE the alphas stalking me across the grounds, not even glancing back to enjoy the smoke.

Who am I?

Where am I?

When we hit the edge of the property, Reese scales the fence like a leopard, perching between iron barbs to offer me a hand up. "This way."

Sure.

Pretending this is normal, that anyone wants to touch me or that I can tolerate being touched, I climb to take his solid grip. Bishop and Jin sneak underneath, supporting my feet, and easy as a dream, I'm over the other side.

Like a feather with sweaty palms.

When the gamma squad runs the SAS obstacle course, I climb the wall alone while Elyse's mates take turns kicking mud.

My heart sours.

Serafina doesn't deserve these alphas.

The guys stashed their getaway car behind a row of hedges. My head swivels, ears perking for sirens.

"We're running a satellite jammer," Bishop says. "We won't be followed'

That's exactly what I'm worried about until Jin opens the door.

Then my problems go fuzzy.

Bishop's car is peach on wheels.

His scent sinks so deep in the custom upholstery, it's harder to hold back my drool than my poison perfume.

The guys jump in and crank the torture.

Between Reese's body heat upping the temp in the back seat and Jin tilting his mirror to kill me with eye contact, I'm zapped to the past when the guys let me tag along on errands. Bishop muttering to himself. Reese stripping off his waiter's coat the same way he used to strip off sweat-stained T-shirts after long days at the field.

Just shave my head and toss me a baseball cap.

We could take one of those cute re-creation photos if Dutch were here, trying to lure me onto his lap.

Shit.

I'd climb on board and risk ruining myself to erase the stain of alpha hands still creeping up and down my thighs like phantom paws

I grip the safety bar when Jin guns the car through the mansion's unmanned gate.

The sole of a sideways boot peeks from under a bush, and the only sight that's sweeter is the steady-growing plume of smoke rising from the roof.

How's that for a distraction?

Commander Fissure will be slammed sifting through corpses, and with luck, she'll write me off as gamma barbeque.

Not that I *ever* bank on luck.

I bank on faking my way forward.

That means womaning-up and facing the alphas I need to ghost.

I swallow the lump of Himalayan-sized salt clogging my throat.

I just have to keep my distance for a few hours.

Then I'll slip away. Maybe leave a note.

The guys will be upset, but they'll forget me the second they scent their real mate.

Just like they forgot Solomon.

I'm ready to lie as soon as they start asking questions.

But once Jin hits the city streets, driving in circles to throw off any tails, the quiet's only broken by the engine's whine.

It reminds me of waiting in the orphanage sitting room. That thick, strained silence just before I'm rejected by another set of parents who want a kid and not a question mark.

Waiting for the killing blow.

It tears the teeny fibers in my heart to leave them hanging, but I don't want to be the one who swings the axe.

I'd rather feel awkward than get destroyed.

So I seal my lips, nose, and pheromones, trying to breathe around their scents while I calculate how soon I need another shot and how far I can run on the wad of cash jammed down my corset.

We're crossing the bridge out of the city when Bishop cracks the silence through gritted teeth. "Dutch isn't coming home."

Reese sighs. "He'll regret it."

"Lisa and Dany?" Jin asks.

Bishop squeezes his phone until its case creaks. "Already on the plane."

"Good." Jin's dark gaze flicks to mine in the mirror, waiting for a response.

Serafina doesn't know their secret history. She'd flash into a rage, hearing other female names from her packleader's lips. *I can do rage.* "Who are they?"

"Lisa is our pack mother and Dany's our little sister. Dutch is—"

Bishop huffs. "A stubborn, classless oaf."

Reese rolls his eyes. "A *loveable* oaf."

"That too," Bishop whispers so softly that I have to bite my cheek to keep from licking my lips.

Jin grips the steering wheel, flashing the Triad tattoos on his fingers. "He's our pack's fourth alpha. Your alpha, if you'll give us a chance."

My heart squeezes, dripping spiked lemonade. "I need time."

First opportunity to sneak away, I'm gone.

Then I'll have all the time in the empty world to kneel on rocks and regret smashing the coward button.

"Not sure we have that." Jin's glance skims past my shoulder. A black sedan is already on our ass, tinted windows and no plates

No way it's Team Fissure. Bridget would never roll around town in a car that can't double as a battering ram. I dip lower in my seat. "Redfangs?"

"Triad." Jin hits the gas, then his phone rings through the speakers

When Korean letters pop up on the console, I'm not the only one sucking a breath through my teeth.

Jin never speaks Korean and almost never speaks about his dad—the only person who'd be in his contacts under a name I can't read.

"Here we fucking go." Bish straightens cuffs that don't need straightening, then pulls a pistol from the glovebox. He passes it to Reese, who cocks the barrel so smoothly, his arm veins pop against tanned skin.

Illegal forearm porn.

Bishop takes in my flinch, watching me like a sweater with a loose thread. My pulse races faster than the car.

He's the one who'll pick apart my lies.

Instead of calling me out, Bish offers the grip of another pistol. "Can you handle a .45?"

"Sure." It's heavier than I like, but any weapon's better than none when my best defense is benched.

"Give me Dutch's piece." Reese snatches it away, passing me his slightly smaller gun instead. "This is about to be the Wild West."

The grip's warm from his bandaged palm, and he handles guns even better than he handles a bat

Looks like I missed a few key chapters of their secret history.

When the hell did my guys go to spy school?

After the past few years, military training should be a turn-off, but these guys never follow my rules.

At this point, Reese could give me a flu shot and I'd swoon.

Pressing a finger to his lips, Jin answers the call.

"Where's the girl?" An alpha voice whips.

"She's here. Unconscious." Jin hits the gas and waves us lower in our seats. "I'm taking her off grid."

"Bring her to me," Kairo barks.

I love how Jin doesn't waver under the command. He finds my eyes and his shoulders rise. "She's too injured. Drugged. We had to sedate her."

"Bitten?"

"No," Jin says roughly, scraping my heart.

"Give me your coordinates. My men will—"

"Father?" Jin lifts his voice. "We're going through the tunnel. You're breaking up."

"Su-Jin—"

Jin flicks his phone to airplane mode, forcing the call to drop, and casually cutting across five lanes of traffic to hit the first exit at the end of the bridge. The Triad car screeches its brakes, missing the turn. "That buys us more time."

I manage not to fan myself but *holy anointed shit.*

If not mates, why hot?

Bishop's head-shake doesn't shift a hair out of place. "Not enough. Should we call for reinforcements?"

"Not that. Not yet." Jin is going to crash us with this no-look driving thing, but I forget to complain when our gazes snap so tight, the *click* rattles my spine. "What do you want?"

What I want is to bail on the roadside, hop a plane going anywhere, and put at least three countries I can't pronounce between me and the pack I'll never stop craving.

I sigh. "A shower. I need to wash off these alphas."

Three feral growls rock my already rattled backbone.

"Let's get you home." Reese white-knuckles his seatbelt.

I turn away to stop myself from unclenching his bandaged fist.

Should've died in the fire.

Asphyxiation would be less suffocating than a car ride with this pack.

γ

AFTER A WINDING DRIVE full of sharp turns and backtracking, the streets turn weirdly familiar.

I realize why when we zoom past a leaning sign spattered with bullet holes.

NEXT EXIT, EAST MEADOW.

The Meadows?

Now?

My rapid breath fogs the window. I'm glued to the glass, praying we're just passing through.

But Jin takes the exit that makes me want to scream. We pop onto a divided highway, one side gated mansions, one side the kind of slums that make you double-check your locks.

Guess which side is mine?

Jin steers away from the fancy part of town where he and Bish belong, toward the shit side where Reese, Dutch, and I came up.

Memory lane is paved with rusty nails, dirty needles, and potholes I'm hoping are still deep enough to connect to Siberia. I'd rather dig through the demon-infested center of the earth than deal with the ghosts that crowd these corners.

The bodega where Reese and I stole candy bars. The charity store where Dutch dragged me to buy himself a new coat after he bundled me in his, with a voice even meltier than his body heat. *"Stay warm, Solly"*

I had more of Dutch's clothes than my own.

There's the falling-down warehouse where Bishop ran his fights in a tailored red jacket. It's also where I had my first fantasy about heat sex, thanks to a sweat-slicked, blood-streaked Jin.

Thank fucking shit we turn away from the ball field.

I can't with those memories.

They belong to the Sol who disappeared. The one with the smooth neck and all that naive hope.

The truth chars the edges of my lips—or maybe all these years later, I'm still feeling Jin's kiss.

I sit on my hands, trying to hide the tremble in my fingertips.

If they'd taken me back to The Barrington, I could've coasted through my role. Any hotel. Any other town.

The universe is definitely screwing with me.

But fine.

Let's fucking go.

I won't break.

Not over Jin's gaze eating me through the mirror, Bishop manically adjusting his cufflinks, or Reese's blood soaking through his bandaged palm.

And not over Dutch.

Even if my crazy side is devastated he's not here, and I'll never get to see how he looks all grown up.

It's for the best.

Hard as ice and blood diamonds, I'm Serafina Redfang in bitch mode, tilting up my nose at alphas who dare to drive me to a zip code with no sushi—unless you count the two-headed fish that wash up from the drainage canals.

Never mind that I would've gone swimming in that muck-water if I'd dared to let them see me in a suit.

Every block stings like swallowing a hook.

I close my eyes and keep them shut until Jin throws the car in park

"We're here." He cuts the engine, but no one unbuckles.

I recognize the worst pocket of town, where more homes are abandoned than livable, but I've never seen the tiny yellow house with its lights glowing warmly beyond a chain-link fence.

Already hating myself, I ask, "Where's here?" with enough disdain to burn my tongue.

Leather creaks, the guys shifting.

Awkward is better than destroyed.

I hope.

"Would've booked you the penthouse," Bishop starts. "But—"

"Kairo has us watched." Jin shakes his head. "This is our safest property."

"Not exactly The Barrington, but it's home." Reese scratches his beard with the hand I keep reminding myself not to snatch. I'm about to exit the car by headbutting through the glass.

Before the madness takes over, I unbuckle and go for the handle. "Find me a shower and a bed. We'll deal with…"

The SAS, the Triad, plus three or four alphas who think I'm their mate, and *oh yeah*. The naked skin reminding me it's been too long since my last shot of lemon-flavored hell.

I'll shit enough bricks to build my own hideaway if I don't get out of this mess soon.

"We'll deal with everything in the morning," Jin finishes my sentence, clicking into packleader mode as he clicks his belt. "Let's get you inside. Reese—"

"I'll grab the tarp."

When I have to bite my lip to keep from asking, Reese fills in another blank as he hops out the door. "No garage. We have to cover the car."

"The neighborhood is all vagrants and gangsters." Bishop gestures for me to walk in front of him, turning the weedy sidewalk to a runway with his stride. "Don't go out without one of us and your gun."

The SAS brass would be horrified I have a firearm, let alone that I'm carrying it loaded. But I feel safer with a weapon that isn't neurotoxin and weirdly smug that they trust me enough not to ask for it back.

They shouldn't trust me.

I follow Jin into a cozy living room that feels much too much like home. It smells like fresh-baked bread, herbal tea, and something sticky-sweet that drips a shiver down my spine.

"Bathroom?" I press my wrist to my nose, trying to blot out

the pheromones I can't let myself inhale. My pulse-point can't squeeze out a drop of lemonade.

Time to re-apply or run.

Definitely run, because everywhere I turn is another glossy image from the vision board I burned. The squishy sofa heaped with crocheted blankets. The bookshelves packed with romance novels and pots of ivy. And the dark-eyed, dark-haired pack-leader who tosses his suit jacket over a kitchen stool and starts to roll his sleeves to cook me dinner. "Do you want to eat first?"

"Later." I swallow lava rock and press a hand to my stomach, wishing my body would react the way it should.

I want to eat Jin, but even though I can imagine licking him from wrist to corded shoulder, there's no gremlin, omega urge to pounce and bite and breed.

Jin, Bishop, Reese, and even Dutch, whose sneaky pheromone ghost keeps trying to creep inside my nose. They're Michelin-star desserts; the sweetest, richest treats I could possibly stick in my mouth

But I'm just waiting tables, passing their plates to someone else, and even if I could sneak a taste, there's no way I can afford the bill.

The truth is the lead ring squeezing my throat.

Not mine.

My neck itches under lace. All I want to do is get clean. Have a minute to myself under water so hot it steams away this train of thought.

Bishop catches me picking my sleeves. "You can take Dandelion's room." His tone is so heart-tuggingly flat, I wouldn't believe he felt the mate connection if I hadn't seen him loosen his tie at the hotel. Bishop can lie with the best, but he wasn't faking the mate-bomb that left his elegant features slack.

Now his mask is just as tight as mine when he shows me down the single hall. "Help yourself to clothes. If the scent bothers you, we'll run a wash. Bathroom's here. Toiletries, clean towels, toothbrushes." Keeping me an arm-length away, he opens a linen closet filled with labeled shelves of expensive, unopened product that screams his touch. "We'll be across the hall."

The doors to the bedrooms and bath cluster in a triangle, the house so small, I'm going to have to work my ass off to escape without getting caught.

Bishop's careful distance makes me that much more desperate to bail.

He deserves better.

A mate who'll jump into his arms. Not a fake who leaves him wearing the same blank face he used to wear when his father left him black and blue under his fancy suits.

"Thank you," my voice wavers.

Something flickers behind his eyes—*a flash of heat?*—but I duck into the bedroom before I screw myself and tug his sleeve to ask what's wrong.

I collapse against the door.

Was it this hard staying away from them when I was younger?

I have to get out.

Before I rip myself in half, pretending.

NINETEEN
BISHOP

I'M BEGINNING to loathe slammed doors.

When my supposed mate shuts me out again, a numb wave crashes over my shoulders.

Can't feel my fucking spine.

If I had claws, they'd be steak knives, gouging the wood.

Instead, I make fists with manicured nails, battling the rabid urge to stake a claim that she so obviously doesn't want or fucking reciprocate.

I check my buttons one-by-one, feeling up and down my shirt again and again and again.

Not until I'm calm—that's not happening with my head buzzing like I drained the bar of lemon drop shots—but until I have to move my ass or risk Serafina catching me standing frozen like a twat.

In the kitchen, Jin chops onions while Reese droops on a stool, looking as defeated as I won't admit I feel.

"She okay?" Reese lifts his chipmunk face.

Can't give him hope.

"No." I push past to the sink so I can wash my hands for three or four hours.

"What do we do?" Reese turns to our leader.

"Feed our mate." Jin works the cutting board as if a meal can fix the iron wall between us and the girl who has my ears perked, Doberman-sharp, catching every single floorboard creak from the vicinity of her room.

The caveman body-swap is *horrifying*.

I don't cook, but I want to order takeout from the best restaurant in the city, drag Serafina into my lap, and feed her bites of filet and foie until she tells me what the fuck I need to fix to convince her I'm the one.

My lizard brain sincerely believes that fine dining and hand-feeding are the magic recipe for thawing our omega's heart.

That level of delusion is exactly why we're fucked. "She has too much power."

"But she said she knows we're mates? Or implied it, at least." Reese rubs his chest, massaging the same spot where our princess's stiletto heel corks my aorta. He lifts a bandaged hand. "It must be real. She took care of me. Felt so fucking—"

"Something isn't right." I cut him off. *Let's not hear how the princess reached out to someone else.* Not even Reese, who I'd lend my last bottle of hand-san. "*She's* not right."

"Don't," Jin snarls. He thinks I'm talking shit about his girl.

It's not that.

She's *perfect*.

Longest fucking legs. Sin-soft lips, and she knows how to handle a gun.

Exactly the kind of girl Senior would've wanted me to mate.

Pedigreed, poised, and dark money rich.

Unfortunately, I *continue* to be a true-blooded Barrington, because even with the caveman need to breed, I still noticed the tailoring on her gown. "Her sleeves were too short."

So was her hem.

Bodice too tight.

Yeah, her whole fucking sale was rushed after Jericho kissed a phone pole hard enough to dial Kazakhstan, but I have credit card debt out the ass and three seamstresses on call.

You're telling me a billionaire couldn't schedule a fitting before his only daughter's backroom auction?

"What's that mean for shmucks without a summer home?" Reese asks

Jin stops chopping.

I don't stop washing, scrubbing between my fingers and around my thumbs. "I don't know yet."

No matter how I clean, the sickening feeling won't go away.

Serafina makes me feel like I'm staring in the mirror.

Look. I'm GQ, okay?

Brands, hair products, styling on point; has to be, or I can't breathe

Our girl is twice as pretty, and I think she's just as fake.

Lying doesn't bother me. I knew how to grift before I could stack blocks.

The distance is what fucks with my head.

An omega who'll barely speak to her scent-matched alphas. Almost jumped out of her skin from a hug.

That's not normal.

Her face when Jin held her.

Those bloodless cheeks.

Before she pulled her shit together, she flashed a haunted gaze that summoned my ghosts and froze me dead.

Overwhelmingly not fucking normal.

I can't let her any closer.

At least, not until I figure out why she isn't riding the same wave of wild instinct.

I want to trade bites so desperately, I'd let her bleed my collar red and never bleach it clean.

The possible reasons she's holding back pinch the tube of my throat.

I hope it's not that dark.

Maybe she's playing rich girl games, protecting herself the same way I'm about to protect our pack.

Until I know for sure, she's banned from meeting Dutch.

He can't forget the beta we never had.

One whiff of our scent-matched mate?

He'll be a simp for life, and I don't want to watch him die inside when the princess pushes him away.

I'm the only one who gets to torture our boy.

I wash until my hands sting, tissue-thin skin barely holding in my drumming pulse.

That's when Jin tosses a clean apron over my shoulder and shoves the can opener into my chest. "We're making tacos. Go drain some beans."

"Go drain some beans," I mock, toweling off and tying on the apron to protect my shirt.

Senior would have an aneurysm.

His heir, doing kitchen labor?

Hmm.

I'd better chop lettuce, too.

I'll send him a letter with all the food service details.

See if I can make his head explode.

When my hands are busy, my chest loosens. But my ears never relax. I tense when our princess leaves her bedroom, tip-toeing to the bath.

The sound destroys my focus, and I'm not the only one.

We stare through the wall.

Waiting.

Hoping.

Guarding.

If she doesn't open up to us, we're fucked.

And if she does?

Even worse.

Senior would abandon me for weeks at the hotel. Before I was old enough to get wise, I fell asleep wishing he'd come home. Nine times out of ten, he crawled back to ream my tutors and kick my ass

But that tenth time?

He'd bring a signed game ball. Custom-molded Italian loafers. Mirabelle plum jam, straight off the plane from Northeast France.

Treats to keep me dumb and tame.

I'd wait. And *wait.* When his briefcase hit marble, I'd vomit out my lungs, wondering if he was dishing out a present or another ass-ripping over my latest failure to perfectly rep the Barrington family name.

I'm a fucking *sucker* for treats.

If this omega reaches out, asks for help, gives me so much as half a smile…

I'll let her hurt me ten out of ten times and never complain.

Fuck

I drain the beans.

Tacos will make her love us.

Right?

TWENTY

SOL

DANY'S ROOM is chaotic comfort. It reminds me of Lilah's cozy closet at the OCC, just slightly bigger—an overflowing nest of bookshelves, notebooks, and K-pop posters.

Smells fresh and floral.

She's beta for sure, because my skin doesn't crawl.

I've never met Dutch's sister, but I heard about her all the time after she was born. He showed off her baby pics like he was earning commission on views.

She must be a teenager now?

Or not.

When I flick through the closet Dany emptied when she and Lisa ran, her leftover clothes are all a little short.

I'd rather wear a moist potato sack than the cursed, itchy gown that's sticky with sparkling peach after a drive-by with Bishop

Sending Dany my undying thanks, I grab a pair of sweats, a T-shirt, and the neon pink track jacket with a lip logo that I wish weren't a crop-top because it's the only thing that'll zip to hide my throat.

Then I check the window.

Barred.

In this neighborhood, it has to be. I'll have to steal a screw-driver or sneak out the front.

But, shower first. I need to kill time. Wait for the guys to lower their guard. On my way out, I spot the City Cryptids cap hanging behind Dany's door.

It's embroidered with Reese's number nine.

Totally stealing it when I bolt.

First, I steal into the bathroom and make deadly sure it's locked

Then I strip, balancing in the micro-aisle between the chipped vanity counter and the avocado-colored tub.

When the gown's zipper sticks, I'd rather ask Bridget to braid my hair than ask the guys for help. I yank the torn skirt, cleansing myself with the *riiip, riiiiiiip, riiiiiiiiiiiiiiip* that reminds me how close I am to *finally* breaking free.

I pile my get-away items from the stash that's been strapped to my thighs or shoved down the front of my gown.

Pistol. Cash. Fake makeup clutch of doom, hiding a poison payload

The shower isn't hot enough to fog the mirror, so I spot my nasty throat before I can duck behind the sunflower-print curtain.

Desperate to cover my body, I quick-wash, using the detachable shower head to avoid wetting my face.

I can't scrape off my makeup layer.

I'll die before I let the guys see me bare.

I don't even dare let out my pheromones under the safety of the spray. But at least they're not as wild after coming out to play.

Trying to erase the feel of lingering alpha hands, I flub and fling the bar of soap. It hits the tub like a bowling ball.

Booooong

Before I can recover, Reese pounds the door. "Princess? You okay in there?"

"Fine." I catch the soap before it flies away again. "Be out in a minute"

Please don't let him start calling me princess.

It's worse than Serafina.

I've never been a princess.

Never even hoped for a crown.

I want to move beyond the old dreams I've given up and build a new me. Not a Darling, a Redfang, or even a flipping Moon.

Marisol no-last-name, who does what she wants and answers to no one

To achieve that, I have to stop being soft.

I scrub myself raw, dragging out the clock.

I'm wondering if I can hang in the bathroom until dawn when I smell frying onions and spices, and my stomach starts to growl.

I haven't eaten since those spa lettuce wraps.

After drying off, I slip into Dany's sweats, then scowl. My makeup is looking melty, and even with a T-shirt underneath, the cropped jacket makes me feel ridiculously on display.

Should've gone with the potato sack.

I end up stealing Lisa's mint green bathrobe, promising I'll send the fam a gift card after I land somewhere safe.

That's the last they'll ever need to hear from me.

The food smell hits harder when I peek into the hall. Something sizzles in the kitchen, where three magnetic voices whisper back and forth.

"—can't put salsa on hers. What if she doesn't like spice?"

"Imagine? *Tragedy.*"

"Enough. Find the ramekins. We'll give her some of everything"

"The hell is a ramekin?"

"A small, oven-safe vessel. Perfect for crème brûlée."

"You mean a fuckin' *bowl*?"

"You need another etiquette lesson."

"Hard pass. Wait. Does the sour cream smell funky? We can't feed her this."

"Toss it. I'll go to the store."

"Bring back a Spanish wine. Something that pairs well with beef."

"I'll ask Hank for the key to the wine cellar." I can *hear* Jin roll his eyes. "It's the bodega, Bish. Not Majorca."

"Maybe we should take her to—"

Hypnotized by their easy conversation as much as their care, I crane forward too far. The battered floorboards groan.

Their cut-off silence is as pointed as their warmth.

I dart into Dany's room.

The syringe case mocks me when I toss my pile on the bed. Doesn't matter what the guys cook. I need another dose of lemon to leave the room, and I won't be able to keep down food after the shot

I wish I had a phone so I could check the news. I need to see if the SAS took my bait, or if Bridget already knows I axed her target. I'm so restless, my bones rattle.

I need to be on my way to a new identity before Bridget finds me or *worse*—finds out how much I care about the guys.

After a while of vibrating through my skin, a soft knock sounds

"Made you a plate," Jin's voice is hushed, like he's afraid to startle me. "We're here if you need anything."

I wait for his footsteps to fade, but I'm not startled.

I'm burning up inside.

When I press my ear to the door, the only sound is the drone of the living room TV. I open the door a crack, find a plate on the floor, and snatch it inside.

Tacos.

Their heat steams the plastic wrap that covers half a dozen tiny ramekins, filled with guac, salsa, and fresh sour cream. They're made with so much care, my heart pushes up into my throat. I shake as I pluck off the stuck-on note.

We'll wait for you.

My stomach eats my ribs, but the throb in my chest aches worse

I can't bring myself to crack the plastic.

Instead, I set the plate on someone else's dresser, next to someone else's gun, and the baseball hat I'm going to steal.

I've never really owned a thing.

Sometimes, I don't even think I'm real.

I'm lies on lies on lies.

Even then

Faking is better than being rejected.

I turn off the light and balance on the edge of Dany's bed, waiting for the house to still.

I can't keep wishing I belong.

I can't keep waiting to be seen.

I have to fight and make a place that's mine.

I have to cut away the past.

Maybe no one else will ever love me.

That's fine.

I'll fight and fight and fight until I'm strong enough to love myself.

γ

SLEEP NEVER COMES.

At dawn, in a trance, I aim one last pheromone shot into the rashy, irritated skin of my scar-gnarled throat.

Lemon-soaked chemicals leave me choking up bile, but there's no more time to kill, waste, or linger.

I have to run.

With my loot jammed in a tiny, lip-shaped backpack, and a gun in the waistband of my neon-pink tracksuit, I already look like someone new.

A raccoon-eyed K-Pop groupie, sprinting the walk of shame.

Dany's leftover sneakers are more than half-a-size too small, but I have no other choice as I tiptoe out of the house.

Breathing echoes from the bedroom across the hall. I slip past, moving ancient-turtle-slow, but the real danger waits in the living room.

Reese lies passed out on the couch with the sports channel on mute

One leg on the floor, one on the sofa. His T-shirt is peeled up to flash his abs and make room for the hand that dips below his waistband

Smells like sex and chocolate syrup.

My belly tightens.

When he stirs, I freeze.

One hand sleepily itches his beard while the other moves *deeper*, unconsciously stroking under his shorts.

"*Unh.*" His husky grunt hits the backs of my knees.

While I shake, my pheromones prick.

If Reese catches my real scent?

I won't have to slink away.

He'll chase me out, knowing I'm a threat

I clench my jaw.

I have to leave before I cause more damage. Before Bridget finds me and grabs hold of my biggest weakness.

Fast, silent, I unlock the door.

When I'm out, when I'm sure Reese is dreaming, and Bishop and Jin are too far away to hear, I don't look back.

I sprint

Filling my lungs with clean, cold air, I tell myself the itch in my eyes is from wearing the same pair of green contacts way too long

Soon, I'll purge the rest of this disguise.

The slums suit my mood.

I hop bottle shards and flattened fast food bags without breaking stride.

Back in the day, East Meadow Steel supplied every skyscraper in the city. Now the manors of fallen metal barons are knee-high with reeds, and boarded-up windows are more common than ones with lights

It's the perfect place to hide from cops or a shady government agency. *As your needs may be.*

Taking advantage of the decay, I follow the permanent street map burned into my memories, cutting through alleys and abandoned yards.

The bus station isn't far.

I'll pay cash for a ticket and be untraceable.

No CCTV in this zip code. I've got no phone. No way for anyone to capture me, ever again.

But the road to freedom has one last memory minefield, ready to blast me with spiritual shrapnel.

The abandoned ball park.

Cutting across the field is the fastest way to the station.

I jog down a hill of ratty grass and cigarette butts, onto the dirt packed dense with memories stronger than my need to flee.

Kayden and Jayden used to drag me here, needing me to hold their gear and be their target when they wanted to act tough. My first set of foster brothers was a year older than me, and they always loved putting me in my place.

Bringing me to the field was the only time they ever put me in the *right* place.

I'd watch Reese pitch for hours.

Dutch played catcher while Jin and Bishop took turns hitting.

I snuck here every chance I could, until Reese couldn't help but notice. Instead of turning me away, he taught me how to pitch and catch and hit a ball.

I was terrible

Your hand-eye coordination sucks when you grow up not being able to play—I was too busy changing diapers and washing Vivian's nasty heat sheets.

But Reese was patient.

Gentle.

Days the guys didn't show, I never got picked to play.

But when they did?

Once, Bishop and Jin fought over who got to keep me in their dugout.

First time I ever smiled for real.

Feet hurting as much as the memories, I stop to loosen Dany's micro-shoes, leaning against the dugout's crumbling wall.

The park used to be legit before the town got condemned.

Lights and scoreboards haven't worked in thirty or forty years, but it has all the right equipment—all it needs is a little care and rehab

Just like me

I snort, breath fogging.

Even the air tastes nicer on the field.

Dirt and grass.

Morning dew and a hint of maple syrup.

Okay That last one is someone's breakfast wafting down the street, but still.

When Vivian had heats, and the bio kids got shipped to their aunts and uncles, I'd sleep in the dugout.

Sometimes Reese did too.

Neither of us had anywhere to go before he moved in with Dutch

This was my home.

I breathe deep, not just maple, but a sudden whiff of mouth-watering bacon.

Sugar and buttered smoke put my stomach on swoop.

Then a noise lifts every hair on my body.

I whirl to a growl as low and buttery as that scent.

A shadow rises from the dugout, rubbing his eyes.

Big.

But it's not the size that has me panicking.

Dutch

He's built like an upside-down triangle with legs.

When his blanket falls away, his stupid huge chest heaves. No shirt, just hard nipples, action figure shoulders, and more abs than I can count when I'm hypnotized, tracking his soft, gold happy trail.

Dutch's sweats droop so low below the V of his tight waist, he flashes more than just a trail.

He's packing the whole mountain.

Someone pass me a carabiner.

No!

No climbing, no rope, and absolutely no trespassing.

I should already be running away.

Dutch's blond hair is sleep-rumpled. Pillow lines dig into his cut jaw

But there's nothing sleepy in his stalk.

He climbs from the dugout with a stroking growl, wild blue eyes sparking with something I don't want to name.

I start to turn.

Start to flee.

But when I breathe deep, trying to outrun the predator, I catch a face full of deadly sweet pheromones.

Maple bacon and pancakes dripping butter.

A whole breakfast feast.

But my body never plays along.

It already had three strikes, three chances to react like they were my mates.

The fourth miss hits right in the diaphragm.

I want him

I want them *so much.*

But something inside me is disconnected.

The part that's omega enough to be irritated when I don't have enough pillows or the room is too bright.

Those instincts can't be bothered now.

We already had mates.

Look how that worked out.

I'm not dead enough to stop being attracted.

But that place inside?

The part of my soul that used to flutter and spark?

Empty.

Gone.

"You." Dutch's broad shoulders drop. A golden lion ready to pounce

Something stirs in the hollow inside, but it's not a butterfly. More like icy snakes, coiling to kill my heart. "This is a mistake"

"Mate," Dutch's sandpaper rasp scrapes my spine like my skin is just as bare as his.

Can't help it—I shiver.

Bad idea.

Shouldn't have twitched.

Shouldn't have responded.

He lunges like he's bringing down a gazelle. There's no chance to dodge

Dutch takes me.

Squeezing the breath from my lungs, greedy arms wrapping me so tight

I'm pinned too hard to flinch when he bites the fabric covering my throat

I squeal.

Scissor in his arms.

It's the non-scarred side.

Doesn't pierce cloth.

But his teeth. The heat of his mouth.

Oh my god.

His *touch.*

His big body, pulling me down when I want to rocket away. Firm fingers biting my ribs.

He purrs, teeth dragging fabric, breath so loud, so agitated—

Shit.

Dutch used to give me half his sandwich to coax me into his lap. I'd balance on his knee while Bishop told him he was smiling like a buffoon.

Double-shit.

Buffoons are my *favorite.*

So much for protecting myself.

I'm already screwed.

Might as well enjoy the fall.

My fingers dig the blanket-warmed heat of his hips.

I claw him tighter.

I can't remember the last time I let myself be hugged. The last time I could even handle being touched.

It was definitely Dutch.

Now I don't want it to stop, because there'll never be another hug this good

One so warm and smoky with maple sugar.

He growls and purrs and breathes me in, all primal half-made sounds

Ignoring the yawning emptiness in my soul, I press my cheek to Dutch's welcoming heat, not sure if this is my worst lie or my deepest truth.

Whatever it is, it can't last much longer.

TWENTY-ONE
DUTCH

MATE MATE MATE *mate mate mate mate.*

Holy shit.

That's my fucking mate.

How gorgeous is she?

And her ass!

I want to lick it.

Want to lick her, hold her, pick her up and toss her over my shoulder, haul her home to meet Mom, then hang a sock on the doorknob and fuck this girl so long and full, anyone who tries to take her away won't be able to peel her off my knot.

My dick is so fucking hard.

Mouth all sore and hungry, only I'm not sure if I want to eat her throat or lick her lemon cake.

I clench cheeks, throbbing from that good spot inside.

She'll peg me, right?

I've been doing prep for a boy mate, but we can totally make this work

What a lucky fuck.

I have two mates!

She'll love our beta just as much as we're going to love her.

We're going to be so flipping happy together.

She says something I can't hear. My body's humming too loud.

Fucking rush. All these instincts and urges, roaring.

Think I'm roaring too?

Need to get her close.

Feel her.

Taste her.

I lunge, and when she sinks into my arms, the scent of cake batter fries my brain like funnel cake—nothing but lemon sugar and empty holes that wanna get filled.

I nip her throat, taste fabric, finally hear her drizzled moan.

Makes me shiver so hard, my tailbone wags.

"Mate." Even the word tastes like silk.

Smooth, glazey lemon silk. Like those little cakes Jin's mom used to bake before she went ghost.

Only better.

So much fucking better.

Want to rub her *all over* my skin.

So I do

Her super-soft cheek strokes my chest when I start to move, and when she curls into me, trusting me, something lines up, deep inside

Instinct drags me to her collar.

Have to rub my scent all over her throat.

That's when my mate shudders.

But not the good kind of shudder?

What?

Why?

When I loosen my grip, she pulls away, and the only thing that keeps down a barf-wave of rejection is the weird-ass déjà vu when I finally notice my mate's brain-hurtingly pink jacket. "Those are my sister's clothes."

"Borrowed them." She tugs the crop top over the T-shirt I wish wasn't covering her stomach.

I'd drop to my knees and dip my tongue in her belly button.

No, wait. Save the button.

Easier to lift her.

Hook her knees over my shoulders. Get my hands under that juicy ass. Paste her thighs to my face and nuzzle into her hot, wet, syrup-dripping—

A whiff of Dany's jasmine blindsides my brain.

Feels like my sister walked in on me jerking off.

I cringe, and my omega pulls away, holding out a hand before I can snatch her back.

"You must be one of my prospective mates?" she says, all cold and distant.

Frigid fingers squeeze the bone between my lungs.

What did I do wrong?

I *felt* her respond to my touch. The way she trembled. Her scent dripping. Melting into me. Making me melt with her sexy fucking softness.

Prospective?

"No. I am your mate. There's three others. Or maybe four? I'm Dutch, by the way. The person, not the nationality. It's a thing. But you can call me anything you want."

She brightens until I think she's going to laugh, and the ghost of her smile plucks my heart halfway out my chest.

But her smile dies before it can shine.

Instead, she scowls so nasty, I want to apologize for every wrong thing I've ever done from accidentally stepping on a stag beetle in fourth grade to eating Reese's pre-game banana last week

Have to be better.

"Whatever your name is, you can't throw yourself at an omega"

"You're not an omega. You're *my* omega."

My mate.

Mine.

Mine mine mine mine mine mine mine.

"This is a mistake."

"You said that already." Thought I couldn't hear her the first time. Must've blocked out the words, 'cause they can't be right. "What are you doing right now?"

She drags her toe through the dirt. "Jogging."

"Come home with me." Have to introduce her to Mom and Dany

Oh, wait. They already flew out.

I still want to drag my mate to the safe house.

For coffee, breakfast, and a bite. Then maybe losing my knot virginity if she's cool with mating before our official ceremony

Dude. Backyard wedding. Dany can be flower girl.

My mate shivers.

Her cheeks are pink.

Cold?

A grumble rips from my chest.

I haul her onto my hips, loving when her ankles hook, and holding her gives me the excuse to cup an ass so sweet, I have to lift her even higher so she doesn't feel the baseball bat swinging in my sweats.

No underwear lines under those pants.

I mean, *holy fucking fuck.*

I'm so hard I could hit a homer with this dick.

Even my knot pounds.

It always swells when I'm jerking off or fooling around with Bish, but it's never blown up like this. Feels like a veiny fucking basketball at the base of my cock, growing, growing, *throbbing* with every brush of skin.

Ready to sink deep.

Stay deep

Lemon teases my nose, but I have to get a grip.

Take care of my mate before I go animal.

Then I'll mark her

Make sure every alpha knows this omega belongs to me.

To us

She lets me carry her, not shivering, but still.

So fucking still when my blood's screaming for her hard enough to bongo-drum my balls.

I don't like it.

Feels like the moment before the phone call that destroyed my world. Knew something was wrong.

Know it's wrong now.

But what?

Super-gentle, I set her on the dugout bench. I wrap her in my blanket, wanting her warm and slathered in my scent, tightening it over her shoulders until only her face peeks out.

My mate has cutting green eyes and cheekbones I want to trace with my tongue.

When I start to unzip the sleeping bag, wondering how I'm going to zip her in sitting up, her feather-soft words insta-melt the fear that she's about to run. "You slept here?"

"Mmm," I agree, tasting her voice like a dessert.

"Why?"

"Fighting with my pack. They brought back—"

Oh.

Oh fuck.

I'm not *that* stupid, but sometimes I'm a real fucking tool. "You're Serafina. The Redfang princess."

"That's me." The light leaves her eyes.

Damnit.

Didn't mean it like a bad thing.

Everything about her is so fucking good.

"That's perfect. No. You're perfect. I mean. Bish said you were ours. I just didn't believe him. But now*this*, right?" I already have the real estate blocked out for her on my throat. She'll own my whole ass when we finally bond the pack.

Can't fucking wait.

"This." She tries to wiggle out of the blanket. "You better go back to the house. Let me finish my run. I'll meet you there."

"No." I hold the blanket tight, stopping her from going away.

Just the idea is a bone in my throat.

Can't lose her.

Can't lose anyone else. "The neighborhood isn't safe."

Why'd the guys let her out alone?

They're the real tools.

A whole-ass shed.

"I can take care of myself."

"Right. Gangster princess. But I want to take care of you too."

"Dutch..." Her breath feathers my face.

I lick my lips, tasting cake batter all zig-zaggy with little strips of lemon

What does Bish call them?

Oh yeah.

Zest.

She's soft cake and sprinkled sugar, drenched in zesty glaze that runs down the back of my throat. Can't even keep my tongue in my mouth.

Too soon to suck her fingers?

Bet they taste so good.

I'm gonna lick every spot on her skin.

Oh, fuck.

What if she licks me *back*?

I think I whine.

But my phone vibrates, saving me from embarrassing my ass. It's been ringing since yesterday, and I finally have a reason to pick up

Have to tell the guys I'm in love.

Before I can open my mouth, Bish banshee roars. "Where the fuck have you been? She's gone. Serafina is—"

"She's right here."

"*What?*" he hisses so hard, even our mate flinches. "Where's here?"

"The field. But—"

"*Stay,*" he commands, whipping out dominance I didn't know he had and forcing my knees to lock.

Click

"Not a dog," I mutter, but oh well. The sooner the pack's reunited, the sooner we can mate, and the sooner we can all have fun unlocking Bishop's beast mode.

Together. As a pack.

"I have to go." Serafina pushes, trying to escape her toasty burrito

"I'll run with you. Anywhere you want." 'Round the block, closest wedding chapel, *wherev.*

"No. I—" her voice pierces, so painful I don't know what the fuck to do except help her untangle.

My hands feel like foam fingers, all numb and useless when Serafina starts to pant.

She's panicking

Have to make her comfortable.

I rip off the blanket.

She jerks, whipping her ponytail to the side to get away.

She's going to leave me.

Now *I* can't breathe.

Going tunnel vision, my sight fades to a pinprick where a cluster of freckles hides behind her ear.

Four freckles

One freckle for each alpha, on an S-curve I used to follow with my fingertip.

Time freezes, and I go light-headed with half my blood jailed in my cock.

I am the toolshed.

Why didn't I notice sooner?

My mate stumbles out of the dugout in a sprint to escape that hammers my skull with panic.

Can't lose her.

Not again!

Three long steps and I dive.

Mid-air, I pillow her with my body, curling to protect her from the fall I can't feel.

Can't feel anything but her heat, her breath, as dirt puffs around us and we skid toward first.

I roll onto my back, seeing nothing but blue-pink morning sky and wide, green eyes.

Another thing that's blue?

The circles around her irises.

Contacts.

Sticky makeup can't hide the long lashes I remember. Or that little dip between her nose and lip I never stopped wanting to kiss

The point of her chin.

The way she squeezes my shoulder, thumb hooking under my collarbone—coming home to reclaim the spot where only she could ever belong.

Click.

Click.

Click.

All my missing pieces snap home. "Solly?"

TWENTY-TWO
SOL

HE KNOWS.

He *knows*.

Oh, shit.

He knows, but *what* does he know?

That I'm fake?

That I'm Marisol?

No. He can't know that.

None of them ever knew that—not who I really am.

"*Solly*" Dutch purrs deeper, rumblier, firing a velvet-wrapped bullet between my eyes.

The weaponized nickname tears down my spine, chipping bone behind the hollow pit that has me all fucked up inside. "I—"

"*Solly. Solly. Solly*," Dutch calls my name, rumbling my thighs. His thick fingers tremble against my cheek. "You're back."

He's so soft.

So raw.

Eyes sparkling and wet.

My lips part, wanting to answer.

I choke on words, but the tightening of my throat isn't all emotion

Needle-pricks scrub my skin in lemon salt while my pheromones stage a death-match with Serafina's scent. Keeping control feels like squeezing coils of barbed wire, but the fight's not half as bloody as the one in my heart.

A breath rips between my teeth.

What in the *shit* am I doing?

Lying on Dutch's chest?

Letting him peel off my mask?

One moment of lost control and he's dead.

My heart ices.

There's only one thing I can do when I'm cornered, when I'm lost and weak and bracing for another hit.

Lie and make him go away. "I'm Serafina Redfang. I'm not—"

"Freckles."

"I don't have—"

"Here." His finger brushes even softer than his voice when he strokes a familiar path behind my ear. Down and over, down and over, sparking a shiver that keeps falling when he lifts his fingertip to trace the spot again.

"One. Two. Three. Four." Dutch pauses at every dot, then cradles the side of my face, stroking my earlobe with a ticklish, too-possessive thumb. "Where have you been, Solly?"

My neck skin creeps, numb shock rolling like a cold, cracked yolk

Freckles?

For real?

I thought I'd get caught using the wrong fork at a fancy dinner. Maybe pop out of Serafina's bra, trip in her stilettos, or spill a secret she's not supposed to know.

But *freckles* sell me out?

I didn't even know I had freckles, and it's weird as shit that Dutch knows me better than I know myself.

Pancake breakfast soaking my tongue, I drag his wrist away. His golden brow bunches, but he doesn't fight.

I'm the one fighting my truth and the twisted scent trying to claw free.

What am I supposed to say?

I love you so much I can't breathe, but my sister is the one you need

Even if I turned back time and stopped myself from being

marked. Even if I'd clung to the guys and stopped us spending all those years apart.

I'd still have the asterisk.

This ability.

This scent.

This janky gamma body, built to repel.

"Solly." Bare back resting in dirt, Dutch doesn't twitch.

He *purrs*.

Balanced on his chest, I'm tickled with waves of soft rumbles.

Every breath in.

Every breath out.

His rocking motion and gentle sounds soothe the tentpole tension in my spine.

Even better?

Dutch doesn't ask questions.

He purrs me loose.

My muscles soften. Fingers un-bunch. Knees relax. Even my throat unclenches, both flavors of perfume lulled by magic that has nothing to do with alpha.

It's not Dutch's dominance soothing me like a warm blanket.

It's *him*.

The kid who gave me his clothes, his toys, his lunch.

The kid who gave me everything he had, even though I never had a thing to give him back.

I swear I'll give him the truth he deserves.

In a second

After Dutch stops purring.

When I can speak without my voice breaking.

"Solly." His heart shimmers in his eyes, warm and blue as ocean water. "I'm sorry."

"You're—" I choke. *He's sorry?* "For what?"

"Couldn't keep you safe. Thought I lost you." Dutch's purr roughens. "Never again. I'll never let you out of my sight."

If I'm so good at lying, why is my head so blank?

Holding me close, Dutch lifts his upper body from the dirt. I slide down his hips, grinding his lap and bare chest. Before I can react, he curls around me, burying his face in my scarred shoulder.

His breath blowtorches my scars.

I want to push him away.

I want to run so far from the tears in his eyes and the way he trembles, bleeding and vulnerable.

But his magic cancels my need to cringe, and instead of doing the right, honorable thing, I disappear into him and this impossible moment.

I missed you.

I missed you so fucking much.

Dutch clings just like he did after his dad's funeral. Only then, he was a kid in a starchy collared shirt.

Not a full-grown alpha in gravity-challenged sweatpants that fell even lower when he tackled me to the earth. His smooth, bare skin is so hot, he steams in the morning air, puffing out scent like a pancake fresh off the griddle.

The bus station is calling my name, but Dutch's need calls louder.

My body doesn't resist his arms.

Maybe my need is screaming the loudest.

My heart dances between doom and delirium.

But before I can follow the fantasy any farther down the foxhole, a sports-car bulldozes the chain-link fence. It off-roads down the hill, tearing to a stop in a cloud of dirt and dragging me back to the reality where I'm always screwed the second I drop my guard.

My scent glands fire, ready to tear down another enemy.

Wish it were an enemy.

"Princess!" Reese's raw call echoes like a grand slam ball, pinging my vertebrae on its way out of the park. Wearing nothing but the shorts he slept in, Reese sprints across the field.

Bish and Jin follow. Jin in silk pajama bottoms, and Bish—

I can't breathe.

It's rare to spot him wearing anything but neat slacks.

Now he sprints in the fluffy mint bathrobe I left folded on Dany's bed, every stride flashing bare thigh. He's so laser-focused on me, he doesn't seem to realize he's undressed.

Dutch sighs into my collarbone. "We can finally be a pack."

I'm trying to find the words to explain why that's impossible. Then a siren chirp kills the bear hug I can't bring myself to stop.

"Cops?" Dutch lifts us to our feet before I can blink, tucking me behind his body to protect me from the threat.

Like I'm not the most dangerous thing on the field.

An SUV with tinted windows and no plates rolls over the downed fence.

Sick knowing twists my stomach. "Those aren't cops."

"Kairo?" Reese isn't winded when he cuts his sprint at our side

"Kairo would've brought a fleet." Jin squares up, instinctively taking the lead position as the alphas form around me.

Bishop completes the protective square. "Kairo would've found the safe house months ago if he had eyes in this zip code." He tries to straighten his lapels, but he falters when his hands catch terry cloth instead of tailored silk. Even then, he doesn't flinch, staring down the enemy.

He ran here for me.

Mostly naked, chasing his mate who fled.

They *all* ran here for me, and instead of asking me to explain, all they do is shield me from the danger.

My heart thumps hard enough to slap me in the face.

Just what I need to get my head on straight.

Even in permanent whiplash mode, I'm solid on my most important facts.

One:

No one hurts my Meadows boys.

Two:

I'm never going back to that base.

The SUV parks beside the guys' car. Undercover as a soccer

mom in jeans and a sweater, Commander Fissure slides out of the passenger seat. Doctor Brandon and Silas pile out wearing polo shirts and poker faces that would let them pass as weekend warriors if Elyse didn't roll from the third row like their evil step-daughter.

She can't pass as anything but smug, quirking red-lined lips in an evil smile as she clinks a well-worn set of ankle cuffs.

Needles gnash my skin.

I keep down my scent, but either the guys feel my fear or they sense Elyse's menace. They tighten around me, forming a solid wall of protection that makes it hard to swallow.

These two worlds were never supposed to collide.

"Who the fuck is this?" Bishop lifts his nose.

I step forward so I can be their shield. "They're here to take me back."

"*No*." Dutch hauls me to his chest, clutching tight as a straitjacket.

"Shit." Reese sizes up the agents crossing the field. "They're packing. Should've grabbed my bat."

"None of you brought a gun?" Jin's shoulders tighten.

Bishop snorts. "Left mine in my *cashmere* robe."

I wiggle free of Dutch and pass Jin the gun from my waist. I have a better weapon, and I want him armed if this turns into a firefight. "Let me do the talking."

Jin knows what he's doing when he palms the weapon. The flex of his forearms dries my throat.

But, I shut down my delusions, moving to Jin's side while Dutch shadows my back. Bishop and Reese stick close, growling to mark territory. Aggressive alpha surrounds me, almost suffocating, but I don't want to run.

Not from these alphas.

I want to enjoy our last time together.

Bridget halts her crew twenty feet away; exactly the limit of my kill range. My reluctant birth-giver folds her arms over her fuzzy sweater, but she's so rigid, she'd scream military wearing a gown. "Twenty-Six. You broke our deal."

Fuck. That. Shit.

"You abandoned me." *Again* "Everything after that was self-defense"

"We're recovering bodies from the fire," Brandon says. "I'm sure the autopsies will elucidate whether you defended yourself or lashed out."

Elyse doesn't have the rank to speak, but she clanks the ankles cuffs to emphasize I'm screwed.

I've never been afraid of *her*.

Bridget shakes her head in familiar disappointment. "The mission was to stall. Not cover mistakes with another arson. There'll be no escaping responsibility this time."

Responsibility?

My neck-veins spiderweb with fire. *You* want to teach *me* about responsibility?"

"You four." She looks past me, back to ignoring me the way she prefers. "Step away from the girl or you'll join her in custody"

"How ill-mannered." Bishop looks down his nose, blue-blooded even in a bathrobe. "Making demands on our turf? You haven't even introduced yourselves."

"That's classified," Silas snaps. "Step away from the asset."

"Take a fucking hike," Reese growls.

"She's ours." Dutch clamshells my ribs, staking a claim that'd melt me dead if I weren't boiling with hate.

"If you want to escalate, we're game." Jin aims at Bridget's chest, flexing his Triad tattoos. "But you're not taking our mate."

The M-word streaks through me like a meteor.

Full-body shiver.

Next comes the crash.

"Mate?" Elyse gasps. "You? With *her?*"

"Impossible." Brandon locks eyes with Bridget, wordlessly

discussing how much to reveal to make the deluded civilians go away

It won't take much.

I'm already scoping out the dugout and the street beyond, picking spots to duck and cover.

"This girl is a test subject who escaped our lab. She can mimic pheromone signatures." Bridget's cold explanation cuts between my ears. "We have your real mate in custody. Hand over the fake and we'll happily trade you for the authentic goods."

The veins at my temples judder.

My pheromones scream.

Before I can unleash the devastation I've been holding back for eons, Dutch's snarl shakes the earth. "Fuck off."

"Don't be fooled," Doctor Brandon starts. "She—"

"Is our mate. End of story." Jin whips out his dominance.

Then it's not the earth shaking.

Their scents stroke my skin like a promise. Fizzy peach and sizzling lightning, comforting cocoa and sweet maple. Their four-way snarl rattles my knees as hard as it rattles my composure.

They don't believe Bridget.

The truth does sound crazy.

Before Bridget, there was no precedent for scent-copying, and the SAS isn't passing their gamma data to the press. As far as the world knows, pheromones can't be faked.

"Still waiting for somebody to flash a badge," Reese says, unimpressed

"We're past the point of showing identification." Bish sneers. "You can't remove an omega from their pack. If you'd like to detain the group, make sure to prepare a cell large enough for my litigation team."

"They're not taking her," Jin says with rock-solid confidence. "They're not touching her."

Holy shit.

They're stealing lines from my vision board.

"Yeah," Dutch snarls, "So fuck off."

"You already said that." Bishop gives him terry cloth side-eye.

"Then why are they still here?" Dutch circles my belly button with his thumb "Throw down or go away. I got cake to eat."

In the first sign of life since the time-before-the-bite, my pussy flutters

Love them.

Always have, always will.

Even if they'll never be mine.

Bridget wrenches her glare to her preferred target. "These lies aren't doing your cause any favors."

No? They've worked 'til now. "I kept my promise. I stalled for time and stopped Nikolaj from leaving town. Now I have a pack and—"

Before my mouth can run with the fantasy, corn syrup perfume punches my palate.

"What the hell?" Reese pinches his nose, Dutch whines, and I lose my *everlovingshit* and the last of my dried-up, leftover fucks

It's one thing handing the guys to their real, fated, scent-matched mate.

I'd rather shoot Serafina's pheromones into my oozing eyeballs than let my mother charm them with her scent. A snarl ratchets out from my soul. "They're *mine*."

"That's your attitude?" Bridget purses her lips.

This is where I'm supposed to apologize and salute.

To offer my hands and ankles and let her march me home to prison in cuffs.

I'm done playing nice.

I've *been* done, no matter what it costs to disobey.

"You want to find out whose pheromones are stronger?" My throat pulses.

I'm ready to compare.

The agents who always sneer at me, smug and superior, go nothing but grim.

Monster-Sol is delighted.

"You'll regret this," Brandon says, reading straight from his cartoon villain script.

"Nope. But you might." My pheromones whirr, desperate to cut loose ends.

Elyse twitches.

Loving her flinch, I make a *gimme* motion. "Give me the cuffs."

"I don't take orders from freaks." Elyse's tone is pure mean girl, but the clink of metal gives away her nerves.

Air hisses through Jin's teeth. "And we don't take insults to our mate."

"Do as she tells you or you'll deal with us." Bishop vibrates with deadly smooth malice.

Another pussy flutter shakes the dust downstairs.

Feral Bishop. Not even a priest could resist.

Elyse goes glaze-eyed.

Before she can think about adding some quality to her himbo harem, or I can body slam her for the thought, Bridget lifts a hand. "Leave the restraints. We'll procure an upgraded set."

"Yes, Commander." Elyse hurls the cuffs with a snitty glare.

I catch, ignore a phantom jolt, then pass the hot potatoes to Dutch. "Destroy these."

"Anything for you," he says dreamily.

I'm even more convinced I'm sleeping when metal squeals. The cuffs that made me miserable for *years* crumble like dry cheese in Dutch's palms.

"We're done here," I say a little too roughly. "Unless you have something else to add?"

Bridget glares at the audacity of my existence. I brace as her lips part.

This'll be good.

"I have something to say first." Jin drapes an arm across my shoulders

I'm too focused on holding back my pheromones to flinch, but some rogue instinct tilts my head, and the traitor who's temporarily driving my body presses my cheek to his bare chest.

Warm static numbs my face. I fight the insane urge to mark my territory by licking the smooth path between his pecs.

Not yours, Sol.

Never yours.

"I don't know why you came after her, and I don't fucking care to find out." Jin's touch shields me from the pressure of his voice, but the SAS picked the wrong side. His dark, heavy dominance sinks their shoes into the dirt. "She's *ours*. You understand what that means?"

"We'll fight," Reese says.

"We'll *win*," Bishop adds.

Dutch tosses the manacles he just dismantled, scattering scrap metal around their toes. "So fuck off and leave us the hell alone."

My chest does a back-and-forth squeeze like a drunk accordion. Supported, surrounded, buzzing and overwhelmed, I can't decide if I'm a liar, a cheat, or the luckiest bitch in the world.

"We're leaving." And if Bridget doesn't get out of my way, I'll launch the pheromone nukes.

No more playing good girl.

"Let's go home." Jin steers me to walk away, but not even his protective warmth can shield the laser-beam glares following our retreat.

My spine jangles.

That hate isn't going anywhere.

Bridget is only letting us walk so she can investigate the guys' identities before she makes her move.

We reach the car alive and un-shot.

A temporary escape.

But Dutch drags me into the back seat, killing my chances of clear thought, let alone a coherent plan for what comes next.

Squeezed hip-to-shoulder between him and Reese, with Bishop taking the passenger seat, and Jin jumping behind the wheel, I'm warped back in time to those summer days coasting around town.

Now the car interior is custom leather instead of frayed cloth, and I have to pinch my knees to keep away from the full-grown alphas with scents as thick as syrup.

Jin guns the car up the hill.

When we hit the street, Bridget and crew are still standing in the middle of the field, huddled over their phones.

"They're not going to let you go," Jin says.

"No." I hug my legs, trying to avoid the body heat radiating from enough bare chests to violate the fire code. "I need to leave the country. Somewhere the government can't extradite. I have cash for a plane ticket."

"You make it sound as if you're going alone," Bishop says, half deadpan, half amused—his go-to tone for calling out bullshit.

"That's not how mates work." Dutch's fingers sneak toward my thigh. "We're a team. Remember, Solly?"

Oh shiiit.

Jin swerves.

Without a seatbelt, I fly into Reese's arms.

He catches me, eyes going so wide his chocolate pupils reflect my shell-shocked expression. "Did he just call you…?"

Who needs a plan?

We're about to have a reckoning.

"Solomon?" Bish's eyes rapid-flick as he mentally yanks my threads and catalogs my flaws.

Jin hops the sidewalk, screeching the brakes.

Before I can hop an alpha and bail into traffic, he hauls me between the seats. He lunges so fast, I should hit the shifter, maybe bang my head.

Jin would never.

He slides back his seat, squeezing out Reese so I fall smoothly cushioned on his welcoming lap.

A morning driver flies around us with a *whoosh* that mirrors the howl in my head.

Jin's ragged breath hits my cheek.

He tastes like rain when he cups my face in both hands.

A warning jangles the base of my spine.

I'll jump out of my skin if his touch slides south.

"It's you." His fingers shake.

The dark gaze I've dreamed about, his heat, his touch—they'd be fantasies if this weren't the beginning of a nightmare.

I panic. "I'm not your mate."

We're so close, the air punched from his lungs blows back my lashes, but I have to tell a version of the truth.

I need the guys to cut me loose before they're roped into my government-funded mess. Before I slip and hit them with my real pheromones

Fighting nausea, I fumble for the door handle. "I'm not anyone you need to worry about."

Jin snags my wrist with one hand and steadies my face with the other. His pulse teases my cheekbone. "You're Solomon."

"Not anymore"

"Then who are you?"

"I don't know."

"I do." He tilts my chin, fingers so gentle, I could easily pull away

I don't pull away.

I don't even try.

Maybe because it's Jin and we've done this before. My body forgets to flinch.

Maybe because I want it to happen.

I want to be normal just once, and touch the alpha I've always loved

Jin offers a brush of lips.

A soft, two-second kiss.

Like a butterfly, landing on a stem.

Like we've always been together, and it's fair game to call my name with a phone-sex drawl and a gaze that claims like the abyss. "*Sol.*"

TWENTY-THREE
SOL

LIGHTNING STRIKES.

Jin's rumbling purr wrecks me with a thundering boom.

Like a flash across the sky, a war breaks out inside.

The part of me that could never regret Jin, that aches to complete my set—to taste Bishop, Dutch, Reese, and abandon myself to a doomed fantasy—battles the part that's hyper-focused on my scars.

That's the part screaming loudest into the storm.

NOT MINE.

I have to draw a line.

Make it clear that this can't happen.

But draw a line with what?

Permanent marker?

Blood?

Polonium?

Time, distance, radiation.

No force on earth can stop Jin from reclaiming the part of me he's always owned.

"Sol," he murmurs again.

Is that my name?

Are we sure?

My lips flame and my pulse taps a call for help.

Looks like I finally chose destruction.

And holy fucking shit, does it feel good.

That's why it has to stop. "I'm not your omega. I'm not an omega at all."

"Then you're our beta," Reese offers, like it's the simplest thing

"I'm not a beta." *If only.*

"Alpha?" Dutch shrugs. "Who even cares? Whatever you are, you're ours."

Flinching away from his earnest, puppy-dog intensity, I lock gazes with something worse.

Bishop can be polite. Bishop can even be kind if you've proven you're on his side. But Bishop Barrington has never once been *good*

He's greedy and he's much too smart.

My soul leaves my body as he casually weaves together my lies. "Not an alpha, omega, or beta. Hunted by a nameless government agency. Lab experiments. And some reason they're afraid… *Ah.* Special abilities section."

"The SAS?" Jin's pulse zings my fingers.

So much for my secrets.

I push his hands away to hold my throat, scraping out words like shattered glass. "If you know them, then you probably know I'm a gamma. It's like the lady said. My special ability is mimicking pheromones. I'm not your mate."

A little truth

A little lie

Maybe that leaves me room to survive.

"No need to argue semantics." Bish waves.

"Yeah," Reese agrees. "And why fight over names? You're our friend. Enough said." Folded in half behind Jin, Reese's reassuring brown eyes glow inches from my seat in the driver's lap

Too close

All of them. Too close.

My neck crawls.

Jin must feel my struggle. He lets me free, seamlessly passing me to Dutch and Reese, who return me to the muscle-choked back seat.

There's the *real* mystery.

Why do I mind the guys' hands when they graze my neck, but not at all when they pass me around like their plush toy?

Dutch grumbles. "We're more than friends."

When Bishop twists to watch me from the front seat, the throat of his robe falls open, flashing pale, sleek skin, and a tempting splash of freckles. "Are you our friend, Princess?"

Don't look at his collarbone.

My voice shrinks. "Don't call me that."

"*Queen,*" Bishop breathes.

Holy screaming shit am I out of my league.

Bish taught me how to play poker.

I owe him twenty grand in favors.

"Can we drive?" I squeeze my arms, trying to stay small. "We need a plan before the next enemy comes for us."

"We. *Us.*" Dutch beams. "That's what I'm talking about."

I lock eyes on the center console, catching a flash of flexing forearm as Jin turns back onto the road. "You're sure Nikolaj is out of the equation?"

"Definitely sure." I rub goose bumps.

I'll tell the guys what they need to know to keep them safe.

The fact that I killed my father, doused him in vodka, and checked behind the bar for marshmallows after I lit up his corpse isn't *need-to-know*"That's why I'm in trouble. I was supposed to buy time as Serafina, not take him out. The rest of the team was building a case for his arrest."

"Your *team*?" Bishop's sarcasm cuts sharp enough to slice the upholstery. "Your *team* sent you to be the prize in a mafia auction?"

"What a shit team," Reese growls.

"The shittiest. When they finish identifying bodies, my face will be on flyers on seven continents." *With a bounty sweet enough to tempt penguins.* "So, if you want to bail—"

"We're already riding the same boat." Jin merges smoothly into traffic. "We were supposed to deliver you for Jericho—"

"But we were never going to comply," Bishop cuts in.

"Because he's a sadistic asshole," Reese adds.

"Exactly." Jin nods. "We were going to bait Nikolaj into attacking the Triad for kidnapping, and scrape my father off our asses. Now with the Redfang assets up for grabs, the Triad needs Serafina even more."

"Do you…" I swallow chalk. *Ask the question.* "Do you want me to tell you where she is?"

"*No,*" four united growls roll down my spine.

I shiver. "But she's—"

"Another problem." Bishop casually flicks away my dread scenario. "We're booked solid with trouble."

"Speaking of trouble?" Dutch jerks his chin toward the back window.

When Jin turns onto the freeway, heading for the city, two unmarked cars follow. One black sedan and one familiar, boxy van

I can smell the potato chips from here. "The van belongs to the SAS. We won't be able to lose them."

"Let's reconvene at The Barrington," Bishop says. "A government agency isn't going to make a fast move in public. If they do get bold, I have the better lawyers."

The perks of being a crime family.

"We need to handle Kairo first." Jin switches lanes. "He'll be waiting for us to slink home."

I chew my lip, testing a hint of a plan. "Will he be waiting for you at the hotel?"

"He has soldiers posted to watch the property," Jin answers. "If there's an opportunity, they'll try to drag you to him at headquarters"

Bishop *tsks* "You act like I don't pay for private security. Kairo's soldiers won't be dragging anything except their Neanderthal knuckles."

"I said they'd *try*." Jin flashes his death god smirk. "Not that we'd lie back and take it."

Before *I* lie back and take whatever Jin wants to give me, I clear my throat. "Call Kairo. Ask him to meet us there."

Bishop always shimmers when he smells a hustle. "What are you scheming?"

"Like you said. The SAS doesn't like moving in public or screwing with the mafia. With the Redfangs headless, who's to say I'm not the real Serafina? I'll sign away her inheritance. Then Kairo can take the cartel, you're on his good list, and we can flee the country before the SAS realizes. Everyone wins."

The best part is, we have to move fast.

Sign some contracts, hop a cargo plane, then tag all these problematic alphas off on their actual mate.

Marisol gets wasted on spiked coconut water, escapes mass murder charges, and fades into the sunset, alone.

The End

"Not everyone wins." Bishop rubs his chin with a thoughtful thumb. "There's a Triad issue you haven't factored."

"What else?" *Please don't take away my sunset.*

"Jericho." Jin's grip strains the wheel. "He and Serafina were supposed to mate. My father doesn't want a deal on paper. He wants a deal in blood."

I grip my throat. "But isn't Jericho…?"

"In a coma." Reese grins until he bounces.

"Poor fuckboy fiancé." Good thing Jericho Moon won't be coming anywhere near my throat.

Dutch wrinkles his teddy bear nose. "You're right on the fuckboy part. But *poor?* Dude deserves to suffer."

I'd love to handle that for them. *Later.* "Then what if I'm already mated?"

Bish sucks a breath. "Are you—"

"No! *No*." I trip to explain. "I mean, you're scent-matched to Serafina, right? What if you and I pretend to be mates?"

"Pretend?" Dutch jerks so hard his forehead dings the dome light.

"Pretend," I test the word, loving it more and more.

Fake mate feels so much more solid than my current role—childhood friend of questionable origin and importance.

Plus, when I slip and do something stupidly sappy, I can play it off as acting.

Will it be torture?

Worse than kissing the electric fence.

I have plans on plans on plans for escaping solo, but if all five of us all have to survive—a must when I'm this obsessed with them—I don't see another way. "Anyone have a better idea?"

Bishop pulls his phone from the pocket of his robe. "Not at all. Your scheme comes with the perfect reason to flee the country."

I don't trust his secret smile. "What's that?"

"Pack honeymoon."

"*Honey—*" I choke on the word and the sudden jackhammer of alpha pheromones.

"Fuck yeah," Dutch growls, all bacon and smoke, grabbing for my arm. "Heat honeymoon."

"First off, I'm a gamma? We don't have heats," I lie straight-faced, wiggling from his grasp. *They'll never know.* "Second. I'm not the real Serafina. I'm your stand-in mate, and anything between us can only be an act. If you won't agree to that, then—"

"We agree," Jin jumps in before I can think of a good ultimatum.

"No." Dutch pouts pillow lips. "You don't speak for me."

"Packleader." Bishop gestures to the driver seat. "He speaks for us all."

"Now you're playing the P-card?" Dutch huffs. "You won't even let us take your name. No. You do your schemes and shit. I'm mating my Solly."

He tugs my hand under his chin. The bob of his Adam's apple tickles my knuckles in premonition:

Dutch is going to be a problem.

"Can I join your pack?" He strokes my fingers against his rough-stubbled throat.

It's hard to say no when I can't suck enough air to breathe.

Bishop scoffs. "You're being ridiculous."

"Try it. Then you won't be so jealous." Dutch tugs my arm, trying to tip me into his lap. "Please, Solly? Otherwise, I'll do something dumb and accidentally ruin your plans. I suck at lying."

Reese rubs his brow. "Last time he went undercover, he ended up working at a diner full-time for six months."

"They were short-staffed," Dutch says defensively.

"It's your choice," Jin offers. "I can always bench Dutch if he causes you trouble."

"Let me be your first alpha," Dutch presses. "I don't need much. A few hugs an hour. Some snuggles. And maybe some other stuff, but that's mostly it."

The boom of my heart sounds miles away.

"You could order me." That's what alphas usually do. If Dutch would cross the line, I could tell him to screw off.

Bitch mode is useless when he acts cute.

"Like this?" His sunshiny voice drops to a raspy, skin-stroking command. *"Let me give you a hug."*

Let me misses the point of a bark, but Dutch's dominance is fully functional. Goose bumps pop on arms that ache to open for him. "That's not how that works."

"Right?" Dutch nods, undeterred. "That's why you have to take me. I'm hopeless."

Dutch isn't stupid.

He knows how to work his assets.

He works them *good*.

I have the same problem four times over—*play their games, lose control*. I'd rather surrender and move on. "You can be my fake alpha until Serafina's free."

"Yesssss," Dutch's purr torches my fingertips. "What do we call our pack? The Moons?"

"Fake pack." I try to reclaim the hand that'll be ruined forever if he doesn't stop humming into my blood.

"*Never,*" the word rips through Jin's teeth.

"Dutch Moon?" Bishop puffs a breath. "May as well call you Amsterdam Sunset."

"What about Dutch Barrington?" he tosses back. "I'd be dignified as hell."

"I'd rather be a Redfang." Bishop brushes invisible lint from his shoulder.

"Not an option." I'd almost rather be a Fissure.

Not that it matters.

The name isn't real.

"I'd help but…" Reese shrugs. "We can't all be Parkers."

"Well, well, well." Dutch grins. *He was waiting for this* "D'Artagnan Pack takes the dub."

"Bishop D'Artagnan?" Bishop brushes his robe harder. "They'll laugh us out of the registration bureau."

"Family names are cursed." Reese shakes his head.

"Then what?" Dutch digs blunt fingers through his hair, putting off a frazzled, distressed energy that makes my fingers twitch. "I can't do this no-name pack bullshit anymore. We're *finally* together. Don't act like I'm the weirdo for wanting to make it official."

My heart hums, the air too thick.

I agreed to fake being mates. Not to name the pack I'll never be allowed to join.

Dutch doesn't make a sound, but I *feel* his sorrow. Just the idea of his whine sticks needles in my bones.

Let's be honest.

I know how much they hate their names. Once upon a time, I dedicated a whole notebook to solving the problem.

"Meadows." I've never said the name out loud, even though I've scrawled *Marisol Meadows* millions of times, surrounded by tiny hearts. "It's Meadows Pack."

"Dutch Meadows." His golden smile beams through the roof, killing that dark-cloud energy. "I'm the fucking tulip king."

I stare at my toes. *Too bright.* "You can change it to something else"

"No way. It's perfect." Reese reaches through the seats. "Gimme your phone. I need to text Coach to change the roster."

"Tulip *prince* Pack only has one king. Otherwise, no notes." Bishop hands away his phone, smiling soft as satin without a hint of sarcasm—all genuine glow.

What have I done?

"That settles our name." Su-Jin Meadows strokes the steering wheel like he's stroking my bare stomach.

I have to end this conversation. *Focus on the plan.* "How do you want to sell this act to Kairo?"

Reese pauses mid-text. "Easy. Convince him you're ours and you wouldn't touch Jericho with a pole."

"Not even wearing a hazmat suit."

"Can you mimic being close to heat?" Jin asks.

My tongue clogs my mouth.

"No." I swallow, thinking fast. "I can't really use Serafina's scent right now. I must've overworked myself these last few days"

Lying out of my ass, I lock down what's left of my last dose of lemon. Being near the guys does seem to burn Serafina's perfume off faster, but even if I were stabbed citrus-fresh, it's true that controlling two sets of pheromones is more than twice as exhausting

Especially under Bishop's bullshit-busting squint.

I'd rather grit down all the cursed perfume in my body than explain the actual mechanics of my ability.

He'll tear my lies apart.

Bishop rubs his hands, but instead of calling me out, he hits me with his shit-stirring-est smirk. "If you can't wear Serafina's scent, you'll have to wear ours instead."

I rock back in the seat. "How…"

"You know how it works." Bish keeps stirring, smiling the wicked way that dries my throat. When he's held me breathless long enough, he flicks fingers at Dutch. "Tulip Prince? Can your royalness remove the bag from the trunk?"

I'm forced to squeeze closer to Reese while Dutch maneuvers to pop down his seat.

Why even have breakfast as a meal?

I've got pancakes, bacon, cocoa, and toast, all shirtless and heated to the temperature of the sun.

That's just the back row.

Dutch wrenches out a jam-packed duffel. When he sets the soft bag on my knees, I wrinkle my nose. "You had spare clothes this whole time?"

Then why have I been making eye contact with their nipples all morning?

Bish tightens the knot of his belt. "Clothes weren't a priority."

"Wait." Dutch rubs his ear. "Say that again?"

"Open it." Bish rolls his eyes.

"I think you broke him," Dutch whispers.

If anyone is broken, it's me.

I unzip the duffel.

Each alpha has a bulging packing square labeled with their name. I'm praying they're *clean* clothes, but two teeth into Jin's zipper, I'm hit with a hurricane of stormy, ocean-salt alpha.

My fingers clench, tempted to burrow, but the instinct isn't so intense I can't stop.

I'm *definitely* the broken one

"Take a piece of each of us," Bish murmurs.

"Take it all." Dutch snags his pouch, unzipping a flood of maple-bacon just as intense as the scent baking off his body.

"I'll pick." Trying to stay in control, I grab the clothes he stole and finger through my options.

I pull Bishop's peachy silk pajama bottoms over my pants. Dutch's hoodie goes over his sister's jacket like I'm buckling into a pancake muffler. Reese's deliciously sweat-branded wrist-bands fit like cozy cocoa mittens.

I tie the *owned-by-alphas* look together with Jin's luxe green overcoat. Lightning sizzles as he watches me through the rearview mirror.

All four alphas watch me like I'm sliding into their skin.

Like wearing their clothes *means something.*

It does not.

It can not.

Because this is when my inner omega is supposed to bust out, all Jill-in-the-box.

Surprise! You were always meant to be theirs.

All I feel is a phantom neck pang and a toothache from gritting down my scent.

Don't get caught in their spell.

If I'm going to act, I better do it right.

I yank the backpack crushed under Dutch's lumber-thigh, dig out my blackest stick of liner, and wing my eyes for battle, Serafina Redfang style.

"What are you doing?" Dutch peeks into my bag.

I snap the case shut before he realizes the secret hidden underneath the fake backing, passing him a makeup mirror to keep his grabby hands full of something other than my skin.

No more weakness. "I'm putting on a show."

TWENTY-FOUR

JIN

FAKE MATES.

If this isn't real, then explain the volcano ripping faults in my chest.

I almost crashed three times while she was strapping into my coat.

I can't wait for Kairo to see her wearing me.

Can't wait for my father to realize she'll never belong to his favorite son.

Serafina, Solomon, Sol.

She's mine, no matter her name or story.

As I pull under The Barrington's awning, alphas climb from expensive cars. Clean. No visible tattoos. Sheathed in suits that fit the zip code.

These aren't street-level soldiers. They're generational enforcers, pulsing with dominance.

Kairo's taking us seriously.

Because Serafina Redfang is the ultimate bargaining chip.

But Sol—*my mate*—is something else. I launch keys at the valet and vault to her, instincts raging to shield and protect.

She'd be tall for an omega.

For a gamma? *Who knows.*

With her hair slicked back and eyes painted for battle, her fearless glint is nothing like Solomon's coy, corner-of-the-eye glances. But now that I'm looking instead of overdosing on perfume, I recognize those bones.

I lick my teeth.

Her lips taste the same.

Tangy, sweet, and made for me.

I lean in, desperate for more. "Are you sure you—"

"I'm sure." Businesslike, she sidesteps me. "Let's do this."

My fierce little tomcat.

Solomon always hated aggressive power.

When I tried to hold his hand, he'd bolt. If I sat too close, he'd slide away. But when I left a space and waited, silence and no sharp moves, Solomon always closed the gap. Cozying up in the dugout, thigh to my thigh, or brushing my shoulder with a peach-fuzz cheek.

I pin the same-different Solomon to Bish's car, barring her between my arms without touching. Close, but not *too* close. "You sure you're happy with this plan? The audience is bigger than we expected'

Any other omega, beta, gamma, I'd be clueless what to do without a guiding scent.

Sol gives *nothing*.

But I don't need cheats to understand how she's feeling. I spent years before my awakening, reading her moods.

I know how far to push and when to stop.

Keeping my feet flat on the outdoor rug, I stop the knee twitching to part her thighs. *No sudden moves.*

"I can handle an audience," she says faintly.

"We can send you upstairs. Convince Kairo by ourselves." I hold my position. *Steady. Let her know she's in control.* "We never want you to force yourself."

"No. I can do this." Clenching her jaw, Sol stretches onto her toes. "I can make it realistic."

Patience pays when my mate closes the distance, looping her arms around my neck. She laces her fingers in a death grip.

She's no omega, melting for her alpha, but Solomon hasn't changed

Maybe a gamma can't relax until she meets her equal.

I can give her that.

Soft power for my Sol.

Let her say she's faking.

Let her take all the time she needs.

There's no rush.

Sol was always mine, when I had nothing and no one else. Kairo and Jericho couldn't take her from me then. They sure as fuck can't take her from me now.

"You don't have to say anything." I lean, stopping just before our noses bump. "I'll take care of it all."

Her green eyes blaze. "What if I've got things to say?"

I want those contacts gone, want to see her bare and yielding.

She'll give me everything.

But not until she's ready. "Don't hold back."

"Never again." Sol lifts higher, her unscented softness rubbing my skin like fur. I swallow a growl, flatten my ears, and wait—the wolf, letting the tomcat explore.

I don't move.

Don't breathe.

Just part my lips and pray.

Before she can claim what's already hers, Reese snarls.

Her heels hit the ground.

Kairo's enforcers have us surrounded. Dutch and Reese shoulder out the guy who pushed too close.

Aggressive bodies clog the hotel entry.

I didn't fail to notice, but we're Meadows Pack. The guys have it handled.

And I fucking love that name.

"There's no smoking on the property," Bishop reminds a seven-foot alpha with a dangling cig.

He snorts. "Are you supposed to be the owner?"

"Oh? Is it obvious?" Bishop puffs, full peacock, lifting his defined chin and straightening the lapels of his robe.

Sol's chuckle grazes my throat. She quickly shutters her smile, but the damage is already baked into my skin.

Her every emotion feels like a win, kick-starting the purring muscles that would've atrophied if she hadn't come home to us.

"Should I carry you inside?" I drop my lips to her ear. "For the act?"

Her arms tighten, then relax.

Fingers tighten, then relax.

I ignore the roaring urge to haul her to my body.

Wait for her answer.

Finally, she sighs. "It would be more realistic. If I were really your mate"

"Exactly what I was thinking." *Realistic as fuck* I wrap Sol's thighs around my hips. The cords of her tense muscles grind my sides

I ache to rub her back. Smooth her out. Purr her soft.

That only works for Dutch.

My dominance is too heavy, and my intentions—

Not pure.

I can only wait.

After a few tight breaths, she relaxes her knees and tucks her head into the hollow of my shoulder.

It's your spot, Tomcat.

Make yourself comfortable.

"Steady," I warn, flattening my palm to her back.

She tenses. I support her until she settles, readjusting her grip around my neck.

It's sweet as fuck when she clings—much more kitten than stray when she isn't throwing claws.

"*Move,*" I bark.

Triad soldiers scatter like cockroaches, and the flex of dominance teases a shiver from Sol's spine. In my coat, in my arms, she's already mine.

I'm fucking *dying* to show her off. "Let's go."

Bishop strides ahead into the lobby. Dutch and Reese shadow me, instinctively positioning to shield our mate.

Sol burrows into my shoulder, either enjoying her act or desperate to hide. Her ponytail bumps the corner of my mouth.

A leftover hint of lemon cake—no more than a crumb—zaps my lungs before burning off.

Fuck

When it's her, a crumb does damage.

I step sideways, trying to make room for the hardening cock and fast-swelling knot that are ready to stake my claim.

Tell me that's not real.

Sol has to feel what she does to me.

Breathing through her teeth, a hair away from my waiting throat, she unconsciously teases me with a bite she's not ready to give

My pajama pants strain.

Picked the wrong day to go commando.

As we pass the front desk, my pheromones rage, pumping out possession, lust, and a rumbling warning. I wouldn't choke them down if I could.

Everyone needs to know.

Don't think thoughts about my mate.

Bishop's staff trains on gun battles and bioweapons. They don't flinch for a foyer full of mobsters. The desk manager nods as her straitlaced CEO struts past in a pastel robe.

"It suits you," I murmur.

"Mention it one more time." He tightens his belt, then smooths his hair, the quaver in his fingers matching the dangerous thrum in his tone.

Ah, shit

I'm not the only one playing cool.

I shift Solly's weight, then pull Bish back. "I'll take point"

Stepping forward allows me the pleasure of watching Kairo react

Of all the seats in the bougie lobby, my father chose the sofa beneath the grand chandelier. Legs crossed, fingers locked over the knee of his tailored suit, and surrounded by high-end lackeys, he conveys absolute power.

Until he spots me and the girl slung around my chest.

He flashes to his feet, straining blood vessels and swinging dominance like a mace. *"Hand her over.* Then we'll discuss your punishment."

Kairo's bark used to put me on the floor.

It was so heavy, that first time.

Apologize!

His pressure dropped me to my knees in front of my entire class. No matter how I fought, pulling muscles to stand, holding my breath to swallow the lies he forced out of my mouth, I was powerless to resist his alpha command.

I'm sorry. I cheated. Jericho should've ranked first.

If he could make me spew that horseshit, he could make me do anything. I had to live small to protect me and mine.

Now I meet his dominance with the confidence I've built brick by hand-formed brick. It pours from my willpower, my competence, and the unwavering loyalty of the guys who've always had my back.

We were relentless before.

Now we have a mate to protect.

I parry Kairo's authority, gathering power from my heels to my balls to my gritted jaw.

If I fall, Sol goes down.

That can never happen.

"*Sit,*" I command.

If my father had braced, he could've defended against my bark

Not expecting me to fight, he stumbles.

His legs knock the sofa, his ass hits a cushion, and before he can stop my momentum, he tips so deep in submission, he flashes the balding patch at the back of his skull.

The sweetest part is the secret smile pressed against my skin.

Tomcat thinks she's hiding it from me.

As if I don't feel her every move.

All she has to do is blink and blood swells my knot.

"Disrespectful." Kairo fights to raise his head. When I ease my press, he snarls, "How dare—"

"Calm down." Careful with Sol, I sink onto the opposite sofa.

Kairo vibrates, about to flip the coffee table. Bish sits at my side while Dutch and Reese move behind, naturally taking the enforcer positions at our backs.

Our seamless unity mocks the chaos on Kairo's side.

His suited yes-men shift foot-to-foot, whispering and openly doubting their once-unquestioned king.

His submission changes *everything*.

Enjoying the moment, I position Sol more comfortably. Her ass settles between my thighs when I turn her sideways, sliding her legs across Bish's lap. "Still woozy from the drugs?"

"Sleepy," her groggy mumble scratches my heart.

If I didn't know she was acting, I'd be sprinting her to a nesting suite.

"Yes. The drugs." Kairo reaches for the life-rope. "Serafina. You're the future matron of the Triad. Don't let a few chemicals turn you into some cheap plaything for these b—"

"Don't finish that sentence." Sol's dead-flat voice hits so far from coy omega, I miss a breath.

So does Kairo.

For wildly different reasons.

While my father blinks like a frozen fish, Bish drags Sol's calf to cover the split in his robe. Using me like a chair, there's no way she doesn't feel my red-hot reaction to her ice.

Sexy as fuck.

"You're bolder in your father's absence." Kairo's bowed lip twitches. "Jericho will teach you how an omega should behave."

Sol tightens, tense as a rubber-band.

So do I, but her *snap* comes faster than mine.

"Jericho?" The name I hate is music when it's drenched in her disdain. In long, catty strokes, she claws my chest.

Dragging nails tipped in diamonds.

Hard enough to mark.

Fascinated in a way that stops my heart, she ignores Kairo to watch her own work, painting me in possessive stripes.

Fuuck. I love her claws

I grunt, letting her play.

When Sol scrapes higher, grazing throat, my dick twitches.

It's fifty-fifty whether I'm already soaking through to her ass.

Sol stops scratching but doesn't quit. She hooks a thumb possessively tight beneath my jaw, and tilts my chin to show me off. "Why would I want Jericho when I can have *this?*"

Fucking rip me open.

I want her to bleed me for the world to witness.

Sol always saw me for *me*.

Always valued me, when everyone outside our pack had me pegged as Jericho's store-brand shadow.

The guests on the fucking skydeck can scent how ready I am to stake my claim on this girl.

Kairo's temple throbs. "You—"

"Don't speak to my mate." I whip him 'til he has to brace his knee to stop himself from folding.

"Yours? You have no power to—"

"Ours," Bishop cuts in. "Nikolaj is dead. We have all the power."

"Ask around to confirm. We'll wait." I lean back, sliding Sol with me as Kairo and his lackeys put their heads together to check the news.

"Bring sparkling water." Bish waves for a lobby attendant. "My mate needs a champagne flute."

He's the master of subtle power plays, and our pajama dress code makes the scene even more satisfying.

By the time the Triad confirms rumors of Nikolaj's demise, Sol is sipping bubbles, and Bish has her sneakers off, stroking the feet stretched across his lap in tall, neon purple socks.

We look like a lazy morning pack.

We *are* that fucking pack.

Kairo shoots a sucked-egg scowl. "You don't have the power to hold on to the cartel."

"It's ours regardless. Konstantín slaughtered the other Redfang heirs. Now Nikolaj's assets pass to his last surviving child. *Serafina*." Slowly, giving her time to adjust, I cup her head and pet her golden hair. "My scent-matched mate."

Sol tenses for a micro-second. Then she runs with the act, rubbing into my palm.

Fake or not, her affection lights me up.

"Ridiculous," Kairo grits. "You're not qualified—"

"Here's my offer." Cutting off my father is my new favorite move. "You transfer me the controlling shares in Crescent in exchange for Serafina's stake in the cartel. Nikolaj's territory, assets, and contacts are all yours, minus anything he had carved out for Serafina's trust. You and the family will drop any claims of an engagement with my mate. We take nothing from the Triad, and you never come after my pack again."

"The share agreement was contingent on your obedience." Kairo lifts his chin. "After this disrespect? *Hmph*."

I smooth a translucent vein at Sol's temple. *This* is the way to negotiate. "You give me Crescent or I poach every multi-million investor at Full Moon."

Kairo pivots. "It'll take weeks to negotiate a handover. Even if the lawyers—"

"Vinny? Is that you?" Bish trills across the lobby. "*What* a coincidence."

The man who's been standing quietly to the side joins our party carrying a fat briefcase.

As the long-time Barrington family lawyer, Vincent Sylvester doesn't bat an eye for mafia *or* Bish's theatrics. He pulls out the sheathe of contracts that Bish texted him to prepare before he contacted Kairo to arrange our meet. "I've sent copies to both sides. Let's make this fast, yes? I have tee time in an hour and traffic's a bitch."

Kairo glares like Vinny just planted a steaming shit on the table, but his disapproval leapfrogs the lawyer, cutting for my jugular. "How can you disrespect your father this way?"

About that.

You want respect?

You have to give it first.

Sol has been milking the drugged omega act to stay silent, but with contracts on the table, she peels away from my chest. "Where do I sign?"

Vinny respectfully hands her a fountain pen while Bish lets our mate use his lap as her desk.

Not missing a beat, she signs every tab as Serafina Redfang.

Kairo phones his lawyers to stall.

Good luck.

We've been planning this for years. Other than the happy wrench of our unexpected mate, Vinny had contracts ready to go, and our terms are too favorable to nitpick.

"If you need more time, we can postpone. But by then, we'll have to cement our new position at the helm of the cartel." I let the threat linger, watching Bish stroke the arch of our mate's foot. She curls her toes and bumps my ribs in a wordless *hurry up* I offer my father a languid smile. "We can't postpone the mating, but we'd prefer a quiet honeymoon."

Kairo goes a few more rounds with his lackeys and lawyers.

I just have to wait for his greed to win.

It always does.

When he signs, his furious pen rips through the paper.

After he initials the last line, Kairo bolts from the lobby.

He'll hit us back.

By then, we'll have our mate hidden and our family protected.

"Clear the lobby," Bishop calls. "And make sure these fine gentlemen pay for their parking."

I lift Sol and book for the elevator, the pack surrounding us.

She peers over my shoulder, watching Kairo's entourage slink out the front door. "They're leaving. You can let me—"

"Cameras," I murmur into her hair.

"They're Bishop's cameras." She wiggles, teasing me with softness as she tries to find the floor.

"Hackers," Bish offers, sweeping us into the elevator. "Can't be too careful. It's best to keep up appearances."

Dutch punches the button for our floor.

Rolling his eyes at our bullshit, Reese ducks to scan her face. "You okay?"

"How soon do we fly out?"

I cover my sway in the elevator's jerk.

She's that eager to get away from us?

"Do you have a passport?" Bishop asks.

"I don't even have a phone."

"I'll take care of you." Bish tilts his head to watch the floors tick

Sol's muscles were starting to relax. Now they tighten until she hugs me in bands of concrete.

I don't want to let her go.

Too soon, we're outside Suite 707.

The door is some thick, ancient hardwood, but after Jericho's assassins cloned our card, Bish updated us from a key to a biometric scanner.

Good thing

We ran after Sol without wallets or weapons, let alone unimportant things like shirts and keys.

Bish opens our suite with a fingerprint and retina scan.

Sol kicks out of my arms before I can carry her over the threshold

"Are you okay?" Dutch rumbles the question she doesn't have to answer

I know she's not.

All that strange tension humming through her body.

"Bathroom?" she asks, too high-pitched.

"Through the bedroom suite." Bishop points.

She takes off like a stray about to spend a week hiding under our bed. My ribs grate my lungs.

Solomon was always skittish, but not like *this.*

Why is she rejecting us so hard?

The shower water roars.

Reese staggers. "Is she…washing us off?"

I pull the pack in for a huddle before we bleed out from that four-way bullet. "Anyone doubt she's our mate?"

"No." Reese clenches my arm.

"Fuck no," Dutch adds. "She's been ours since forever."

"She's lying. *Again*" Bishop plays with his robe, but he has more sparkle than he did the first time Sol iced us out.

He wants to pick her apart.

I hand him the place to start. "It's Solomon. Remember the time we tried to follow him home?"

"I just wanted to see where he was living," Dutch grumbles. "Make sure his place was safe. *Her* place? Why didn't she tell us she was a girl?"

"Think." Bish flicks his forehead. "Would you want Dandelion running the Meadows alone in a skirt and a bow?"

Dutch scowls, covering the mark. "What's the outfit have to do with anything? Boy or girl, our mate's fucking adorable."

"I get why she freaked and avoided us back then." Reese stares through the wall. "But why in the *fuck* is she doing it *now*?"

"She's always kept her secrets close," I remind them. "We know who she is. We know everything she likes." And this time, our thoughtful mate left the door wide open. *Pretending to be ours?* "Don't rush her. She'll come to us. She always does."

Sol knows where she belongs.

If she claims she doesn't?

Purring, I stroke the tracks she carved in my chest.

I'll make her remember.

She kissed me first.

TWENTY-FIVE

SOL

EVERYTHING IS TOO MUCH.

My gnawing pheromones.

Their gnawing pheromones, and the lingering heat of the full-body fantasy where I rubbed all over Jin and didn't get chucked like a ripe sack of trash.

His touch tattooed my spine.

I almost bit his nipple, because it was hard and *right there* and it probably would've tasted like ocean-salted caramel.

I almost *lost my shit* and let Monster-Sol have her way because Kairo needs to die.

I'm definitely taking care of him for the pack.

After I figure out how to take care of myself.

The guys' shower is the same as the one in the penthouse. It has glass panels instead of a modest curtain, surrounded by ceiling-height mirrors that display every angle of the body I don't want to face right now.

I run the water for steam but can't strip naked. Wearing three kinds of shirts, a knee-length coat, and double pants, heat steams me like a pork bun

Against my long-term welfare, I cave, pushing up my sleeve to press Reese's wristband to my nose.

I'm not a pork bun.

I'm a *bacon* bun, salty-sweet with cocoa, peach, and lightning spice

Fuck.

Me.

When I lean against the marble vanity, my knee bangs their cabinet.

I'm not a good person.

I want to snoop.

My traitor fingertips are creeping south when Reese's voice freezes me mid-reach.

"You forgot your backpack. I'll leave it on the knob." A rattle spikes my adrenaline. Reese doesn't try to come into the bathroom, but he doesn't go away. "Can you make a list of things you need? Clothes and whatever. I'm doing the shopping run before our flight. We won't be able to get much after we land."

His voice is flat instead of its normal raspy silk.

He sounds like the kid who got cut from the team.

Say it with me, one more time.

Fuck.

Me.

I open the door.

Just a crack.

Reese's gaze eats through the gap.

My current look is worse than naked scars.

I rolled my sleeve to nose-fuck his wristband. Now his nutty, cocoa scent waves *howdy* from the tip of my nose, screaming exactly what I've been doing all by myself.

"*Princess.*" His liquid rasp drips down my shoulders.

What sad little kid?

Reese's full-grown alpha gaze chews me up like ballpark gum. "What do you need from me?"

Blow me until I make bubbles.

Shit. No. *Nope.*

My pheromones claw.

I lock my mouth before it makes an offer I'll panic out of the second that beard comes too close to my throat.

Ground yourself in reality, not in brown eyes. "Yoga clothes. With zip-up jackets and high necks."

"Easy. What else?"

"Nothing." Feeling like there's chocolate smudged around my lips, I try to shut the door.

"Wait." Reese shoves bandaged fingers through the crack.

Cheater.

I can't smash his hand.

He widens the gap, pushing in Dany's backpack, plus an addition that hits harder than his swing.

His hat.

Dingy blue with a bent brim, it's embroidered with the number nine and his high school team's wolf mascot.

It's the same baseball hat he set on my head like a crown every time he spotted me waiting at the fence before his games. He'd jog to me, beaming—just the way he smiles now.

His boy-next-door grin has me opening wider when I need to be shutting him down.

"Never used to see you without a hat." He scratches his beard, right over the dimple it can't hide.

I started wearing hats to hide my shaved head.

Kept wearing them because I wanted to wear *Reese.*

My scent glands pinch the sides of my throat.

What if I just...let out the truth?

Blood leeches from my face, leaving my cheeks numb.

Yeah.

Brilliant.

Then I can witness the dream that is Reese Meadows retching on my shoes, red-eyed-glaring to ask why the hell I smell like unwashed pubes.

I've seen the same reaction hundreds of times.

The wrinkled nose. The twisted lips. The face-pinch that turns a stranger into an instant enemy.

I have to draw lines, stop leading him on, and for the love of the freaking game—stop letting my real self peek out, all pathetic.

"It was a phase." I shove the hat back before the broken-in fabric can kiss my fingertips.

Reese refuses the trade, forcing the hat into my hands.

"It's yours," he rasps in a different flavor—stubborn instead of hurt.

I have to be stubborn too. "Reese—"

"Gotta pack." He steals my best move, slamming the door before I can uncap a marker, let alone draw a line. His voice comes through muffled. "You skipped dinner *and* breakfast. Come out soon or Jin'll go Martha on your ass for lunch."

After he's gone, I bang my forehead against the wood.

Get a grip, Sol.

I kill the water I've been wasting and grab the syringe case from the backpack I never should've left in the guys' hands.

I thought dealing with Meadows Pack would be easier without perfume.

That was ultra-wrong.

I need all the vodka lemon.

Any shield to stop them from treating me like the old Solomon.

Almost needing the pain, I load a cartridge and jab my throat.

Vodka-lemonade-citrus-kitchen-cleaner.

Barf.

Yellow spots pop behind my eyes.

When I can stand without drooling into the sink, I straighten my hair and fix my makeup. I change into a fresh pair of contacts, then darken my liner to hide the blood-shot whites of my fake green eyes

I'm not going to hide in the bathroom.

I'm going to walk out and prove that I can handle my shit.

But before I brave the suite, I jam Reese's hat to the bottom of my bag

I can't wear it while I'm here, but it's too important to leave behind

He'll never know

Since I panic-sprinted, I didn't catch much of their space. The master bedroom isn't where I plan to start.

I pinch my nose and jog past, pretending I can't see the rumpled sheets on the bed big enough for five.

The living room is a different kind of minefield.

It's too comfy for a hotel.

The penthouse was sparkling and sterile.

The Meadows' suite is clean—*because Bishop*—but there's nothing nondescript. Their personalities leap from every surface, and their pheromones aren't the only reason I can't drag air into my lungs.

None of the furniture matches. A futon sits next to an expensive, high-backed armchair. A cashmere throw blanket rests beside a quilt made from Reese's old jerseys. The shelves surrounding the flatscreen hold the weirdest mix of cookbooks, business texts, baseball trophies, and Dutch's family photos.

It makes no sense, but it's *theirs*, and it's perfect.

Or it would be.

If it were also mine.

Still wearing socks, I pad across the carpet.

Bish stole my sneakers.

I'm expecting him and the rest to pop out, but the suite is silent except for a constant *chop-chop-chop*.

Around the L-bend in the living room, I find the kitchen. Jin slices green grapes on a cutting board, but he hasn't found a shirt.

Red claw-marks cut down his pecs, following the slope of the built chest I helped myself to explore.

It says a lot about today that I forgot *I fucking marked Jin*.

It made sense at the time.

A show of possession.

For our act.

Yeah. That doesn't even sound believable in my head.

Reality?

I saw my shot, and I took it with a freaking grenade launcher.

I don't regret what I did, but I *really* need him to put on a shirt and stop reminding me how hard his pulse hammered for my claws

"Hungry?" Jin pushes a plate across the breakfast bar.

I take the tall chair at the end of the row, keeping a slab of marble between me and his body heat.

His sandwich chokes me as much as his bare skin. White bread filled with a yellow sauce and grapes. It's the sandwich he always brought me in a spare lunchbox, even when money was tight.

"Curry chicken salad is your favorite." He slices the bread diagonal.

Just the way I like. "You remembered."

Jin leans against the bar with a hypnotic gaze set to stun. "It's you. How could I not?"

Lines.

Boundaries.

Be stubborn.

Even better—*be Serafina*

I push the plate away with a fussy finger. "I'm not who I used to be"

Jin doesn't flinch. I'd say his lips thin, but they're lush again when he smiles, slow and confident. He pushes back the plate, rejecting my rejection. "Nothing important has changed."

I wish that were true.

Instead of arguing, I take a huge bite.

The familiar spices almost juice out my dried-up tears.

Jin peeled my grapes.

He balances his chin on his palm, presenting his lean torso like he already co-signed my plan to lick him down the middle.

You could roll a marble between those pecs.

It would slide straight between his chocolate-bar abs, dip through his shallow belly button, and snag in the waistband of his lazy-fitted pajama bottoms

Lonely, gold-toned skin winks from Jin's hip bones.

Begging for more of my claws.

I'm not omega enough to *act* on the fantasy, but gammas must be natural freaks.

I want to peel down his waistband.

Mark *everything*

Jin's eyes flash onyx under my too-obvious attention. He drags down his ribs, then hooks his thumb, tugging the pajamas lower on his hip.

Something, *somewhere* tingles, and I forget I'm eating.

A half-chewed grape falls from my mouth.

Not very gangster.

"No rush." Jin passes me a paper towel. "You can have as much as you want."

"What if I want everything?"

Jin's evil smile kicks my stomach into a trench.

You done fucked up, mouth.

Slow and sweet as molasses, Jin slides along the counter. He doesn't stop until he almost bumps my knees.

But he doesn't touch me.

Not at all.

Lightning crackles between our bodies.

Leaning on his elbow flexes his forearm and pops his cut shoulder. "Everything's already yours."

Reese stared like he wanted to eat me.

Jin stares like I'm already peeled.

I double-check my layers, tugging the coat around my throat. "How soon can we leave the country?"

"Tonight. Bishop is expediting your fake ID." Jin watches me shift.

I press back on the stool. "Can he make more than one? I need a new identity."

Jin's smile chills. "So that you can leave us."

"Eventually, yeah." That last bite of chicken salad settles like lead

"Why?"

I wouldn't know how to put my cards on the table if I dropped the deck.

For an answer, I offer my wrist, easing the Serafina half of my tightly held control.

One whiff of topped-up lemon shrinks Jin's pupils.

"*Sol.*" His razored growl leaves me tightening my abs, fighting to keep down an answering flare of perfume that won't smell like lemonade

"Do you feel that? Your reaction?"

"Let me feel it again." He dips his head.

I snatch my wrist. "That's *her* scent. You're feeling Serafina. She's your—"

"*No.*" Hooking his foot in my chair, Jin drags me close.

So close, a deep breath will have me sucking his nose.

Then he holds, hovering.

With no touch, my body doesn't panic.

But I can feel the storm under his skin. My claw-marks rise and fall in rapid pulses. "Do you have any idea what you mean to us?"

I breathe shallow, trying to minimize the crackle of a Jin so electric, my flyaways climb to caress his face. "I get it. You think I'm your mate, but—"

"Not that. Solomon. *You*. Sol. Do you know what you mean to us? To me?"

The air goes plasma.

Too thick to breathe. "I'm just some kid you let follow you around'

If Jin touched me, I'd have a reason to run.

He doesn't, even now.

While he braces my chair arms, I count the silver lines swirling the depths of his black irises. "You're the only one we ever let close. The only light we had when everything else was fucked."

My heart jackhammers.

Jin doesn't have to touch me to put me in chains.

I'm frozen

Hypnotized by his bottomless eyes.

My pheromones prick.

This is not good.

I swallow. Jin close-range watching me gulp doesn't help me find a voice that comes out small and dry. "Solomon is gone. You can't keep waiting for someone who doesn't exist."

Just like I can't keep hoping for the happy ending.

"Then who are you?"

"What's left."

"Your name?" Jin hovers, keeping my air like he owns it. "Give me your real name."

"You don't need—"

"I *want*," he says roughly.

"Marisol." The name slips out with no care for the consequences

Consequences like a syrupy purr and a black-eyed smile as Jin rolls my name like sweet lemon taffy in his wicked mouth. *"Marisol."*

My knees rock.

Jin smiles sharper, licking his teeth.

Someday soon, I'm going to punch myself in the throat.

"Just call me Serafina. I'll be gone soon enough."

"Because you're faking," Jin states the facts, but his all-tooth smile won't switch off. "Because you say you're not our mate."

"I'm not your mate," I repeat, mirroring his words but not his husky, bedroom rasp. *Are we speaking different languages?*

"Okay."

"Okay?"

"What else would you like me to say?"

"That you understand this is an act."

"Marisol. I understand."

I shiver.

Since when did Jin grin so *filthy*?

Shit.

Since always

Bloodthirsty Jin, licking his teeth in the ring. Ripping through fighters who thought they stood a chance.

Meadows Jin is nothing like the buttoned-up Su-Jin Moon who had to march on his father's orders, keeping his fire banked.

His bloodlust is my catnip.

His regular lust?

Holeeeeeeshiiit.

"When's our flight?" I ask faintly.

Jin releases his foot, freeing his lock on my chair. "Bish needs a photo for your fake passport."

I drag in a breath of cold, fresh air. "Where is he? I'll go to him."

"He'd like that." Jin opens the junk drawer, but it's Bishop's kitchen, so the pencils sit in neat trays, organized by lead thickness. Jin grabs a plastic card and presses it into my palm. "Spare key. Sixth floor office suite. Take the private elevator."

He opens the secret door I thought led to a pantry. Before I can escape, Jin forces the sandwich plate into my hands. "Please eat more than two bites. I don't want to have to feed you by hand. Unless you ask me for it."

I blink.

Jin licks his teeth.

We both know what he just said.

After the door shuts, I sway, going nowhere.

Because elevators. You have to hit a button.

I punch six with the lip of my plate.

As of this morning, I would've said Dutch was the hardest alpha to handle.

Wrong.

They're all a problem.

I take another bite of Jin's sandwich as the elevator pings. Thick perfume almost has me spitting it back on the plate.

Omega.

Mint and chocolate, but it's not the luscious, buttery kind, like Reese's rich flavor.

This chocolate tastes like a cold, fussy truffle that costs a million dollars and cracks your front teeth.

The source sits at the desk in the center of the businessy office suite. An ice-cream omega in stilettos, showing off a tight body in a V-cut, white jumpsuit.

"You are…?" Her once-over takes in my sandwich, rag-bag alpha layers, and the hit of vodka lemon I crank out just for her.

It all screams *mate* so loudly, I don't bother introducing myself. "I need to see Bishop."

"Do you have an appointment?"

"I'm wearing his pants." I wiggle a leg, showing off the glossy blue silk. "Do I need an appointment?"

"Straight to the end of the hall." She gestures to a set of double doors. "But he might be…occupied."

The woman isn't giving me territorial omega vibes, but I don't want to chat through her pheromones. I use my key to swipe past.

If Bish has business, I won't interrupt.

I'm happy to wait, all by myself.

I need a break

A short hallway leads to a second, already open door, but it may as well be a wind tunnel.

My vision whitens with the savory-sweet scent that rips my throat and roars past my flaming ears.

Maple bacon and peach mimosa.

I lick my lips, mouth watering.

It smells like Bishop and Dutch, and no third person.

But…

My body goes weirdly tight.

What *is* that?

Their scents twine with each other. A rhythmic *thump, thump, thump* is either my heart exploding, or something more serious going down in the office beyond.

"Bish?" I whisper.

That syrupy, smoky scent moves my feet.

Mimosa brunch.

A full breakfast spread.
The door hangs open in invitation.
I'm peeping before my brain connects the wicked dots.
Thump, thump, thump goes the wood.
My body goes *sploosh.*
So much for a break.
I'm about to be broken.

TWENTY-SIX

SOL

BISHOP FUCKS DUTCH over his desk.

Bent in half, Dutch splays across the wood. Sculpted ass bare. Holding on for a ride, he clenches the edge with thick fingers. Desperate. Almost splintering.

Thump.

Thump.

Thump.

Dutch's pants puddle on the office rug.

He never had a shirt.

None of them ever have a fucking shirt.

He's bigger than Bish. Much more dominant.

But he's the one being rocked.

With every precision thrust of Bishop's cock, Dutch moans my name like cotton sugar. "Solly."

Thump

"Solly."

Thump

"Oh, fuck. *Fuck*. Sol. *Bish*. Shit. *Unh~*"

Thumpthumpthumpthumpthump.

They don't…seem to realize I'm here?

Feral omega is never going to happen if it doesn't happen *now*.

If I were the real Serafina, the wild sex would pump my pheromones harder than Bishop is pumping Dutch.

Gamma instincts work in reverse.

Because I'm *me*, and I do my best not to kill unless I really mean to murder, I reflexively reel in my scent. My muscles lock, from my tight jaw to my curled baby toes.

I don't breathe or twitch or leak perfume.

And they…

Keep going

Bishop.

Holy fucking shit.

King Bish.

He fucks in his belted bathrobe and doesn't show a lick of skin

Neat. Controlled. Fierce.

His complexion of freckle-dusted porcelain isn't even flushed.

Just focused.

Brutally pinning his packmate's bouncing hips, Bish pounds so fast and hits so deep, he sheathes every stroke before I can catch a flash of the skin I've only imagined in my dreams.

Thumpthumpthumpthumpthump.

I *never* imagined Bish palming Dutch's skull, grinding the bigger alpha's face into his hardwood desk.

Bish growls, ragged and silky. "You want me to fuck you while you fuck your mate? Or fuck her between us?"

"Both." Brutal thrusts strangle Dutch's moans. *"Unh* Please. *Both*"

Tingles feather my blood.

They'd let me join.

They think I'm *theirs*.

All I have to do is ask.

I drag in a record-scratching breath.

Bishop's hips still at the bottom of a stroke so deep that Dutch's eyes cross when he spots me with a muzzy moan.

"Mate." Dutch reaches, straining. *"Bite."*

His hips lift

Bishop slams him down.

The *thwack* and his smirk tickle something, but my body feels so far away.

Am I in control?

"All yours, Queen." Buried deep, Bish yanks Dutch upright. "Try the equipment before you sign the contract. It won't disappoint."

I've seen all the videos.

I've read all the smut.

I thought they were exaggerating.

They. Under. Sold

Reaching around the alpha pinned to his hips, Bish grips a freaking tennis ball can so girthy he can't close his fingers around the shaft. His long, firm stroke ripples Dutch's messy abs.

Dutch is slick all over.

The tip of his dick glistens with the same pearly wetness that drips down his thighs and smears Bishop's desk.

I swallow a mouthful of maple syrup.

"Tell her what you told me." Bishop squeezes, dragging down until he captures the growing bulge of Dutch's purpling knot.

"*Unh*!" Dutch tips back his head, but he's too tall to rest on Bishop's shoulder.

"Words."

Dutch's blond lashes flutter. "Solly. *Ohfff~*"He hunches forward, shooting a pearly rope in time with my name.

"Those aren't words." Bish flicks the mess off his fingers, painting Dutch's heaving chest.

My body is..

Boiling?

Frozen?

Gone?

My scars tingle and burn.

Not in control.

Am I leaking scent?

Shitshitshit.

I can't even feel the rope.

But Bish and Dutch are still standing. Still pumping out syrupy sex pheromones that punch down my throat.

I haven't ruined anything. *Yet.*

Somehow, I find my feet, socks, heels, and manage a backward step

Bish knocks Dutch to the desk and forces his slick fingers into Dutch's ready mouth.

Dutch sucks what he's given.

His sex-hazed eyes stay locked on me.

"Let me finish, and I'll be right with you. Unless you'd like to join?" Bishop flashes a *help-yourself* smile.

Air hits the tip of my numbed nose, so I know I'm still breathing. "I have to..."

Sprint through a human carwash.

Put a bag over my head.

Escape to anywhere but here.

"Wait. Solly. *Mate!*" Dutch gets louder as I flee. His ragged snarl beats me to the hall. *"Asshole!* Stop fucking hammering my spot when I'm trying to declare my love."

"Your asshole likes hammering." The sound of slapping skin follows me as Bishop proves his point.

When I stumble from the hallway like a cooked lobster, slamming the door behind, the secretary arches a brow. "Were they busy?"

I double-check that the door is locked.

Don't want some strange omega scenting...*that.*

But the office must have lab-quality ventilation. Not a whiff of mimosa brunch hints how *busy* the Meadows are inside.

Busy as my heart, pumping sludge.

Not knowing where to go, where or even *who* I am, I take cover in the private elevator and spam the close button.

I don't know what happened to my sandwich.

Now I'm hungry for something else.

Peach-stuffed pancakes.

Bacon and champagne.

I'm lucky the elevator has dark panels instead of mirrors.

I can't imagine my face.

It's enough imagining *their* faces.

Bish's lowered lids and bared teeth. The delicious twists of Dutch's lips, reflecting every sensation he feels.

My body warms, but the heat comes from layers of alpha-scented sweats, not the *Heat* with the capital H.

I lean against the wall to cool down.

File that reel away for later.

I'm still staring into space when the elevator lifts. Up a single floor, the door slides open.

Reese.

His fingers twitch, feet and shoulders shifting with killing intent.

My body responds, pheromones surging. But Reese flips his switch just as quickly, realizing I'm not his enemy.

Not yet.

"Sol?" His eyes and shoulders soften, but I already saw too deep

Even forced to sit at the back of the SAS classroom, you pick up a few techniques.

Reese is a killer.

And I don't shiver because I'm disappointed with his life choices

His nose wrinkles. "That scent..."

"What scent?" Reeling in, I throw myself against the wall hard enough to shake the elevator cables.

"Bish and Dutch." Reese rubs under his nose. "Did you walk in on them?"

"Oh." Pricked tension leaves me oozing down the wall. "That."

Stepping in, Reese jabs the sixth-floor button, and the doors shut us in together.

The elevator narrows with a second body inside.

It wouldn't fit three.

Unless we tried *real* hard.

I can think of a few ways...

I shudder.

I'm so ruined

"Did it bother you?" Reese asks.

"What?"

"Them being together?"

I snort. "Why would it?"

"Everyone says omegas get territorial. Maybe gammas do too?" His heavy breath ghosts me in cocoa. "We'd never do anything you didn't want."

"*We?*" My voice lifts. "Do all of you… Together…?"

"That a problem?"

The only *problem* is, I can't join. "You'll have to ask Serafina."

Reese blinks. "Ask her what?"

"If she minds…pack relations." Going by her texts, my sister is all in on sharing. *Long as they're man enough to eat ass.*

Reese twists the cord of his City Cryptids hoodie.

Finally, one of them has a shirt.

"Honestly?" Reese releases the stretched string with a *pop* "I don't give a shit about Serafina. You're the one we were waiting for."

I breathe through the heart-squeeze. "Reese..."

"You coming?" He jumps out, playing his run-away strategy to perfection. "I have to borrow Dutch. Bish'll be free now."

It's been hours, and I'm already so tired of arguing in Sera's favor.

I've warned the guys enough.

Let her do the rest herself.

"Alpha Reese." The desk lady shimmers when we step into the office. Her mint sours my throat.

I step between them, tall, but not tall enough to cut off her view.

"Capri." Reese doesn't turn to face her. He's busy *glowing* over my possessive move. "It's Alpha Meadows now."

My heart squeaks.

Why do I do this to myself?

Before Capri can clap back, Reese tugs me down the hall. His fingers melt like stick butter on my skin.

I shiver again.

Reese eats a smug smile, pretending he doesn't feel my reaction

We're all getting *fantastic* at pretending.

Entering the office, I brace for a second helping of sex brunch.

Bishop is too on his game. Every surface is wiped and de-scented from the bookshelves to the coffee table to Dutch's pants folded in a small, perfect square on the leather office sofa.

The inbox, pen jar, and CEO name plate line neatly on Bishop's desk, as if they weren't recently knocked to the corporate carpet by his seismic thrusts.

"Dutch?" Reese calls. "You ready, bro? We've gotta bounce."

The side door pops open.

Barreling through a puff of steam, Dutch rushes out with soaked hair and droplets rolling down his golden skin. "Solly!"

I dodge his tackle, but I can't escape his arms.

Instead of crushing me to the couch, he pulls me against his bathwater-warm chest.

"Missed you." He nuzzles, all cat-bear-puppy-dog-alpha, desperate to rub me in his scent.

Thank hell for my layers.

All these shirts, and he may as well be huffing my scars.

I can't escape—and most of me doesn't want to—so I drag his arms to my waist, far from the creepy-crawly part of my neck. "I was just here."

"Why'd you leave?" He rests his chin on my shoulder.

My throat works. "You were busy."

"Bish was busy." Dutch's laugh tickles my ear. "I was just getting used. You're more important."

"Used? But it looked like you were enjoying—"

Stop talking, mouth.

"Totally was. But Bish would never treat you like that." Dutch whirls me, fluttering wet lashes. "We'll *worship* you. Together."

My mask must be holding better than I thought.

Otherwise, he'd realize how *not a problem* it would be for he or Bish or all of them together to pin me their favorite surface and treat me any fucking way they want.

Mentally, I'm theirs.

Physically is the mess.

Dutch leans in with a sticky whisper. "Don't worry. My knot is pristine. Been saving my dick virginity for you."

My pheromones rear.

I wrench back lemon and the start of something worse.

Bishop's office is cursed.

"What are you still doing here?" The incubus strides out of the bathroom in a crisp, grey suit that sets off the evil flecks of green in his hazel eyes.

In a silky tie with his dark hair styled away from his clean forehead, Bishop is sleek and sexy professional.

Only the dent in his cheek gives him away.

That crooked grin hits like a secret whisper.

It's all yours.

"Go, minions. Fly to the department store." Bish flicks the air. "Don't skip anything on my list. It's all necessities."

Reese checks his phone. "Even the five-grand air purifier?"

"Especially the air purifier. What if our mate is allergic to tropical pollen?"

I'm always on team air purifier, but *tropical?*

I was envisioning a quick flight across the border. Not some exotic destination a worryingly long plane ride away.

My pulse picks up, but before I can ask, Dutch squeezes me to his chest. "You run errands. Let me stay with Solly. I'm the bodyguard."

"Sure." Bishop arches a groomed brow. "Then you'll take care of booking the plane and arranging the supply shipment and bribing customs and—"

"Never mind," Dutch mumbles, then beams a smile. "Dibs on sitting next to you on the plane."

"Anything else you need us to grab?" Reese pries Dutch from my body

"No." I brush tingling arms.

Buy yourself working sweatpants and a truckload of shirts.

"Meet us at the airstrip," Bishop calls. "We're on a clock."

It didn't seem like he was in a rush to finish with Dutch, but I have more urgent questions. "Where are we flying?"

Bish moves behind his desk. Bracing at the angle we *both* know is the best for whipping his hips, he offers his slyest ruler-of-the-world smile. "It's your honeymoon. Would I take you somewhere basic?"

"Where?" I'm in no mood to play. *Not with this.* "Is it safe?"

"Would I bring my mate somewhere unsafe?" When his smirk fades, Bish is pure intensity.

He stares like I'm a ball of yarn, and he already has my loose threads twisted around his claws.

"I'm not your mate," I repeat firmly, hoping this time will stick. "I'm grateful you're willing to help me run, but I need details, or I'll have to go my own way."

"You want to share information? Love to." Bishop stalks around his desk.

I thought Jin and Reese were the predators.

Wrong again.

"What's your real name?" His forward step slows my heart.

I back up. "Sol. Can you—"

"That's not it."

"Fine. It's Marisol." That cat's already out of the bag and purring like a slut.

"So it is." Bishop shivers in satisfaction, but he's not done. Captivatingly dark, he herds me toward the back of his office. "How does your special ability work?"

My scent glands prickle under his attention.

"It's my turn." I tighten my control. "Where are we flying?"

"One of my properties." Bish takes another step, and my back bumps his bookshelf. *Out of room to flee.* "How exactly does your ability function?"

"I mimic pheromones."

His gaze flicks side to side. Slowly, maddeningly, he shakes his head. "That's not right."

A scent sweeter than peach bleeds off his collar.

Freaking *Bish.*

He's wearing pheromone-boosting cologne.

As if he needs the help.

"You don't need to know." It's always like this with him.

He interrogated me for three days just to find out my favorite color.

I said yellow, trying to be gender neutral, and by day four, I had a yellow silk handkerchief and a tulip bouquet.

I can't cave again. "You—"

"What did the SAS do to you?" His blindside rattles between my ears.

"Nothing," I answer fast, forced, and incredibly fake.

"I saw your ankles," he offers, teasing the scab of my ugliest wound. "Who, when, and how."

"Nothing," I repeat, just as fake, but much firmer.

"Lie," he hisses, brushing my cheek with his knuckles.

I dodge his touch.

Need him to stop looking at me.

To stop *seeing* me. "I handle my own business. Get me out of the country, and I won't be your problem anymore."

Bish traps my head between his arms, so close to grazing the danger zone. "That's where we have our miscommunication. You can lie to me. I'll even help you lie. But never. *Never* shut me out. Your business has been my business ever since you showed up at my field."

I don't want to shut him out.

Don't want to lie.

But I have to hold back the truth.

Bishop dips his head. Lips the darkest red. Hazel eyes lit with yawning pupils, hair and collar pristine.

But his breath is wild.

My blood fizzes.

I need to move, but my wiring's fried by champagne. Bubble-pops stop the signal warning me to escape.

"Who hurt you?" He breathes so close I have to bite my lip to keep our mouths from touching.

I shiver.

It's a *good* shiver.

Not a get-away, run-away, clammy-with-cold-sweat shiver, but a warm, liquid feeling—a delicious drizzle of hot peach, melting my bones.

His dominance holds as firmly as his arms.

Supporting me.

Protecting me.

He seriously thinks I'm his mate.

We're sharing air.

Heat.

Lips so close, we'd kiss through tissue paper.

The flinch I'm waiting for never shows.

My useless body remembers this boy.

This *man* in a fitted suit, with a dolphin-smooth shave, and tastefully expensive pheromones that leave me drunk on fizzy liquor.

I have to remind myself. "I'm not yours."

And you're not mine.

"*Liiiiiiiie*," he drags out the word in a dangerous drawl.

"I—"

"I know a con. I know a hustle. Run all the games you want. Just don't act like I can't see you playing." Bishop slips a champagne shudder. "You smell so delicious. Lemon sorbet and cream. Want to taste you melted, Queen. All over my tongue."

Something flutters.

A strange, lost feeling.

I want to taste you back.

See if your lips fizz.

But Bishop wants to taste *her*.

My voice comes out small. "I taste like ashes."

Bishop tenses for the kill. "Let me taste for myself. One lick. Yes? Say yes or tell me to fuck off. There's no halfway."

I should run, not hand him my heart and a knife.

But my body doesn't take orders from me.

It takes orders from *him*. "Yes."

A hard, hot mouth knocks me into the wall, and a boom ricochets between my ears.

His body covers mine.

Peachy, but not soft.

Hard all over.

Bishop's firm chest. His iron grip. His knockout moan when he presses into my mouth.

Blood rushes to my head, my heart confused.

"Let me in," he murmurs. "Let me take care of you."

Liquid, I open for his kiss.

Bishop Barrington—worse, Bishop *Meadows*—looses a billion-dollar purr that plants a row of hotels, claiming real estate in my throat.

His hard-gentle tongue drags between my lips.

I let go of the wheel and everything else but a last pinky finger on the emergency brake, just in case I have to bail.

Strong, soft, peachy-sweet.

Bish is everything I need.

He sighs against my mouth. "That's my girl."

I swallow the desperate sound that might be a whimper.

I take the hard turn toward destruction, gripping his suit to hold on and enjoy the ride.

Gonna be a loooooong way down when I have to let him go.

TWENTY-SEVEN

SOL

BISHOP OBLITERATES MY SELF-PRESERVATION, my critical thinking, and every other ability I've got, except the one to moan.

He grips my chin, tilting our kiss to the angle he wants.

I want it too.

Jin's dominance feels like being devoured.

But Bishop's control makes me want to offer him my wrists.

The jagged softness of his purr smooths the pinch of his fingers and it's just—

So right.

Seduced by champagne, I submit to his lips.

Bishop blanks my head, giving me an addictive peek at how good we could be if I weren't broken.

Then his palm finds my shoulder.

Creeps north

Kiss canceled

Before he tastes my shudder, I rip from his mouth and clamp his wrist.

Bishop pants, burning with feral intensity he can't hide behind a smirk.

"Bish." My voice cracks. "Help me lie."

"Tell me." Embers burn in his eyes.

"I need you to not touch my neck." The words scrape, dragging antlers up my throat. "And I need you to not ask why."

Darkness flashes, a hint of smoke, but Bishop can hide a quickie in a hot minute.

He pivots fast.

"Done." When Bish smiles, there's no smirk, no sarcasm, no sneer.

He smiles *soft.* Peach fuzz and a promise I'm not crazy letting him inside.

"Just like that?"

"Just like that." Bish rests knuckles on my cheek. "Unless you have more to share?"

"No." When I shake my head, his skin rubs.

"Queen." He thumbs the corner of my lip, rubbing a shine of drool—his *and* mine.

Then the germaphobe sucks his thumb.

I've made so many mistakes.

Bish makes me *want* to make bad choices.

When I duck under his arm, he lets me escape.

Lending him a grip on my fraying threads stops him from picking the rest of me apart. I put the sofa between us for sanity. "How long is our flight?"

"Ten hours." Bishop straightens his jacket, but there's no hurry in the glide of his hands.

Wish I were that calm.

My fingers jitter until I jam them in my coat pockets. "That's a long time."

"Trouble flying?"

"I don't know. I've only flown twice."

Once, when I was sent to the OCC.

Once, after I was kidnapped away.

Guess which time was worse?

"We're flying private."

The lingering brush of his knuckles twists into a different touch—carpet scraping my cheek.

Tasting the ghost of rubber and wet grass, I hold back a gag. "Private isn't better."

"Should we cancel?" Bishop whips out his phone, ready to kill the whole plan if I say the word.

That's why we can't.

"We have to go." I have to get ahead of Bridget before she

unleashes her arsenal. Before Kairo comes after the pack for revenge

Besides.

It'll probably be fine?

"I'll make sure you're comfortable," Bishop promises, swiping on his phone. "Let me take your passport photo."

I stand against a white stretch of office wall, rumpled in sweats and alpha scents. *Not very Serafina.* "I should fix my makeup."

"It's for a fake." Bish waves off my worries. "I'm bribing customs enough for you to get through on a photo of Dutch in a wig"

Why didn't we do that?

Would've saved two lethal trips to his office.

Just in case customs grows a conscience, I narrow my eyes to max their Redfang glint. Bish snaps a few pics, then returns to his desk

"This is for you." He pulls an unboxed phone from his drawer. "I've forwarded our updated contact cards."

I almost drop the hardware at first swipe.

The contact names stab my secret teenage heart.

Jinnie

Dutch Baby

All-Star

King Bish

I calmly save the numbers I always wanted.

While Bishop handles last-minute travel planning, I perch on the squeaky-clean leather sofa that smells extra freshly rinsed, web-searching and trying not to imagine what he and Dutch did on the cushions to warrant an end-to-end shampoo.

Thought I'd have to dig, but 'Lilah Darling OCC' spits out pages of results

I almost shatter my new phone the second time in its first five minutes

"Problem?" Bish frowns.

"No. Something good." I click a press release that unhinges my jaw.

The flagship branch of the Omega Cultivation Center announced its temporary closing as it transitions to new management. In an interview from the Wyvern Compound, former director, Hikaru Wyvern, introduced his successor, Lilah Wyvern née Darling, as "the omega who will lead not only the organization, but the Darlings themselves ahead into the bright futures they so richly deserve."

I'm sorry

Lilah *Wyvern*?

I live in a bunker, and even *I* know Wyvern Pack. How did little miss *you-can't-make-me-an-omega* end up mating a pack of warlord billionaires?

And who the hell is doing her PR?

If they'd interviewed her, my Lilah would've told them to condemn that broke-down shit-hole.

Hiding a smile, I save the listed contact number.

I have a thousand questions, and I'm going to ask them all myself.

Finally have somewhere to run.

Aspirationally, I download a few books to occupy me on the totally-not-a-problem, zero-anxiety, ten-hour flight.

Authors are writing stories that *aren't* omegaverse.

I flip through a lacrosse romance to see how it works.

Lots of puns about shafts, balls, and head, but zero knots, and nobody's body odor decides their future.

It's just sports.

Imagine?

I download dragons, shifters, hockey players, and billionaires, hoping to fuel the trend.

The omegaverse must be stopped.

Padding my TBR keeps reality at bay until the shirtless alpha with my nail-tracks carved down his chest strides into the office smelling like sea salt, ball lightning, and the promise of marathon sex

I retract my previous statement.

The omegaverse must go on.

But can I be a *normal* omega?

I just want to enjoy the knots and bites and fun-scented men without freaking.

"Ready?" Jin hauls a duffel bag over his bare shoulder. "We've got unmarked cars wrapping the block."

"You're not ready." I start to tug off my sleeve. "Here. You wear—"

"That belongs to you." Jin drops to his knees to pull the coat shut. He only touches fabric, but with so much possessive heat, he may as well be thumb-fucking my bare chest.

"Can you fly shirtless?" Leather squeaks when I slide away on the couch.

"When you fly private, you can do anything you want." Bish closes his laptop, gathering a few last items for his briefcase.

Jin isn't rushed. He's steady on his knees. "Aren't I pretending my scent-matched omega is hitting her first heat with our pack? Wouldn't you be calmer, seeing your alpha flaunt your marks? All part of the act."

Freaking *master* of disguise over here.

I stand to escape.

Staring level with my belly button, Jin almost tips me with a black-hole grin.

"Let me use the bathroom, then I'll be ready," I answer his question the way I should've the first time, then duck into Bishop's en suite.

My nose twitches from the steamy leftover scent of warm soap and clean alpha, but I focus fast.

Unzipping the backpack I'm keeping latched to my side from

now on, I pull out the syringe case, already tasting bleached lemonade

I can't slip, even if these alphas grease my handholds. Without the pheromonal reminders of who I am and who I'm not, I'm afraid of sliding *allllllllll* the way to the bottom of the Meadows hole

Peeling back layers of alpha hand-me-downs to reveal my throat, I turn away from the mirror and jab.

It stings, then burns.

My neck cords and lemony starbursts spin.

I swallow the stomach acid, blot sweat from my forehead with one of Bish's bergamot-scented hand towels, and force my face into a mask of confidence.

I only have to push through three more steps.

Flight.

Flee.

Then freedom.

I leave the bathroom, head held high until Bishop's lips press. "You didn't wash your hands?"

"I didn't—" *Ugh.*

I one-eighty, scrub with soap, then dry my hands on my coat while we all pretend my cheeks aren't flaming.

It's from the chemicals. "Can we go?"

"After you." Bishop sweeps his arm, leading down the hall.

He and Jin snap to my sides, playing perfect possessive mates, protecting the omega wearing half their closets.

Capri has front-row seats for our act.

"Happy honeymoon," she calls sweetly. "And congratulations, Mister Meadows. I'll take good care of operations while you're indisposed'

Her tone jangles some instinct, but she doesn't throw sex pheromones. I'm not sure how to read her until Bishop slows at her desk.

"Have you been introduced to my mate?" Bishop palms my

shoulder, showing me off. I'd like to say I'm faking when I preen, pushing back my shoulders. "This is Serafina Redfang."

Oof.

I deflate like a stomped balloon.

"Redfang." Capri snaps her mouth shut, falling down a few pegs with me. "How fortunate for you."

"Isn't she?" Bish pulls me from the omega's sharpening gaze. "Best recount. You don't have the votes to make a move."

Jin chuckles.

I hide ruffled feathers on the way to the elevator. "That's your secretary?"

"That's a spy." Bish hits the button. "With illusions of removing the last Barrington from The Barrington Hotel."

I fiddle with a button on Jin's coat. "Sounds like the wrong time for a vacation."

"It's the perfect time." Jin plucks my sleeve, pulling me into the elevator.

"When their victory's in sight, it's the best time to strike." Bishop flashes a murderous grin.

I pencil Capri's name on the list of problems I need to take care of for the pack, but she'll have to wait.

My personal shit list keeps getting longer.

Together, we step onto the lobby's mosaic tile. Walking three across, the guys bookend me, playing both mates and high-end bodyguards

Spotless in his luxe suit, Bish struts like a CEO frothing for a hostile takeover.

Jin doesn't pretend to be civilized.

He wears fitted athletic pants, ready for the ring or a battle-field. His clawed chest is a primal threat.

Walking between them, I feel more confident in Dany's purple socks than I ever did in my sister's stilettos.

I know where I stand.

Always on their side.

And nowhere near the enforcers lowering the resale value of the hotel's sitting area furniture.

These aren't Kairo's fancy helpers.

The men perched on velvet puffs look like the Redfangs I met in Brandon's cells. White tanks, cobra tats, and greasy gazes that dart to my chest, heat-seeking my boobs through layers of fabric

Jin's growl rattles the chandeliers.

He and Bish shift to shield me.

I'm supposed to be their mate, so I don't have to pretend I'm not enjoying their overprotection.

But the guys can't block every angle.

My one-time partner and full-time nemesis, Silas Fissure, reads the newspaper from an armchair. Playing golf dad in a polo and khakis, he glares over the page as if I'm the one who twisted *his* arms three-hundred-sixty degrees.

Bishop cuts the sight-line without breaking stride. "Care to introduce your friend?"

"Not the time." Silas isn't the only buzz cut sprinkled among the gangsters. I spot a few other SAS agents, who look more familiar when they glare.

I dip my fingers into Jin's pocket, letting him tow me across the lobby. The pitch of his growl deepens with my touch.

When we pop outside, the valet has a sleek, black car idling. Jin goes for the wheel.

Before I can duck in back, Bish sweeps me into the passenger seat. "Stick close."

I'm supposed to be clinging to my mates, so I don't argue.

Bish secures me between his thighs and buckles us together, crushing my backpack to his stomach.

Afraid he'll guess what's hiding in the lumpy shapes, I cheat and blast Serafina's lemon.

Then the syringe case isn't the hardest thing between us.

His scent spikes, peach as fuzzy and desperate as his whisper. "*Queen*"

When Bish readjusts, his firm length seeks room to breathe, spreading a lane in the valley of my ass.

I don't dare shift, afraid I'll freak.

But now that Bish has my manual, his hands don't stray near my throat.

His scent is another story.

Remember that book where the kid gets trapped inside the big peach?

Now the peach wants to be inside *me*.

"Hold on," Jin grits.

"As our leader commands." Bish locks arms around my waist.

When we gun away from The Barrington, a fleet follows.

"Why follow us in the open?" I watch them through the side mirror.

Jin speeds through the city. "Because they want us to know."

Gravity crushes me into Bish.

"Our enemies want us afraid," he whispers, halfway inside my ear.

Fear isn't a problem with Bishop's hardness cutting through two layers of my pants. "How soon after we land will they have people on the property?"

"They won't," Jin says.

"They *can't*." Bish blows my ear, drawing out a shiver. "No airstrip where we're heading."

"Where's that?"

"My private island."

Sure. Let's pretend that's normal. "Then we're taking your boat to your island?"

"The feds reclaimed my father's fleet." Bishop's nostrils flare in distaste. "We have to rent."

"How awful." I pat his knee.

I've never even seen a boat outside my foster brothers' tub toys

Jin snorts. "It's isolated. Only one working trawler within a few hundred nautical miles."

"There's no ferry or helicopter or…?"

"No way on or off besides our ride. It's safe," Bishop promises.

I was worried about safe *before*.

Now I'm worried about being stranded on an island with four alphas who play too easily with my lies.

My thoughts spin faster than Jin's wheels, but he's barreling onto a private airstrip before I can scheme a way to keep my distance

Best I've got is pretending to be really into snorkeling.

As soon as we pass the gate, Jin zooms across the tarmac toward the tiny plane with steps rolled to its lit-up door. He doesn't slow until we're almost docking as cargo, finally hitting the brakes. "Let's get in the air before Kairo pulls shit with air traffic control."

Bish throws open our door. Before I can jump to freedom, the sharp scent of jet fuel stabs my memories.

Suddenly, I'm not in Bish's arms.

I'm in another alpha's.

When the pack that bought me flew me home, Tommy Orlov tried to force me to ride in his lap.

I ruptured his ball sac before he tied my hands and feet.

Then I rode on the floor.

Eating carpet.

Tommy kicking me, roaring for revenge.

Rance only stopped him so he wouldn't hurt *Serafina's* face.

There were more cooperative omegas on the flight. The Orlovs used them to show me exactly what would happen once they got me home to their nest. Rance rested his heels on my hip, every bump of turbulence rattling my broken ribs.

The whine of the engine and the whine of—

"*Queen!*" The voice calls me back to the alpha who smells like a picnic at peach fields instead of wilting crabgrass.

Bish anchors me, pinching my chin. "Lie and tell me everything is fine."

"Everything's fine." I breathe out, shaking.

Bishop holds my gaze, deep and unmoving. "Say that nothing is wrong."

"Nothing's wrong," I repeat.

He thumb-strokes my jaw, letting me keep my lies and supporting me anyway. Seen but not questioned, I start to relax.

"Left inner pocket," he commands, not barking, just dishing Bishop-brand certainty. *The smartest course of action is always what he tells you to do.*

I feel up the satiny lining of his jacket until my fingers slip into his pocket and find a handful of white pills.

"I confirmed the dosage for your height and weight. If you trust—"

I toss them back and dry swallow.

I'd never trust Bishop Barrington buying snacks or playing cards. He picks weird, crumbly cookies with French labels and always hustles the table.

But he used to disinfect my knee scrapes like a surgeon.

Bish would never hurt me.

Plus, I really don't want to raw-dog this flight. "How long until they start working?"

"Before Dutch steals you away." He slides out of the car, lifting me with him, princess-style.

I hug his neck. *Don't want to fall if I'm going to pass out.* "You don't have to lie for me. Just don't tell the pack my secrets."

"My sealed lips are already yours." His voice drops to a spine-stroking purr. "They can still taste you."

Whether it's Bish or the drugs, everything mellows.

Jet fuel and the plane idling on the tarmac only make me sleepy—at least until a bear-cub alpha bulls down the rolling steps. "Solly!"

"Close your eyes," Bish whispers.

I obey

Dutch bounds over, anxious enough to pounce. "What's wrong? Are you hurt? *Is she hurt?*"

"She's sleeping," Bishop lies, tilting my head into his softly rumbling chest. "Don't wake her with your bellowing."

"Okay, okay, but can I carry her? You—"

"I'm more than capable of tossing you around, let alone our precious, delicate mate. Get on the plane before we lose our taxi slot."

His order doesn't have a drip of dominance, but I shiver like I'm already under his whip.

Just as affected, Dutch bounds up the steps.

Bish singes the ridge of my ear with a whisper. "We'll be safe on land by the time you wake."

"Bish," I murmur, but my lashes are too heavy. "Don't..."

"Sleep, my queen. I won't let your knights peek underneath your armor."

Tying off the reins on my scent, I fall into the welcoming darkness

TWENTY-EIGHT

DUTCH

I'LL FLY *us to the island.*

Strap Solly on my back, go full battery bunny and flap south to snuggle with my girl all winter.

If Bish would let me *fucking hold her.*

He hits the top step of the rolling stairway, cradling our mate. I launch a palm to protect her head from the door hatch.

Bish snarls like the last time I jizzed his silkies. "Do you think I'd let our mate so much as shed an eyelash?"

"It's not that." Feels like he has five fingers clenching my kidney. One wrong squeeze, and I'll fucking *die* slow and screaming

Like, I'm terrified to lose Mom and Dany.

I'd be destroyed if anything happened to our pack.

But I need Solly to *breathe.*

Until we bond, and I can feel her with me all the time, letting her out of sight is more dangerous than loaning out my heart.

"Just let me hold her a sec." I trail Bish between the seats.

Who knows where he rented this bird.

Only one side of the aisle has bucket seats. Plush, sofa-beddy benches line the other side, pre-stacked with pillows.

Gonna need Solly pressed all up against me on one of those.

"Not until it's your turn." Bishop sinks onto the cushioned bench, and a shot of peachy satisfaction knocks me sideways.

He's rubbed all over her.

Which is fucking ace, except for the part where there's no maple in the mix.

I drop in front of them while she rests her head on his fancy jacket.

Does Solly like that high thread count shit?

I grip the throat of my hoodie.

Have to start dressing nicer.

I could blow my load just from casting the fucking *shadow* of my dick on her soft, sweet body.

For the chance to hold her?

I'd crawl on plastic blocks.

Teeth rip my middle until I pry her hand from Bish and curl it into my palm. *Have to feel her pulse.*

Need to mate her, bond her, wife her, fucking every way she'll let me have her.

Sol can tie *me* up.

Long as she keeps me close and promises to stop vanishing.

I'm trying my best not to wake her, but I'm so desperate for her touch, I squeeze her fingers.

Solly peeks through her lashes.

Her bright eyes are dilated, and the black middles eat up the fake green, almost giving me back her natural brown.

"Dutch Baby," she murmurs.

I have fucked up nightmares about the monster who gave me that nickname.

But from my mate's lips?

My cheek clench nips the tip off my tailbone.

Call me anything, long as you stay. "I'm not going anywhere."

"You're a problemmmmm," she slurs, beaming a mushy smile that pauses my need to panic.

"I'm not a problem. I'm your alpha."

Her eyelids droop.

Must be exhausted

To make her comfier, I pry out the backpack jammed between

her and Bish. But soon as I yoink, she claws. "You're not my alpha"

My heart blends like a smoothie. "Sol—"

"Want you. But you're not." She hugs the bag.

I want to rip it from her fingers and scream. *Hold me. Feel me, right here.* "I'm always yours."

"Keep those eyes closed." Bish rocks her with the softest purr. "You're safe. You don't have to fight."

"Never…safe…" Her lids flutter.

She wants me, then says I'm not hers.

Gives the sweetest smile, then phonebook-rips my heart.

Before I find out how many petals Sol has left to yank on the flower of my fate, Reese pops out of the back of the plane. Finished loading our shit, he zooms to her.

When he cups Sol's face, her head droops.

That's not right.

"What *in the fuck* did you give her, Bish?" Reese asks in a barely muzzled snarl.

"Benzos."

My lips pop open. "You *drugged* our mate?"

That's why her pulse is so slow and her eyes are so black.

"Consensually." Bish rocks, trying to pull Sol away from me. "Don't roar in her ear."

Gonna do more than roar.

"Explain," Reese grits.

We'd already have Bish on his ass if our mate weren't cozy in his lap

"Be quiet before you make her more upset." Bish's glare could kill a peasant uprising, but it's not what stops me lunging for my mate

The plane surges down the runway.

Its engine is hella loud and high-pitched.

The sound should drown everything, but it can't touch the muffled whine trapped in Solly's throat.

It's a whimper and a wail.

A held-in scream.

The smothered cry claws my insides with a rusty hook. My alpha instincts rage—to rally, shield, protect—any fucking thing.

Kill the enemy. Soothe the gamma girl. Make her safe.

But there's nowhere to rally.

No enemy but the one in her head.

Fuck

I'm shaking

Need to make her better

"*Give.*" I whip Bish and rip Solly from his frozen arms.

Dragging her flat to the padded bench, I touch her everywhere, hooking my leg over her hip, hugging her back, tucking her head under my chin.

I hug her so tight we could fly through a brushfire, and she'd smell like maple bacon instead of smoke, but that fucking *whine* won't stop.

Solly's lemon sharpens, blades instead of glaze.

Holy fucking panic.

My mate's distress drags out my fuzziest purr.

I lean into the instincts, purring louder, harder, but it's not enough. "What is this? How do I make her stop?"

Reese fucking bodies Bish, collar-tossing him across the aisle. "Why's she making that sound?"

Bish slams into a seat, shirt all fucked, but he doesn't twitch to straighten his clothes. Haunted, he stares at the girl keening in my arms. "I don't know."

"*Fuck.*" Reese rips off his shirt. "Move."

I push into the metal wall, making room. Reese squeezes on the bench. Hugging wherever he can latch a body part, he sandwiches Solly between us.

He smells like chocolate bread rolls, and his rumbly purr insta-syncs with mine.

One alpha wasn't enough.

Between two alphas, Solly softens like pudding.

When she relaxes, her whine dies.

"You're safe," Reese whispers.

My organs stop bleeding, but I'm dripping cold sweat.

I can't hold my mate any tighter without squeezing her out of her skin.

So why does she feel a million miles away?

My throat throbs, desperate for her bite.

Bish tucks a blanket around us, then settles at our feet to stroke Solly's ankles. I can't hear his purr over the engine, but Solly eases even more when he joins our cuddle-pile.

Either Jin senses her need, or the pilot kicked his ass out of the cockpit for takeoff.

"Kairo tried to ground us, but—" Jin's nostrils flare. He staggers as the plane picks up speed. "What happened?"

Reese rumbles. "Bishop fed our mate his anxiety meds."

"Why would he do that?" Jin drops to his knees.

"I'm afraid you're about to find out." Bish grips Solly's ankle. "Hold on to her."

The engine screams. I try to brace, praying he's wrong.

When the plane lifts, we tilt and gravity yanks.

Her soundless whine rips me into meat confetti.

I rub her skin, but she doesn't respond—too far away.

Feels like I'm losing her again.

Gonna be sick

Jin checks her forehead. "It's not her heat."

"No shit," I snarl.

If you have a problem you can solve with a dick, then you don't have a problem.

Solly sounds like she's fighting wolves in her stomach, otherwise I'd knot her happy. "Do the packleader magic."

"She's not ready to mate." Jin cups her face, eyes dark.

"Do *something!*" Maybe Sol's not ready for Jin's magic wand, but she relaxes with his touch. His palm slides down her cheek. I shift, making room for him to move deeper.

Bish lunges. "Don't—"

Jin brushes her throat before Bish can snag his wrist.

Solly screams.

Kicking, she spears to escape my hold.

Her pain saws my spleen.

"Solly." I rock with her, letting her hit me, kick me, trying to stop her from hurting herself.

A sharp, sour scent attacks the cabin.

Hospital disinfectant and funeral flowers.

It makes my eyes water, makes it harder to breathe, but nothing feels worse than watching her suffer.

I can't let go. *Won't let go.* "I'm here."

The pack whispers and strokes our girl.

Finally, finally, the plane levels and the engine cools its shit.

Sol shudders in release. "Killed them."

What in the fuck?

"Tell me their names, Queen." Bishop strokes her calf, coaxing like a vampire.

I'm the one losing blood.

Someone hurt her?

Jin's gaze darts between Bish and Sol's fluttering lids.

Least I'm not the only tool without a fucking clue.

"Rance." Solly shoots the name like a poisoned dart.

Then she slumps, letting go.

Her breathing evens.

Mine spikes to the clouds.

"Who the fuck is Rance?" Reese purrs with an edge of held-back rage.

Fucking same, Dude.

I crush the fire into a flaming nugget and swallow, letting it steam my gut. If her soft breath weren't holding me back, I'd already be ripping through the hull and crashing like a meteor on whoever the fuck put hands on my mate.

"Unique name." All prince of darkness, Bish strokes her foot. "I only know one Rance."

Jin squeezes his hand until his knuckles snap. "Orlovs. Heard their pack caught a hit."

"I'll confirm their deaths," Bishop promises. "Or arrange them."

Reese thrums so hard, he shakes me through Sol's body. His hand drifts up her shoulder.

"Don't touch her neck," Bishop barks.

I freeze hard enough to shit ice cubes.

"Why?" Jin asks, breathless.

"Don't touch her neck," Bishop repeats. "The why isn't mine to give."

An unholy roar steams behind my ribs.

It comes out a chainsaw purr, blowing Solly's hair. Gold halos her sleeping face.

My angel.

She was hurt.

She was in danger.

She was almost fucking *taken* and we wouldn't have had a motherfucking clue we sharted the bed and failed our mate.

We don't even know who her enemies are.

The door inside me rattles.

I swore to keep it locked.

We all agreed to behave.

But when I look around, I'm not the only one fingering that key. Three sets of pitted black eyes see our mate, and nothing else that matters. "We need backup."

Don't care what it costs.

Can't risk losing her.

"Agreed. Our original plans are already fucked." Bish holds her ankle.

"Reese?" Jin squeezes his shoulder.

"Do it." Reese exhales. "I won't be the reason she gets hurt."

"You have until we land to change your minds. Then I'm making the call." Jin pets Sol's hair.

I melt when she sleepily rubs his fingers. "Worth it."

I don't care if we have to sign away our future to keep Sol safe.
Without her, our future blows brontosaurus balls.
Besides.
We still have our honeymoon.
I'll love my Solly as long and hard as it takes until she realizes.
I'm about to be on her ass like epoxy 'til the end of time.

TWENTY-NINE
SOL

I SMELL BREAKFAST.

Groggy, I nuzzle a warm, squishy pillow, pushing into softness that fills my mouth with drool.

Pancake.

Feels like I'm floating, but something heavy and cozy holds me down.

Pancake *blankets.*

I moan and stretch, dreading the alarm for PT at dawn. When I crack my lashes, the room is deliciously dark.

Too warm.

I kick off the sheets, and a subtle rumble teases me back to sleep

I'm halfway to a sweet dream of marshmallow men.

Then my pancake pillow *purrs.*

I jolt, popping energy-drink, triple-shot, adrenaline-burst awake

Instead of flying off the bed, I bounce the arms barring my waist, and butt-hump a maple-bacon alpha with the morning wood of a freaking sequoia. "Dutch?"

Where the hell…?

The ceiling is sloped but not like the tube of a plane. It's an upside-down bowl, covered in weird, wavy patterns that flicker in the dimness.

"Solly." Dutch hugs me from behind. "You're awake."

Am I?

The dreamy light calls bullshit on this being reality, especially when his stroking purr blends with another rocking, soothing sound. "Waves?"

"Overwater nest. Or underwater? Some kinda water." Dutch sleepily pulls me deeper into satin sheets.

He spoons me, our feet twined, and my loose hair tangles all over the super-heated alpha chest I've been using as a pillow for unknown hours.

We're touching everywhere.

And Dutch's scent isn't the only one that lulled me to my best sleep in years. The slippery slope sheets reek of chocolate, rain, and peach champagne.

They took turns staying with me.

Too stuffed to breathe, I pry myself from Dutch's heat. He clings until I smack his fingers. "Bathroom."

Sighing, he releases my waist.

The round bed is so huge, it takes a few seconds to find the edge

My socks land on clear glass.

Underneath, bright fish swim between vibrant corals.

The gentle lap of water tangles with Dutch's rumble, and a scream echoes between my ears.

Swear to shit, Meadows Pack ganked my vision board.

I had a collage of honeymoon resorts, and those nests are spooky identical to the one where my sweaty feet fog the peek-aboo panel into the sea.

Thick, navy fabric drapes the rounded walls, and delicate track-lights ring the base of the super-sized bed like strings of pearls. Dutch crawls after me. With his legs tangled in the dark sheets, his bare torso morphs into the top half of a jacked merman.

My pheromones are ominously silent.

Almost dormant.

Please say I didn't leak.

I try to sniff myself, but I'm still wearing Reese's wristbands, and all the same layers of alpha, minus Jin's overcoat. That's tossed over the lounge sofa in the pile of *their* discarded clothes.

I pop beads of cold sweat.

Taking Bishop's drugs was monumentally shit-brained.

Pretending I didn't almost kill the men I love on the fake heat honeymoon of my fantasies, I escape the nest through its only door.

The glass-bottomed hallway offers amenities on either side. Beverage station for mid-heat hydration, soaking tub, snack bar, group shower, and *finally* a private cubicle with a toilet.

Dutch races to follow me inside.

I block the door, but end up body-to-body with the blond merman in stretched boxers.

The fish below scatter, terrified of his bulge.

"Can you bring me my backpack?" I work to keep my voice even

"I got you." Dutch beams. "Be right back."

While he trots off, happy to be given a task, I calmly lock the door. What's left of my acting collapses.

I sag against the sink.

The girl in the mirror must be Serafina.

She can't be me.

Rumpled doesn't cover the mess.

My sleek ponytail morphed into a tangle of seaweed in the night, and my smoky eye is so mutilated, I'm cosplaying a skull. The contacts I forgot to take out left my eye-whites bloodshot and burning rabbit red.

And my scent.

I have zero memory after Bishop carried me on the plane.

Can't afford to remember.

Four flavors of alpha cling to my skin like I spent the night *rolling* in Meadows.

"Found it," Dutch calls.

I crack the door.

"What else do you need?" Dutch bounces as he hands over my lip-shaped cache, sending a family of eels fleeing for safer waters.

He's five times the size of the kid who snuck lollipops in his pockets before draping his jacket over my shoulders.

Otherwise, Dutch hasn't changed.

His blue eyes sparkle, just the same.

So eager to please.

My fingers twitch to pet his head.

I'm so far past pretending this pack doesn't own me.

So screw it.

Let's pretend I can still walk away.

When I reach for Dutch, he ducks so fast, his shoulder bangs the doorframe.

His golden hair is soft on top. Short and prickly at the back. I stroke him flat-palmed, then drag my nails along his warm scalp until I'm scratching behind his ear.

He moans, rubbing my palm like a greedy cat.

I'm done hoping my body will respond like an omega's.

That ship is sunk, deep below this perfect nest.

All I can do is make Dutch feel good.

His shuddering purr melts my fingertips. "Mate. *Fuhhhhh Uh* Gonna come from just my ear."

"Your ear?" I stop pinching his lobe. "Does that happen?"

"*Mmm*" Dutch nods, encouraging me to stroke him between my fingers. "It will with you."

His lust is liquid. Shining and smoky.

So are his beautiful eyes—wanting, trusting, *responding* to my smallest touch.

I drag down the ridge of his ear.

Dutch quavers like I'm stroking his cock.

Maple syrup sex sears my throat, and *bam.*

My shoulders make that creepy clench that forces me to snap away like I've been stung.

Dutch heaves.

We gasp together. He's so focused, I know he doesn't realize that his scent is the only one gone wild.

I have to keep mine locked. "Do me a favor?"

"All of them." He drapes the doorway, eyelids low, with a wet spot flowering halfway down his thigh.

"Find the clothes Reese packed for me?" I ask breathily. "I need a shower."

Dutch bites his thick lower lip. "If you're gonna wear yoga pants, we have to mate."

"Then I'll borrow someone's sweats."

"That's *worse*," he moans. "Then you smell like pack, but we're not bonded, and I can't *feel* you and—"

"Dutch"

He yanks my hand to his throat. When he rasps, his Adam's apple scrapes my palm. "I can't lose you again."

I swallow.

Do I tell the truth and kick the puppy?

Or lie and drag out his pain?

I tug free and lob down the middle. "Your mate isn't going anywhere"

His eyes darken. "Solly—"

"Aren't we on an island? I can barely swim." I shoo him and pull out the big guns. "Hurry. I'm hungry."

"Why didn't you say so?" His eyes widen. "Hold on. I'll grab papaya and ass pants."

The trick earns me a moment to breathe.

But I've barely started scraping off my makeup, and Dutch is already tearing down the hall with a suitcase and a plate of cut fruit. "The supply shipment just came. I have to help unload so we have real food for you, but eat papaya first. And maybe wear a long shirt? Want to bite that ass so much my teeth are gonna wiggle loose"

My scent glands tighten. "You want to bite…"

"Or lick." He forces me to take the plate, dragging his tongue over his lips. "Eat fruit. Bet it makes your pussy taste even sweeter."

He runs before I can respond.

Which is ideal, because I *can't.*

My pussy spasms—thanking him for his concern—then retreats to the cloister.

Dead silent.

Why bother saying hello if you're not going to participate?

I take my suitcase and suspect snack into the wet room, bar the door, and run all ten shower heads to fog the mirrors.

Picking an outfit is harder than stripping.

I've always dressed to play a part, but since I reunited with the Meadows, my role has gotten hazy as the shower glass.

They're treating me like their real mate.

If I dress like Serafina, all leather and lace, I'll forget I'm fake.

Bishop packed me enough fancy lingerie that the real Marisol —*hopeless slut*—is happy to walk out and greet them wearing *just* lace

I don't even know how to style my hair when Vivian's not giving me buzz cuts, and I'm not required to wear a military bun so tight it prevents wrinkles.

Solomon is my best option.

Dressing like a boy will hide my scars and remind me to keep my distance from the pack.

After a full-body scrub, scraping off sweat and makeup, I change into my new identity.

Loose athletic pants cover my gnawed ankles. A baggy T-shirt goes over a yoga zip-up to hide my throat, and I tie my hair in a low pony for extra protection. When I pinch out my contacts, I don't force in a new pair or paint on more makeup.

The last touch is Reese's hat, pulled low on my forehead.

I shiver through a cocoa hug.

That leaves me waffling over whether to give myself another shot of Serafina. My stomach rumbles before I open the syringe case

It votes to have one solid meal that doesn't repeat.

I wrap a clean shirt around the case, jam the bundle in my backpack, then hide that at the bottom of my suitcase, pushing everything into the corner under the shaky towel bar.

I live here now.

I'd rather sleep on tile and a bed of Bishop-approved linens than brave the minefield of the too-perfect nest that isn't really mine

Territory and secrets more secure, I head to explore.

The hallway opens to an overwater villa clipped from a travel mag

White curtains billow in the ocean breeze. Every wall is made of windows, overlooking the sea. Past a living room furnished in delicate white and turquoise furniture, opens a huge, modern kitchen

The only decorations that aren't photo-copied from my vision board are the burlap sacks piled on the bamboo countertops. They spill out bunches of bananas, toilet paper, rice, and other supplies.

Where are the guys?

Before I can scramble a one-woman search, Dutch's overexcited voice nears the open front door. "Come on. Come on. You have to meet her."

"Don't be a pest," a female chides. "I'll upset her, this close to her heat."

My nervous system fires a panicked blast of static.

That gentle voice is my only warning.

Dutch tugs a woman into the living room.

She's a fraction of his size, with strawberry blonde hair in a loose bun, and kind, blue eyes that sparkle just like her son's. In an adorable, island-print dress, even her slight wrinkles are soft.

I've had two mothers, and neither ever looked at me with an emotion more gentle than contempt.

When Dutch's mom spots me, she covers her mouth with both hands

A railroad stake sinks between my ribs.

Dutch spots me standing like a sculpture, and his doofy grin hammers the spike through my marbled backbone. "Mom. This is my mate, Solomon. Solly, this is my mom, Lisa."

"Solomon?" Lisa gasps. "It's really you?"

Shit. She has tears in her eyes.

I scrabble to correct the misunderstanding. But instead of screaming *FAKE MATE* and punting Dutch off the private dock, the only words I can vomit are, "It's actually Marisol."

"Marisol," Dutch echoes, starstruck.

I'd lose myself in his fuzzy smile, but Lisa pounces. Head barely reaching my chin, she crushes me in a Dutch-strong hug. "I'm so glad he found you. We were so worried when you disappeared'

She smells like crusty sourdough and brown butter.

I don't like strange betas.

I hate strangers *touching* me, let alone hugging.

But Lisa doesn't trigger my ick, even when she rubs my back.

"You heard about me?" I ask, fighting shakes.

"We thought he made you up." Dany streaks past her brother, a fireball of red hair, freckles, and neon K-pop gear. Sweet as jasmine tea, she rockets into the hug, blushing. "I finally have a sister"

Light-headed from lack of oxygen, I reel.

Mate. Daughter-in-law. Sister.

Just pile on those titles I can't have.

Through a nervous laugh, I try to signal Dutch.

SOS!

Grinning and zero help, he squeezes us together, taking the group hug aerial. "All my favorite girls."

"Women." Dany wiggles. "Let go. Your pheromones stink."

"My favorite women," Dutch agrees, setting us down. "Solly doesn't think I stink."

Lucky I haven't been breathing

"I'm so glad you're safe." Lisa gently clasps my hand, but her tone hardens when she squints at her son. "Forgive us for intruding on your honeymoon. You weren't supposed to know we're here."

"Doesn't hurt to meet sooner." Dutch rubs his neck.

Dany makes a disgusted noise. "Even *I* know you're not supposed to bring strange betas around your mate before a heat."

"You're not strange. You're my sister." Dutch palms her whole head to rumple her hair. "And you're seventeen. You better not know *anything* about heats."

She ducks him, ready to throw elbows.

Before they can get into it, Lisa squeezes my hand. "We'll be nearby. Send one of the boys if you need anything. Otherwise, we won't invade."

Dany nods, but her eye-sparkle has a different flavor than her family's

She has questions.

And I've seen her bookshelf—they're probably *detailed.*

I don't have answers for her or anyone else.

I tug free of Lisa. "Thank you. We'll be fine."

She and Dany hurry out, either being polite, or sensing the storm rumbling my belly. "We agreed to *act* as mates. Not lie to your mom."

"I never agreed. And I didn't lie." Dutch's sunshine fades to something darker.

He takes a step

He's so gentle, so smiling, I forget he's stupid huge.

Dutch can be alpha when he wants.

He was unawakened the last times I saw him turn on his dominance—for fight nights or when boys tried to bully me at the field

I forget because he obeys my orders like a puppy, begging for treats

Now, Dutch reminds me how alpha he can be when he wants something bad enough.

When he wants me.

All that want skates down my spine.

There's no sunshine in Dutch's growl—it's all need and night.

"I'm yours." Dutch moves, moving me with his gravity. Only instead of repelling me how an alpha should, he snaps me to him like a magnet. I rise on my toes. His aggressive rumble laps my hard-peaked nipples.

It feels *so, so good.*

I hang, hypnotized by the Dark Dutch who clings to my tongue

All smoke. No sweetness.

"*Yours*," he repeats, as if the first time didn't spaghetti-twirl my insides. "Any time. Any place. Anything you want, I'm yours. But I can't lie, and I won't let you get hurt."

My heart pumps, sluggish.

The air too hot.

Dutch drags my hand to his mouth. "Brown eyes."

I flash back to Bish, feeding Dutch his cum-soaked fingers.

That strange place inside me throbs.

Remembering the same, Dutch chuckles, baring his teeth. He drags the pads of my fingers over his canines.

"Fuck. It *hurts*." He sucks two fingers into his mouth, scraping my knuckles. His tongue licks between, around, almost *through* me

Instead of pulling back, I stare into the darkness.

Was that part of him always there, hiding deep?

Or was it born just for me?

Dutch licks my fingers like they're dipped in sugar. I could explain away his hunger if I'd taken that last pheromone shot, but my skin is lemon-free.

All me.

Dutch releases my glistening fingers with a moan.

His head drops to my right shoulder. He nips my collar, dragging the fabric off my throat. Rubbing me. Nuzzling me until I can't tell if I'm panicking or about to swoon. "Teeth so sore. So fucking empty without you. I wanna devour this throat. Bond that perfect ass. Kiss your tits raw and drink your pussy 'til I drown.

Let you mark me. Let you fucking take me while Bish takes you. Need you inside me. *Here.*"

Dutch flattens my trembling hand to his superheated chest, and his raw, vulnerable growl ravages my layers.

"Marisol." His cock grinds my belly button, heavy and hot. "Where's the lie?"

I have no answers.

None.

"Lying again?" Bishop's voice curls into my ear, dirty as an order to suck his fingers.

I jump away from Dutch, heart hammering.

I thought the puppy dog would end me.

How many other sides is he hiding?

Shit. They're *all* going to kill me.

"Don't play my favorite games without me." Bishop drops a crate inside the door. Jin and Reese follow behind, hauling more supplies

Their nostrils flare at Dutch's scent.

Or maybe the tent in his sweats.

The round hump is more of a yurt when Dutch makes no attempt to hide the swell. He cups, then rubs his crotch. "Can you die if your knot explodes?"

I promise, I'm the one who's dying. "Who told Lisa I was going into heat?"

"She must have assumed." Jin sets his bundles in the kitchen. When the top bag tips, spilling flour and packs of bacon, his mouth twitches. "I was planning on pancakes and bacon for breakfast, but..."

"Think she's full of those. How 'bout Nutella toast?" Reese rubs under his nose, hiding a smile that sets my ears on fire.

I can't win.

I can only pretend I'm not bothered.

Clutching my arms, I move past them to peer out the door. Our villa sits far out on the water, connected to shore by a floating dock

There's a small boat puttering away through the surf, but no other sign of life besides sea birds and hints of buildings peeking through the jungle behind the beach. "There's a resort?"

"There was before the last hurricane." Bish squints at the horizon. "My father acquired it less than legally. He lacked the funds to finish repairs."

"So we're alone?"

"'Cept for Mom and Dany. They're staying in the bunker." Dutch collapses on the couch. Bish tosses a gentlemanly throw pillow over his bulge.

"Most of the buildings are in ruins," Jin says. "We were always planning to retreat here, but we had to speed up our timeline."

"I'll give you the tour after breakfast." Reese tips my brim on his way past, brown eyes sparkling. "*Love* the hat."

I take a deep breath and pull the hat deeper to hide my eyes. "What if we need to escape?"

"We don't." Jin licks his teeth. "We stand our ground."

A deserted island would be the best setting to max my pheromonal damage *if* I had the balls to tell the guys what I can do

But I'm stuck on the fact that we're *alone.*

Together.

No way out.

Bish flashes his finest Barrington grin—polite and deeply bloodthirsty. "We have eyes on every airstrip in range. If guests are arriving, we'll have plenty of time to prepare the entertainment."

"So, we wait for the bad guys. Then what?" I need to find my exit point

Jin stills. "I'm calling some old…friends. The price is steep, but they can shield us in the long term."

"Even from the SAS?"

"*Yes,*" Bishop hisses. "They'll pay for touching you."

When I shiver, Jin grins. "Breakfast? Let's do Nutella pancakes on the deck."

"And mimosas," Reese offers. "Gotta do fancy shit on a honeymoon."

"I'll pop the good champagne." Bish heads for a stack of crates

"And I'll just…jerk off 'til my cock is raw." Dutch rolls off the couch and crawls for the hall that must lead to the guys' rooms. "Less someone wants to help?"

I jam my hands in my pockets.

New plan

Don't let Meadows Pack see through my bullshit.

Jin grins, whipping out a jar of chocolate spread.

Yeah

That supply boat?

Not the only ship that's sailed.

THIRTY
SOL

AFTER A BREAKFAST of pancakes and smirks, I join Reese for an island tour while the guys finish unpacking.

Going by the un-repaired bungalows, the hurricane hit yesterday. But beyond the caved-in roofs and scattered palms, I see what this place must've been.

Sapphire sky and turquoise ocean. Wild, jewel-green paths dotted in tropical flowers.

Private bridges isolate the ocean villas from the beach—far enough for privacy, but close enough to call for room service or a massage after a wild heat.

And here I am.

With *them*.

At least if I'm boned, I'm taking it raw on white sand.

We wind the paths between jungle villas. I hop a downed palm, wanting to peek inside the door hanging open to darkness.

Maybe establish a secret hideout—no alphas allowed.

"Princess. It's not safe." Reese plucks my sleeve.

I brush off his hand. "Still not a princess."

"What do you want me to call you?" His mesh shorts don't have pockets, so he jams his hands behind his waistband, flashing a peek of the cut muscles above his hips.

I look away. "Not that."

"*Gamma,*" he rasps.

My wobbly knees almost drop me in a pineapple bush. "*Anything* but that."

His thick brows bunch. "Kind of running out of options, little buddy"

The name twists my underbelly.

Even my toes curl.

Buddy?

Seriously?

That's what does it for you?

Reese is too alpha to miss my sudden heavy breathing, but he doesn't call me out—just grins slow and covers his smile.

I blink, trying to get back to the point

Any point will do. "Why isn't it safe?"

"We came a few years back to set traps." Reese squats to tug flowers away from the post of the villa's gate. After the brush is cleared, I spot the subtle scoring across the wood. "See that notch? We marked the gates where we rigged surprises."

"What kind of surprises?" I peer toward the villa's porch.

"Nothing too complicated." Reese straightens, rubbing his beard. "We didn't have a lot of time or resources, so mostly pit traps and falling logs. Probably all busted now. We'll have to start from scratch."

"So, you were always planning to stand your ground."

"Eventually." Reese nods. "Kairo was never going to give us an easy path to freedom."

Wish I didn't know how that feels.

Wish *they* didn't know how it feels.

At least, now I have a project. "I'll help you rig the island. I don't know much, but I'm good at following instructions."

"That so?" The corner of his mouth twitches.

Damn it, Reese. "What else is there to see?"

"Let me show you my favorite spot." Reese navigates twisting golf-cart paths like an expert. I watch the scenery to keep from staring at his ass.

The island is small enough to walk around, so we're never far from the beach. Reese heads for the central area, where overgrown plants stop at the plaza of the abandoned resort

The buildings would fit in The Barrington's basement, but repair the glass and signs, and drain the muck from the pools, and I can already see waitstaff running around serving drinks in coconuts

Serafina will love it.

Sour, I fall behind Reese and give in to nature, wistfully watching the sway of his athletic hips.

It would be a crime to not appreciate that beauty while it's mine

Reese catches me watching.

His three-quarter smile scrapes my heart—equal parts cocky and shy

What expression would he make if I dropped the act and finally did what I want?

Running leap into his arms.

"Coming?" he asks.

Not yet.

Later.

When I replay that smile, alone in my perfect nest.

Wearing a T-shirt marked with Reese's number, and his buttery, chocolate scent.

I catch up, weaving between rusted lounge chairs.

We reach a concrete building that doesn't match the island theme, but it's the rare structure with unbroken windows and a solid roof.

"Exercise room." Reese opens the glass door. "Bish hooked me up to practice."

It's hard to notice the darkness when Reese glows so bright.

We pass a waterlogged reception desk, but the tile floor is swept. Everything's so weirdly empty, I feel like an explorer when we pop into the former weight room.

Benches and dusty machines are pushed in front of a cracked mirror, freeing the room for the rectangular net frame rigged to the ceiling.

A big, boxy pitching machine—the kind they have at real cages

—waits next to two buckets of brand-new balls and a pile of batting gear.

Reese rubs his palms with a World Series grin. "Should we check if it still works?"

"Right now." I'm dying to knock the shit out of something.

My soul needs an outlet, and nothing's better than smacking a ball into the rafters.

"Help me with the net?"

Whoever they had install the ceiling frame left the netting crooked. Reese lifts one side, while I pull the other.

It's so normal.

Like those afternoons we spent together on the field, not really talking. He'd pitch to me, or practice popping balls to the outfield, then we'd switch, wordlessly determined to keep moving.

We were always alone together the most.

Everyone else had somewhere better to go.

"You still play?" Reese asks when the nets are fully draped.

"Not really." I lasted half a season with the OCC softball team before the rich girls ran me off the field. The SAS officers have a beer league, but they'd never ask me to join, and I wouldn't volunteer.

"Thought you would." He scratches his beard, tempting me to do the same.

Just one stroke.

I curl my fingers.

I'm not that unhinged.

Yet.

"We should grab the machine." I hurry to keep moving, so I won't stare at his beard or moon over long-gone memories.

As soon as I lift my side, Reese tosses a wicked curve.

"You're gonna reject our pack."

My grip slips.

The machine drops, and my stomach lurches in the long second before the pain hits my toe.

"Fuck." Reese scoops me into his arms. "Is it broken?"

There's the pain.

I scrunch my face and knead his shirt.

Reese sinks to the ground, rocking me, rubbing down my calf. There's a pain-touch-delay, so he has fingers on my sneaker laces before I realize he's at my ankle.

My cuff-grizzle is healing, but I can't begin to explain the ringed scars.

"Sorry. It's my fault—"

"How is it your fault?" I kick from his reach, wincing from my shriek and the crushed-toe sting.

Brilliant.

Reese's heart beats faster against my ear. His cocoa smells more sharp than smooth, but he doesn't let me go.

"Sorry." I wiggle away. "It's not broken."

He holds. "Thought of a name for you."

"Huh?"

"Butterfingers."

My heart tightens. *It was easier when he ran away.* "Reese—"

"Did you ever think of us?" He squeezes me, waist and knee. "I thought of you. Every fucking day."

My breath hitches.

I think about you once an hour.

Every time I'm cold, lonely, hungry.

Especially when I'm horny.

I push at his chest until he's forced to let me free.

I wince when my foot lands, but the pain will fade.

Pain always fades.

"A lot of things have changed."

"No doubt." Reese rights the fallen pitching machine, squatting and giving me his back while he checks its moving parts. "I wanted to play in the majors. Walk out to the mound, look up to the skybox and see you up there, wearing my jersey." His shoulders droop. "Guess it was a stupid dream."

"No." The word slips through the kink in my heart.

"No?"

"You'll make the majors."

"That's the only part you heard?"

It's the only part that doesn't hurt.

Even if Serafina's the one in the stands, I want to watch Reese on TV. "Don't give up your dream."

Reese unfolds, then pats the machine. "I'm gonna stretch. Maybe toss you a few. You want to hit?"

"Yes."

He moves the machine under the netting, this time with no drops. I grab a bat from the gear pile, then trade Reese's cocoa ballcap for a dusty batting helmet.

Reese dumps a bucket of balls into the feeder. "I should tape off a box for you."

"Later." I duck under the net, staying out of range until Reese gets the motor churning.

After the machine fires the first ball, I know where to stand without tape. Clearing my head, I adjust my grip and square up.

The world quiets when the ball launches.

I swing to hit the freaking *moon* and whiff so hard I spin.

Laughing, I line up again, this time, focusing on the ball instead of my bottled rage.

Perfect timing

I crack the ball so hard my bones click, and the only sound more satisfying than my hit is the *boom* when the ball slams the ceiling

"Beautiful." Reese gives my fingers another reason to tremble.

"Weren't you stretching?" I choke the bat.

"Yeah." He pins an arm across his chest. "See?"

Have to ignore my lickable audience.

Reese half-asses his stretches just like I'm half-assing my swings

He won't stop watching me hit.

I can't stop watching him exist.

Before I end up taking a ball to the chest, I finally stop peeking.

Once I find that focus, I mostly zone out. I can't let go all the way—never can when I'm not alone—but I fall into a rhythm that's just what I need.

I hit the ball, I feel better.

Maybe if I pounded a few alphas, my problems would disappear.

"You're swinging too early."

The *whoosh* of my bat matches the gust from my lungs.

Reese climbs under the net, swirling hazelnut. "Can I show you?"

I grip the bat in self-defense.

The answer should be *no.*

But I've never had a defense against Reese. "Sure."

He slips behind me, toasting my back and taking control. Smoothing down my arms, Reese guides me into position, choking my grip up on the bat, and working his hips to drop my stance

"Feel the power?" Controlling our connected arms, he takes a practice swing.

"I feel it." But the power isn't coming from me.

Reese presses so close, when he tightens his abs, he lifts the back of my shirt. "Ready?"

I've never let him this close.

Not even when he taught me to hit.

The machine whirrs. Reese holds me a moment longer than I would've waited to move. He swings, wearing my body like a suit. Our joined force pings the ball high into the nets, shooting tingles to my toes

I've been missing out.

Reese surrounds my shoulders.

Arms holding my arms, hands covering my hands, and *hips*—

He guides me with the barest movements. Telling me exactly what he wants me to do with a touch, a nudge.

"Few more hits," he grunts after another stroke. "Build the muscle memory."

Reese steers me, moves me, basically already owns me.

It's safe in his arms.

No squidge at my neck.

But I'm not building memories.

I'm imagining futures I can't have.

Sinking in melted chocolate, I lean into the twist of his abs and the snap of his hips. His forearm veins pop like he's cast in bronze

It's no stretch to imagine our clothes disappeared.

That instead of swinging, he's driving into me from behind.

I'd *drip* for him.

My body finally matching how I feel.

"*Reese*," his name escapes, more moan than request.

I don't even know what I'm asking.

Just know I need to get away.

I rip from his arms. The pitching machine whirrs.

"Sol!" Reese lunges.

The shadow of the ball blooms at the corner of my eye. Reese twists, folding to protect me.

Instead of shattering my cheekbone, the ball craters Reese's shoulder. There's an ugly *fwap*. A muffled groan.

His lunge knocks me off my feet.

We fall together, but Reese twists, catching me on his heaving chest.

"Dangerous," his caveman rasp hits deadlier than that pitch.

My heart judders. "You... Why…"

"*Why?*" Reese snaps.

He flips our positions in a stomach-clenching roll.

I land on my back.

Reese braces over my head, a knee tucked *high* between my legs

Panting, he tugs off my batting helmet.

Then he lowers himself.

Slowly.

Slowly

Until his chest grazes my peaked nipples and his dark eyes burn so bright, he melts me to the floor.

"Little butterfingers," Reese purrs. "Why'd you wear my hat?"

I choke on chocolate.

I forgot.

Solomon was never a safe disguise.

Least of all from *him*.

REESE

MY QUESTION HANGS.

Thought patience was my virtue.

Nah

Not since my little buddy reappeared and punted Serafina's bougie ass

Only Solomon ever made sense for our pack.

"Why?" I spit back her question, hurting for the answer.

I would've held back. Not pressured her.

But then she walked out of our nest, dressed all fresh and clean *except for my motherfucking hat.* No more fake green eyes. No more makeup. Just clean skin rubbed in my scent and no other alpha's

Sol hits with the same heel pop as ever. The same *me-against-the-world* swing

I want to wrap her up until she remembers.

It's *us* against the world.

Ever since the first time Solomon slept in the dugout and asked why I wasn't going home. Easy answer. *"I never had a home."*

Sol was huddled in a blanket, only brown eyes peeking out. Don't think she knew what she was saying, but I'll never forget.

"Then we have to make our own."

That was September ninth.

Double-nines

That year, my team only let me use one nine on the back of my jersey

I never changed numbers.

Every time I want to quit, I remember.

Whenever I feel like shit.

Even when I believed Solomon was lost and gone.

I wanted to make something of myself, so I could make a home for *us*.

My pack.

My brothers.

Sol.

"Reese…"

Fuck

My name on her lips would be the sweetest if she didn't say it like she's trying to let me down easy when she trades me off her team.

Jin says wait. Let her come to us.

Maybe that flies when you're the hot-shit packleader. All suave and educated, with the CEO charm.

Nothing ever comes to me.

I have to put in work.

So how do I prove myself to her?

My hard fucking cock offers a hint.

She's too beautiful, underneath me. Pony tail spread out like feathers. So soft at this angle.

My cock can shut the fuck up.

I haven't slept since her internal scream on the plane. No way in hell am I gonna be the reason she makes that sound again. The reason her scent twists.

But I can't move off her body now that I have her pinned, and Sol can't seem to pull the trigger.

So, we hang together.

She swallows a few times.

Looks at me, then away.

Every time her eyes lift, I clench a little tighter, ready for the blow.

It's gonna be a no this season, Reese.

Try harder next year.

Don't need you on the squad.

We hang so long, my bad shoulder shakes like a rusty hub-cap, spinning to pop off.

Sol hisses. "How bad is it?"

Busted, same as ever.

I roll my joints to check the damage. Then my *good* shoulder spasms

Oh, right.

Took a fucking bean-ball to the scapula.

Then forgot about it, soon as I had her out of danger.

Another thing I almost forgot?

The rest of what Jin said.

We know who she is.

The kid who cleaned my batting blisters.

The princess who timed out of her own auction to scrape glass from my booze-slicked palms.

The secretly soft-hearted warrior with pockets full of pepper spray and rainbow bandages.

Instead of swallowing the pain, I wince again. *Harder* "Stings"

"Stop putting weight on it." Solly pushes me away—but not the way I feared.

Soft hands on my forearms, she helps me sit up, not blinking as she rakes me for damage. Like she's devastated to find a crack in her favorite cup.

I'll fucking take it.

Anything that keeps her looking my way, forgetting the plan to cut me loose.

"Where did it hit you?" she murmurs, fingers tap-dancing my bicep

"Dunno. It's kinda radiating." Abandoning whatever's left of my pride, I rip off my shirt from the hem.

Can't make any promises about my winning percentage, but my body?

That's one-hundred.

Shout out to the training plan from hell.

I inhale as I strip, hoping to catch Sol's scent spiking.

It doesn't.

But those brown eyes snap to my abs, then she's inhaling too.

One blade-sharp breath.

Her eyes blacken.

I chew back a purr.

I can be so much more pathetic if it makes her suck her pretty lip like *that.*

Hell, I'll take notes from Dutch.

"First aid kit." Wobbling to her feet, she pulls the cord on the pitching machine and darts under the nets, only stopping to point at me. "*Stay*."

Her order locks my joints.

Sitting on my ass like the good boy I'm not, I roll the feeling around.

Sol's command isn't exactly Jin's whip. That always hits with the shoulder-dropping reminder he's top dog—and *my* top dog, which makes a difference.

Then it's strong yielding to stronger.

But Sol's simple *stay* has me frozen on my haunches.

Omegas don't do that.

If my mate tells me she wants something, I'm already running. Not because she ordered, but because I need her happy and fulfilled.

Now I'm locked so hard I'm not sure if I'm allowed to breathe, and it's weirdly fucking satisfying knowing I can pass out and still deliver.

Gammas are something else.

I'm cool with it, with her, with almost fucking anything. Just don't want to find out what happens if she orders *go away*.

After a visit to reception, Sol jogs back.

I haven't twitched.

Soon as she kneels behind me with a rusted metal kit, her order eases and my chest can finally stretch.

Have to ask Jin what's up with our pack hierarchy.

Sol's fingers graze my bruise. "Lucky it wasn't your pitching arm."

Luck had nothing to do with it.

I reacted how I was trained to react.

Muttering, Sol rummages through the kit until she snags an ancient ice pack—one of those snap-to-freeze deals. She breaks it brutally in half. "This better work."

"Or you could just blow on it?"

She mashes the pack. "Don't act like you're not hurt."

I shrug, then wince. *Oops.* "The old injury hurts worse than the new."

Her fingers drift toward my scars—surgeons had to butterfly me open to jam in the rods. "I should've been there."

"At the hospital?" *Nah.* I'd rather bleed out than let her see me wrecked. "But where'd you go? After you disappeared?"

"You mean, after you *all* disappeared? I'll tell you if you tell me."

"Done." She'll find out soon anyway.

Jin already made the call.

We're just waiting to hear back—*find out how much we owe for their help.*

"Boarding school." She presses the activated ice-pack to my sore spot. Her touch is gentle, but her voice flicks like a switchblade. "Where the hell did you get *this?*"

Sol jabs the scar I forgot.

The one from the bullet that skewered my left side. "It didn't hit anything important. Went straight through."

Her nail scrapes the old wound.

My spine snaps straight.

"Why were you in a gun fight?"

"Military. Training exercise."

She fingers the bullet hole while she ices me down. Her voice is hypnotic, rusty and ragged. "And the shooter? Are they still a problem we need to handle?"

Is she…offering to kill the guy who hurt me?

Praise fuck.

Her possessive threat pops goose bumps down my spine like giddy little shrooms.

And the big mushroom is just as fucking stoked.

"It's handled," I say too husky, wanting *more.*

More of the dark goddess whose demons wink at mine.

"Good." Her nails sink deeper in my side.

Just fuck me up

A purr rattles my whole chest.

Sol stills. Draws back her claws. "Reese…"

Not this again.

If she's gonna say my name all breathy, please let it be knotted on my cock—after enough orgasms to scream her raw, leaving those long, long legs too jelly to walk.

Otherwise, the bullet might as well have hit a couple inches higher.

Pop my fucking lung and take me out of my misery.

Want to bite her, but I can't.

Hold her, but not hurt her.

Pry out her pain without triggering her trauma.

I twist, knocking Sol across my lap.

She falls over my thighs with a sucked-in gasp. Instead of dropping the ice pack, she straddles me and swings her arms around my neck, holding steady pressure.

Taking care of me that good?

Just *fffuuuuuuuck.*

I grab her wrists. Drag her hands to my neck. My squeeze

opens her fingers, forcing her to lose the ice. Then I switch her grip, digging those pretty nails into the meat of my throat.

"If this isn't real, end it now." Careful not to hurt her hands, I choke myself out with her softer skin.

"Reese!"

Yeah

I like that one *so much* better.

I don't try to breathe.

Just stare in her eyes, holding, waiting for her to *see.*

The cracks go all the way down.

All she has to do is squeeze.

Figure then she'll end it clean.

You're off the roster, kid.

Sol shifts in my lap.

I'm ready for the hit. Instead, I get her whip. "*Stop.*"

My fingers freeze. She bats my hands away.

"*Breathe.*"

I suck in a saw-toothed breath.

Her hands fall on my bare chest. I can only follow her orders.

My panting slows under her fingers—under her *care.*

Sol lifts my chin, leaning forward in my lap to check the damage. "It's going to bruise."

Hope fucking so.

"Doesn't hurt." I tip back, bracing my arms. Sol's weight drags down the hard shaft that shows just how *good* I am, until her thighs squeeze my sides and her heat settles right where I need her.

"Idiot." Sol claws my shoulders, fucking *blazing* "If you don't take better care of yourself—"

"Don't know how." No one gave a fuck about me before I found the field and Dutch and *her.*

Once, I had a fever so bad I passed out in the yard at home. Got lucky it rained, or I might never've woken up.

My so-called parents were there.

They just forgot I existed, the year they found out about meth.

All I know is working 'til I bleed. "You want it changed, you're gonna have to take one for the team."

Her fire softens. "I can't even take care of myself."

"Easy." I lean into her hands. "I'll take care of you. You take care of me. Fair trade."

"I can't..."

My heart stops chugging.

Sol shudders, then continues, every heavy word dragging kettlebells. "I can't be what you need."

"Already are." I breathe back to life. "Already make me feel so good'

"Not possible"

"Uhhh..." I lift my hips to remind her. "Yeah it is."

She shakes her head. "My scent."

"Not really missing out." It's weird she's not throwing pheromonal signals, but her naked breath is enough to keep me hard. One more of those little head shakes, and I'll be halfway home

I lick my lips, then taste her name. "Marisol."

Her thighs clench. "You know?"

"Dutch only said it thirty-thousand times." Was hoping she'd tell me herself, but it is what it is—*no work, no reward*. "I know I've got nothing to offer you, but—"

"I don't want to hear that from you."

"Why?"

She knocks my chest. "Like you wouldn't give me *everything*?"

"Then what's the problem?"

"I can't accept. I can't even be *touched*. I'm so broken, I—"

"Broken where?" I growl, fucking raging at whoever fed her that horseshit. "By the way? You've got no problem touching now."

"That's different." She lifts on her knees, taking the weight from my lap.

"Different how?"

"I can touch you." She brushes achingly sweet fingers down my beard, then drops her hand. "You can't touch me."

"So touch." I'm already bracing on my hands. I slide them farther behind my back, ready to be cuffed. "I won't move. You can touch me anywhere you want."

Her gaze rakes my bare abs, up the corded throat that's red from her grip. "Anywhere?"

Oh, fuck yes.

"If you're not sure where to start…" I lick my lips. *Shoot your shot.* "You kissed Bish and Jin. Not trying to pressure you or anything but… Made me jealous as fuck."

"I don't know what I'm doing," she murmurs, mostly to herself.

I claw concrete.

Fucking fingers, don't move.

"I'll teach you." I tip my head and hold, heart flipping as she tilts her lips.

"You were always good at that." Hot breath feathers my beard.

Sol moves closer.

And a little fucking *closer* until her nose brushes mine.

Just a tickle slings my balls up tight.

"Reese."

Hell. Fucking. *Yeah.*

That's how my name's supposed to sound.

Takes everything I've got to keep still.

To not lunge and steal.

Be patient.

Can't fuck up my chance to show my mate what's real.

There's only a couple things she needs to learn.

One, that she's mine.

And two, that I'm hers.

THIRTY-TWO
SOL

SHITSHITSHITSHITSHITSHITSHIT.

SHIIIIIIIIIIIIIIIIIIIIIIIIIIIIIT

My mouth is off the rails, and my body's not cooperating.

Not that it ever does. But this is an *extra special* betrayal.

The purr that rumbles the ridges of Reese's abs vibrates my belly

I only say belly, because if I say *clit?*

Reality will trigger my rejection. Then I'll have to leave Reese's lap

I don't want to run.

I want to be *normal.*

I want to be that girl, wearing the jersey in his dream.

"You can use your fingers." Reese's lips move, *so close* to touching mine. "Feel."

When I rock my hips, his hardness hits that spot—right in the low, low, *loooooow* belly. I reach for his mouth.

"Like this?" I drag a finger across his lower lip.

Reese parts for me, nutty breath searing hot. "So good."

I snap my teeth before I slip the baby deer honk creeping up my throat.

Unnnnnnh

I edge his upper bow. His lips are wetter than I expected.

A little bit sticky, smudged in his own flavor.

Pre-licked.

"Taste," Reese rasps.

His dominance simmers, but he doesn't flex. So different from Jin who makes me *want* to obey, from Bishop who I trust to take control.

Reese is a natural teacher.

Just like how he taught me to hit.

Move your hands a little higher. How's that feel? Yeah? Okay, twist like this. Can you keep your heel down? There. So good, Solly. Want to try another swing?

I taste him on my fingertip.

Reese groans.

Or maybe that's me?

His scent is all my favorite things.

Crisp, buttery toast spread with smooth cocoa.

But his *flavor?*

I suck like I'm cleaning him off a spoon.

Reese follows the sweep of my tongue, the hollowing of my cheeks, and his soft warmth curls into spine-licking heat. "More?"

"More."

"Can I use my tongue?"

Yes, please.

I nod instead of screaming.

"Slide your finger deeper." Reese parts his lips.

I do what he says.

It's good advice.

Pushing into his waiting mouth, I graze his teeth and shiver.

Then Reese comes to me.

His lips close around my finger. Warm. Wet. Holding my eyes, he swirls his tongue around my fingertip.

My belly jolts.

This is working.

I'm not freaking.

Not omega-slick-dripping, but for once?

I'm enjoying.

Reese gave this to me.

He works side-to-side in the fold of my finger-joint.

Before he releases my finger, his tongue-tip gives me one last *boop*, like he's patting me on the head.

Good work in there.

Slowly controlling that tongue, he pushes me out of his mouth.

This time, I don't have to be told. I suck him off like chocolate soft-serve.

"That's how it'll feel on your tongue." He swallows, deliciously rough. "Think you want to try?"

I don't want to try.

I want to *keep*.

But I'll take my taste. Later-Sol can suffer. "What's next?"

"Hands." He tilts his neck. "One on my face, one on my throat. Need you to hold on. Can you do that for me, Solly Baby?"

I turn off the voice warning me to stop.

All I have to do is listen to Reese.

"Yes." I take his throat and finally dig into his beard.

Soft.

A harder press, and coarse hair pricks my fingers.

Dangerous.

"You're safe with me," Reese purrs, velvet and smoke. His arms haven't moved—just like he promised. "Now bring me that mouth."

His pulse thrumming my fingers, I lower into the heat of his breath.

"Open for me." Reese's whisper feathers my lips.

Just following instructions.

I let Reese in.

His tongue glides over my lip, chocolate smooth.

He pushes deeper.

Everywhere.

Mouth and chest and thighs, but he's not even using his hands.

Reese twirls the same pattern he previewed on my finger, flicking around my tongue, then licking the ridge of my teeth.

Side to side, round and round, working like he's feeding me dessert.

His purr breaks to a groan. The beard tickles. Soft, then scraping

I gasp

Reese pulls away, heaving. "Too much?"

He shifts, and the hard rub of his shaft sizzles between my thighs

My physiology is wonky as shit, but I know what I want.

"More." I trace his abs to the band of his shorts, loving how his ridges shift at my touch.

"That—" His breath hitches. "Might be a little advanced."

I tease the elastic. "You said *anywhere*."

"Hell yeah, I did." Reese leans back, eyes half-lidded. "But not if you're not comfortable."

I'm much *more* comfortable when I slide my ass down Reese's thighs, and his flag pole isn't trying to wave me like it's Fourth of July

I want to focus on *him* while I have this moment of peace.

Maybe this once, I won't ruin everything. "Tell me how to make you feel good'

Reese's voice was low before.

Now it sinks deeper, seductive and sandy as siren song from an ocean trench. "Take out my cock."

The air's so heavy, I'm breathing underwater.

Afraid the moment will break, I can't risk moving slow. I've been pining for Reese too long to lose this chance.

One tug of his shorts, and Reese's shaft strains to say hello.

His tip is slick.

Ready.

My tongue-tip flicks my teeth.

Reese's growl makes his cock bob. "Keep looking at me like that, and I'll feel too good too soon."

"What do I do?" I have ideas, but I'd rather follow Reese's lead if he's playing teacher.

"One long stroke, base to tip, yeah? Feel what you're working with."

I boldly cup his knot.

Pulsing heat teases my fingers.

"*Mmm.*" His shoulders pop. "Don't just squeeze. *Stroke.*"

I slide my grip along his soft-textured hardness, grazing around his head, all the way to his glistening tip.

"Again," Reese encourages. "*Harder.*"

I stroke curled fingers. Base to tip, hard as I dare.

His head tips back. "So good."

The rasp of his voice and the twitches of his muscles…

Addictive.

Reese's husky instructions send me into a haze.

"Good. *So good.* Can you squeeze a little harder next stroke? Yeah. Just like that. You won't hurt me, Solly. Up and down. Up and down. And around my knot? *Mmmh.* Taking such good care of me. Ready to go faster? Pump— *Ah.* Yeah. Pump it just…like… *Fuck.* Like that. Keep it slick for me."

Whatever he needs, I can finally give.

Reese's thighs tighten, then tremble. The purr that won't quit goes ragged as ripped velvet. Then he dishes his whip—a nibble of sweet command. "*Make your alpha come, good girl.*"

Feathers twist inside, but I'm focusing on *him*.

I pump his cock the way Reese told me he wants it.

Hard and fast.

My sweet Reese quakes until his lips peel from his teeth. "Gonna make me come. So hard. Oh, fuck. See what you do to me? So good, Solly. You ready? Fuck. *Fuck. Now—*"

Reese rears.

His hands lift, then smash the concrete, keeping his promise.

Abs twitching, cock jumping, he shoots rope after rope, pheromones so thick, they may as well be pumping down my throat.

"Keep stroking," he moans.

Wasn't planning on stopping.

I rub until he's drizzled *all over* my fingers.

Reese gasps, shattered but nowhere near done. "Taste your hard work."

My lungs seize.

Just his scent, and I *know*.

My mouth floods.

His kiss was already sweet.

On my fingers, from the source—Reese is so cocoa-butter rich, it's not enough to lick the spoon.

Have to eat my alpha straight from the jar.

Reese tracks every flick of my tongue, unblinking.

My cursed pheromones perk.

Down, girls.

Don't ruin this for everyone.

"You like?" Reese asks with a razor-edged purr.

I wouldn't face-suck my hand if he wasn't such a treat. "Did it feel good?"

He chuckles. "You're a natural."

"Isn't it supposed to..." I fold my hand in half, letting my fingers droop

"Not when my mate's sucking herself off on my thighs."

The M-word stills my busy tongue.

"Can I use my hands?" He leans forward.

"To do what?"

"To take care of you."

I freeze on his knees.

I'm not exactly desert dry after Reese's lesson, but I'm far from unleashing the flood like a real omega would.

He shoots like a freaking garden hose.

Meanwhile, my soil's barely damp.

Maybe the asterisk is for vaginal dryness.

Shame hits worse than my water analogies.

Hot, heavy dread withers my belly until my hand feels covered in drying glue.

The familiar wiggle scrapes the back of my neck in warning. "We can't. I don't think I can—"

"Not like that. I didn't mean—" Reese rushes to explain. "Just… I want to hold you after."

The worm wriggles south.

I crunch my shoulder blades, trying to kill the scritch.

Please don't ruin this.

But I can only fight my body—and reality—so long.

Reese lifts his hand.

My neck crawls until fire rips my chest. Then my whole body nopes the hell away from the alpha of my dreams.

I backslide, rolling from his lap.

"Sol. Did I—" His voice rips. "Did you not want…?" He reaches for me, injured shoulders shaking.

"No. No." *You're everything I want.* "It's me. I just—" *I can't keep you.* "I need to run to the villa. Promise you'll ice your shoulder."

His eyes darken. "Rather you did it for me."

That's someone else's job.

I kick the fallen ice pack to him. "I'll check on you later."

"Little late to pull the trigger now." Reese yanks his shorts to cover his slick abs. "If you want to toss my ass—"

I laugh

The most nervous, shrill, *sickening* laugh.

I'm running out of lies and layers.

Honesty is the price of kissing alphas I can't keep. "I'd never get rid of you"

Reese licks his cocoa lips, eyes lighting with crazy hope. "Then.."

Then why are my signals so crazy mixed?

Meadows Pack has never rejected me for anything.

They never make me feel unwelcome or unwanted, even when everyone else wants to chew me up and shit me out.

But it only takes one mistake.

One whiff of nightmares bleeding off my skin.

One peek at my scarred throat.

They see me as their mate, as Serafina's stand-in, or their little gofer buddy.

They don't see ME.

I don't want them to.

Because they won't understand how deeply I'm broken.

That I crave them in one breath, and the next is full-body rebellion. I could kill them if I sneeze too hard.

Monster-Sol is on an iron leash, but even my Meadows boys will have to face reality when I slip and make that one mistake.

When they realize they brought home a hyena cub instead of the kitten they were promised.

That their love—no matter how well-intended—isn't enough to make my body work the way it should.

I would *never* throw away Meadows Pack.

Won't have to.

They're going to throw me away first.

"Reese."

"Just say it." Blackness eats the warmth of his eyes as he staggers to his feet.

Reese is the one who gets me.

He gets *wishing* you were an orphan, being abandoned, passed over, and forced to follow someone else's playbook to survive.

Our pain has always ripped along the same frequency.

So, if the choice is between hurting myself or Reese?

I pick up the ice pack like I'm picking up a knife. "Make a deal with me"

He's still bracing for a hit, body tight. "Yeah?"

"Don't read into my moods. They're not because of you, or anything you did or didn't do." Melting ice wets my fingers. As the tension leaves his shoulders and Reese regains his sparkle, I remember how to fake the kind of smile that says *everything's fiiiii-iiiiiiiiiine* "Let's find you a better ice pack. This one doesn't work'

"That one's perfect." Reese licks his lips.

I shudder. "Let's go back."

Refusing to flee, I put on my bravest mask and lead the way. Reese follows at my heels, but I don't talk and he doesn't ask.

Have to hold my shit together from now on.

Back at the villa, the guys are finished unpacking.

Dutch sprawls on the living room sofa, and the only surprise is that he's not howling, waiting next to the door. "Solly!"

Already on my game, I dodge his running leap. "Do we have ice?"

Bishop peers over his laptop at the breakfast bar. He's as casual as he gets, with his shirt sleeves rolled to his elbows. When his nostrils flare, so does his smirk. "Enjoyed your…tour?"

"No way." Dutch lunges. "You kissed Reese too?"

"What's wrong with that?" Reese mutters, holding Dutch from tackling me as I slip into the kitchen.

"Rubbed all over each other." Dutch sags on Reese's shoulder, pressing into his beard. "Let me taste."

"Just this once." Reese finds my eyes.

Dutch yanks Reese's chin and plants a kiss so deep, I feel it in *my* toes

He moans.

Reese grunts, holding my gaze as he pins Dutch's hips.

"How much ice do you need?" Jin's question breaks the frantic rhythm of my heart.

I rip away from the kiss, but Jin's dark, knowing eyes are worse than the sound of Dutch eating me off Reese's face.

Jin doesn't touch me.

Doesn't move any closer.

He watches, seeing through my braveness and all my other masks

My pheromones don't just prick.

They claw.

Shit is not holding together.

"Dude." Reese wrenches free with a sucking gasp. "Fucking knocking my tonsils."

"What am I supposed to do?" Dutch pants. "Tastes too good."

Maybe we should run a flavor train. Taste allll the kiss combinations.

My mouth opens to drop that gem, but Jin's attention snaps it shut.

He licks his teeth like he read my thought.

"Make her an ice pack," Reese insists. "Sol rocked her foot at the cage."

"Doctor?" Bish already has his phone out.

"It's fine." *Pain's already gone.* I wave them off, smile fraying. "Make an ice pack for Reese. He's the one who took the hit." I move past Jin, around the kitchen island, walking normally instead of sprinting for cover. "I'm going to shower real quick."

Four flavors of gazes burn my back.

Crackling, fizzing, gliding, *consuming*.

I walk calmly to the nesting suite.

Bolt the door.

I walk less calmly to the shower, starting to shake.

Another lock.

Then there's no stopping the collapse.

I flip the temp to glacial and stumble under the spray, fully clothed.

Teeth chattering, I drop on my heels and clamp my head between my knees. My pheromones claw loose just in time to wash down the drain with my regrets.

This is how moths must feel.

I keep volunteering to burn.

Shit on a shipwreck.

Burn me again.

THIRTY-THREE
SOL

AFTER I SCRUB off Reese's beard and my toxic scent, I finally find the way forward

I can't be Solomon, and I sure as hell can't be myself.

Serafina to the rescue.

I change into leather pants and a high-necked yoga zip. I can't care about island humidity when I need to play a badass.

Heavy makeup, green contacts, and the highest pony.

Most importantly, Serafina's scent.

I stab her lemon in my throat.

As she hijacks my body, my vision blanks. I stumble to the drain to puke bile.

But I'll take the stinging, bitter pain over walking around naked with my heart hanging so obviously on my sleeve that Reese can use it for batting practice.

When Dutch calls me to dinner, bellowing *Sollllllllllllly* down the hall, I walk out a different girl.

Shields up

Mask on

I can't hurt the guys.

Even if I have to torch myself.

Meadows Pack shoots pointed looks as I cross to the long table in front of the open-air deck. I sit with my back to the breeze-blown curtains, so I'm not romanced by the glimmer of the moon.

More business, less fantasy "What's the plan? Have you heard from your friends?"

"Eat first." Jin sets down a steaming bowl of soup. "You must be starving."

All I want to do is lean over the rail and spout hard lemonade into the sea.

I'll probably kill the fish and bleach the reef.

"I can multitask." I stir, not planning to taste, but curiosity and the mouth-watering scent of Jin's chicken noodle win over my nausea. "You made this?"

He steals the chair next to mine at the head of the table. "Mother's recipe."

"But she…"

"Is a contender for shittiest parent in the pack?" Bishop sits across from me, steepling fingers over his soup.

Jin's mom abandoned him when Kairo offered her a check, trying to hide his affair from his actual mated wife. She left her son and her job in The Barrington's kitchen with all the cash and no regrets

Her name lives at the top of my shit list.

"She left recipes." Jin shrugs. "Not much else."

Boxing Reese out, Dutch drops beside me, pressing me with his thigh and spooning chicken from his bowl to mine. "Eat more"

"Hell of a depressing contest." Holding a plate of bread, Reese takes the open seat beside Bish.

He butters the thickest bread slice, then sets it beside my bowl.

I curl my toes in my sneakers, weirdly satisfied by his gesture. *Hold steady.* "So, are we expecting backup or not?"

"We are." Jin looks away. "After we settle terms."

I frown. "What terms?"

Ignoring the roll of paper towels, Bishop elegantly spreads a cloth napkin over his lap. "There's debate over how much we'll owe for their assistance."

"If they're that expensive—"

"Not in dollars. Years." Reese passes me another buttered slice.

"What does that mean?" The guys who love staring holes

through my esophagus suddenly won't meet my gaze. My neck crawls, but not with rejection.

It creeps with a weird, unsettling fear.

They agreed to something stupid to save the wrong girl.

Not happening. "Cancel the deal. We stand our ground. Booby trap the island."

"Booby." Dutch snorts. I throw an elbow, but he moans and opens his arms, giving me access. "Hit lower, Solly."

I grip my spoon. "Don't sign up for something you're going to regret. It's not worth it."

I'm not wor—

"You're worth it." Jin hooks his foot in my chair and slow-drags me into his stormy scent, stopping an inch before I bump his thigh.

While Dutch sticks to my other side, Jin leans into my space, but doesn't reach. Just exhales until my skin fries.

My body drifts to him, magnetized.

Somehow, I stop before I climb into his lap.

Sandwiched between him and Dutch, my pheromones claw.

Excited? Or terrified?

"How 'bout we deal with *now* problems?" Reese butters me a third slice of bread. "If we don't set up a defense, we won't be around to negotiate. Handle later problems later. After we survive"

"I have trap ideas." Give me a few hours, and I'll seal a villa like a turtle shell I can flood with killer pheromones.

Just can't let them know how my ability works.

"Did we get everything we ordered?" Jin looks to Bish.

Bishop lifts his soup spoon like we're filming a Regency romance. "Everything's accounted for in the warehouse. I even acquired a cache of C4."

"Light 'em up." Reese grins so sexy-sharp, he almost pops my lung

Military school did Meadows Pack *good.*

"Let's start in the morning." I swirl my soup, trying to make it look like I'm eating.

It smells delish, but it won't go down smooth. My throat's too tainted with Serafina's sour candy and vodka.

"In the morning," Jin agrees. "After dinner. And breakfast."

Freaking food police.

I smooth my face before I sip the broth.

It's the first time I understand the phrase *melts in your mouth.*

But when I swallow, my stomach sends the liquid back with a chaser of acid. I swallow again, through the burn, tensing every pheromone-holding muscle.

Cold sweat beads on my lip.

I mop myself with a paper towel, stirring and blowing, trying to hide the lack of progress on my bowl. It's harder to pretend I'm eating with the buttered bread tower that's grown to four untouched slices

"Put down the butter knife." I pass Reese back a slice, then slide the others to Dutch and Jin.

Bish won't eat bread that touched the table, so I only have to handle one slice myself. I rip it into small pieces that'll sog and sink to the bottom of my bowl.

Every time I nibble a token piece of crust, Jin's aura thickens.

Watching. Guarding. Drawing me closer to his flames.

My stomach churns a dough ball.

I swallow nausea.

I'm still in control.

For now

AT NIGHT, the guys leave me the nest.

The safe, perfect, overwater nest that sounds like the ocean and smells like the dream of my perfect pack.

Instead of suffering over everything I can't have, I drag pillows and blankets into the shower suite and set my alarm to ring every two hours. Brandon sent me so much Serafina juice, there's no need to miss an injection.

By morning and shot number four, the howling in my ears isn't just the waves, and last night's token chicken noodle has *looong* returned to the sea

I should stop choosing suffering.

But I won't.

Because when I find Jin shirtless in the kitchen, scrambling eggs with my claw-marks proudly scarring his chest, his pupils yawn for Serafina's scent.

The lemon football lodges in my throat.

Keep your acting on point.

I grab a banana so he won't try to feed me. "I'm heading to work on traps before it gets hot. I won't be far."

His grin rakes my goose-bumped skin. "I'll know where you are"

I don't know if that's a fact, a threat, or a scary-sexy promise, but two can play it cool.

I banana-salute and drop my smoothest lie yet. "I'll be back for lunch"

With Jin's gaze lasering my back, I power-walk across the dock to shore

Reese and I passed the warehouse on yesterday's tour. It's a glorified shed, but it has a solid roof and all the tools I need.

First issue of business, I grab a shovel and bury my banana in a hole. Then I dig out plastic sheeting, shears, and a bucket of thick caulk.

I wasn't lying about setting my own traps.

Picking across the property, I hunt down a jungle villa with surviving doors and no marks on its gatepost. Then I get to work, sealing broken windows.

The place needs to be air-tight.

My ears perk all morning, waiting for visitors, but I'm left alone to caulk and sweat through waves of nausea. I'm just hiding the syringe case and trying to stand up after my second injection when I finally catch footsteps too light to be an alpha's.

"Marisol?" A lightly freckled face peeks into the villa.

In purple shorts and a matching APOCALIPS T-shirt, with sunglasses and two strawberry blond buns perched on her head like fuzzy ears, Dany makes the cutest beach bunny.

Meanwhile, I'm sweating my ass off in neck-to-ankle spandex. *Like a tomato-faced mime.*

I jam the syringes in my bag.

Dany's pale eyes crinkle in a genuine smile. "Nice backpack."

I totally owe her concert tickets to make up for everything I've borrowed. "What's wrong? Did something happen?"

"Not at all." She waves open hands. "Sorry. My brothers wouldn't let Dutch come after you, so he gave me the eye. I wanted to see what you've been up to."

Wow

I must've finally communicated my need for personal space.

Not that my ears were straining for hours, hoping to hear Dutch barreling this way.

Nope.

Not me

"There's not a pit trap or anything, right?" Dany stops a flip-flop at the doorframe.

"It's safe." I hold back a smile while she picks through the debris in the living room. Dany's built small like Lisa, and when she concentrates like she's casing for landmines, her nose wrinkles

There's something so soft and shy and innocent about Dutch's little sister. Even *I* want to protect a beta I've barely met. "You call them all your brothers?"

"Except Bishop. He gives me more birthday money if I call him Uncle Bish." She stops shy of my pile of cut-up tarps, then her shining eyes snap to the most interesting target in the room—*me*

"Would it be really rude to ask about your heat? I've never met an omega. I mean, I've read about them, and I write about them, but since I had to homeschool, I'm probably never going to meet another one in real life. Mom said not to bother you, but— Oh. I'm already bothering you, aren't I? I'm so sorry. I don't usually have anyone to talk to that's not family, and when I do, I just— " Blushing, she covers her mouth. "I'm stopping."

I chew back a smile. Today is not the day a fuzzy bunny throws me off my game. "You *write* about them?"

"Read." Her eyes widen. "I meant I read and read about them. I read about them so much that I said it twice."

Uh huh

I didn't snoop through Dany's stuff, but one night in her bedroom, and I couldn't avoid seeing the bookshelf and stacks of handwritten story notes.

Girl has a fanfic addiction worse than mine.

All I have to do is squint and Dany panics, twirling a strand of hair like she can helicopter to freedom. "Um. More importantly, do you want to come to the beach? We're going to barbecue—Jinnie makes the best kebabs—and yeah... The guys have been digging for hours so they want to swim to cool off. Mom said we should give you the option to join but let you know there's no pressure because my brothers probably already did ten stupid things this morning, and even a saint needs a break. And, um, we left a watermelon in the surf to chill, so it should be pretty juicy by now and—"

"Dany," I cut her off. Didn't mean to deflect so hard I set her on a ramble. "Is it safe to have a beach party?"

"Why wouldn't it be?" Puzzled, she stops twirling her hair.

"Redfangs and Triad and—" *Secret agents, oh my.*

"Ohhhh. Them? They've been after us since forever. We still get to have fun."

Her words explode like I tripped Bish's C4.

We still get to have fun?

Well, shit.

I've been living with the wrong motto.

All smiles, Dany skips to tug my hand.

The only betas I reluctantly spend time with are chippy-dick Simon and Brandon's assistants in the mad-science lab.

They know better than to reach for me.

After my last injection, I'm cranking kitchen cleaner lemon strong enough to melt skin. "Don't my pheromones bother you?"

"No? They're nice." She smiles shyly. "Besides. You're my brothers' pack. That means you're my pack until I'm old enough to find a mate. From what I've read, you would've made me go all beta-freezey if you didn't recognize the bond and read me as a threat."

Prairie dogs are more threatening than Dandelion D'Artagnan Meadows—*bless her bunny heart.*

"I mean, if you're okay with me being in your pack. You're the omega, so it's your choice. I should've asked if it was okay before I said you'd be my sister, but I was too excited to finally meet you after so long, and—"

"Dany. Breathe." The girl couldn't bully a paper bag.

That's what makes her so much harder to handle than the guys

Only one version of me was ever *nice*—the Marisol that still had Lilah.

It's my least favorite era, but not because I wasn't happy.

Because I was never happier.

And I never will be again.

I have to scrape the back of the vault to remember how to bend my lips in gentle kindness. The effort rips something in my heart, but a few breaths through the pain, I manage a real, rabbit-soft smile. My spiked shields fall, and the Sol buried in a ditch of ash-dusted wildflowers resurrects to pet Dany's hair. "We can go to the beach."

A sharp breath whips my head to the door.

Jinnie.

Four alphas hover beyond the frame, but he's the one who made that sound.

I know because I'm already leaning, already being claimed by the dark-star gaze that just saw much too deep—and he's already starting to purr.

My muscles clench.

I slam the shields, but it's too late to pretend I'm anything but a dirty liar hiding a gooey marshmallow core.

"Look at their faces," Dany murmurs. "So miserable without their mate."

As if I could look away when they're together. When they're watching me watch *them* through air so lightning-struck, I slurp plasma through the tube of my throat.

"Super fucking miserable." Reese ropes Dutch's arm, holding back the bigger alpha's lunge.

Jin tosses me a dirt-crusted banana. "Found the breakfast you lost."

His warlock grin transmits his not-so-secret thoughts.

You can't dig a hole deep enough to escape me.

I won't win

I can't.

Not against him.

Not against Dany's soft tugging fingers, Dutch's whine, or Bishop fucking Barrington, who brushes past the pack to offer me a frosted glass garnished with peach slices stabbed on a plastic sword. "Arnold Palmer? It's half lemonade and half peach iced tea"

I am *so* shit-fucking-*fucked*.

So screw it.

I still get to have fun.

Right?

I take the glass and gulp.

Bishop watches like the cat who's already tasted my cream.

He offered me a sword, so I take it between my teeth, dragging off a hunk of peach. Then I offer the tip to Dutch. Reese lets him loose. He lunges to wolf the fruit from my fingers, leaking juice down his chin.

"Wow." Dany goes googly-eyed. "These are such good notes."

Just wait, Bunny.

We're having fun now.

I swipe Dutch's thick lip and suck maple-sweetened peach from my thumb. "Piggyback me. We're going to the beach."

"Oh, fuck." Dutch falls to his knees. "It's finally happening."

The old Marisol clawed back from the grave for a limited-time special engagement.

She won't last long before the corpse rot catches up, but just for now?

Let's pretend.

Just once.

Just fucking *once.*

Let's pretend I get to have the happy ending.

THIRTY-FOUR
SOL

MEADOWS PACK HAS BEEN DIGGING.

Not just tunneling my walls and bulldozing my shields.

They've been digging all morning, setting traps in the tropical heat.

Thanks to the shirt shortage you've heard about, they're bare-chested, bronze, and glistening.

Dutch's smoky-sweet pheromones seep through my clothes until I smell like I did snow angels on the breakfast buffet.

The juicy humps of his shoulders stretch *tiiiight* when he grips my thighs under my ass. Inhaling him, I nose a path from the nape of his neck to the lobe of his ticklish ear.

Then I take a bite.

Just a nibble, not trying to break skin.

"Oh, *fuuuhhhhh*—" Dutch staggers with a full-body ripple.

"Did you just…?"

"So hard. Almost blacked out."

I can smell the maple-scented evidence, leaking down his thigh

Whether I play the good girl or I take what I want, I always end up in the same hole.

Might as well make it the *fun* hole.

Already screwed beyond screwed, I hug Dutch's broad back, wrapping his neck and digging my nails into his sun-warmed shoulders

His molasses moan strokes my motherfucking clit.

From now on, I'm calling it what it is.

No more bellies.

No more bullshit.

No more worrying about the consequences.

I'm off the leash until my body yanks the choke collar.

"Giddy-up." I squeeze his hips with my knees.

"*Fuck,* yes." Dutch takes off like a stallion, galloping the overgrown jungle paths.

I'm ready to let him drag me into the sea like a kelpie. To let him take me deep and devour me whole.

His cotton candy growls feather through my skin. I stroke and scrape him, loving his strained, fuzzy moans.

"Fuck. *Fuck*" Dutch jogs, drunk and panting, shuddering every time I drag my nails along his ear.

Let me repeat.

His *ear.*

How sensitive is the rest of his body?

And how freaking good is his stamina?

No matter how many times he shatters, the tent in his shorts stays popped

The Big Top is in town for the long haul.

By the time he staggers onto the white sand beach, even *my* thighs are shaking. I'm not omega slick, but my body isn't rejecting his skin or scent or touch.

Maybe because Dutch doesn't challenge my control. He devours what I offer, and all I want to do is give him *more.*

Dutch wades into the waves carrying me on his back. "Looked it up. I could die~~*unh*~~ I could die if no one~~*Fuhhhh*~~ Die if no one milks my knot."

"Milk your own knot." Bish removes his shoes above the water line, then starts to roll his sleeves. Jin and Reese kick off their clothes while they sprint for the surf, stripping down to pants and shark-toothed grins.

Did I agree to swim or be their chum bucket?

I shiver as spray hits my shins.

Either I'm telegraphing my longing more than usual, or Su-Jin Meadows has an X-ray for everything I'm hiding. His slow smile strips me down to sinews. "Been waiting for you, Tomcat."

My nipples pierce my shirt.

There's no having fun with Jin.

If I give an inch, he'll steal my entire soul.

But Dutch?

Dutch was *made* for fun

He swings me to his chest to save me from the waves. My knees land around his ribs, lifting me above him.

Dutch doesn't give a salted shit about the submissive position.

He's busy *worshiping*.

Blue eyes shimmering, so sweet and hungry for my touch.

I totally get why Bishop screws with him.

"You like being ridden." I stroke his square jaw.

He arches into my fingers. "If it's you, I like it."

"Anything?"

"Ride me. Mark me." His fingers dimple my thighs. "Just like you marked Ji-*nnhhh*~"

I claw his shoulders and almost lose my shit from his orgasmic purr.

"Solly." His pupils blacken. His grip bites harder.

But before Dutch can act on that breath-stealing darkness, Bish splashes in to take control.

He pinches Dutch's chin. "Don't press our fake mate too hard"

"She's not fucking fake. How is *this* fake?" Dutch slides me down his abs until I hit his hard proof, and Dutch grinds the truth against my leggings.

The pressure feels good, but some broken circuit stops me from going omega wild.

When my stomach swoops, it's not from Dutch's lust.

Not from his want, searing so intensely I can't swallow.

Not from the sexy woodsmoke note in his scent that would one-hit kill his actual mate.

I'm hypnotized by what Dutch *doesn't* do.

He doesn't lunge, doesn't take.

He doesn't have to prove he's a big, bad alpha.

Dutch's unbothered confidence lets him casually give away the iron control I battle to keep with clenched teeth and palm-cutting nails.

He yields.

Not just to me, but to Bish, letting the other alpha tilt his chin.

Purring like a satisfied lion as he lets himself be dominated, Dutch gives us the control we crave.

Bishop freaking *preens* when he takes charge. With a cocky, clit-flicking smile, Bish drags our alpha to my mouth. "Then show her how a real kiss tastes."

Dutch's lips meet mine, pancake plush.

I'm expecting gentle.

The golden retriever puppy.

But as soon as I taste his mapled breath, Dutch takes me like a full-grown bear.

No soft, cinnamon roll kiss.

No teasing

No exploration

Dutch claims my mouth, planting a flag on my tonsils. Bruising my hips. Working his jaw. He drinks my spirit—and feeds me himself in return.

Tangled in alpha, I lose the sky. All thought. Everything disappears but Dutch's heat and hands and deep-stroking tongue

One carbon-fiber thread of willpower keeps my nightmare pheromones from ruining the kiss.

I let everything else go.

It tastes real.

"Too rough." Bish stops Dutch's syrup with a yank.

Says who? *I like rough.*

"Allow me to demonstrate." Bish's wicked smile sears away my will to argue. His purr is smoother than Dutch's ragged rumble. More liquid than gravel. When he brushes knuckles down my arm, he may as well be dragging a vibe across my clit.

His kiss is smoother than Dutch's too.

Stroking. Lingering

But his claim?

Even *deeper*.

Bishop kisses with his eyes open.

He watches me react to every caress, every teasing sweep of his tongue, and the roving touch that sparks fizzy shivers up my sides never strays near the danger of my throat.

Like a spider controlling his web, Bish is ready to kill the kiss and any other moving thing that so much as makes my eyelid twitch

I'm always tight. Always coiled and afraid of letting go, but Bishop's attention promises the emergency brake I never knew I needed

Because I might lose control.

But Bishop Barrington-Meadows?

He never fucking will.

I slip a moan—a begging, breathy, out-of-character whine that's much, much, *much* too real.

But until my body pulls the cord, I'm not bowing out.

A familiar stroke rubs my calf, and a breath of chocolate ghosts my cheek so close it's almost sharing Bishop's kiss. "Go team."

Bishop nips my lip, drawing a last gasp before he releases. "Make her moan for us."

"*Mmm.*" Rising from the waves all merman sleek, Reese licks my mouth like ice cream. "Taste so fucking good, Solly Baby."

Their hands support me under the water.

Stroking.

Rubbing.

But only my legs and hips and sides.

Never nearing my throat.

Reese kisses me light-headed. Then Bishop reclaims the lead before passing me to Dutch.

Lush cocoa, chased with sparkling peach mimosa. Then maple and bacon and full-circle, back to brown-buttery, hazelnutty toast.

Their switching leaves me gasping. Fast then hard. Light then deep. Playful, then so serious I don't know how I'll survive if they ever let me free.

They tag-team me in kisses and growls while my skin crackles from ocean spray and the lightning-streaked pheromones that never stray too far away.

Like the sky giving us room to play, just Jin's aura holds me safe

I don't care about my name or any other problems.

I have no problems, as long as this never stops.

"Get comfortable between us, Queen," Bishop whispers so dirty I'll need hydrogen peroxide to scrape his voice from my ear.

Whether it's the rolling waves or some leftover shred of instinct, I can't help moving my hips. When I'm passed back to Dutch, I grind down his abs until the seam of my leather crotch finds the hard ridge of his cock.

He makes a primal, purring chuff.

I kiss deeper, tasting syrup, cocoa, peach.

But I'm missing a flavor.

Jin knows.

Jin knows *everything*

When he catches me peeking, he pries my claw-grip from Dutch's shoulder and kisses my knuckles. I shouldn't be able to feel such a soft brush of lips with so many alphas begging for my attention, but I'd feel Jin call me from the seabed.

"Come," he murmurs.

It's not a command.

It's permission to let go.

All the way

Sprung loose, I climb into his waiting arms.

The guys yield me to their packleader. Dutch presses my back. Bish and Reese support my sides—my own personal island of alpha

When I stop fighting Jin's pull and climb aboard, my body drops into the cradle that feels like it was made for me. Sinking deeper in the water, sinking deeper into Jin, I loop his neck, drape myself on his chest, and slide down his waist, stroked by his encouraging purr.

Down, down, down, tight, tight, *tight,* until I'm sealed so hard to his cock, our friction strains the fabric that's the only thing between us and a full-on undersea fuck.

"Come to me." Jin lowers his chin, not touching, not taking, just hovering close enough to feed me his breath.

I rise to meet the storm.

Jin's kisses always crackle.

But when I take the initiative, his lips blow my freaking power grid

Electric.

Almost numbing.

I feel his pulse in his tongue and his primally satisfied purr. Letting him take me as deep as I dare, I moan into his throat.

"It's me." Jin hums against my lips. "Remember?"

"I know."

"Then what do you want?"

My heart crashes wilder than the surf.

Stroked and held from every angle except the ones that hurt, I focus on the sweet tightness between my thighs.

I want Jin

I want them.

I want *everything*—as much as I can take before I fall apart.

Focusing on sensations, I grind Jin's hardness. It's not dry-humping when we're soaked in ocean water.

The wet fabric between us stretches, but not enough. I have to work for the friction I need. Dutch "helps" from behind, stroking his cock against my ass and pumping me against Jin.

Racing the clock, I ride Jin until I hit the spot.

His zipper.

The metal bump digs juuuust deep enough.

My clit sings—and *shit* can it belt.

A freaking anthem.

I chase the pulsing rhythm, stroked by alpha growls.

Rub, rub, rub my clit, wildly in the sea.

Finally, finally, finally, finally—*about to fucking cream.*

"Jin!" I claw his shoulders, grasping for the impossible bliss.

Just for a second.

Half a second.

Let him be mine.

"There you are," Jin purrs apart my soul. "*Marisol.*"

I shatter.

From my name.

From the *idea* of keeping him.

Jin's cock pulses between my thighs.

I shudder, and the tang of saltwater, the entire freaking ocean can't hide the four-way spike of alpha lust stuffing my lungs.

It's not my favorite place to get stuffed.

But can I handle more?

Strip off the layers between us?

Then I could ride more than Jin's zipper.

Panting, I tense for the inevitable cringe.

But as my breath steadies, my freak flag stays furled. My post-orgasm pheromones are docile. Silent instead of sawing.

Am I fixed?

If I am, I'm flashing the green light.

Meadows Pack can drag me to shore and spread me on white sand. I'll sink on Jin's waiting knot, and while Bish and Reese feed me kisses, Dutch can eat any part of me he wants.

I'll let them run a four-way fuck-train longer than the Trans-Siberian rail.

And when we're locked, body-to-body, alpha knot-deep in my begging pussy, then I'll let them—

Bite.

My muscles spasm.

Sharp. Stabbing.

The sudden pain rolls down from my clenching throat.

I try to breathe through the cringe, but while I was having fun, my system was doing steroids on the sly.

One thought of their teeth and my real scent screams, trying to break free.

Desperate to hide the sour, fantasy-killing truth, I flop from Jin's arms, a fish escaping the hook.

"What's wrong?" Jin stops me from tipping underwater, but his gentle touch only pincers my pheromones.

I splash out of his grasp, dodging Meadows hands and worried looks.

It's easier to move away from them when I'm being hammered from the inside. I stop breathing, even blinking.

If I could, I'd stop my heart.

Anything to keep this moment pure.

Because life does not get better after *that*.

I just peaked

Now it's enough if I don't make my situation worse.

I retreat to the shallows. "I'm fine. Just caught a chill."

Bishop catches up the fastest.

He knows what my goose bumps mean.

Following me onto the beach, he brushes seawater from his ruined clothes. "Let's towel dry, shall we? You must be freezing"

My throat stings.

It's one-hundred degrees in the sun.

He's helping me lie.

"Solly." Dutch chases after us, dripping shorts clinging to his battleship

"Stay." Reese snags him mid-lunge. "Bish will take care of her."

"Indeed. With me, Queen."

I want to flee screaming into the trees, but my need to keep the status quo is burned too deep.

Just be normal.

Instead of making a scene, I follow Bish across the sand. He leads me away from our villa.

Barefoot, soaked, I've never seen Bishop so undone. But as much as I want to memorize the shape of his abs through that see-through white shirt, it's all I can do to breathe and not implode.

Something's always wrong with me, but now it's even *wronger*.

Maybe I overdid it on Serafina's formula. Or maybe my first alpha-blessed orgasm overloaded my ovaries.

Doesn't matter why or how.

All that matters is Meadows Pack can't find out.

Bish heads to a shed with a weather-worn *laundry* sign. He opens the door for me, but he's too aristocrat to be mistaken as a butler.

Bishop is king.

He slams the door.

Advancing with a spine-stroking growl, he backs me up to a washing machine. "Act with me."

I swallow pheromones and the burn in my throat. "Aren't I already?"

"One more scene." He steadies shaking fingers at my hips. "You take care of me like I'm yours. I'll pretend your pain isn't ripping me apart."

His suppressed panic punches deeper than my fears. I lunge for his buttons. "Take off your shirt."

"Just like that," he croons. "Make me believe we're real."

Shit on a sandcastle.

What part of this is lying?

Trembling, I pop open his buttons.

His scent is so razored, the urge to soothe him slices sharper than my rogue pheromones. He vibrates as I strip off his soaked dress shirt.

Bish cooperates, letting me move his arms.

Dark hair messily plasters his forehead. Underneath Bishop's fancy layers, his skin is translucent pale. Delicate blue veins show at his throat, drawing constellations with his freckles.

He's the leanest Meadows.

Cut chest. Narrow waist.

When he's still and silent, he's a different alpha.

Almost...*fragile*.

"Is this how you'd take care of me?" Bish asks roughly.

I hide my rapid-breathing, reaching for a towel from the hamper of clean linens he was probably washing and precision-folding while I slept.

"Yes," I answer, just as hoarse, patting dry his pebbled skin. "What would you do? If I were really yours?"

"If you were mine?" Bishop's voice drags like undertow. "I'd already have you in the shower, licking that salt off your skin. Then, I'd wrap you in cashmere blankets. Drip you in diamonds. Keep you safe and so fucking satisfied in our nest, you'd never want to leave."

I don't need diamonds.

I want his vision to be real.

My throat sears harder. "If I were yours, I'd never try."

Bishop pries away the towel. Careful not to brush my throat, he wraps it around my shoulders, surrounding me in peach-soaked warmth. "Tell me more."

"I'd tie your tie every morning. Fancy Eldredge knots." I already know how. Once upon a vision board, I dreamed of dressing Bishop Barrington in killer suits, and I taught myself until my hands cramped. "If I was in a good mood, I'd even let you dress me."

"Queen," he rumbles. "If you were mine, you'd never frown."

"If only."

"If only."

Swallowing knives, I shrug off the towel, looping it over his shoulders instead of mine. "You should take a shower."

"Take one with me. Keep up the act."

"I think I've done enough acting."

"I hope so." Bishop leans in slow, reading my response.

Maybe grooming him just does it for me, or maybe his over-cautious attention is exactly what I need to feel safe.

Now my glands are quiet.

Confident I'm finished freaking, Bishop brushes my cheek. "Nothing hurts more than always being fine."

Isn't that the freaking truth?

He's opening a window for me to come clean, but until my house of cards is fully in flames, I'll never climb through. I allow myself one stroke of his smooth jaw. "We'll hold together. We always do."

"Left you a selection of clothes." He purrs into my knuckles. "They'll satisfy your needs."

So would Bish, if I took what he's offering.

That's why I shut it down. "Be right behind you."

When he's gone, I pop like a water balloon at a porcupine rave

Bishop left me a basket heaped with long-sleeved, high-collar tops, perfect for hiding my lies.

But being rejected isn't the worst-case scenario anymore.

Like, what's Meadows Pack gonna do?

Reject me harder than I reject myself?

Not possible.

I'm terrified they *won't* reject.

They'll accept me as I am, with all my damage.

My body that doesn't work, my cursed perfume, and the scars that prove I'll never be the omega they deserve.

Then all roads lead to doom.

Either I leak my scent and hurt them or destiny wins.

They meet Serafina.

Then I'll get to die inside, watching them realize they chose wrong

That's the difference between a fake and fate.

After changing into dry clothes, I backtrack to my trap villa, following the jungle path that Dutch flattened. My syringe case got abandoned in my moment of madness.

Even though it hasn't been an hour since my last injection, that orgasm must've burned through my artificial lemon.

I'd rather pass out than face the guys bare-skinned.

Serafina's scent is the only shield I have left.

Nothing says *remember your place* like throat needles and Meadows Pack reacting to my sister's perfume.

My throat itches at the injection site, but I force the needle home

The shot knocks me on my ass.

Lucky the bathroom floor has a drain.

I vomit yellow-green liquid juiced from my liver. But emptying my already-empty stomach doesn't stop the dizzy pulse of nausea.

It's a while before I can stand.

Corpse-pale, with dark purple shadows under my blood-shot eyes. A fake grin strains my lips across my teeth.

Shove it down and smile

Anything to make the honeymoon last.

THIRTY-FIVE
SOL

I SHAMBLE back to the beach, cold-sweating and screwed the second Jin's dark gaze finds me through a haze of stomach-twisting grill smoke.

Like a culinary thunder god behind the barbecue, he flips steak kebabs, side-eyeing the cold sweat beading through the emergency bronzer that doesn't do shit to hide my dizzy paleness.

"Marisol," Jin's dark drawl may as well be a command.

Come here.

If I move toward the scent of roasting meat, my organs will spit out a whole new spectrum of rainbow juices.

Not just green and lemon yellow.

Purple, grey, and maybe even blood-flecked crimson.

Dutch and Reese splash in the surf. Bish is off somewhere, probably still cleaning himself up, and Dany's busy scribbling notes under the shade of a cabana.

Before Jin's magnetic field claims me, I spot my out.

Lisa appears, dragging a cooler from the villa.

I spinny-head jog to meet her on the sand, then grab the handle. "Let me help."

"Please." She adjusts her grip, and together, we skid the cooler to the picnic patio that's blissfully downwind from the grill. She drops the weight, then brushes off sweat. "You're such a good girl."

The praise stings the back of my throat.

Has to be from the chemicals.

It can't possibly be tears.

Lisa drops on the picnic bench, hitting me with the more mature—and much freaking scarier—version of Dany's glitter-eyed curiosity. "Did you get some quiet time this morning?"

"Some." I sit across from her, keeping my back to Jin.

"Goodness knows how anyone handles that many alphas." Her gaze goes distant. "I always had my hands full with the one."

"They're…good to me."

"They never stopped missing you." Lisa's bathwater-gentle smile leaves me squirming.

I have a million ways to deal with insults.

Contempt, neglect, disgust.

Those are my home base.

Whether it's my genes or what I am, people aren't *supposed* to like me. Other than Lilah—the only omega who stands hand-in-hand with me on strangeness—and the Meadows pack, who knew me before I became a walking threat.

Every other alpha, beta, gamma, omega, and sane breathing organism who spends more than an hour in my company flips the second they subconsciously sense the danger I work so hard to hide

On the first day of gamma training, Elyse smiled and introduced herself.

By day two, she had her wannabe mates tripping me on our training runs. My relationship with the team only spiraled down from that doomed start.

It's about time for Lisa to sense I'm not safe.

To instinctively push me away and stop me from hurting her loved ones.

But she keeps smiling like she's happy I'm here. Feels like sailing off a cliff until the reason clicks.

Then I splat bedrock.

Lisa thinks I'm her boys' perfect match.

Betas have the weakest threat instincts. If she's convinced I'm THE ONE, a few twisty somersaults will be enough mental gymnastics to explain away my off vibes.

Wait until she finds out I can't center a pack bond, and I'm the reason her *real* daughter-in-law is stewing in military prison.

Simple as that, I remember my lines.

Just be what Lisa wants me to be. Don't kill her light.

I whip out my safest, good girl smile—all plastic, perfectly rehearsed

Or maybe not?

Frowning, Lisa reaches to check my forehead. "Do you feel alright?"

"Fine," I robo-answer, ignoring the drone in my head, and Lisa's innocent fingers burning like cherry-red pokers. Even her barely there beta scent has my stomach boiling like a thermal swamp

Push through

Hold in the pain.

"How can you be so cold?" Lisa asks. "You should be close to feverish with your heat spiking."

"Took a cold shower." I duck her hand. "And the guys were wrong. My heat's not due anytime soon."

Or ever.

"Don't be so sure." Lisa's gaze flicks from alpha to alpha. "Those boys haven't looked away from you long enough to blink. They're waiting to give you what you want. Even some things you don't know you need."

"They're good to me," I repeat, all broken-record.

"Have you planned birth control?"

I jerk, almost tipping my ass to the sand. "I've planned."

It's called trauma.

Omegas only conceive during their heat.

I don't know where gamma fertility is supposed to fall on the A/B/O spectrum—Bridget never offered me *the talk*—but if my oven can't turn on, it definitely can't bake. Even if the Meadows pass me a fully loaded turkey baster and a handful of Bish's anxiety meds, there's no way I'm getting penetrated with their baby batter.

"Never trust a rutting alpha to remember protection." Lisa pats my frozen fingers. "They're driven to breed, and that first mating heat near guarantees a pregnancy."

I take a serrated breath.

Air hitches in the cavern of my ribs, while my pheromones wail through the hollows.

If Meadows Pack were mine, I'd *beg* them to breed me.

But baby clothes live on the dark side of my vision board.

The side I would've kept blocked forever if not for this hellish conversation, testing my acting skills to the utter shit-limit.

"I have an implant," I lie to kill the topic.

"What?" Dutch looms at the worst possible moment, baking me in smoky maple heat. "Why?"

Before I can choke an answer, Lisa *tsks* "You know better. Simmer those instincts, and don't even *think* about forcing her."

"Mom! I'm not! I wouldn't!" Dutch turns to me. "I didn't mean it like that, Solly. Just… We're already family. Why wait?"

Shiiiiittttt.

I can't breathe.

Can't do this.

"No rush to build our home." In ocean-soaked board shorts and bare skin, Reese drops onto the bench. His eyes narrow. "Less you're planning on going somewhere?"

"No fucking way" Dutch's agitated growl scrapes like broken fingernails. "Can't lose you, Sol—"

I smooth his popped arm veins. "You won't lose me."

You'll find the real thing.

Dutch rubs my palm like a cat

I soothe him until he climbs the bench, tangling our ankles and rubbing me in cuddly warmth.

Then, I'm afraid he's soothing *me.*

"Meat's ready," Jin calls, kicking up a flurry of activity.

Dressed in a fresh, white shirt and sharp-pressed slacks, Bish rejoins us in time to help Dany unpack side dishes from the cooler.

Before I can join, Reese brushes my hand with callused finger pads. "I got you. What do you need?"

I want to say *nothing.*

Then Jin presents a platter of kebabs. The juicy scent leaves me fighting a wave of upchuck and canceling plans to do anything but clutch my stomach against the rise of lemon sludge. "Bring me some water? Please?"

Reese's lip quirks. "Ask that sweet? I'll give you anything you want."

His cocoa-warm scent burns out the barbeque until he jumps to grab drinks. Then I'm left choking on the wrong kind of meat. My head spins dizzy three-sixties while my stomach wants to projectile-puke pea soup

This is...*very wrong*

More wrong than this morning.

More wrong than my worst day in Brandon's lab.

"Eat. You look pale." Jin loads my plate with kebabs, then passes it to Lisa to fill in white space. She adds coleslaw, chips, and cut watermelon.

I'm holding strong until she scoops into a bowl that taunts me with a gooey *glorp*

"My famous potato salad." Lisa ladles chunks dressed in mayo thicker than setting concrete. "It'll get some more meat on your bones before your heat."

My insides squeeze toward freedom.

When I go green-gilled, gulping instead of digging in, Lisa's head tips in unconscious submission. "If you don't like—"

"No. I love potato salad." The words fall out just like the gummy *blep* of potato salad falling off my spoon. Letting Lisa apologize for my damage feels worse than the stomach churn

I've beaten black-ops agents, guinea pig drugs, and enforcers with tear-drop tattoos.

I'm not surrendering over room-temp mayo.

But the guys' stares give me an easy reason to delay the bite of doom. "Why are you watching me eat?"

"Why not?" Dutch asks.

Dany kicks her brother under the table. "Don't make lunch weird'

"Be weird if I didn't watch." Dutch licks his lips, gazing dreamily at my mouth. "That's my mate."

My stomach swoops for a whole new reason.

Maybe I'm coming down with the vapors.

"Water." Reese cracks the seal, then sets an ice-cold bottle at my side.

I sip, painfully aware of the silence.

They're watching my throat.

I tuck my neck into my shoulders, letting the sloshing water settle

"Go ahead." I wave, trying to deflect. But Dany's the only person at the table with food on her plate.

"I've read about this." She munches sour cream and onion chips, enjoying the show. "It's one of those primal alpha things. Maybe because you skipped meals? If you don't eat first, they won't be able to take a bite."

"That's not a thing."

Is it?

I got spoiled asking Lilah for homework answers instead of paying attention in class. Never thought weird alpha behavior would send me spiraling into a life-or-death gastrointestinal crisis.

I'm not even theirs

"Totally a thing." Dutch leans a chocolate chip cookie on the edge of my overflowing plate.

"Yeah." Reese spreads his hands. "Take a bite and see."

I try not to make eye contact with the potatoes, let alone the guys, but Bish and Jin trade one of their psychic, lie-piercing looks

Tension squeezes their harmonious beach party.

I refuse to be the buzzkill.

Always aware of my audience, I lift a spoonful of potato salad, and force myself to chew.

It eats like drywall mud.

Thick.

Pasty.

I fight to keep my face smooth.

Look at me.

Just like a real omega, having a totally normal meal with my dream pack.

Never mind the burbling pool of lava-vomit.

I force my gag reflex to obey, the same way I clench my pheromones

Just sweatier.

Maybe a little shakier.

My hard swallow echoes for the crowd.

Bishop snags my wrist. "Don't force yourself."

I shake his grip, and stubbornly—*stupidly*—reload my spoon. With the confidence of a thousand lies, I force another gluey bite.

Chew.

Swallow.

"If you're not feeling well—" Jin starts.

"I'm eating. Now you—" *Blerg*. "Now you can all—"

Vomit speed-bags my throat ball.

SHIT.

Need to run

To the bathroom.

To the ocean.

Anywhere.

As long as the pack doesn't witness my fall.

But when I lunge to escape, I tangle in Dutch's legs.

My swan-dive dies in Bishop's chest, and the chin-jarring impact shatters my seal.

My control.

My precious lies.

Everything shatters when I spray Bishop in stomach acid and second-hand potato salad.

"I'm sorry." I brush the ruined fabric. "I—"

"Be still," Bishop snaps.

My joints lock, but not because I *have to* obey.

Bishop has dropped guys for splashing mud on his slacks.

His jaw tightens until it shakes, but instead of exploding, he scoops me into his arms.

Does the island have a volcano?

Maybe he'll do us both a favor and toss me in the crater.

His speed-walk rattles my vertigo, but I'd rather ride the tilt-a-whirl than say a single word.

Ignoring questions and growls from the pack on our heels, Bish carries me home. He stops shy of the nest, heading for the shower suite. His porcelain expression chips when he spots my bags and blankets spread in the corner.

"Water," Bishop barks.

Dutch jumps to crank the rain showers, checking the temperature while he chews his lip.

Meadows Pack reflects in the mirrors.

An infinite number of alphas, seeing me at my worst. The only way to look away is turning into Bishop's shirt.

The sour smell sinks my heart. "I'm sorry."

Fully clothed, Bishop walks us under the water. "It's only a shirt."

I'm grateful for the flood that hides my face.

Ten shower heads make quick work of my mess, but they can't fix how I wobble when Bish lowers me to the tile.

"Marisol," Jin growls. "You're sick."

"I'm—"

"Don't fucking say *fine*," Reese snarls.

My knees quake.

Yeah.

I've fallen too far to get away with *fine.* "The steam's making me feel better. Just let me shower and go to sleep. I'll be okay by morning."

Bishop pushes back dripping hair, scowling at the blankets bundled in the corner. "You'll sleep where? Your nest or the bathroom floor?"

Not *my* nest.

"The nest." I push his hands, gritting my teeth to prove I can stand. I'm not even lying, this once. My aching body wants a real mattress tonight. "Just give me a few minutes."

"You shouldn't be alone," Dutch whines.

"You can wait for me in the nest."

Dutch brightens. "Promise?"

"Be right there."

"We'll be outside," Jin warns.

"Sure, sure." I rush the pack out, then throw the sliding lock.

I am not okay.

My body drags like I ran back-to-back marathons on zero sleep.

I've barely had a few bites of food this week.

I feel sour.

Weak.

I want to lie on cold tile until the walls stop rippling. But knowing the pack is waiting, I force myself to move.

Stripping off my puke-sprayed outer layer, I groan as I scrub clean.

Why did it have to be Bish?

I'll never be able to look him in the eye after this.

Ugh.

After scrubbing myself raw, I ooze to grab a towel.

My dragging feet hit a puddle. Instead of pulling the towel, I fall into it, grabbing on to save my life.

The rickety towel bar pops free.

My feet fly one way while the rod escapes the other.

I smash tile hard enough to rattle my teeth, and the towel bar clatters louder than I could've screamed.

"Solly!" Dutch's voice blasts.

So does his kick.

The flimsy lock doesn't do shit when the door splinters off its hinges

Dutch skids through the same puddle that pulped my ass, pack on his heels.

I flail for the towel, hurrying to cover my body.

It's too late.

They see all of me.

The real Marisol.

The one with the manacle scars and the ruined throat.

No lies or scents to hide the carnage.

The me I hate the most.

Four agonizing gazes hammer my heart in flaming cannonballs

Exposed to air, to light and shame and my worst nightmare, my throat crawls in a collar of maggots.

"Marisol," Jin's softness scrapes my raw spots.

I find his stopped feet, but I can't lift my gaze.

I don't want to see.

His pity.

His disgust.

"Get out." I finally snatch the towel to my front, covering my throat, trying to gather the shards of my shredded mask.

A tentative purr echoes. Reese takes a step. "Solly Baby. You—"

"Get. The fuck. *Out.*" Pheromones strain my seams, fighting to fuck me over one last time for funsies.

"You're hurt," Dutch's voice rips. "Solly—"

"*Leave!*" I bark.

Dizzy, drained, desperate, it's all I can do to stop my pheromones leaking.

My aura breaks the leash, and the truth of what I am forces them to move their feet.

Meadows Pack walks, leaving me curled on the floor.

Cracking ribs pincushion my heart.

I lash the towel around my disintegrating throat.

Now who am I supposed to be?

THIRTY-SIX
BISHOP

"LEAVE!"

Sol's command manifests a mech pilot at my brain controls. When she jerks my nerves, I'm a meat marionette.

I flex dominance to fight her pull, but I may as well be shooting silk threads.

Like the girl has her hand up my ass, she waggles her willpower, and all I can do is walk.

Hijacked by an impossible whip, my ass turns in a circle.

I can't scent my queen's panic, but I know those spring-tight shoulders are suppressing out-of-control shakes.

I *know* because the same fucking shudders rattle my vertebrae like poker chips when my loafers start moving the wrong direction—*away from her.*

Helplessness twangs my spinal cord, twisting with an even more confusing feeling.

I *want* to obey.

More than that, I *should.*

It's natural.

A field mouse fleeing a hawk.

Our pack has never run on pure dominance. If we did, I'd be taking orders from Dutch. But even Jin—with enough leadership juice to eviscerate all comers—can only eat his growl and do as he's told.

Alphas aren't the apex predators anymore.

My feet won't stop until we hit the front porch. Then Sol's

command *lets* us stop. Otherwise, I'd be pied-pipered off the fucking pier.

I smooth my sleeves against the loss of control chopping through my veins, but my fingers drag in shower-soaked fabric.

My hair's fucked, my slacks slosh, and I can *taste* Marisol's vomit at the back of my throat.

I'm desperate to scrub us both.

To clean and care for Sol, to groom her and ground her, and let our fucked-up pieces snap together until we stop lying, claiming we could ever be whole alone.

Her scars go deeper than I feared.

My fingers strum my sternum, trading buttons for bone.

Never let them see you flail.

Her violation tastes more bitter than my own.

Fucking coward

Who the fuck am I? Trying to tease out her secrets when the wet fabric pulling across my chest leaves me weak.

My queen should never reveal shit, unless it's on her own terms

Now I've got the realness I was gagging for.

I don't give a gilded fuck if being a gamma elevates our mate to the top of the dominance pyramid. She deserves the throne.

But what the fuck happens to us when she shuts us out for seeing through secrets she wasn't ready to tell?

My heart seizes.

Then who'll brush her hair?

Jin pins my hand to my chest. "Breathe."

His dominance brute-forces my airways open.

Reese scrapes fingers through his beard. "Was afraid she could do that."

"Who… How… *Fuck* She's so fucking beautiful." Dutch cups the rod in shorts. His lust rises thick as maple sucked from the trunk

Jin ropes us into a panic huddle.

While Dutch and Reese thrum, and I breathe through a toothpick-width of working throat, Jin holds up the sky. "Do you want to let her go?"

"Fuck no," the answer is instant, echoed by three ragged growls

"Then be what she needs." Jin purrs with evil certainty.

"She needs fucking revenge," Reese snarls. "Whoever did that to—"

"Make a call." Jin's lightning paddle-charges my sluggish thoughts

Yes.

I've been clinging to shit that doesn't matter.

What good is looking good if we can't protect her?

We need their help.

I flick my sat phone to speaker. A crisp voice answers on the first ring. "Call sign?"

"Sierra Delta Romeo Bravo. Put me through to Jäger. He's expecting our call."

"Hold."

The line clicks. My pulse quick-steps, but I'm not worried about signing a contract.

I'm worried about leaving Marisol alone.

When I kiss her scars, I want her to *feel* how far I'll go to handle her business. I'll fix her problems before she has to lie.

Before she ever has to suffer again.

The wait leaves Jin crackling. "It never takes this long."

"They on vacation?" Dutch asks.

"Them?" Only if hell has a circle with a spa.

My palms sweat until the line connects. There's no answer, but the call timer starts.

I clear my throat. "Commander?"

"Burrowing Bishop." An empty laugh cuts the silence. "Is Dutch Baby there with you?"

Lips white, eyes wide, Dutch shakes his head.

Much as I love to fuck with my boy, I'd never sell him out to a sociopath

Jin pries the phone from my fingers. "Pass us to the commander. We're ready to cut a deal."

"No shit?" His nightmare laugh rings brighter. "Yo, Daddy. Your babies are crawling home. Come genuflect for the bishop."

There's a noise of disgust, a clatter, and then an actual human takes control when Hunter Wyvern claims the phone. "Barrington?"

"Meadows." My chest finally loosens. "I told you we found our mate."

"Lot of that going around," Hunter replies, uncharacteristically smug. "Already inked a mate into your contract. These days, nowhere's safer to nest than our compound."

"She was *bitten*," Jin snarls. "We need to find out who and where. Then they bleed."

"Our favorite kind of job," Hunter rumbles.

I'm not as confident. "What if our new enemies are military?"

"Depends what kind."

Reese cracks his knuckles. "Special Abilities Section. I'll do the time. Doesn't matter, long as those chucklefucks pay."

Hunter whistles. "How do you guys always get so tangled in this shit?"

"Isn't that why you like us?" Dutch mutters.

"We need your written pledge of support," I press. "There's no deal if there's no revenge for our mate."

"If you want blood, Finn can run your mission. Once you're ours, you're ours. Shit knows we could use a few more adults on the A-Team. Balance the fucking insanity."

"How soon can you pick us up?" Jin asks.

"Is it an emergency?"

Sol's pain puts a temporary hold on my scheming need to overthrow the federal government. "We need a few days to take care of our mate. Then we're yours."

"Fan-fucking-tastic. Shoot me your mate's name and details, and I'll sic J on the feds."

A female murmurs in the background.

"Gotta go. Ring when you're ready for an airlift." Hunter cuts the call.

I can *feel* Marisol.

Not her emotions—that will have to wait until I take her throat —but some uncorked caveman instinct lets me guess her location through layers of bamboo.

I'm resigned to a black-ops future that'll have me wearing full-time camouflage and cargo pants—like the kind of hillbilly who licks his fingers, gobbling gopher jerky in a lifted truck with a brass knot and testicles swinging from its hitch.

But the thought that has me counting buttons isn't the mess of my custom-tailored shirt.

It's my queen's shattered voice.

The way she shut me out.

As if she needs to hide.

From me?

I have matching scars.

I'll lick hers clean.

I'll lick her *everywhere.*

The instinct to return to her side frays worse than the water dripping under my collar. "I'm going to her."

Jin yanks me back. "Take a shower first."

"I'm fine."

"She won't be if she sees you all wet and agitated."

"*Ah.*" That's why I trust Jin to lead.

We could charter a jet through my blind spots.

Just because I'm ready to risk showing my flaws doesn't mean my queen is ready to accept.

"Sol is overwhelmed," he continues. "Let me speak to her as packleader. I'll bring you in when she's calm enough to handle more"

"How much more?" Dutch grips his chest. "Gonna die if I can't bite her. She was so fucking hurt and we didn't even *know.*"

"No talk about biting yet. Blow off steam however you need." Jin shakes out his arms. "I'll take care of our girl."

"Yeah." Reese jumps off the porch. "I need to take a walk. Maybe do some fucking murdering."

"What about your steam?" Our packleader crackles like the only generator powering the island AC through a sea-boiling heat wave

"I'm not angry."

I arch a brow. "Tell me another one."

Jin's eyes flash midnight black. "Fine. I'm fucking furious. But revenge later. Right now, I need our mate fed, in dry clothes, and convinced how much she's loved."

"Take care of her." I grip his arm, trusting him to be there for my queen until it's my turn to serve.

"Obviously." Jin pats my fingers. Then he ruffles Dutch's hair and squeezes Reese's good shoulder. "Go take care of yourselves. When you can purr instead of snarling, wait outside the nest. Got it?"

We scatter to see to our needs.

Reese sprints to the batting cage, and Dutch runs off to find his family

I shoot Wyvern House an encrypted message, containing all the intel I've scraped together on Marisol and her enemies.

Serafina Redfang. The SAS. And Rance Orlov, whose pack is either dead or about to beg us for that privilege.

I have my own sources. The dirty associates I inherited from Senior, plus years of contacts I've cultivated along the way toward securing my hotel and clawing my boys beyond the ever-clenching rim of Kairo Moon's greedy-sphinctered ass.

Compared to Wyvern House, I'm a diaper baby trying to spy for secrets with two plastic cups connected by dollar-store yarn.

Their mercenary business runs worldwide. With their resources, they'll have targets ready for us to eviscerate before my hair is styled.

Until I can castrate the shit-gibbons who insulted my queen, all I can do is scrub away the unholy rage threatening to burst my skull like an overstuffed éclair.

I head inside for a marathon shower.

First, I scrub my skin pink.

Then, I *keep scrubbing* until it's red, depleting the local water table and straining the island power grid to maintain a sufficiently sanitizing steam.

I scrub until the hot water quits.

Then I huddle under cold spray, teeth clacking.

Scrubbing doesn't fix shit, but it's preferable to *not* scrubbing and infinitely looping the haunted, horrified look in Marisol's eyes as she covers her body and banishes my pathetic ass.

I shouldn't have seen what she wasn't ready to show, but now that our lies have unspooled, I can't be the kid waiting for daddy to come home and dish another beating.

I can't wait for Sol to accept what I'm offering.

If she slams the door in my face, then I have to keep knocking

If she hides her pain, then I have to bare mine.

And when her rejection rips me into wet confetti?

What else?

Hide the damage with online shopping.

Marisol Meadows is about to receive an *obscene* quantity of gifts

The allure of flexing my black card finally drags me out of the hail spray. I dress neatly, dabbing on cologne so that when I roll into her nest, Sol only gets my best.

That's all she'll see from me until she's willing to accept my worst.

I've been carrying the gold and ruby lighter she stole from Old Nik, then tried to toss. It's expensive. And it evokes the vision of my war goddess mate, haloed in flames.

I tuck the lighter into my pocket, then grab my phone, ready to stockpile cashmere bedding for the royal nest.

But the lock screen pulls me up short.

Twenty-three missed calls and one voice message from an unknown number.

When I hit play, a stone-cold voicemail floods my ear canal, chilling like liquid nitrogen. "We've been searching for Marisol."

My fingers freeze.

Now that we're signing away our souls, Jett Wyvern is technically our ally.

But the cold-blooded motherfucker who manages Wyvern House's wet work makes hardened mobsters brown their tracksuits

I don't want my queen's name in his mouth.

He shouldn't be on the same *continent* as my mate.

"JJ. Let me," a female asks sweetly. There's a rustle, the phone changing hands, then her tone heats to a hiss. "Hunter just told me you're Sol's mates. If you're the reason my friend got hurt..." She snarls. "I don't care who's responsible. You'll pay. Tell her Lilah's on the way."

The line *click* leaves me whiplashed.

We may have graduated Wyvern House Academy with the owners' kids, but we haven't kept in touch, let alone exchanged holiday cards.

There's no such thing as a halfway Wyvern. You're in or out, and we were always tapped to work for the Triad.

Now my information is wildly out of date. Last I knew, the Wyverns' only mate was a male omega.

And now this Lilah wants to come at us?

I snort.

Let's make this clearer than my skin.

Marisol is mine.

I haven't begun to show her how deeply.

Until my queen can smile freely, until she can trust me with her secrets and trade me her throat for whichever piece of my soul she thinks glitters the prettiest*~~don~~'t even fucking think* about coming between us.

Growling, I ring the unknown number.

It never connects.

I try headquarters, but instead of the operator, I receive an endless ring that deepens the stubborn rumble of my chest.

I need to speak with Jin before I pass a word of the Wyverns' dubious message to Sol.

The guttural caveman band using my ribs for percussion won't be quashed until I have her in sight. Preferably in my arms, surrounded by silk sheets, feather down, and my pack's equally possessive pig-grunt purrs.

How far we fall for love.

I hurry to the nest.

Dutch and Reese wait shoulder-to-shoulder, watching the door.

"Any movement?" I park beside Dutch, whose tension tugs threads from my shirt.

"He's soothing her," Dutch mumbles. "*I* could soothe her."

"Soon." Reese pats his shoulder.

"Soon," I agree, smoothing my buttons and breathing, trying to soothe myself until Dutch scents the opportunity for a hug.

I'm no pocket-sized alpha, but Viking Dutch clamps my shoulders like a sarcophagus—impossible to fight. "Is it supposed to hurt this much when she hurts?"

"She's our mate." Reese piles into the hug. "I'd cut off my fucking arm to stop her hurting."

We're all quaking for our queen.

But we can do better than quivering like a pack of useless rabbits

Squeezing my phone between their bodies, I search for the boutique that furnishes The Barrington's five-star nesting suites.

A common nest uses a rubber sheet as its base layer. As if *my mate* is going to smell cheap polyester and pass out in a wet spot during her heat.

I pull up the thickest mattress pad. It has a high-tech core, with a reservoir rated to wick away gallons of slick.

Costs more than a mortgage.

I choose four—two black, two white.

Add to cart.

Reese whistles. "Do million-dollar pillows next. Our baby needs the best."

"Our queen," I correct. From diamond-tasseled heat sheets to the spot of her choice on my waiting, well-moisturized throat. "We'll give her everything."

THIRTY-SEVEN

SOL

I LAYER clothes on clothes on clothes, but full body armor wouldn't cover my raw nakedness. My horror bleeds through fabric

Spilling the ugly truth leaves me empty of everything but freakish pheromones, my ragged skin crawling with millipedes.

They saw.

They *know.*

Now, even if they don't reject me?

I'll have to reject myself.

You'd think I'd stop wanting Meadows Pack, knowing how we end, but parts of me are too baked-in.

I have to wear socks to sleep, I hate warm lettuce on my cheeseburgers, and no matter how many times reality screams *you can't keep them,* I'll always be the same stubborn bitch.

I want the impossible.

I want them to want *me*—the real evil, crazy, loyal, obsessed, weirdo freaking gamma, Marisol.

The footsteps stalking down the hall boot all versions of me out of my post-throat-reveal trance.

I can't handle the bathroom. No mirrors. No glass.

The only place left to flee is the nest.

Jin follows.

The packleader of my dreams gleams darker than the underwater blackness. Energy crackles around his shoulders, dragging me back to a forgotten afternoon.

Nobody had warned us there was a tornado watch. We were playing ball when the eerie silence hit.

No more birds or backfiring engines. The world held its breath until the clouds split, pelting us in knife-sharp hail.

Jin sprinted from the outfield. Curling to protect my body with his body, he shielded me to safety.

Now he's the storm, about to shatter the sky.

His scent rips, ozone sharp.

Danger fires the glands in my throat. My wrists. My thighs. They prickle in desperate warning, coiling to protect me from a threat more dangerous than hail.

I've weathered too much shit to snap now.

I square my shoulders and sink roots, refusing to give in to the shame. "What do you want to know?"

"The ones who bit you. Where are they?"

"They're ash." I grip the fabric over my throat, trying to blunt the vibration of his saw-toothed growl.

"I'll take that answer. For now." Jin stalks closer. "Let's talk about what you need to know."

Be firm. "Doesn't matter. I'm not your—"

"Marisol Meadows."

My hair lifts with his lightning.

Storm's about to crash.

"You forgot where you belong."

A bitter puff escapes my throat. "I never forget that."

"Good. Come here." He wears the same low-slung work pants I rode to climax. After our day at the beach, his sun-kissed abs give way to my claw marks on his chest—light and dark, old and fresh

He looks like mine.

But I resist the electro-magnet desperate to snap me into his arms

Barely brushing my skin, Jin checks my forehead. "What do you need"

I shift away from his sizzling touch. "To talk."

"After."

"After what?"

"After you let me take care of you."

"I can take care of myself."

Channeling Bish with the bullshit detector, he curls his lip. "How's that going?"

I laugh, semi-hysterical.

"I can wait for you to ask for what you want." He grazes my arm, fingers sparking. "Just let me give you what you need."

The promise of destruction sinks my stomach undersea.

But it's Jin. So I have to ask. "What's that?"

"The pack that's always been yours."

I grip my neck to stop from closing the space between us. Fresh out of masks and brave faces, fighting gnawing pheromones, I force the truth through the claws shredding my throat. "Jinnie. That belongs to someone else."

His jagged breath needles worse than my cursed perfume.

I have to say the rest before he purrs me into a spineless puddle. It would be easier to flip off the SAS firing squad than to bare this last, awful scar, but my one last moral is stubborn. *I refuse to lead him on.* "I can't have heats. Can't bond. I want you so much, but I can't be your m—"

"How much?"

A ripple rocks my spine.

"How much do you want me?" Jin's scent storms, all rain and salt and firefly sparkles.

I want him much too much too much. "Does it matter?"

"If you can't answer, ask me the same."

My voice goes as breathy as the wheeze between my ears. "How much do you want me?"

Jin's wolfish grin bites through the dark. "Marisol. You're why I have teeth."

Well.

Shit.

"I'll be waiting for you to ask for them." Jin licks sharp canines. "But not now. You need to rest."

Yes. A life rope. *Time for him to leave.* I dart for the too-big bed. "I'll be golden by morning."

Instead of giving me space, Jin follows. He peels down the sheets and tucks *himself* in. "I'll make sure you are."

My glands throb. "You can't stay."

"Can't? Or you don't want me to?"

I'm scrubbed raw. Almost to bone.

"Can't." I scrape my shoulder, digging the runneled scars through my shirt. There's one way to force out Jin, and it's more sure-fire than a rocket launcher. "But I'll make you a deal."

"Tell me." Jin grabs my wrist, stopping me from clawing myself.

My chest aches.

I'm so tired of pretending "Taste my real perfume. After that... Do whatever you want."

"Hit me." He pulls me deeper, onto sheets already stained with his scent. *At least when Jin leaves, I can keep that little bit of him.*

Before I can second-guess, I unleash the poison.

This close, a puff is enough.

Just a little flex while I hold my breath against a lifetime of dread

Jin's nostrils work.

Ready for the worst, I swing my legs off the bed.

But Jin doesn't follow the pattern.

No scrunched, blood-shot eyes or retching, hacking cough. He doesn't glare with hate or accusation.

His sculpted face stays carefully blank.

A dinosaur-murdering meteor craters the pit of my gut.

Blank is worse.

"I'll go." Before my socks hit glass, Jin yanks, tipping me onto the bed

I land beside his long body. His fingers curl with mine, the only place we touch, but his magnetism locks me in place. "What's it going to take to prove that you're mine?"

My pulse thrums.

I want to ask what he scented, but I know Jin well enough to guess his nightmares.

His father's pepper. His mother's perfume. Reese's hospital room.

Maybe he's not tossing me, but he doesn't realize what that means. "You'd have to meet Serafina."

"Not reject?"

"Just meet. Then you'll know who to reject."

"Marisol." His growl melts my bones. "Ask for what you really want."

Now that I'm lying flat, purred by my ideal packleader, exhaustion pokes holes in my willpower.

I've warned Jin.

I've showed my evidence and all but passed him throat-first to his real mate.

Even the regret police deserve a donut break. "Hold on to me."

Jin's purr hitches, sultry and seductive as his rainstorm scent. "Come."

I move across the sheets.

When I cross his invisible line, Jin drags me to his body, wrapping me in dominance as heavy and satisfying as a weighted blanket.

His rumbling purr doesn't spark rejection.

Jin feels so safe, my eyelids sink.

I want to sleep for fifty years.

We lie together for minutes, maybe hours. Jin thumbs my hip while I breathe his reassurance, soothed by his presence and the gentle lap of waves. One-by-one, my inner tangles loosen until I'm liquid, floaty and content.

"The pack is waiting," Jin murmurs. "Do you want them in your bed? Purring you to sleep?"

"What if I hurt—"

"Nothing hurts them worse than being away from their mate, knowing she's in pain."

I shudder.

Feels like teaching a toddler.

Don't touch the stove.

I'm not your mate.

They have to get burned before they learn.

Too sleepy to fight, I sigh. "I want all of you."

"That's our girl." Jin's scratchy voice strokes me in time with his palms. "Come in."

Unleashed, alphas pour into the nest.

Dutch pile-drives the bed first, but the body that slides against my back isn't maple syrup burly. Lithe and crisp, with a hint of expensive cologne, Bishop purrs so rich, he curls my toes. "Feeling better?"

"Am now." Pressed between him and Jin, while Dutch and Reese rock the mattress, climbing my thighs.

I'd freak if I weren't so tapped.

Bish noses my ear. "Honesty tastes good on you."

"Don't get used to it," I mumble.

"Never. I want to taste all your flavors."

"I'm in charge of tasting." Dutch shoulders Bish's legs, hugging my ass and looping an arm *high* between my legs.

I'd squirm, but even if the guys can't be *mine-mine-feral-gamma-mine*, maybe my body's finally allowing me partial ownership.

"You sure you're okay? You took a lot of hits today." Reese massages my calf, working out a knot—*not the fun kind.*

Four purrs sync, scratchy and stroking.

Surrounded by their scents, tangled in hands that won't let go, even when they should, I shut down the inner robo-voice that wants to answer: *I'm fine.*

If I had the energy, I'd scream.

They're supposed to be mine

THIRTY-EIGHT
SOL

WORST-MORNING SCENARIO, I wake to an empty bed.

Or in an SAS cell.

Instead, I wake with my head pillowed on a packleader thigh.

My thighs are pillows too.

Dutch fell asleep face-down. Every time he inhales, his nose bridge rubs my clit, and with my legs hitched over his shoulders, it's a miracle he can breathe at all.

Reese holds my hand somewhere humid and tangled, elastic pulling my forearm.

I'm inside the shorts.

Bish is the only alpha who didn't shift in the night. Glued to my side, he clutches my arm to his chest. Our fingers twine, and the knuckle pushed between his lips grazes his teeth.

I shut down a shudder.

If they won't pull away, how can I?

Jin shifts, his black hair falling over his smooth forehead. My cheek is the same supernova temperature as his leg, and his pheromones spark like I'm already licking his lightning rod.

The angle puts his face upside-down.

But upside-down, right-side-up, even Uno-reversed, Jin's slow grin is catastrophic for my heart. "Morning."

"You're still here."

He knocks my forehead. "You thought we'd disappear?"

No.

Yes.

A long-forgotten flutter rustles deep inside. Butterfly wings or feathers

Maybe one last hope.

I spent the night tangled in Meadows with no mistakes. Pheromones calm. Glands quiet. Even my throat behaves.

No one ever tasted my perfume and stuck around after.

Until Jin

He watches over me with a dark gaze that liquifies my plan to run the hell away.

I'd jump him if my arms weren't pinned.

"Jinnie." I arch to meet him. "Kiss me 'til it feels real."

Jin's sandpaper purr curls my toes. "Been waiting for you, Tomcat."

He dips for a chaste kiss.

Jin's gentlest touch sings with that lightning edge I can't resist.

But his softness doesn't last past my gasp.

When I yield, Jin claims my mouth. Parting my lips. Working his jaw.

He tastes like summer rain.

Like lightning over the ball field, and all my dreams, crushed into a black hole I don't want to escape.

He tastes like everything I ever wanted.

My body strains toward him, not away.

Jin lifts me, drawing me closer. His possessive pull shifts Dutch between my legs.

When Dutch's nose grinds my clit, my spine full-on rainbows.

Holy shit.

I writhe, desperate to anchor around Jin's shoulders, but my arms aren't mine to move. My fingers scrape Bish's teeth, while my captive hand offers Reese's wood a tight, good-morning shake

The alphas' sleepy groans harmonize with my muffled gasps and Jinnie's roughening purr.

Dutch nuzzles, grabbing my ass in a toe-curling huff.

Must be vaginal CPR.

She's alive.

Fluttering. Pulsing. Maybe even slick.

"Papaya pussy," Dutch mumbles into the seam of my pajamas

"Easy." Jin lifts me from danger before Dutch starts compressions between my thighs. But Reese won't release my hand, and Bishop nips to keep his grip.

I shiver as Jin helps me sit. "How do you feel?"

Yesterday was a shitshow.

My *whole life* has been a shitshow.

Between injection side-effects, waiting for the dawn PT alarm, and always having to act for whoever's watching and waiting to punish me for another mistake, I didn't think it was possible to sleep that deep.

After a night with Meadows Pack, I'm brand new.

I don't recognize the Sol who purrs like a vixen in Jin's arms. "Really fucking good."

"Solly." Dutch burrows under my shirts.

I tense, always expecting that killer squeeze.

The only *squeeze* is the one between my thighs, when Dutch's rough tongue laps my belly button.

I crush his shoulders as the licks spread, slicking my quavering belly.

Reese heaves Dutch away before he can dig in for the winter. While Bish straightens my shirt, Jin offers a reassuring purr. "You want more proof this is real?"

Of course I fucking want more.

I'd beg for it.

But without the bear-cub alpha breathing life into my labia, I remember how reality works outside this nest.

The guys saw my scars, but that doesn't mean I start flaunting my damage. The *idea* of their teeth near my throat tucks my chin all the way to my pelvis.

I can contort my boundaries to steal kisses, but I can't pretend they don't exist. "I'm not ready for more touch."

Dutch groans, face-down in the rumpled sheets. "Can we touch ourselves? It's a medical emergency. My dick's *purple.*"

"As if it's your turn to come." Bish rakes my fingers with his teeth, his breath sizzling through my veins.

"Like I can't smell you, dick-ocrites?" Dutch squints from my thighs. "You're just as hard for her."

"Hypocrites?" Bish purrs.

"I said what I said." Dutch kneels, popping his ass and clasping his hands in a puppy-dog plea. "Please, Solly? Just let me taste your cunt. One lick. Then I'll use my hands on myself."

My stomach wobbles, still wet from his tongue.

What puppy?

Wild-eyed between my knees, Dutch is all wolf.

I *want.*

But I don't trust my body.

If I ride Dutch's face, one lick won't be enough. I want to buck for the right reason. Not freak and flail and run away. "You can't."

"Okay, but someday?" Dutch sighs. "I'll make it so good for you. Reese will teach me how."

The vision tugs my breath.

My favorite teacher, gently coaching my cuddliest alpha how to eat me out.

Do not give in.

Reese shakes his head, hiding a crooked smirk. "First thing? Real aggressive, coming out swinging with the C-word."

"Oh." Dutch licks his lips, never breaking eye contact with the area in question. "Is cunt wrong?"

Call it my lady cave for all I flipping care.

"Nobody's eating anything until you meet Serafina." I wince against a barrage of growls. "Maybe not even then. I'm not..."

I don't have to explain what happens when you're a fucked-up gamma who murdered your wannabe pack and ripped out your own throat to kill their half-made bond.

"Solly Baby." Reese bumps my pinky. "You don't owe us shit. We owe you."

"You don't—"

"We do." Jin strokes me with a growl. "Meeting her won't change what we are to each other."

It's not that I don't believe.

I can tell when Meadows Pack speaks from the heart. Jin isn't screwing around with the rumble from his diaphragm and that dark, unblinking gaze that dares me to argue.

I'm done arguing.

But hearts change.

Wait until they meet their real match.

Bish nips my finger, stealing me from the gloom.

"Dutch." His lips spread slow—an evil mastermind with a knitting hook and an unlimited budget for picking me apart. "*Crawl.*"

Dutch obeys on hands and knees.

My tongue goes chalk.

"Someone has to take care of him." Bish yanks Dutch's hair. "Right, Tulip Prince?"

"Fuck yes." Dutch's eyes roll back.

"*Reese,*" Jin barks. "You know what we need."

"Yeah, I do." Reese rolls off the bed, loose shorts almost bailing off his hips when he dips from the nest.

"Tell her what you want." Bish grips Dutch's throat.

"*Solly*" Dutch's desperation stabs my heart. "I want it from you. Will you give it to me?"

He wants…*what*?

From *me*?

I freeze until Reese returns, carrying lube and an armful of toys. "You packed so much shit. What'd you think was gonna happen on this trip?"

"This," Dutch moans. "*Please.*"

The nest traps their blossoming scents. Smoky maple clogs my throat when Dutch begs.

"Choose your weapon." Reese spreads toys across the sheets. "I'll teach you what he likes."

"He's not complicated. Any touch will do." When Bish manhandles his throat, Dutch pushes into the rough touch, all greedy cat.

Like I'm going to walk away from *that*?

And do what?

Stare at the ocean and pretend I can't hear the pack fucking Dutch brainless?

Without me?

Absolutely not.

I hesitate over a wand vibrator. "You won't try to make this about me?"

"Not until you ask for it." Jin feeds me a head-spinning hit of storm cloud with his wicked whisper.

All I ask is that the batteries are fully charged.

I click the wand to check. The hum numbs my fingers before I flick it off.

Reese whistles. "Want to fucking wreck him, huh?"

Uh huh

And maybe also myself?

I wave the wand at Dutch. "On your back."

He rolls over.

The instant obedience drops my stomach beneath the sea. "Hold him down."

"Nothing I'd enjoy more," Bish purrs, pinning Dutch's arms above his head.

The position stretches his abs, straining his bulge against the teeny boxers he slept in. When I peel them down his shaking thighs. Dutch's cock slingshots to his stomach.

His poor knot.

It really is purple.

Aching to fill his lucky omega, it swells painfully from the smooth-shaven base of his juicy-thick cock.

Pre-cum slicks his head. My mouth fills with the musky sweetness of his scent. Quavering maple alpha, desperate for my touch

"Don't turn on the vibe yet." Reese splays open Dutch's thighs

"Make him work for it." Jin grabs an ankle, forcing Dutch open wide

Pinned, Dutch pants, his cock twitching.

All I've done is *look*.

Holy fucking fantasy.

I'm all in.

Without hitting the switch, I twirl the vibe around his leaking head and tease pre-cum down the pulsing veins of his shaft.

"Yes. *Yes*. More. *Please*." Dutch jerks, pinned by his pack.

"He has two good spots." Reese guides my arm the same way he coaches me how to hit. "Here. Base of the knot. And here." He levers Dutch's thigh and helps me slide the vibe under the alpha's drawn-up balls. "Between the balls and his rim."

"But only if he behaves." Bish slams Dutch's wiggling arms. "Make him earn his pleasure."

"How?" I ask, breathless.

Bishop's grin steals what's left of my air. "Give him something to suck"

I'm so, *so* tempted.

But not for myself.

I want Dutch to earn his reward by working Bish's cock. Taking it *hard* down his throat. Just how he took it over Bishop's desk

"What do you want?" Evil Jin gives life to my secret thoughts.

I shudder.

Not today. Not yet.

But maybe tomorrow.

I hope?

Before the guys seduce me into breaking my rules and participating, I offer a finger to Dutch's mouth. "Do you deserve more?"

Starving wolf, Dutch snaps.

Working his tongue like a tentacle, he sucks in three of my fingers at once.

"Don't bite," Jin warns in a spine-scraping bark.

Dutch takes my fingers to the knuckles.

Mouth so hot.

Sucking.

Slurping.

Exploring every ticklish inch of me with happy, desperate moans and teasing my skin with his teeth.

Reese nudges me. "Hit him with some juice."

Focused on devouring my fingers, Dutch doesn't hear the tip.

My turn to be evil.

I push the vibe to Dutch's knot and hit the switch.

He rips a moan that ripples off the walls and rolls down his abs, torquing him so hard, he almost throws the pack's caging hands

That's the lowest setting.

I squeeze my thighs. "Too much?"

"What? No," Reese chuckles. "Fucking break him. We'll hold him down until your wrist gives out."

Welp.

The guys set the stage to let me play. I don't know who or what they see when I move between Dutch's trembling knees, but there are no cameras in the nest.

There's no pressure, except for the deep clench inside that I'm pretending I can't feel.

My perfume stirs but doesn't fight. In a rare show of unity, my body, mind, and ever-shifting identities settle on the same page.

I don't have to please anyone but myself.

But I *want* to please Dutch.

I want to please him into a puddle.

Not to prove that I can or even that I'm normal.

Just because I *love* touching Dutch. The way he full-body spasms, so responsive to the barest brush.

Bracing against his thigh, I crank the vibe another notch to tease his knot.

"Sol—*ghfeeee*." His dick jerks, his tip leaks, and Dutch can't speak, only gasp musical moans that cord his throat while he calls my name in tongues. "Slll. Eeegh. *Uhhh. Fuhhhh.* Sullll—"

Addictive.

The power.

His pheromones.

Most of all?

The pack.

Their dominance doesn't scrape my spine in threat, triggering a fight or flight.

Some part of me *knows.*

Whether they take or give control, Meadows Pack is mine to command

I open a hand to Reese. He knows what I want, pumping me a palmful of lube.

I slick Dutch's straining shaft, gliding up and down to coat the hard length I can't surround with my fingers. He pulses like a hummingbird under my palm.

The excess lube drips beyond his balls. When the wetness kisses the tight ring of his ass, Dutch clenches. Then his ass pulses open. Closed. Open again. Helplessly twitching in hungry little nibbles

"More," Dutch croaks.

I can't deny him what he wants.

I want it too

Scraping across the sheets, I reach for a toy. A slender, matte black plug the length of a finger.

"You're underestimating him." Reese stops me, trading my choice for a bigger, thicker option.

Much bigger.

Bishop smacks down his wiggling arms. "Be good and show our queen how much you can take. No orgasm until she gives permission."

I choke, pulling back the vibe. "You can tell me if you need to stop."

"*Cute*" Jin purrs a laugh. "Stop isn't in Dutch's vocabulary. He'll let you fuck him to death by dehydration."

Without the vibrator scrambling his brain, Dutch's glassy eyes clear. Gentle sunshine piercing clouds, his smile sweeps my heart. "*Yesss* Fucking juice me forever, Solly. I love everything you do"

"Just until breakfast." Jin secures Dutch's thigh. "We can last as long it takes to satisfy our mate."

That *we* hits as hard as the Meadows' screaming scents.

Silk chocolate, dripping peach, and stormy ocean, plus the succulent, candied bacon I want to suck off my palms.

Their desire demands an answer, but I can't share my perfume without insta-killing the vibe of their happy nest.

I batten my hatches, shutting down any possible response from my body

That's enough thinking.

Working Dutch double-handed, I grind the vibe to his knot while I kiss the plug to his welcoming hole. Then all I care about is drawing out more of his ragged, strangled moans.

But the plug is so *thick.*

Teasing isn't enough to force it inside.

"Grease him up." Reese pumps lube on Dutch's balls.

As he squirms, I spread the slickness.

"Good," Reese coaxes. "Work it in little circles. Then thrust both at once? He'll take you like a champ."

"Like this?" I vibrate Dutch's knot and stretch against his rim, moving both toys in synced circles.

"Look at him," Reese purrs. "Makes me wanna trade positions"

My grip slips at the thought of Reese underneath.

Shhhhit.

Biting my lip, I fix my grip to thrust.

The plug sinks deeper, its tip almost inside. Alternating pulsing the plug and vibing Dutch's knot, I tease him to the beat of his happy, dying moans.

When the plug *streeeeeetttttchhhes* Dutch wide, almost home, I crank the vibration. "Show me how you come."

"*Ohfffffuuuu—*" His ass swallows the plug.

Dutch comes twitching. Bucking. Painting his own abs.

I push the plug to the hilt and rock it to settle its seal. When the toy drags against his walls, his muscle-spasms pulse my fingers, connecting us. Like I'm feeling him from the inside.

Dutch can't drive onto me while the guys have him pinned, but he pulses and flexes his ass, greedy for more.

I'd do the same if we flipped the script. If I were on my back for dark-mode Dutch, who probably *gives* even better than he takes

Held down by my alphas. Clit teased. Pussy fucked.

Dutch's groans hide my desperate whimper. I run the vibe along his shaft before my traitor hands can steal it for myself.

Maybe Dutch can take more.

I can't.

Going for the kill, I dial the power until the vibration numbs me from fingertips to tongue. Then, I run the rocket-powered vibrator up and down Dutch's straining shaft.

"Gon— Gonna*nh*"~ Dutch flails. *Fuhhk* Gonnacomea-gainnnohfuckfuckfuckfuckfuck. *Fuck me.* Hafto. Haf—*Haaaa* Plee — Can I? Can—*uhhhh*. Please. Pleasepleasepleaseeeee."

I choke on his scent.

Dutch spills a constant stream of pre-cum. His abs are a fucking mess. But no matter how I milk his shaft, he only twitches

Begs.

"He's waiting for permission," Bish whispers.

"Solly." Leaking tears, barely lucid, Dutch beams me the sweetest smile. "Am I… Do… *Nnh*. Doing good?"

My belly pulses.

Barely breathing, I pump the vibrator against the base of his plug, rumbling him so deep his eyes cross.

A sultry voice scrapes out from my soul. "Good boy."

"*Sollyyyyy,*" he moans

"Come for me"

Dutch bellows.

Ropes shoot to his chest. But he keeps pumping, pumping.

More.

Again.

Again

Syrup glides down my throat.

"Mate." Dutch snaps his teeth, throwing himself against the guys' restraining hands. "Knot. Bite. *Unnnnnnnh.*"

Pins and needles stab my throat, half ticklish, half tearing.

Breathe.

Don't lose it now.

The other Meadows grind Dutch into the mattress while I ride him over the crest, trying to empty him by working the vibe. But there's no such thing as empty with this alpha.

When my arm starts to tremble from working the vibe, I sink back on my knees.

The base of the plug twitches deep between his cheeks.

Do I take it out?

Leave it there?

Go thirty more rounds?

Dutch has the stamina. Panting, his ribs glazed in maple bacon, Dutch *begs* for more with his perma-hard cock waving like a fresh-stuffed deli sausage.

"Look what you fucking did to him," Reese's rasp drags my skin like teeth

A phantom bite stabs my throat at the center of my scars.

That fast, a familiar, squeezing choke cuts the haze of desire.

Jin must sense my panic brewing. "Time for breakfast?

"Yes." I cop out before my airways can narrow.

"Go get cleaned up." Jin pats Dutch's thigh. "We'll take care of Dutch"

My knees shake as I crawl off the bed. The glee of ass-fucking my alpha fights the invisible pinch in my throat.

Why?

I love teasing Dutch until I'm drenched in his scent. But at the same time, weird congestion chokes my throat until my fingers twitch. Like a plea to scrub clean.

I wobble out of the nest.

Maybe I'll never understand my body, but this morning counts as a win.

I *can* play with the pack.

As long as I take breaks to breathe and wash.

One problem.

The shower suite's door lies horizontal in the hall, thanks to Dutch's battering-ram kick.

My suitcase looks like it exploded, surrounded by towels flung in last night's disaster sequence. In all the chaos, I left my syringe case open on the floor. It only shows tubes of makeup on the top layer, but the false back is half popped out in one of its corners.

I snatch it closed and dart for the toilet cubby with the functioning lock.

Maybe I'm still panicking, or maybe I always had the peripheral vision of a freaking sunfish.

I collide with Reese.

"Whoa." With a sideways swoop that stops me cracking my nose on his sternum, Reese dances me to safety.

But the syringe case drops on its corner, cracking open like a book

Eyeliner sticks scatter and the false back pops away, revealing rows of lemon-yellow vials and a sheathe of spare needles.

Reese's grip tightens. "What the hell are those?"

"Told you I could mimic pheromones." I duck to grab the case, trying to avoid his hands *and* his reaction.

"With injections?" He sucks a breath. "I thought you meant mimicking was your gamma thing."

"It is. Partly." I can mimic, maim, kill—so many fun features that I don't want to explain while my traitor body is still humming from a fantasy.

"You've been shooting this shit? Wait. Is that why you got sick?" Reese advances, backing me into the wall.

He's not supposed to be the insightful one, but he grew up watching drugs wreck his family. I wince. "I have to—"

"*No*," Reese snarls, edging me in alpha. "You don't have to do shit."

I clutch the case to my clenching stomach. "But you like the lemon. If I don't smell like S—"

"I didn't scent lemon when I climbed between your sheets last night," he says huskily. "Didn't scent any this morning when I was fantasizing about spearing you on my knot, flipping that vibe on your clit, and making you scream my name like you remember I'm yours."

My heart quakes. "Reese…"

"See? You keep saying it like that. Like you don't want me back." His chocolate scent stabs, sharp and bittersweet. "If I'm not good enough—"

"*Don't*," I bark. When he freezes, I flip our positions, forcing *his* back to the wall. The syringe case clatters. "We had a deal. No reading into my moods."

Reese's heavy breath stirs my hair. "Then spell it out for me."

"Which part?"

Reese slides down the wall.

I stop breathing when his knees hit the floor.

He pulls my fingers to his lips, tickling them with his beard. "Do you want me or not? I can be your alpha or whatever you need me to be, but if I'm yours and you're mine, then I need you to trust me."

My throat scrapes. "I do trust you."

Always have.

Probably more than I trust myself.

Reese purrs against my fingertips. "Then trust that I'd never trade you for anyone, and let me yeet those fucking needles into the sea."

I wasn't built to say no to a Reese on his knees.

It's not like I was going to keep injecting. Last night taught me a valuable lesson about mixing mayonnaise and experimental drugs

And after this morning…

I'm in good hands with the Meadows pack.

The *best* possible hands.

I don't know how much I can show the parts of me I've always had to shove down, suppress, and mask, but if I'm going to try opening up, I want to try showing everything I am to *them* without worrying how our story ends.

Just move forward.

One breath at a time.

I press my knuckles to Reese's lips. "You can keep the case."

"I'll lob it over the equator."

"Okay."

"And one more thing?"

"Sure." *Just take it all.*

"Say my name like I'm your alpha."

I tear my fingers from his mouth and grab his cheeks so I can cop a feel of that beard while I tilt his face and force him to see what he does to me.

No more shields.

Stripped bare. *For him.* "Reese."

"Fuck yes." He grips my wrists. "Call me like that all day."

"If I'm yours, then what are you going to call me?"

Reese beams brighter than stadium lights. "You're my Solly Baby"

My knees shake. "Reese…"

"Nice. Love that one too. We'll have to play around with this." He snags the syringe case, pops up to kiss my forehead, then dashes down the hall like a little kid afraid I'm going to call take-backs on the conversation that converted my brain into nougat. "Get ready for breakfast. I'm gonna butter you so much fucking toast."

Toast?

Reese Meadows can butter me, stuff me, and drizzle me in his favorite glaze.

He doesn't need to edge me to make me scream his name.

In my dreams, I call him all the time.

Wobbling into the bathroom, I'm finally alone with the strange girl in the mirror.

She has brown eyes, sex-messed blonde hair, and too-wide pupils, shot with an impossible mix of hope, thirst, and fear.

I hope she knows what she's doing.

Because now *everyone* can see.

THIRTY-NINE
SOL

NOW THAT I'M CITRUS-FREE, my hollow stomach has demands.

I want my goddamn egg and cheese sandwich.

After a quick wash in the sink, I don't waste time designing another disguise the pack will see through, wear down, and disintegrate

Shorts, T-shirt, *done.*

My scabby ankles haven't seen the sun in years, but with all my secrets flying free, I'm letting them hang loose.

Everything but my throat. It feels too scratchy and weird around Meadows boys.

Dutch chucked a worn hoodie on top of my suitcase.

Now it's mine.

I tighten the cords, but his pancakey afterglow isn't enough to fill my stomach—or my other hungry holes.

Yeah. I'm doomed.

When I pop into the kitchen in my newly unhinged glory, Bish and Jin stare like they've been following me through the walls.

"Bacon?" Jin lifts the sizzling frying pan. An apron covers his bare chest.

I can't tell if he's wearing shorts underneath.

Not that it matters.

Jin could seduce me through a snowsuit.

I take the stool beside Bish, and Jin passes me a bacon haystack. After I mow through a few pieces, I clear my tight throat. "Any news?"

Bish stops scrolling his phone. "Jericho is awake."

My perfume claws for freedom.

Here we go.

The guys haven't reacted to my majorette show of red flags so far. Ignoring the quaver that warns to keep my shit lidded, I tentatively crack the cage. "I could fix that for you."

"Do it." A ragged purr rips from Reese, who ghosts behind my chair like he popped off of a baseball card. His chocolate isn't comforting when it's shot with sex and violence—it's *irresistible.*

"Only if you let us watch," Bish adds, ultra-casual.

I pinch my knees.

Got it.

Red flags are their favorite color.

I bail from the chair and Reese's body heat, bringing my plate to Jin at the stove. "What else are you cooking?"

"Whatever you want." His husky edge promises more than a snack

My gut squelches, queasy from the baked-in instinct to hide what I want and handle everything myself. *It's just breakfast.* "Make me an egg and cheese sandwich?"

"My pleasure," Jin purrs.

"Use the brioche. And the Jarlsberg." Bish moves to the fridge, then huffs. "Which of you savages unpacked my cheeses like this?"

Reese steals Bishop's chair. "Don't make froofy shit. Our girl likes it greasy."

"I know what she likes," Jin says.

"As do I. Use the brioche." Bish tosses him a loaf of bread, then starts organizing his cheese cache.

My gaze slips to Jin at the stove.

He hypnotizes me just breathing.

When Jin cooks for me, I'm lost.

Even Gary the grill beta never gives me that much butter. With long, slender fingers and flexing forearms, Jinnie flips a sandwich sexier than most alphas fuck.

I'm drooling by the time he presents me with the ooziest, most golden-brown, egg and cheese on the crispiest, crustiest, butter-drenched brioche.

The first bite rolls back my eyes.

Then Jin's husky rumble twists my toes. "You like?"

"I've had dreams about this sandwich." I swallow molten cheese—Jarlsberg and whatever else Bish had airlifted just to please me

He knows what he's doing.

They all know what the fuck they're doing.

"Bite?" Jin leans in.

Shivering, I offer him my sandwich.

Jin holds my gaze as his teeth *snap* crispy bread. He sticks close to chew, keeping the space he stole from me.

I take another bite through his teeth-marks.

"Share with me too?" Reese sneaks behind me.

Swallowing thickly, I can't say no.

Reese bites through my print with a buttery purr. "Next time, let me and Dutch make you the sandwich."

Yes.

Please.

"We'll take turns." Jin leans to snap another bite, careful not to touch skin.

I'd have to ask for that.

But I don't dare ask for more. I eat my perfect sandwich, trading bites between the guys until I'm licking grease off my fingers

"More?" Jin licks his lips.

"More." One more egg and cheese.

Then maybe a nibble of Jin and Reese.

Bish snags me before my teeth get me in trouble. He wipes my buttered fingers with a hot towel. "Where's my treat?"

"You don't share food."

"Let me have a bite of something else." Bish nips my cleaned knuckles

I've slept.

I've eaten.

The chemicals are purged.

So why am I light-headed?

"Solly!"

The bellow I've been expecting gives me a split-second warning I'm about to be tackled.

This time, I don't dodge.

Just let him have me.

"You're wearing my sweatshirt." Dutch hauls me on his hips with a growl deeper than the ocean. *He* notices my shorts. He slinks up the leg holes, under my panties until he's double-palming my ass. "Have to eat you up."

"Want to make her a sandwich?" Reese covers Dutch's hands, then slides around my hips until he's stroking my belly. Dutch grinds me, his ready dick hard as a toothpick.

But thicker.

Much thicker.

"Umm..." A soft voice calls from the porch. "Should I come back later?"

"You're good." Reese caresses my stomach before pulling away. "We're dressed and everything."

"Bish is dressed." I wiggle out of Dutch's grasp.

One alpha wears a vest over a collared shirt, ready to roll for high tea or oysters on the dock. The others are shirtless, painted into shorts that offer as much coverage as a tube sock.

Dany peeks around the corner, curious, but not curious enough to crash a full-on pheromone demo. "Dutch said I could help set traps. But I can go read if—"

"No. Please help." I swat Dutch's ass-grabbing hands.

She manages three steps before her nose pinches. "Are you sure?"

"Stay and eat with us." Jin dials down his scent. "We need to plan."

The guys follow his lead, clicking down their intensity.

While Jin whips up breakfast sandwiches for everyone, Bish spreads a map of the island on the dining table. I let Dutch pull me onto his lap to spare poor Dany his bulge.

Bish taps the red dots clustered over the jungle villas. "These are the villas rigged with explosives. Our reinforcements are en route, but we may as well finish wiring the perimeter to address our future bug-out needs."

"They're already on the way?" I freeze on Dutch's thighs. "What did you agree to?"

I won't let them throw away their lives.

"They moved before we could finalize the terms." Jin turns to Bish. "You want to explain?"

"I missed a barrage of calls last night." Bish pulls out his sat phone. "Headquarters left a curious voicemail."

"Wait. *What*? Since when?" Reese jerks from the map. "That's not their style."

"No. It was their mate. She said— *Shit*." An incoming call flashes before he can play the message. "Incoming call from the airstrip."

Jin's jaw tightens as he takes the phone. "Situation?"

The silence sucks the air from the room.

Dutch's legs bounce while Jin asks clipped follow-up questions, but hearing half the conversation is enough to gather that we're screwed.

My stomach swoops. They were always going to come for us.

Which enemy found us first?

By the time Jin grimly ends the call, danger needles my glands

"How long do we have?" Bishop asks.

"About two hours until the hostiles land," Jin answers. "It's an aircraft carrier. With helicopters on deck."

"So, it's the SAS." I jump off Dutch's lap.

"Our guy only spotted Triad soldiers. But it's safe to assume Kairo cut a deal with the feds or he wouldn't be rolling up like he's getting carried in a military parade." Jin turns to Dany to start dishing orders. "Grab your mom and enough supplies to last a few days in the bunker."

"On it." Dany darts off, no questions asked.

It's not her first crisis with the pack.

Jin looks to Bish. "Do we have an ETA from headquarters?"

"I've been trying to make contact. They're offline." Bish flicks through his phone. "Maybe already on the way. I'll keep calling while we run more wires. Minions, with me."

Dutch and Reese follow him out of the kitchen war room, leaving me all alone with Jin's switched-on dominance.

He doesn't order me *yet.* But the idea that he might straightens my backbone like a flagpole. "If you're about to banish me to the bunker—"

"Did you finish setting up your trap house?"

I blink, hitting cotton instead of a dominance battle. "Just about. Why?"

"You up for using your gamma skills?"

My gut churns, but it's long past the time to hide what I can do

I can't waste any more time caring what Meadows Pack thinks

All that matters is that they survive.

I meet Jin's eyes with no pretense and no lies. "I'm a walking weapon, but if I unleash, I won't be taking prisoners."

"Blood for blood." Jin closes the space between our bodies. "That's fair. They brought the fight to us."

"I won't make them bleed. I'll make them suffer."

If Jin is going to flinch, it has to be now.

My Jinnie doesn't even blink.

He cups my cheek. "What do you need from me?"

Everything.

I swallow razors to stay focused.

After this?

I'll ask him for it. "Help me set up a platform in the rafters. Then stay upwind."

"How many alphas can you take out?"

"How many are on the boat?"

Jin grins just like the blood-splashed boy who I gave my first kiss. "Show them what happens when you fuck with Meadows Pack."

My lips ache to steal one last taste of him.

That's why I hold back.

If I ever let myself have Jin?

One kiss will never be enough.

γ

JIN HELPS me carve out a sniper platform in the ruined rafters of my villa. Then he hurries to set more explosives in strategic locations around the island.

I lash tarps until my kill room is sealed tighter than Brandon's lab.

My very own nightmare prison.

Dany drops off a spare set of body armor while I work. Her gear's a little small for me, but the head-to-toe camo with bulletproof inserts gives me an extra layer of confidence ahead of the fight.

My glands tingle, ready to have some fun.

When the enemy ship is twenty minutes from land, my walkie-talkie chirps the pre-agreed signal to reconvene.

The pack gathers at the bunker—a reinforced hurricane shelter hidden under what's left of the main resort.

Last to arrive, I'm the only one without a machine gun.

Dany is strapped into a semi-automatic, and even Lisa is full-on Rambo, with ammo bandoliers strapped across her palm-tree-patterned blouse.

I'm glad they can protect themselves.

I just hate that they have to.

Good people should get to be left alone.

"Buoy cams show the main enemy force heading for the north

dock." Bish pulls up the rocking squares of video feed on his sat phone. A few of the cams are knocked out, but the rest flash the freaking *warship* steaming toward our island. "I finally made contact. Our reinforcements are a couple hours out. They had to land their jet and source a boat."

"Then we stick to Plan A. Run the clock." Jin walks us through the island map one more time, highlighting our roles and hiding spots. "Reese roams the island, the rest of us stay in our places, triggering traps unless I sound a retreat to the bunker."

"What if we all shelter in the bunker? Wouldn't that be safer?" Lisa clutches her machine gun.

"Mom. We got this." Dutch hugs her around her bandoliers. "All we gotta do is stall and run them around."

"Take care of each other," she sighs into his chest.

"That's what we do around here." Reese joins the hug and rubs her back.

After we secure her and Dany down the hatch, Jin pulls us in for a pack huddle. "We ready?"

I'm a million times more prepared than I ever was for a mission with the SAS. I know the plan, a dozen back-ups, and better yet—if shit hits the fan?

I won't be left alone to clean the mess.

We're a team.

Which is *such bullshit.*

I should be running life-and-death missions with disposable teammates. Like Bridget, Simon, Elyse, and her GigaChad mates.

They can all die.

Meadows Pack cannot.

I nod. "Ready."

"Spring traps and stay under cover. No hero shit." Jin's narrowed gaze pins the last person I'd expect to go rogue.

"I always *plan* to follow the plan." Reese stretches his shoulders until they pop. "But I've gotta get my workout."

My adrenaline fires, ready for the fight, but before I can dash to find the action, Jin snags my fingers. "No hero shit. Promise?"

"Not my style."

"Good." He curls my fingers around a walkie talkie. "I need you to stay safe"

"Same." I suck lightning-struck air, so desperate to close the gulf between our skin.

Jin's sly grin only adds to the building storm. "Is there something else you want to ask me?"

"Later." Even though the ticking clock demands that I move, I can't help following the slow spread of his lips.

"I can't wait to hear."

"But Jinnie?"

"*Yes,*" he rasps.

"It's not going to be a question." I scrape his throat until his Adam's apple spasms under my claws. "It's going to be a command'

Jin snatches my fingers for a kiss of glacier-melting heat. "You think I'll obey?"

"You will."

"Why?"

Pushing past my doubts, I hold Jin's all-consuming gaze. "Because it's me."

Jin's stroking purr seeps through my skin—a dark, velvet blanket I never want to leave. "You finally understand."

Yeah

I finally do

I've twisted myself in more knots than Bishop's ties trying to be the Marisol that could survive. While Bish protects my lies and Jin makes me forget the years without the pack, Reese needs me in his cheering section as much as I crave him in mine.

Dutch just wants to scoop my papaya and take turns getting railed

And honestly?

I want to try that too.

Meadows Pack doesn't care if I'm a boy, a girl, or a biohazard.

They don't ask me to be anything or anyone I'm not

After I smoke the island of every mafia bastard who wants to steal what's mine, we're going to have a pack meeting and figure out how to stomp the creepy-crawly throat bugs keeping us apart.

I want to believe that our bond goes beyond mates and cheap perfume

I have to believe that I can heal—not for them, but for myself.

For *us*

FORTY
DUTCH

I PROMISED I'd follow orders.

And I do—for, like, ten seconds—on my way to my post. Then my mate jogs past in body armor.

Only thing I can follow is that ass.

The idea of licking Solly—of fucking *tasting* her—has me so lit, my dick hasn't softened in days. Knot, balls, even my fucking tonsils. They *ache*, ready to take her any way she wants.

Any place. Any position.

From now until forever, even after death. Because if ghosts can fuck, I'll astral project and beg Solly to peg me on the spiritual plane

Mission adrenaline keeps me semi-focused, but even when I'm not rolling my tongue, shadow-munching my mate's funnel-cake cunt, all I think about is her.

The *real* plan is that we secretly set traps to funnel the baddies away from Solly. Another banger from the Meadows brain team.

But the instincts fucking dogsled-mushing me to trail and protect my mate don't give a wagging shit about the dots on Bishop's map.

I have to see her myself.

Make sure she doesn't evaporate.

Sneaking through the trees, I follow Solly to her villa.

She doesn't notice.

'Course Bish does.

My walkie crackles. "Which flowers would you like at your funeral?"

The asshole sounds like he's asking the weather, but let him bullshit all he wants. *I'm his favorite.*

I hit the button. "Tulips."

"Retreat to your assigned position."

"Can't. It's too far from her."

"Dutch," Jin's warning vibrates the speaker.

I power down before he can bark.

Screw the chain of command.

I'm a civilian for a few more hours, and it's bullshit they didn't put me on bodyguard duty.

If not for Kairo's threats, I would've signed a cushy deal protecting rich omegas until I banked enough to find Solly, send Dany to school, and buy Mom one of those smart houses where the fridge reminds you to pick up milk.

But somehow, I manifested a future where Solly found *me*.

Everything happens how it's supposed to.

Even Wyvern Academy.

Military school was worse than rimming Satan's boiling asshole, but now that I know how to protect my mate, I appreciate the value in being educated directly at the devil's steamy taint

After Solly ducks into her villa, I swing into the rafters of the house across the path. A sniping platform is hidden in the gable. All I have to do is wait and kill the shit out of anyone who comes knocking

Soon, choppers take the air.

One flies overhead, low to the trees.

I don't twitch.

Look all you want, motherfuckers.

Reese will find you first.

My bro isn't just a killer pitcher. He's a beast with a rocket launcher

Somewhere in the jungle, he takes aim, and a rocket goes *screeeeee*

Boosh

Shrapnel confettis the beach, and screams echo behind enemy lines, but for once I'm not worried they belong to the pack.

Reese is a cartoon action figure, and Bish and Jin are tied for biggest brain. Mom and Dany are bolted safe underground.

I have Solly in my sight.

No reason to panic.

After a second chopper goes boom, a dude in a tracksuit sneaks out of the ferns. His gold chain catches rays, marking my target like it's Christmas morning.

Kairo must've sent the Z-team.

The guy has one pistol, coke fingernails, and an obvious death wish

Once, I held a funeral for a monarch butterfly that hit my bike tire. *Bummed me out for days.*

I have much more empathy for cute little bugs than for the human-shaped shit-sacks huffing and puffing to find my mate.

I aim, then pull the trigger.

When the guy drops halfway in the underbrush, my conscience pats me on the back.

Nice.

Now he can fertilize the earth and actually contribute to our planet.

I peer through the gable slats, waiting for a fresh target while explosions pop off in the distance.

Eventually, two Triad goons step out from the trees. A smaller guy drags a bigger one, who's about to bleed out from the throwing knife buried in his throat.

Reese with the assist.

I line up to finish the kill.

But as my finger squeezes, my neck hair levitates.

I throw myself to the side.

Out of nowhere, a silenced bullet screams past my ear.

Fuck.

Didn't see that one coming.

FORTY-ONE
SOL

EXPLOSIONSRAIN ACROSS THE ISLAND.

I'm weirdly calm between booms, waiting for the firefight to find my hiding hole.

I've never been afraid of dying.

I'm afraid of being *taken*.

But more than anything, the SAS trained me how to wait. Lying flat in the rafters, I'm way more comfortable than I ever was scrunched in the back of Simon's potato-mobile.

My scent glands fire, ready to unleash.

I ease my death-grip control, leeching perfume into the tight-sealed villa below me.

A bullet whizzes outside.

That's close.

Reese is supposed to be guerilla-roving the jungle and working toward the north dock. The rest of us are hidden in strategic villas, far enough apart to blow explosives without risking friendly fire.

Pulse in my fingertips, I peel aside a tarp to check who's here to visit

A body splays across the path near my villa's gate. The torso disappears in a patch of ferns. I can't see its face, but SAS agents don't go on missions wearing white shell-top sneakers.

I track the angle of the body's fall to the only possible sniping spot—under the eaves of the villa across from mine.

My perch puts me at the same height as its gable. I squint to see who's inside, but the only motion comes from the choppers cutting across the sky.

Eventually, a Triad soldier in a tracksuit struggles through the underbrush, hauling his fatally wounded buddy. Both are scrawny for alphas, with sunken sockets and protruding veins.

They belong on a corner in the Meadows or in one of Brandon's cells.

The gable slats shift. A rifle barrel flashes, then a peek of blond ices my lungs.

Dutch.

Metal glints on the ground.

Not from the bleeding Triad soldiers.

They're the bait.

The glint flashes from the SAS agent, hidden in the brush.

He fires.

The gable implodes, and the splintering boom cracks me in half.

Forget the trap.

Forget the plan.

If Dutch—

My perfume chokes and my heart won't beat.

I drop from the rafters, already sprinting. The bait alpha scattered after he dropped his dying buddy, leaving him to bleed out.

I unleash full-force poison on the soon-to-be-dead agent who thinks he's safe in the ferns.

One whiff and he chokes, giving away his position.

I change directions.

Crawling on his stomach, the guy came ready for me in a full-face gas mask.

But I haven't been playing the long game for fucking nothing.

After years of half-assing Brandon's tests, the agent's mask filter isn't rated to handle me at my salt-the-earth.

Too easy

Flex. Choke. Gurgle

Goodbye.

I leap the body. I don't recognize the guy's face, but the tropical camo screams SAS. So do the fat-barreled tranquilizer guns strapped to his chest.

Guess who those are for?

With no shits left to give for safety, I dart across the open and bust into the villa. A weathered dresser sits under a hole in the ceiling. I climb into the rafters, cutting my palms. Not feeling a thing

My heart pumps glass.

Dutch is fine.

He has to be.

Pleasepleasepleasepleaseplease. "Dutch?"

"Get down!" Dutch rolls, dragging me into his arms on the subfloor. "Solly! You can't—"

"Shut up." I seal his lips with a desperate kiss. His answering *mmf* hits me in the ovaries. When he happily parts his lips, I shift, wanting to shake some sense into him.

But my fingers brush something hot.

Something *wet.*

I yank from his mouth, gasping. Blood slicks my fingers and drips down his cheek.

The bullet grazed his ear.

Trembling, I reach for the gash. "What were you thinking?"

What the shit was *I* thinking?

Hiding out and setting lame-ass traps.

I *am* the fucking trap.

"I have to protect you." Dutch tugs my hand. "My mate."

"No." Maybe I'm not meant to be his.

Theirs.

Anyone's.

Who gives a shit?

Dutch is *mine.*

"No?" His voice spikes. "But—"

I cover his mouth. "I'll protect you."

"*Solly.*" He licks my fingers, lapping his own blood.

"You follow me, and you do what I say. Got it?" I hold my scent but drop my shields, letting him taste the authority that gives a fat middle finger to every alpha who thinks they're still standing on top of the power pyramid.

Dutch doesn't shrink.

He traces the freckles behind my ear. "That's how it's supposed to be."

"Good." I snatch his walkie and click to talk. "Bish? Jin?"

Static answers

I stroke Dutch's hair. "We need to re-group."

I can handle the Triad.

I can even handle the SAS.

What I *can't* handle is the thump in my chest, banging the danger drums.

Commander Fissure must be royally fucking pissed to lower her noble standards and join hands with the filthy gangsters she despises even more than she hates me.

"Just tell me what to do." Dutch rubs my palm. "I'm yours."

"Cover me, but breathe shallow, and stay at least twenty feet away." I disarm his rifle and jam it to his chest. "Can you handle that?"

Dutch hugs the gun like it's his favorite stuffed animal. "I'll die before—"

"Absolutely not." I yank him by his bulletproof vest. "They'll tranq me, not kill me. But they're firing live rounds at *you* You stay hidden, and you stay alive. If they drag me off, there'll always be a chance to drag me back."

"No one's fucking taking you from me," Dutch snarls.

"Same." I drop to the ground, ready to rage.

I've got a pack to protect.

FORTY-TWO

REESE

COMMS ARE DOWN and the plan is fucked.

I go ghost, dropping choppers, Triad, and the slick SAS fucks who think they're invisible running the jungle with palm fronds plastered to their asses.

Never expected Kairo to get in bed with the feds.

They're like orange juice and toothpaste.

Like Bish and bone-in Buffalo wings.

Like Serafina Redfang and our pack.

My instincts roid-rage, knowing Sol's out there alone, but that's why I've gotta put in work.

The shadows talk to me.

I dodge tree to tree, villa to villa, weapon cache to weapon cache, unseen until I *let* the assholes with the scopes spot me long enough to dance them into a C4 surprise.

The weirdest thing?

The shoulder that screams by the third inning has no trouble tossing knives or bracing a rifle.

Maybe I picked the wrong job.

I kill mindlessly, thinning the hostiles pouring from the anchored carrier.

Everyone I've ever loved is on this island.

You want at them?

Good fucking luck.

After I clip a third chopper, I ditch another rocket launcher and take cover, clearing clusters of enemies as I circle closer to Sol's spot.

Just before I duck into a villa, my sixth sense skitters. Burnt coconut singes my beard.

"Stop"

My muscles deaden.

A girl stands in the middle of the path. Dressed in camo and runway makeup. Like those e-girl shills, paid to flash tits and trick incels into enlisting.

Business must be fucking *booming* because eight bright-eyed recruits bleed from the mist around her.

Only, there is no mist.

Just pineapple perfume, clawing down my throat, dulling my senses and making it feel *real fucking natural* to do whatever she asks

"Drop the gun." The hypnotic command tugs my bones.

Gamma shit.

I don't fight her pull, letting my gun slip as I sink deeper in the zone. My gut hasn't jangled a danger alarm this nasty since Jericho lured me into "one last job" with stalker vids and threats on Dany and Lisa.

So what if it was a setup?

Sometimes, you do what you gotta.

I destroyed his files, his guys destroyed my skeletal system.

Not a bum trade. Otherwise, we wouldn't have known he already had eyes on our fam.

I'm down for way worse than a coma if that's what it takes to frag the cock-juggling thunder cunts who cooked up those bull-shit lemon pheromones and punted my girl into the world with nothing but scars and fucking needles.

Black-ops Barbie purrs, trying to play sex kitten. "Good. Drop all your guns and kick them to me."

The command forces me to unload. I follow to the letter, but I'm not going for extra credit.

She didn't say shit about knives.

One of her soldier scouts shifts foot-to-foot with his safety off. "Babe. Orders said—"

"So? Commander will let me keep one." She twirls the hair that falls in waves over her bulletproof vest. "He's pretty."

"He's killed at least thirty of our guys."

"Really?"

I'd say her eyes sparkle, but only Sol has that magic twinkle that tingles behind my knees.

This chick sparkles like a shit-splattered nickel at the bottom of a sewer.

Gives me meat sweats.

"He'll be an asset once he's broken." Her sickly pineapple thickens. "*Come here.*"

My feet move.

I can't twitch a pinky. Can't whip out my dominance.

The closer I move, the more her scent fucks with my head—feels like sinking into a porn shop dumpster after a handful of sleeping pills on the day they swab the glory holes.

The gamma strokes my beard with black widow fingers. "I'm Elyse. Tell me your name."

"Reese." The answer rips out before I can think.

"Elyse. Reese. We're meant to be." She drags a finger down my throat. "You're much too good for that freak."

My snarl breaks free.

"*Shhhhhh* You'll love being my backup mate." Her perfume squeezes my lungs, until all I can see is her mocking gaze and the oil-slick gloss on her parted lips.

Who wants to be her backup?

I'm #TeamSolly all the way, whether I'm center field or my ass is warming her bench.

"I'll show you how a real gamma feels." Her cocktail scent violates my ear holes. "Kiss me like you mean it, Reese."

My hands obey, reaching for her.

I don't fight.

I lean *in* to the screaming compulsion that scrambles my skull.

Because the second this bitch called my sweetheart a freak?

Palmed my favorite knife.

I kiss her like I mean it.

With a blade.

Across her throat.

She sprays blood and goes down gurgling.

Her guys take aim while I'm still frozen.

Can't dodge this one, but at least I bagged the gamma who's been bullying my girl.

I grin into a gun barrel.

RIP MVP

FORTY-THREE
SOL

UNLEASHED, my pheromones storm the island.

I keep just enough control to read the wind and steer my scent away from Dutch.

As we race through the jungle, choking noises shine neon targets on my prey.

There are two types to hunt.

Triad bait alphas, stomping to grab attention, and the camouflaged SAS agents who think they're safe.

My dialed-to-eleven scent shreds their lungs. They're paralyzed before they can twitch for tranquilizer darts. I rip off their masks, precision-pumping shotgun-blast perfume.

Dutch backs me up from the trees.

Headshots, every time.

The puppy dog has perfect aim.

I guide him with hand signals, never looking back—only forward

With explosions popping off across the island, I can't afford to hold back my firepower. But when I let go of those reins, every fiber focused on flexing my scent, there's no hiding my bloodthirsty grin.

Can't help it.

I get all warm and tingly snuffing out evil fucking alphas when Dutch is on my team.

We're almost to the pack's fallback position when raunchy coconut perfume corkscrews my sinuses.

A piña colada mean girl on the prowl.

There's only one reason Elyse would pump her perfume that hard

She caught someone

Waving Dutch to keep his distance, I sprint toward the source, not caring about cover or catching a stray dart

She's not touching what's mine.

The booze-trail ends near a cluster of half-collapsed villas.

I whip out poison until my throat rips down my ribs, but I'm too late

Elyse already holds my alpha in her claws. *"Kiss me like you mean it, Reese."*

Shrapnel pumps my heart

But Reese's brown eyes shine clear. Not glassy, hypnotized like her other G.I. thralls.

When he drops toward Elyse's rotten mouth, steel flashes between his fingers.

Blood sprays.

Elyse clutches her throat with a musical gurgle I can't stop to celebrate. Her mates howl, targeting Reese.

"STOP!" I whip the command ahead of my perfume.

The alpha with the rifle in Reese's face jerks sideways.

But he's already pulling the trigger.

No gunshot has ever been so loud.

It roars through my body. Across time. An endless boom, screaming through my head as Reese's body drops.

I stagger, my scent weakening in the half-breath where my world ends. An alpha squeezes off a tranq.

The dart nails my forearm in a familiar, bruising sting.

Shit.

Dutch takes down the tranq shooter and wails into the other alphas from the cover of the trees.

I rip out the dart and control my pheromones while I can. I know how fast the SAS tranqs work. I have a minute, maybe seconds, to get to Reese.

While Dutch mows down the helpless targets choking on my scent, I hop Elyse's thrashing body and drop to my knees. "Reese!"

He groans, lashes fluttering.

Shaking, I reach for his red-spattered sleeve.

So much blood

"Say something." I rip away his shirt, desperate to check the damage

"Mouthwash," he coughs weakly. "Chick's breath stank like shitty frozen drinks."

My vision spins with sedatives and the hot wash of relief. "It's your pitching arm."

Reese's melted chocolate smile floods me with a different kind of heat. "Blow on it?"

I wobble

He's okay.

Everything's okay as long as they're okay.

Dutch drops behind me, steadying me between his knees. "If anyone's getting blown—"

"Can you walk?" I hold my spinning forehead.

"Solly?" Dutch hugs my hips. "What's wrong?"

"Tranq. I—"

"You were hit?" Reese snaps upright. "Where? Show me."

"No time." I brush off the growly alphas. "We need to find Bish and Jin and take cover. Just pick me up if I start to go down."

I've been sedated enough to know the drill. I hold my temple, determined to stay clear-headed and protect the guys, but even though my sight fuzzes to shit, I'm nowhere near blacking out.

It should only take seconds if the dose was tailored for me.

Either Doctor Brandon brewed the wrong recipe, or pumping myself full of fake pheromones jacked up my tolerance for seedy chemicals

I don't care why, as long as I'm still a threat.

"I'll carry you." Reese moves to pull me onto his back. Like my contact high is a more serious problem than his bullet hole.

"Tourniquet." I smack Reese's fingers. His wound isn't fatal, but I'm not leaving him bleeding.

Dutch passes me a rope from his belt. I loop it around Reese's upper arm until it's tight enough to cut his circulation. Then, I'm finally sane enough to check the area.

Elyse isn't moving—*hope she never does again*—but even though her eyes are shut?

Her body cam blinks at me.

Awareness claws my spine.

Shit. How could I forget about the cameras?

"Run." I push Dutch and Reese ahead of me.

Before I can flex my scent, I taste fake sugar on the wind.

Zzp zzp zzp zzp zzp zzp zzp zzp!

Darts fly thick as mosquitoes. One pings my chest plate. Another grazes my arm, but doesn't pierce my sleeve.

I try to dodge.

Never fast enough.

My thigh stings when a hot needle pierces my quad. Heat flashes from the spot, washing through my arteries. I pluck it out, but another dart pierces my hand. My fingers deaden.

Sedatives surge until the world drags.

Reese and Dutch roar, until they don't.

Pin-cushioned and fading, they can't keep pace ripping out the needles. As my heart slows to a sloshing chug, they drop.

Camouflaged figures ooze from the trees. The smallest one breaks formation

"Medic!" Commander Fissure races to Elyse. "Get her on a ventilator. She has a pulse."

The air goes sludge.

My thoughts foam.

Even then, the drag is too slow. I've been hit so many times, I should be a puddle, but my consciousness holds.

I put on one last show, closing my eyes and falling to the ground before the knock-out drugs shut me down.

Then I watch.

Predictable as shit, SAS agents swarm to save their favorite gamma. Dutch and Reese sag forgotten in the dirt.

They're just sedated.

They'll live.

I vaguely hear a helicopter landing.

"Secure Twenty-Six." Bridget's voice echoes down a well.

"And the males?" Silas answers, fading.

"Leave them for the Triad. We've accomplished our objective."

"Yes, Commander."

Rough hands haul me into the chopper. I'd smile if my body weren't so far away.

Meadows Pack will survive.

So will I.

I've got the drug tolerance of a pissed-off elephant and no more reasons to play sweet and follow the rules.

If the SAS wants me to be a weapon?

Let's fucking go.

I'll bring the fight to them.

FORTY-FOUR

JIN

WE WIRED the island with enough charges to roast Kairo's cannon-fodder soldiers *or* deflect a special forces assault.

Not both.

All these years of scheming an escape from my father's world, and I never would've called the Triad coming after us with a military assist.

Now we're desperately outgunned, and I'll claw out my own fucking bones if my lack of foresight hurts my family.

With no answer on comms and no more explosives to blow, I abandon cover.

Bishop's sniper nest is closest to my position.

I'm praying he has eyes on Marisol.

I'm praying he's not down.

Triad trash give away their locations with their dying, shrapnel-blasted groans. The SAS agents are more stealth, but my dominance hammers through the jungle, freezing alphas just long enough to line up my shot.

Aim, fire, kill.

Everything turns red and green.

Blood and leaves.

Then I find Bish pinned by Triad soldiers and red is all that's left.

Three guys fire into a hole-pocked villa.

I roar.

Bang.

Bang.

Bang.

Before the bodies drop, I'm leaping through the door, heart not just in my throat, but pounding in my chest and lungs. "Bish?"

There's a rustle in the rafters.

"Almost fucking ganked by a grown man wearing velour." Bishop pops up, straightening his hair under the helmet with a quarter-sized ding in its forehead.

Too fucking close.

"Marisol?" I steady him when he jumps down.

Bishop knocks away my hand. "She went next door to visit Dutch. Then I lost video."

It's better they're together than alone, but my adrenaline churns. Nothing's worse than being helpless, not fucking knowing where my people are.

"Cover me. We'll track from their last-known location."

Bish shakes himself, reloads, and follows me, ready for fucking war.

I run toward the gunfire.

Strange perfumes crisscross the jungle. Too sweet, then too sour.

Suddenly, the constant drone of chopper blades changes tone.

"Bird landing," Bish mutters.

"Wyverns?"

"They're at least twenty minutes out."

"Hurry." I give up on stealth. But even at full sprint, I can't outrun the chopper.

We hit a pathway soaked in sour coconut just in time to watch a helicopter rising over the trees.

"Too late." Bish's voice punches my lungs.

I can't see Marisol, but I can *feel* our mate slipping away.

Dutch and Reese sprawl in the dirt. I drop between them, hearing nothing but rotating blades and the punishing thump in my chest.

I should've fucking listened to Dutch.

If we'd done a blood ceremony to bond the pack, I'd know they're alive. My body shuts down when I grab Reese's wrist, praying he has a pulse.

Finally, I find his sluggish heartbeat. "He's breathing."

"Dutch too." Bish plucks a tranquilizer dart from the grass. "Sedatives"

"Check for more needles." I pluck out half a dozen darts buried in Reese's clothes while Bish glares at the sky, holding on to Dutch's throat.

Counting heartbeats to keep himself from falling apart.

I have to be the rock.

For him.

For Marisol.

For our future pack.

No one takes what's mine.

"Bish," I bark. *"Pull out the darts."*

The command rattles him into motion.

Ripping out needles, Bish snarls. "I'm going to fucking *ruin* every motherfucker who had a hand in this conflagration."

"We," I correct. "We'll ruin them."

Wyvern House can have my ass, my soul, and everything I own as long as they lend me the power to bring my mate home.

Jericho cackles from my subconscious.

Fucking loser. You failed your pack. Again.

Fury has me strangling my brother's sorry-ass monologue.

Marisol is *mine.*

I've tasted her lips, and I'll wait as long as she needs to remember where she belongs. Whether she asks me to take control or unleashes that dark gamma compulsion and fucking *commands* me to give her what she craves.

I'll always find her.

We're inevitable.

"Grab Reese and follow me," I order, not giving Bish the time to despair.

Dutch weighs the same as a bull rhino, but I haul his ass to the resort while Bish shoulders Reese, muttering plans for revenge.

When we hit the main property, my heart untangles, finding the bunker hatch undisturbed. I drop Dutch. "Signal the girls to unlock. We'll get them to safety and go after Marisol."

Bish is knocking in sequence when another wave of chopper blades cracks the island's silence.

A fleet speeds from shore in a flying V. All black machines. Unmarked

Wyvern House.

Finally

I launch a flare.

Attack choppers sweep the island with mounted machine guns. A double-bladed transport helicopter races toward my signal.

Bish helps Lisa and Dany from the hatch.

I wait

Everything moves too slow, except the crackle under my skin.

Before the chopper lands on the plaza, four alphas hit the ground. Their boots *thud*, as heavy as their dominance signatures.

Wyvern House is more than a mercenary group.

The heirs take no shit, obey no rules, and get the job done—by any means they want

Exactly my fucking mood.

We trained at Wyvern Academy, but even though we ran missions with their pack, we are not *friends*.

These are the alphas who flame-tempered us for four years, kicking our pack's collective ass until we could dodge Finn Wyvern's throwing knives in the dark.

Now, Finn winks at me across the plaza.

Atlas and Hunter Wyvern approach me together. They're forged from the same massive mold as Dutch but dipped in iron instead of a candy shell. I can't read which is their reigning pack-leader when either has the chops to bark down a charging grizzly

Jett hovers behind them, silent and icy as ever, but I'll volunteer to hold his pliers in the interrogation chamber.

If we make this alliance, we're all-in.

Anything it takes to bring my tomcat home.

I meet them halfway, fighting dominance with dominance. "Our mate was taken. Headed due north, about twenty-five minutes ago. Track them on satellite and pull strings to find their destination. I need my family lifted to safety and a medic to treat my guys. I'll sign whatever deal you want when we're in the air."

Setting my jaw, I clench for push-back.

Instead, the Wyverns' red-headed demon chuckles. "Daddy? Is Jinger Spice our new leader?"

"Finn!" A pocket-sized female omega leans out from the chopper. "Stop screwing around and help, or you'll miss the high-speed chase. We have to go after Sol!"

Green eyes lighting with evil glee, Finn dashes past me. "Dibs on Dutch Baby."

I whirl to stop him from scaring the girls, but Atlas is already tailing his ass. Hunter thumps my shoulder. "Hop in. Questions can wait."

"Thank you." I grip my burning chest.

"Thank our mate." He brushes me off. "Turns out, your Marisol is Lilah's missing Sol. We're practically pack-in-laws."

Gratitude churns against the current of my rage, but I grit it down and get to business. We can't waste time.

With the Wyverns' help, Dutch and Reese are hauled into the chopper. A medic lays them out and relays their vitals to Bish.

Meanwhile, Lilah Wyvern helps Dany and Lisa into bucket seats, offering them headsets and gentle words.

I move toward her.

Five glares stab as soon as I take a step. I was expecting it from the alphas, but not from Orion.

Tall and blond, the Wyverns' original male omega snakes an arm around Lilah's waist like a serpent protecting his branch.

He didn't just hang around.

He grew fangs.

But I don't give a fuck about the Wyverns' pack dynamics.

All that matters is that Lilah is genuine about protecting Marisol. After ten seconds onboard, it couldn't be clearer that the badass mercs run on her orders.

I stop a few steps away from her—while Finn is only fingering his knife and not whipping it out. "You left the voicemail."

"Who took her?" Lilah's grey eyes storm, and her caramel perfume scrapes my sinuses.

I've lived with criminals and with Bishop Barrington.

I can tell most lies from the truth.

Lilah's concern feels real.

I clench my fists and let her see the matching storm in my soul. "The SAS and the Triad. Both need to pay."

"She says *I* get in too much trouble," Lilah mutters.

"We'll find her." Atlas sweeps the omega the size of his quad into his arms. Purring. Stroking. Comforting.

The sound that melts Lilah's tension rips into me like saw blades

I can't offer my mate the same.

I don't know where the fuck she is.

If she's conscious.

If she's suffering.

As the chopper lifts off and tears north, I strap into the tech chair. "Get me on your satellite."

Wherever Marisol was taken, I'll find her.

Then we'll set the place on fire—*together.*

FORTY-FIVE
SOL

AIR HAS a special flavor in the SAS underground.

Part plastic, part antiseptic, and part despair.

Between my sledgehammer headache and the groggy malaise of tranquilizer, I'm in no rush to experience hell. I don't have to open my eyes to know I'm already there.

My body lies flat, but either I'm dizzy or tripping balls, because I swear I'm on the move.

"Her pulse is erratic. Are you positive the sedation is holding?"

"Doctor Brandon said not to administer more until we've assessed the damage. She's had enough to keep her down another hour."

I vaguely recognize the voices as Brandon's assistants. Chad or Thad and the other dryer-sheet smelling beta who always draws my blood.

As I become more alert, I'm careful not to twitch and raise my pulse. I'm being rolled somewhere on a hospital bed, with ropes or tubes crisscrossing my skin.

The betas huff as they push.

"Why is it all the way down here? Place gives me the creeps."

"Be glad for the opportunity. This is cutting-edge research."

"Don't you ever feel bad for her?"

"For Twenty-Six?" The beta snorts. "You've seen her tapes. We're doing the world a favor."

Twenty-six is the number of times I'm about to kick through this asshole's teeth.

No rush

Playing dead, regaining my senses, I let them do the legwork while I wait for the time to strike. The wheels roll until we must've crossed football fields underground.

As we move deeper, a strange sensation snags behind my breastbone

My throat crawls, shooting an involuntary twitch from my scalp to my baby toenails.

"Is she…"

"Standard response. It's good news. The control bond is holding"

I'm still wondering which bond he means when a scanner beeps. The betas stop somewhere that reeks of dry rot—with a moldy, grassy scent that almost claws a whine from my throat.

Rusty fish hooks tug at my ribs.

What the hell?

"How many vials of blood were ordered?"

"Two from each. One now, and one after the re-exposure period. Set the timer for thirty minutes."

"Can we wait upstairs? I'll buy you a coffee."

"Fine. Just get it done."

Brandon's assistants clink around, while I pray they don't check my pulse. Adrenaline fires.

Suddenly hyperaware, I feel every touch.

My breezy hospital gown. The dizzy draw of blood from the port at my wrist. The familiar manacles weighing my ankles.

It gets worse.

My chest.

My throat.

The crawling congestion.

The sickening, impossible yank, deep inside.

It can't be

When the lab door bangs shut, I'm left alone with a ticking timer and my racing-to-the-bottom thoughts.

The drugs have faded enough that I *could* move, but I'm not acting for the surveillance cams when I lie frozen, terrified to face another killer truth.

My throat spasms.

Not because I'm being touched.

More like the memory of a noose.

But it's not a memory.

It never was.

Mother. Fucking. SHIT.

My eyes shoot open.

There's nothing special about the lab. Stainless steel tables. Beeping machines. It's all mad-science standard, except for what I sense behind the dividing curtain.

Tearing wires, feeling nothing but bony fingers hooked in my marrow, I leap to rip the curtain off its track.

I find four beds.

Four bodies

Four alphas I already fucking killed.

A horsefly hums between my ears.

They're husks. Burn-scarred. Unrecognizable. Running on ventilators and feeding tubes. Alpha-shaped lumps of barely breathing mud.

I only recognize them from the pull in my chest

Orlov Pack.

My mates.

Their scents are gone. Their muscles withered. I can't read emotions through the bond that never fully settled, but the horrific, half-formed cord they forced has never disappeared.

How?

I stumble to the packleader's bedside, blindsided, hamstrung, and building a slow-burn rage.

Rance Orlov deserves to be a corpse.

But the ventilator that breathes for him keeps his dead-grass blades piercing my soul.

I grip the bed rail, shaking, trying to figure where my timeline went to shit.

The Orlovs drugged me into heat.

Rance and Tommy stole their bites.

A partial bond formed, but before they could unzip and make it permanent, my pheromones sparked. I awakened as a gamma instead of an omega they could thrall with their barks.

They were down before I knew what I'd done or what the pheromones meant.

I took the candle they left burning to set the mood in their nest.

Ran away

Set fire to their place instead.

I wandered out of the smoke, bleeding, half in heat, and staggering on a dozen broken bones. An SAS van appeared.

When I was clear-headed enough to look back, I figured I'd lost time between the trauma and trying to rip out my throat.

The SAS couldn't have been waiting for me to fuck up.

They couldn't have been watching me all along.

Sitting back, letting me be kidnapped, auctioned, forced to bond

Bile climbs my throat.

I never felt the bond snap.

If anything, *I* snapped those next few days and weeks, clawing my neck until I hit glands and arteries and almost bled myself out.

Instead of explaining where I was or what was happening, Doctor Brandon bound my wrists and put me to sleep.

Maybe some part of me knew the mate bond was still inside, poisoning my body. Maybe trauma made it scar and stick instead of healing.

Kind of lost my chance to follow up.

I was busy dealing with gamma shit and going out of my fucking mind in military prison.

Meanwhile, the SAS recovered the Orlovs' still-breathing bodies

My mother kept my mates alive.

No.

What mother?

What mates?

Commander Fissure rescued my attackers and fed me lies.

She called me a murderer so I couldn't run.

She let me believe I'm a freak who can't go into heat, let me be hated, let me think I'd never be able to mate, and that I'm too dangerous to live unsupervised.

So I'd never escape her control.

My scars pulse like zombified flesh.

I was never a bond widow.

I was *bonded.*

That's why the creepy-crawlies choked my throat and shut me down every time I thought too hard about an alpha's teeth.

That's why I could only go so far with Bish and Jin and Dutch and Reese.

Because my body thought I was *cheating.*

On my "real," half-barbequed mates.

The Orlov claim seeps down my throat, thick as liquid shit.

The cage inside me rips off its hinges.

But behind those bars?

I was never a monster.

Just a girl who wanted to survive.

Finally free of the lies and shackles, I bleed my perfume.

The Orlovs are just skeletons wrapped in jerky. Faded nightmares with no power, now that I'm face-to-face with the truth.

I pop their air tubes, triggering frantic alarms and trading their pumped oxygen for the death they deserve.

Seems anti-climactic

No choke or retch or death rattle to confirm they're gone.

Should I slit their throats?

Just to make sure?

Before I can source a scalpel, something else cuts the cord.

With a cataclysmic *snaaaap,* their leftover soul-hooks disintegrate. The backlash hits like a volcano planet, slingshotting my ribs

White-hot air *oofs* from my pancaking lungs.

I lean into the whiplash like its phoenix fire.

Years of sludge cook off, leaving me light and free and finally comfortable breathing in my skin.

I'm finally *me.*

For two glorious seconds, I'm the Marisol I was always meant to be

Then I start to boil.

My temperature spikes beyond volcano—lava surging through my veins and pooling in the pit of my belly.

So.

Freaking.

HOT.

Almost like—

No fucking way.

My heat? This soon?

No no no.

Not here. Fissures will toss me behind bars with a fresh pack of nightmare alphas.

I have to get off base.

I'm not doing this without my Meadows.

Alarms blare.

But they've *been* blaring.

Last time I tried to escape, enforcers put me on my ass in a minute flat.

Where are the guards?

Just in time to answer, the door flies open. With my body cooking, there's no such thing as control.

Just *heat.*

My flames could blow through a battalion.

The lab assistants collapse in my scent cloud. Thad goes down seizing and foaming. The heat boils my control, but I fight for it, gritting my teeth as I grab the other, still-breathing beta by his lab coat. "Why?"

"Be—" he chokes, "Because—"

"Why would you keep them alive?" I shake him. "What the fuck did I ever do to anyone?"

Is it so wrong to *exist?*

"Control," he gasps. "Doctor Brandon said. Stop you. Taking mates. Fi—fighting back. Escape. Too—too dangerous. Just like. Just like—" His eyes bulge.

My safety's broken, and what little empathy I had left died with those four corpses. Instead of pulling back, I bark, "*Just. Like. Who?*"

"Your father," he gasps, then collapses.

I let his body fall.

So that's why

Bridget, motherfucking-not-a-mother, Fissure.

My belly cramps.

Every alpha who's not one of mine better get the fuck out of my way while I run.

But if I run into Bridget first?

I've got some shit to say.

Fighting the disgusting sear of beta pheromones, I snatch the assistants' security badges and the controller for my cuffs.

Wobbling, I hit the button to loosen the straps. I can barely stand long enough to kick free.

I stagger into a hallway blurred like it's smeared in grease, vision fractured between leftover drugs and the building heat.

Alarms scream. Warning lights flash.

It's too loud, too bright, too *hot.*

The chaos claws my insides.

I want to be somewhere dark and safe, where the only sounds are my alphas' heated breaths.

A clawing cramp staggers me into the wall.

I can't think. Can't plan.

Just go. Get out.

Freedom is so close.

I'm not dying in this cage.

FORTY-SIX

JIN

MINUTES DRAG and hours last forever.

We jump from the Wyverns' helicopter to their jet, tearing toward the mainland.

She's gone.

Gone.

Orion curses. "They jammed sat comms after they ditched their chopper."

"Is there a flight plan?" I lean over his shoulder as if I can claw into the tech panel.

The omega tenses, but I can't scent his perfume.

Only Marisol's. Phantom lemon, lodged deep in my throat.

"It's classified." Hunter whips out his cell. "I'll try to pull strings, but any ideas in the meantime? It's not that we don't know where the SAS has facilities. Problem is, they have a shit-ton of hidey holes. We can't hit everywhere at once."

I've got a few ideas.

First, put my father on ice.

Then, scrape the Triad ink off my knuckles with a cold blade and use it to slit my brother's fucking throat.

But ideas about where my mate was taken?

Nothing.

I clench my fists until my joints pop. "Use any means to find her. I'll repay the favor. No matter the cost."

"It's not like that, J." Hunter pats my shoulder. "We're family now."

"Even then." My blood rattles like the moment before the bell at a cage match, only there's no enemy to savage.

Bish flags me from the back of the jet.

His hairstyle is fucked and leaves cling to his body armor. He hasn't changed out of mission gear. He hasn't even hung up his phone since we took off, busy calling favors from everyone we've ever met. Anyone with ears inside the government. Anyone who might've heard a whisper about where the SAS hides its gammas and research.

Thank fuck we have some connections.

Without the Wyverns, we'd be stranded, roaring at clouds.

I join Bish next to the reclined seats holding Dutch and Reese. They're finally twitching.

"Solly," Dutch moans.

"Easy." I check his pulse, then rub his throat. I don't want him to rush and hurt himself, but I need to know what he knows.

While he fights the drugs, Reese snaps upright, grabbing for his gun

Finding his hip empty, he meets my gaze, dead-eyed. "They took my baby."

"Who? Did they say where?"

"SAS bitches. *Fuck*" Reese grinds his bandaged arm. "I think I killed a gamma. They tranqed us. I went down before I saw what happened to Sol."

"You did good."

Reese snorts. "Bullshit."

"You did. You came back alive." I palm his head as I soothe Dutch's groans. "Now we've got Wyvern House in our corner. We'll find her."

I say it like I believe.

I have to believe.

"Fuck it. Where's Finn?" Reese staggers from his seat. "He always wanted to teach me how to skin a guy. Feels like the right fucking time to embrace the goddamn darkness."

"Bedroom." I nod to the back of the jet.

Reese steadies as he walks down the aisle. When he knocks, I glimpse through the door crack before Finn flashes to block what's behind.

Atlas—the stone-cold commander who made us run seven miles of suicide sprints for skipping class to call Dany on her birthday—cradles his mate in his lap, whispering gentle reassurances

Lilah nuzzles his throat.

The sight stabs sharper than Finn's bladed snarl.

When we find Marisol.

When she's ready to come into my arms, not just willing, but *eager* to take everything I want to give.

I'll take care of her.

Just like that.

"When?" Bishop jumps from his seat. "No. *No* Don't move. Hold on." He covers the phone. "There's movement at the hospital. Kairo's there with Jericho. Someone spotted Triad soldiers smuggling in a blonde."

My heart kicks, then crashes.

The timing's wrong unless the SAS has gammas who can teleport.

But it's a lead.

And Kairo's been dealing with the feds.

We can claw something out of him.

A contact.

A location.

Maybe his fucking liver. "We'll head to the city."

"We infiltrating?" Reese dashes back to us.

Finn follows, tempted by the promise of murder. "Why infiltrate when we can firebomb the fucker?"

"Get Atlas." I hurry to grab Hunter. "Let's plan our attack."

I lick my teeth.

It's time to settle business with my father.

When we bring Marisol home, there'll be no more threats.

Then my tomcat can finally sheathe her claws.

γ

THE WYVERNS GET shit done for us on a massive scale.

Their pack pours out resources like my brother pops pills, shutting a city block to trap Kairo. Their guys on the ground bag trucks of Triad soldiers. By the time we touch down on the hospital helipad, the building swarms with agents in Wyvern House's trademark black camo.

Power is fucking beautiful.

While the Wyvern omegas hold down comms, Atlas, Hunter, Finn, and Jett storm the stairwell with our pack.

Me, Bish, and Reese helped ourselves to semi-automatics from their armory.

Dutch took a machete.

He's barely said a word since he shook off the sedatives. Only asked about Marisol, then numbly listened to Finn's talk about skinning

"There was some kind of incident downstairs," Atlas calls. "Let's move."

Reese bulls through the door. "Let's fucking go."

Snarl echoing to the basement, I sprint ahead.

I want blood. "Kairo is mine."

Reese follows close. "I want Jericho."

"All yours." Whether we smother them or slit their throats. Today's the day we finally cut the fucking cord.

"I just want Solly." Dutch's sigh ghosts down the stairs.

"Soon." Bish pats our golden retriever's bouncing shoulder, uncharacteristically affectionate. "The tulip prince can never crumble"

We're all a little fucked up right now.

"Not crumbling. I'm fucking pissed." Dutch leaps a landing, waving his machete.

"Time to do something about it." I shoulder through the door.

The hospital's VIP program caters to the rich and dirty. It's usually overstaffed with omega nurses in tight uniforms.

Now it's empty, except for the Wyvern agents clustered around a stretcher in the hall.

When they part, my rage condenses to a molten mass.

Kairo Moon is already dead.

His ripped shirt is missing buttons. Blood spatters his arms, mauled face, and the white of his stress-bleached hair. Unmoving, unbreathing, he looks frail and unthreatening.

Weak

I was expecting a throw-down battle with the invincible alpha who dictated the rules of the underworld and the course of my fucked-up childhood.

He lost before I could win.

But the victory means nothing.

With nowhere to vent, I choke on trapped fury. "*Where. Is. My. Mate.*"

I stalk forward. Kairo's lip is split. He's beaten to hell, but the blood on his knuckles says it wasn't a one-way fight.

The lead agent flicks his eyes to the room across the hall. "She.."

My mind blanks.

Not breathing, I rush into the suite.

A blood-stained sheet drapes the body on the bed.

The room is torn apart. Ripped out cabinets. Broken machines smoking

Blood *everywhere.*

Something rattles.

Maybe it's my lungs.

But I must be breathing after all, because perfume blasts my brain stem.

Acid lemon.

Familiar but strange.

It can't be her.

It can't be

Before I can gather the balls to lift the sheet, a voice slurs. "That better be my coconut water. Your room service is fucking atrocious"

I leap a tipped crash cart, following that sound.

Pack at my heels, I kick the bathroom door.

A blonde omega slumps handcuffed under the sink.

Also familiar.

Also strange.

"You must be Fuckboy's fake brother." Missing teeth, the girl sprays blood on her F's. Her eye is swollen shut, but she grins through bruises and gore.

Omega stress pheromones fume like lemon vodka.

I see the resemblance.

The cheekbones. The sharp eyes.

I snort, clearing out lemon that tastes nothing like my tomcat's cakey sweetness.

There's no pull. No resonance.

My blood doesn't hum for the girl on the floor.

Not mine.

I growl. "Serafina"

"I'd shake your hand, but..." Her cuffs rattle the pipes. "Get me the key, a morphine drip, and a plastic surgery consult. Then we'll talk."

"Reese. Find a key." I breathe through my burning throat. "Where's Marisol?"

Savaged, surrounded by strange alphas, Serafina doesn't flinch. "I want drugs and coconut water."

"Where is she?" I bark.

My patience is for my real mate.

Not this fake.

Serafina sucks a breath through the gaps in her teeth. Instead of answering, she tightens her jaw until it clicks. After a few hissing breaths, she shakily exhales. "Fucking alphas. You're all the same. All bark, no manners."

I don't retract my dominance until Serafina starts to shake, sweating through blood. It's not all hers—Kairo's peppercorn and Jericho's pond water swirl with Serafina's hard lemonade—but *enough* is hers. The more Serafina resists, the more she pales. I have to let go or risk her passing out.

She has the information, so she has the power.

For now.

I holster my whip, swallowing a slicing growl.

When she relaxes, Bish swoops in. He's so intent that his boots smudge the blood freckling the floor tiles. "I'll give you a private island of palm trees and the key to the hospital pharmacy. What happened to our mate?"

"An island, the key, and someone find my fucking teeth." Serafina licks blood from her swollen lips. "I'm going to shove them in my father-in-law's orifices."

"Nice. We'll be tooth fairies." Finn yanks Dutch back into the hospital room swarming with Wyverns while Bish and I breathe heavy air, waiting for Reese to find a key.

Serafina doesn't make a sound until Reese returns and lets her free. Then she hisses, carefully disentangling from the sink pipe.

"Jericho's ripped-out throat." Reese jerks his chin. "That your work?"

"So was his spine." Serafina grins, oozing blood between her teeth.

Reese whistles. "You cut his brakes?"

She winces, pushing upright. Her leg is twisted, and she favors obvious broken fingers. Every shift hits another injury, but I don't swing protective for the omega.

Wariness tenses my shoulders.

Serafina Redfang is some kind of victim, but she reads like a feral raccoon. She doesn't care if she can win. Corner her, and she'll claw out your eyes.

"What happened?" I keep my voice even. Not threatening. Not coaxing. *Neither will work with this omega.* "How did you end up here?"

"Fabulous question." Serafina pushes her blood-streaked ponytail over her shoulder. "Stop Nikolaj Redfang from finding out I survived, and I'll answer twenty more just like it."

"Done. He's dead."

Her green eyes narrow. "I don't believe you."

"Fucking cargo pants," Bish mutters, reaching into his pockets. He pulls out a gold lighter shellacked with a gaudy ruby R. "Do you believe this?"

She snatches it, ignoring broken fingers to flick the lid and summon a flame. After a long stare, she blows it out like a birthday candle, grinning like a girl whose wish came true. "How?"

"Your sister." I fight to stay even when all I want to do is shake her down for answers. "If you want to say thank you, help us bring her home."

"Ask. *Anything*" She passes the lighter to Bish, scrubs her palms on her ripped dress, and beams. "Best fucking day of my life"

"Where's Marisol?" I ask.

Serafina shrugs one shoulder. "We haven't crossed paths since she fucked up my escape plan."

"Start at the beginning," Bishop says. "Why are you here instead of her?"

"Far as I can tell? The feds told Kairo your mate was a fake. Then they did some dirty deal to work around warrants and trade us back. After they dragged me out of their bunker and bundled me into a sundress to mate my fuckboy fiancé, Kairo wanted me to mount the drugged-up motherfucker and offer him my throat. I *did* mount him, but only to offer my nail file to his carotid." She grins, winces, then grins wider. "Kairo kicked the shit out of me but didn't finish the job. His mistake."

"Wait. You iced Jericho *and* Kairo?" Reese rocks back on his heels. "How?"

She rolls her eyes. "Check the CCTV."

"I'll scan the footage. If the Wyverns can identify who transported her, we'll know who to kill." Bishop slips out of the bathroom.

"Any idea where you were being held?" I ask.

"A couple hours out of the city on a bumpy fucking road. The van smelled like trees and potato chips."

Rural narrows the location.

Better than we had.

I keep asking questions. Serafina answers, but her impressions of the facility are so vague, they're no help finding Marisol.

The longer she talks, the more she sways.

Enough. My muscles fire, ready to move. "Can you walk?"

"Morphine. Oxy. Give me the good shit and I'll dance."

"I'll send a doctor." Leaving Serafina and her eye-itching lemon behind, I flag a Wyvern agent to dig the hospital staff out of hiding.

My brother's room is a horror set. All ripped wires, tipped furniture, and gore.

Reese follows me to Jericho's bedside.

Someone flipped the sheet to reveal his mangled face.

Serafina didn't stab him once or twice. She gave him new air holes, scratching and slicing enough to vent a few lifetimes of fury

Jericho was already battered after the crash. Head shaved. Eyes sunken. After Serafina's vengeance makeover, there's nothing left of the fuckboy who forced me to scrape out a life in his shadow.

Now that I'm looming over his body, there's no rush.

No thrill.

It feels the same as standing over Kairo.

Just cold satisfaction.

It's pure fucking justice that an omega brought them down, but I won't feel much beyond numb anger until we dish the same to the people who took our mate.

A *snap* fills the silence.

One by one, Reese breaks Jericho's fingers. "Gotta desecrate a corpse real quick. Don't roll without me."

"Jinnie..." Dutch approaches, holding his cupped palm far away from his body. "What do I do with these?"

"You stick them under your pillow, Dutch Baby." Finn pokes the recovered teeth. When Dutch ducks behind me like a ruffled Pomeranian, Finn's smile sharpens. "Little known fact? The tooth fairy accepts all kinds of bones. Try a femur. Bet you earn more than a silver dollar."

Snap.

"I'm down." Reese moves around the bed to Jericho's other hand. "How much for finger bones?"

"A buck three-fifty." Finn beams.

"Give them back to their owner." I pat Dutch's shoulder, then stride away, letting Reese enjoy his payback. "Be ready to move."

Wyvern Pack is clustered in the hall. I beeline to Bish and Jett, who huddle over a tablet, replaying security footage. "How many SAS sites within driving distance are located in the woods?"

Stone-faced and efficient, Jett pulls up a map. "Only two in close range. One a couple hours west. One a couple hours north."

"Even quicker if we fly." Hunter joins us, followed by Atlas. "I'll lend you Finn. We can hit both at once if we split forces."

I pinch to zoom in, but the image pixelates. "Can we access satellite imaging?"

Atlas shakes his head. "Classified. We could request access or hack the feed, but either way takes too damned long. Better to hit both locations fast and ask forgiveness later."

"Then we split." I swallow a rumble and tap the base with the thickest tree cover. I hate guessing. *Not knowing* "We'll go west. You go north."

"I'll make a few calls." Hunter rubs his palms. "Meet you on the roof."

"Let's go." I stride toward the elevator.

Bishop, then Dutch and Reese materialize at my sides. We hum at the same urgent frequency, our scents as sharp as our tension.

I rub my Triad ink until my knuckles crack, but I don't look back

Wyvern Pack joins us before the elevator shows.

With my guys and their resources, we have everything we need

Like I said

We're going to fight.

We're going to *win*.

And we're going to fucking pray that Marisol Meadows knows we're on the way. Whether she needs a rescue or orders us to sit back and watch her bulldoze our enemies, we can write the next chapter any way she wants.

As long as we do it together.

We're coming for you, Tomcat.

FORTY-SEVEN

SOL

UNDERGROUND, the base is a labyrinth. Not recognizing the empty halls, I pick a direction and move, bare feet slapping concrete

My hospital gown itches like a layer of asbestos.

Suffocating.

Heavy.

Hot.

Skin is the only thing I need touching my skin.

I stagger past endless rooms until I finally hit an elevator bank and scan a stolen badge. Buzzed inside, I jab the button for the highest floor. The tight space doesn't help instincts raging as wild as my pheromones.

I need Jin

Pack.

Touch.

Soon

As the elevator rises, a boom rattles the cables, and the patter of gunfire echoes down the shaft.

No wonder no one's coming after me.

The base is under attack.

I'd work the chaos into some grand plan, but I'm a rocket already launched, burning up and running out of fuel. I can't care where I land or who I have to blast.

I *will* break free.

Wild instinct drives me onward.

Have to find my alphas.

Only Meadows Pack can stop the painful cramps biting harder every second I'm not in their arms and nest.

I'm drenched in sweat by the time the elevator stops. It opens to a familiar garage where SAS agents swarm rows of vehicles, gearing up for battle.

Their numbers should be worrying.

But it's *really* hard to worry about anything when I'm steaming open like a clam.

Besides.

There are tanks.

Try to stop me from running away in one of those.

But someone, somewhere must've kept half an eye on the security feeds. Before I can sneak between the rows, a squad races for me with gas masks, riot shields, and tranq guns aimed.

"Masks on! Masks on! Rogue gamma on the floor!"

Their shouts and scents scream *threat*, and I'm fresh out of fuse.

There's no more rope.

No more pretending.

I'm not going to be caged.

I'm not going to be fucking *used.*

My scent boils through the garage and their gas masks. I'd blow through their ranks and flip off the security cams, but I'm not a *running* weapon. The best I can do is a slow, limping walk, clutching my stomach against the claw-blade spike of heat.

I'd be an easy target if the alphas took a shot.

But once they hit my scent, their strings cut. I breathe through my mouth to avoid their nasty pheromones.

Not *my* alphas.

Step-by-shaking-step, I take them down.

I've still got it.

I'm almost to the cars when another team appears, wearing full-on biohazard suits with built-in breathing systems.

Even then, I recognize the shapes of Bridget's mates.

Brandon leads the pack, ready with a tranq gun and a fresh set of manacles

He shoots.

The dart hits my thigh before I can dodge.

I rip it out, flexing pheromones.

He fogs his mask, spluttering. The alphas shoot, firing wide. Silas' last-ditch shot grazes my ribs through my gown, cutting a line of ice and fire.

In heavy-duty suits, they hold out longer than the last batch of alphas. My pheromones fly loose. It's easier to use them than to not.

The hardest part is moving when all I want to do is take fetal position—*preferably inside an igloo.*

I advance, sweating.

When I make it close enough to tip the alphas over, they're already on the ground.

Brandon wheezes, taking a knee. His gun fell, and his fingers shake too hard to pick it up again. He watches me wide-eyed—like he's never seen me before.

He hasn't.

Not the real thing.

My hair wild. No fake smile, because I've no plans to deal with him again tomorrow.

Even spinning with the heat, I've never been more *me.*

I bend to release his mask, but a scream kills my reach.

Commander Fissure sprints to rescue her mate. Her plastic sugar flares like corpse-flowers—sweetness twisted with rot. "Twenty-Six—"

"You gave birth to me, and you can't even say my name?" I dodge behind Brandon, loving this chance to use him as a meat shield

Bridget Fissure goes rigid—*she really didn't know I knew.* Setting her jaw, she unholsters her tranq gun. "You're that man's child. Not mine"

The garage spins

Sweat drips down my back.

I'm fading fast. But I'm not going anywhere, yet. "You can't say his name either? Even though you fu—"

"I never should've let you live." Her perfume sharpens, nauseatingly sweet.

"Agreed. You're the one who made the mistake. Not me."

I sway. I need to run, not argue.

But just once.

Just let me crack her open, one time.

She's close. Gun shaking. Blood flaming in her perfect, porcelain cheeks. "You're exactly like him. No conscience. No remorse. No shame."

"Shame? *Me?* I laugh, bitter and boiling. *Someone's been huffing their own perfume.* "I get it. You went into heat with the wrong alpha. But then you let the same thing happen to me?" I grip my stomach against the clenching, rolling cramps. "You tracked me, right? If I hadn't awakened as a gamma, you never would've picked me up that night."

"That would have been for the best. Criminal mates for a criminal's daughter." Her gun shakes with the hate slowly cracking her military mask. "Step away from my alphas. If you cooperate, this doesn't have to hurt."

My vision blurs, but I'm weirdly unhurried. With Brandon's body blocking her shot, I duck to grab his gun. "I tried cooperating. It hurt. A lot."

I get it now.

I was wasting time, pretzeling myself to be someone I'm not.

Nothing I do will satisfy this bitch.

I'll always be wrong and bad and evil.

Nice try.

She's the one who needs to look in the mirror.

Bruised and barefoot, surrounded by bodies, I lift my gun. My arms don't shake like hers. I can barely see through the haze of heat and drugs, but no part of me wavers.

"Whose pheromones do you think are stronger?" I pop open

Brandon's suit. Without the air filter, his wheeze becomes a gurgling, wet choke

Not dead. *Yet.*

Bridget trembles. "Don't—!"

"Look at me," I bark.

Crisp as a slap, her eyes are forced to snap to mine.

It's so good. "Nikolaj Redfang was an evil shit-stain, but at least he didn't pretend to be pure. I'd claim him as blood before I ever claimed you."

I don't need either of them

Got a pack waiting for me.

Somewhere.

A cramp folds me in half.

Have to get to them.

I square up

Bridget Fissure trains with alphas she brain-rapes into adoring her.

I popped my street-fighting cherry when I was twelve. After the neighborhood boys tried to steal my lunch made by Jin.

While Bridget's been basking in the sun, fun-fucking and sparring with alphas who wouldn't ruffle her lashes, I've been soloing military prisoners in the unforgiving darkness of her mate's underground prison.

We are not the same.

Maybe an ass-kicking will fix her self-awareness.

Or not.

I'll have fun either way.

Puffing out sugar with her snarl, Bridget fires a tranq.

I dodge.

Her dart scrapes my shoulder but doesn't stick. Ignoring the scratch, I charge and catch her off-balance, knocking away her gun before she can squeeze off a second shot. She twists to avoid me, but the motion shifts her bulletproof vest.

I aim for flashing skin.

Three darts hit Bridget's belly.

She struggles for my gun, lashing out with her best sucralose. Fueled by adrenaline, instinct, and a lifetime of stuffed-down rage, I hit back.

Clawing and punching.

Freaking *venting* so many years of complaints.

As the supercharged sedative invades her system, Bridget's fight dies. I knee her in the stomach, driving the darts that much deeper.

Bridget drops. A punching bag cut from her chain.

Planting a foot on her ribs, I unload the leftover tranqs in her throat. When I'm squeezing the trigger, I can't even feel the heat.

Commander Fissure is built small and she hasn't been training her chemical tolerance. After a few seconds, she topples

Then *I* almost freaking topple.

The gun clatters from my fingers, leaving me gasping in the silent garage.

As adrenaline fades, sedatives and suppressed sex hormones take turns setting me on fire and begging me to curl into a ball.

Have to run.

Hurry

With a one-finger salute for the security cams, I drag myself to the closest vehicle. Not a tank, because I can't make it that far, but some camo-colored modified military Jeep.

Sitting is worse than standing. My knees shake with every cramp, and the windshield glass ripples as I sweat.

Definitely shouldn't be driving

But I'd rather take a wrong turn off a cliff than wait for the next alpha team to show and take me down.

They'll be better armed.

And I'll be fucked even harder.

I hit the gas and tear out.

My iffy vision tunnels to a strip of dark pavement, but that's enough to get me moving. I follow the lane into a war zone.

Helicopters scream through the sky, and the red smudge in my rearview mirror isn't the heat frying my brain~~*the*~~ *base is in flames*.

Fences are down and figures in black camo dart between buildings. Flattening the gas pedal, I gun for the green stretch of trees and my last chance at ever escaping.

I tear through the downed gate, onto the tree-lined road, but I can't see the yellow lines through the pain and my shakes veer the car side-to-side.

Well, shit.

I need to go easy on the gas, but I'm out of time and brain cells, with cramps and shooting pain tag-teaming my overheating brain

A scream cuts through the blur—a person darting into the road. "Sol!"

I can barely squeeze the wheel, but I recognize her.

Someone I could never hurt.

I brake. Swerve. The tires hit the edge of the pavement, then everything flips and whirls.

Guess who forgot to buckle their seat belt?

Spinning, spinning, spinning.

The next time I blink, the world is upside down, and the heat is gone. My body icy and far away.

What just…?

The door rattles upside-down. Slowly, my head turns.

Ah. I'm on the ceiling. *Makes sense.*

"*Sol.*" A hand reaches through the shattered window.

I follow the arm and luckily, it's not mine, detached—there's a whole person connected to the shoulder.

Wet grey eyes and soft brown hair. She smells like toasted caramel and sharp, omega panic.

"Lilah? You—"

"Don't talk." She reaches for my shoulders. "We'll get you to the hospital."

"Yeah." That's a good idea.

There's more.

A thousand, million questions.

But I'm too drifty to care.

Wrecked. Rattled. Just exhausted.

"Pack," I gasp. The one important thing.

"They're coming for you," Lilah says gently, then calls over her shoulder. "Help pull her out."

Something flutters in my chest.

Maybe hope

Or maybe I'm impaled.

Either way

I can't die.

My pack is coming for me.

FORTY-EIGHT
SOL

SMOKY CARAMEL DRAGS BACK the curtain of chemically induced sleep, firing my body's alarms.

Pain.

Haze.

No more heat, but a fuzzy, dangerous warmth and sudden panic when tubes tug my skin. Pheromones spiking, I throw off a suffocating sheet.

The lab?

Nonononono.

I rise, expecting to fight another war.

Instead, I wake to an alternate reality where the best friend I've missed for years knocks over a tub of cheese puffs, springing from an armchair to the rail of my hospital bed. "Sol?"

Lilah Darling—Lilah *Wyvern*—glows. Her sharp-but-cute face has filled in. She looks healthy. Happy. Nothing like the scrawny, bruised omega of the past.

But why is she *here?*

"Are you okay?" Lilah leans in, wafting the strange alpha scents that cling to her oversized hoodie.

Cedar. Orange. Apple-musk.

My throat pinches.

Those aren't *my* alphas.

"Where are my—" The words choke. They aren't my mates. *Not yet.* "Meadows Pack?"

"Waiting room. The doctor won't let unbonded alphas near

you without your consent, so my guys are keeping them from tearing up the floor."

They're here.

I flop back on the bed.

Then the neck of my hospital gown also flops, sliding down my shoulder to bare my scars. I grab for the sheet, but before I can satisfy the baked-in urge to cover up, my weirdly stiff arms stop short.

My left wrist is cast in white plaster and my right wrist has more plugged-in cords than a call center.

I freeze.

Breathe.

I don't need to lie anymore.

Gripping the cast, I look to Lilah. "How broken am I?"

"Just a fractured wrist and a shit-ton of cuts and bruises. The doctor said it would take a day to clear the sedatives from your system. She was just waiting for you to wake up before she'd say anything about your hormones. Hold on." Lilah calls over her shoulder. "Orion?"

A tall, blond omega opens the door and walks into my hospital room eyeing me like *I'm* the threat.

He doesn't make sharp moves, but his unfamiliar apple cider prickles in a not-so-comfy way when I don't know who he is or how I got here.

My throat-glands squeeze and my pheromones rear.

I grit them down, but something feels different. *Looser.* "Lilah. Step back."

"Go find the doctor." Ignoring me, Lilah shoos Orion. "Sol won't hurt me."

Are you sure?

Because I'm not.

Orion shares my doubts, trying to drag her away. "Lilah—"

"Please?" The girl who taught me how to gut a handsy alpha with a whittled toothbrush lifts onto her toes, possessively nipping the bite-scar on Orion's throat.

He softens, warm and gooey as a chocolate-chip cookie. Then Lilah matches his melty smile, and for ten seconds of madly-in-love eye-fucking, they don't give a shit about me, my pheromones, or anyone in the universe.

I want that for her.

I want it for me, too.

Realizing the omega male isn't a threat, my danger instincts chill, but not before I catch a whiff of the scent I just leaked.

Did the SAS tranq me with shrooms?

"Be right back." Orion slips from the room.

I hope he's calling the crash team, because I'm about to have a heart attack. "What does my perfume smell like?"

Lilah sniffs.

My blood ices, waiting for her answer.

But she doesn't go septic.

Doesn't choke.

Doesn't even run screaming.

She tilts her head. "Weird."

"Weird how?" I croak. "Are they disgusting?"

"Huh? No." Lilah takes a breath so deep, my blood surges. "They're sweeter than I remember from before your awakening. Kind of like lemon pound cake? But it's weird that I'm not responding like you're an omega."

Because I'm not an omega.

Air whooshes between my ears. "You're sure?"

"Yeah. Why?"

Trembling, I lift my wrist.

Underneath the plastic scent of the IV, my skin puffs out citrus, sugar, and vanilla.

Lemon.

But cakey, soft, and sweet.

Nothing like Serafina's hard lemonade.

That's me?

Doubting everything, I feel along the familiar pheromone

paths. I'm achy and exhausted, but that makes sense now that I remember the fighting and running and car flipping.

My body has always felt tight.

Every muscle taut, constantly working to stuff down my scent, stay in control, and stop me from accidentally razing anyone's nervous system. My jaw, my throat, my abs. I've been clenching so tight, for so long, I never realized it wasn't natural.

But now?

My jaw isn't cracking, my shoulders are liquid, and my throat doesn't scrape, even though Lilah smells like a caramel apple, double-dipped in omega perfume.

I'm empty in the best possible way.

Like everything I've been dragging was cut loose.

Unbound.

Freaking floating

I'm not about to make Lilah my guinea pig, but when I twist a little, testing my pheromone flex, I sense the same-old kill button.

Only it's not an on-off switch anymore.

It feels more like a dial.

Alone with my best friend in the dim-lit hospital room, the dial stays happily parked at zero. I rub the tingles in my throat, trying not to get too excited before I'm sure I understand my body's newest trick. "Hypothetically. If you were forced into a partial mate bond, but instead of fading, the bond stuck around after a traumatic heat—"

"What the fuck? *Sol,*" Lilah grabs for one of her hidden blades. "Who was it?"

"Already handled." *Twice.* "But, in theory. Even if you weren't an omega. Would something like that affect your scent?"

Lilah's grey eyes narrow. "It would screw your whole system. Hormones. Cycles. Perfume."

"Even if you're not an omega?" I press, glad one of us paid attention during the boring classes.

"*Mar. I. Sol,*" she enunciates my syllables. "If you're telling me you had a ghost bond—which is really fucking rare for a reason—

it would mean that your body hadn't healed the incomplete bites. And so, *hypo-fucking-thetically* you would've been physiologically perma-stuck in the moment the bite was forced. So, *yeah* Existing in constant fight-or-flight mode would be traumatic for a slime mold, let alone an omega or anyone else." Her grip rattles the bed rail. "I don't know if I should shake you or hug you until your head pops off."

"One more thing." I inhale the lemon rising off my skin like a total grinning loon. "Do siblings or half-siblings usually have the same scent to their perfume?"

"Not always, but it's pretty common."

I float higher and higher, tingling and light-headed.

Apparently, my body's been spamming the panic button non-stop since the moment I awakened as a gamma.

Now that the Orlovs are *dead* dead and their ghost bond is exorcised, I can still whip out my neurotoxin when I'm threatened

But when I'm safe and happy, surrounded by people who support my right to continue living free and breathing, my scent doesn't default to nightmare.

It's plain, normal lemon, and it's a freaking *dream*.

Because Meadows Pack loves some lemon, and I'm starting to think my flavor was always the one they craved.

Finally

I have a real scent

I *always* had a real scent

Now everything that was ever meant to be mine is coming back

I can have my pack.

I cackle until Lilah shakes her head. "I'm going to grill you *so hard* when you're not in a hospital bed."

"Same. How did you even find me?"

"Like I was going to let you stay disappeared?" Lilah wrinkles her nose. "Turns out your mates trained with my mates. I came to pick you up as soon as we realized. Now—"

A door knock interrupts her. "Miss Marisol?"

"Come in," I call.

This time, I'm ready for the danger alarm.

I full-body clench, but when a middle-aged beta with her scent suppressed strides into her room, my body has enough common sense not to spike an alert.

It's too busy spiking my temperature.

I rub my suddenly sweating forehead.

"We'll talk later." Lilah smirks. "If you're not back on bedrest after your heat."

Holy shit.

I can have a *normal heat.*

Lilah slips out, leaving me with the woman in the white coat. "I'm Doctor Carter. How are you feeling?"

"Good." My legs bounce. The exhaustion I was feeling earlier evaporated when my skin started pre-heating. "Maybe better than I've felt in years."

"Wonderful. We'll keep this short." The woman smiles. "When was your last heat?"

"My *only* heat. Five-ish years ago? I guess I had a ghost bond until yesterday."

Doctor Carter stiffens. "That's…"

"Extremely rare?" I'm out of the few shits I ever had to give. "Now that it's gone, will there be any side effects?"

"I'm so sorry you had to experience that." She scribbles a note on my clipboard. "With the residual bond and sedatives leaving your system, your numbers indicate that you're already rebounding. We'll need to discuss long-term therapies, but if you're pleased to accept the pack tearing up the carpets in my waiting room, your next heat is imminent. We'll need to bundle you into an emergency nest as soon as possible."

While my insides swirl, my pulse and temperature rise.

My monitors blare.

Doctor Carter kills the volume with a smile. "Do you plan to mate with the Meadows pack?"

"Can I?" My voice cracks.

"Of course. And medically, I'd recommend sealing the bond with your packleader as soon as possible. This heat may be shorter due to accumulated exhaustion. But if it's extended due to the length of time your cycle was suppressed…" She clears her throat. "It may be quite, ah, *strenuous*. You'll have a more pleasant experience with a mating bond to guide your pack on what your body can handle."

I

Can.

MATE

Clouds part, angels sing, and a beam of golden light pierces through a mini-magnifying glass, lighting my body in holy fire.

I squeeze my thighs against a flash of heat. "Where are they?"

"Your pack? They're waiting just down the hall. First, let me call the nurse to take your—*oh*! Wait. Please don't—"

No time for nurses.

I yank my tubes and swing my feet off the bed.

There's no pain.

Flashing raw throat, trailing blood and the hem of my oversized gown, I don't give a shit how I look or what anyone thinks about it.

It's *allllll* bullshit.

The only thing that's real is the pull.

I follow the call. Down the hall. To the left. To the waiting room. Before I clear the door, they sense the shifting gravity.

There are other alphas, pumping scratchy pheromones. Maybe Wyverns. Lilah. But people, floors, and furniture don't exist anymore

Only *them*.

Jin's pacing halts mid-step.

Bish drops his phone.

Reese jumps off Dutch's back, and Dutch, suddenly unpinned from the floor, acrobatically rolls to his feet with a desperate half-snarl, half-moan.

They see me.

I see them.

A shiver starts at my scalp, crashing down my spine in a tidal wave that leaves my heart stuttering, my gut fluttering, and my knees knocking so hard I grab the wall to keep from dropping.

My sweetest pheromones blossom.

With my Meadows boys, there's no such thing as danger.

Even before their scents hit, I *know.*

Mine.

They're mine.

Feral, gamma, *get-the-hell-over-here MINE*

And I need to be touching them.

Jin stalks to me.

It's sexy as hell, but who has time to stalk?

I rocket into his arms. Jin catches me with a ripping growl. "Mari—"

Yanking his hair, I drag him to my lips.

Jin was delicious before.

Now, I *devour* him, addicted to stormy ocean salt. Lightning tingles my tongue, streaked with his magic. Jin digs into my hips. His rumbling, possessive purr boils my blood.

I need more.

I kiss deeper, harder, opening his mouth and clawing his neck. The tighter I cling, the needier the ache.

More.

Even *more.*

Anything to fill the painful hollow, yawning inside me.

Desperate, my pheromones spike. With a gasp, I break the kiss. "My scent—"

"Lemon buttermilk cake," Jin growls. "Fucking irresistible."

"Sera—"

"*You,*" Jin cuts me off with a kiss.

"Mate." Dutch glues himself to my thigh. "There's no one else"

"Right?" Reese strokes my calf, adding his rich cocoa to the press of alpha. "That other chick smells like floor polish."

Bishop kisses my fingers at the base of my cast. "You're the real thing, Queen. Truth or lie?"

Their rumbles and scents and rock-hard reassurance—plus the rock-hard alpha between my legs—spark a wave of wild hope. "True"

"Then skip asking." Jin's heated voice hits my skin like melted candle wax. "Take what you want."

Yeah.

Let's do it like that.

I grab for another alpha. My fingers scrape Dutch's T-shirt. While Jin holds my hips, I haul Dutch to my mouth.

Hungry, he opens for the kiss, shooting off the rumbling, cannon-fire moan that ruins me. Buttery maple bacon curls my toes, and the body I always thought was broken perfumes the universe with lemon-glazed sponge.

It's still not enough.

I need more.

More kisses.

More skin.

More *everything* and every part of them.

I dip to Dutch's throat.

When my teeth graze his skin, salty-sweet pancake batter coats my tongue

"Oh, *fuck*." Dutch grabs Jin's shoulder for support.

While he shudders, I purr and tease his throat.

Then Bish pushes in, twisting my upper body to him instead. His boozy pheromones fizz, and his attention leaves me wriggling as he scans me head-to-toe. He frowns at the cast.

"I'm not hurt." Maybe I should be hurt, but all I feel is *heat* and the four alphas jostling for my touch.

I yank Bishop's tie, tearing open his collar.

His frown breaks to a deadly smile—like he just bought a new pair of custom loafers, perfect for burying his enemies. "Let me take you home to my hotel."

"Can't wait." I wiggle my hips, sweating and itching. "I'm... I'm..."

"Too hot." Reese's voice goes sandpaper coarse as he smooths my flushed forehead. "It's game time if that's what you—"

"*Want*." I snag the meat of the thumb he left too close to my lips

Reese gasps

I finally understand why everyone's so obsessed with biting.

My jaw must be connected to my clit.

Biting Reese roughs his breathing. I grind Jin's belt buckle as Bish feather-kisses my knuckles, and Dutch's coats my skin with roaming hands and pancake purrs.

I'm dripping, hot, and halfway to binge-fucking my pack in a waiting room with a wall full of windows.

But the scents of unknown, maybe-enemies stick in the public space, and the bright lights irrationally piss me off.

After a last hard nip of Reese's cocoa butter, I dive into Jin's throat. "Jinnie."

As I nuzzle his pulse, his rattling purr clamps my pelvic muscles. "What do you need?"

"You. Here." I drag his hand to my shoulder, guiding him to stroke my scars and cup my throat. It's not exactly comfortable, even though Jin's touch is cool and careful.

It's ticklish.

Unfamiliar.

But not bad. Not like before, when the unwanted bond zombie-piloted my responses.

While Bishop, Dutch, and Reese stroke my arms and legs, Jin holds. He thumbs the sensitive spot behind my ear, right at the base of my jaw—and *holy fucking shit*.

That's *definitely* connected to my clit

"Marisol Meadows," Jin purrs. "Will you be our mate?"

My skin flames.

My perfume spikes.

And every place that's supposed to flutter—my heart, my gut, and my knot-hungry pussy—gives Jin a full-crowd wave.

Mine.

My alpha.

My pack.

I kiss his jugular. "I always was."

FORTY-NINE

SOL

EVERYTHING MOVES FASTER when you admit what you want.

Jin carries me to the nesting ward.

Before we're allowed in a suite, Doctor Carter insists on cleaning the holes from my ripped-out wires. "Save your blood for mating bites."

Lobster pink, twitching whenever all four alphas aren't connected to my skin, I inhale Jin's stormy-sweet lightning and let the nurses do their thing.

Can't stop licking his throat.

By the time we're cleared, I'm sweating through my gown, and my insides quake like half-set custard.

The nest is nothing special.

No ocean waves or penthouse luxury. Just a big bed—clean and white—in a soundproofed, round-ish room. There's a basic kitchenette with a fridge of bottled water, and an even more basic hospital bathroom attached. A few neat, sterile blankets and pillows pile at the foot of the bed, under ultra-dim lighting. And just in case of emergency, a pull-cord dangles beside the headboard

Zero frills, zero pretension.

But when Reese kicks the door closed, I have everything I need

Everything I've ever wanted.

Jin starts to set me on the mattress, his grip loosening.

Panic flares. I snag his shirt. "Don't. I need—"

"I'm not letting go." He drags me over his thighs, leaving me straddling him at the edge of the bed.

Dutch pushes into my back while Bish and Reese slide in at our sides, continuing the four-way touch that keeps me from throwing claws.

"You're doing so good already," Reese murmurs. "Does it hurt?"

"It doesn't hurt." I shift on Jin's lap. I'm wearing panties under the paper gown, but the position forces my legs so wide, I can't ignore the urgent drumbeat, pulsing deep inside.

I bite my lip. "But if I lose control and hurt you—"

"You can't," Jin rumbles.

"But *if*—"

"Queen." Bish drags my lip from my teeth and rolls the bitten spot between his fingers. "To us, you're only sweet."

He hasn't straightened the collar I ripped open, flashing throat like an invitation to fucking *ruin* him.

I need him to ruin me.

I scrape a tempting stripe across Bish's freckled collarbone. "What if I'm not sweet? What if I'm spicy or sour or—"

"I wanted you when you were a dude." Reese's beard tickles my earlobe. "And when you were a gangster."

"You're ours no matter what," Dutch rumbles. "Our only mate."

Their purrs crumble my walls, and before I can stop my mouth, the needy heat pheromones dredge up the question buried at the bottom of my heart. "Why would you like me?"

No one *ever* likes me

I'm always wrong, never enough, never what was ordered.

"*Love.* How could we not love you? *Marisol.*" Jin's dominance flares. A wordless command hooks its fingers under my chin, forcing me to meet the black-water whirlpool in his eyes. "You're our light."

Kitten claws paw my heart.

I want to be soft and sweet and give this pack every part of me —be the omega of their dreams.

But even dripping on Jin's lap, ready to claim and be claimed until they have to yank that emergency cord and summon a crash team to pull me off their cocks, I can't keep pretending to be something that I'm not.

I'm not an omega.

I'm a gamma.

A weapon.

I'm only soft for four alphas in this world, and if anyone tries to separate us, ever-a-fucking-gain, I'm not going to hide under the sheets.

I'll pull the trigger.

A scary-possessive snarl rumbles from my core. I don't try to hide the monster. *Let them see it all.* "I won't always be good. But I'll always be yours."

"Be bad. Be anything you want." Bishop nips my knuckle, the promise of his teeth curling my toes. "I want to taste all of your flavors"

"Cheezus rice," Dutch groans. "Just let me taste that fucking cake"

Reese's breath sizzles in my ear. "Save me a slice."

My alphas' scents swirl, hot and cold, comforting and electric.

Fresh and crisp, sweet and savory.

Pulsing heat curls me forward. Their hands shoot out with their purrs, soothing the hormonal spike.

What kind of shit-for-brains would let them go?

"Get this off me." I yank my gown, snarling when it catches on my cast.

"Reese," Jin's husky command bottoms out my stomach.

A knife flashes, and the alphas growl as Reese slices. But when the air hits my skin, my shoulder reflexively tucks.

I catch myself halfway to hiding, my cheek pressing my shoulder and my hands flying to cover the scars.

Jin's gaze shimmers, all ink and quicksilver.

Heat pulses in my fingertips.

Not the familiar heat of shame, but the heat of *need*—his and mine. My exposed nipples perk while the cotton panties itch like burlap

Reese drags his knife to the elastic. "Take it all?"

"Take it all." I hug Jin's neck and arch my ass to give him access

"Thank *fuck*" Dutch barehand-tears the panties, tossing two white flags over his shoulder. Purring like a leaf blower, he greedily palms my ass.

I hiss

His palms are hot but cooling.

Overwhelming but not enough.

I grind back on Dutch's kneading hands, then rock forward, seeking Jin's hardness as my neck throbs.

My voice shrinks. "Jinnie. Kiss my throat."

"Only kiss?"

"Kiss. Mark. Bite." I know what I want, but my body remembers the old fear, stiffening as his breath hits the tender skin.

Jin noses up from the base of my scars. He doesn't rush, dragging his lips along the ticklish ridges. Up my chin. Down my shoulder.

Dutch kisses my back and rubs my ass while Reese licks my ear and Bish nibbles my fingers.

How can I do anything but melt?

Feeling me loosen, Jin *hmms* in satisfaction.

Then he opens his mouth.

Butterfly-kissing, sucking, nipping, he teases from my collarbone to my jaw.

Soft.

Gentle.

Adoring

My hips buck.

I quiver, so desperately empty, I'm waterfalling slick.

"Smells so fucking good." Groaning, Dutch kneads my ass like a master baker, working toward my slick inner thighs. "Please, please, please, *please*—"

"*Dutch*," I bark to hurry him before *I* start begging. "Come get your taste"

With a dark chuckle that pangs deep inside, Jin flips me in his lap. Crushing my back to his chest, he hooks my legs with his and splays my knees wide open. "Let him get you loose. Then you're mine"

Dutch crawls to the edge of the bed, licking his lips.

My pussy pulses a fluttering welcome.

But Dutch needs no introduction.

Born ready, he dives in, tongue-first.

No licking, no teasing.

Dutch plunges in to fucking *eat*.

"Ah~!" My spine bends. As Jin holds me down, teeth teasing my throat, Dutch pushes between my lips.

Slurping, licking, *devouring*.

My walls squeeze his tongue. "More."

So much more.

"Shit, dude. You skip breakfast?" Reese yanks his collar. "Don't drink. Make it good for her."

"I will, I will." Dutch bobble-head nods, licking glazed lips. "Can't waste a drop."

He stares between my legs, so determined I can't breathe.

When he dips to work again, I gasp.

His tongue traces my outer lips.

Slow.

Thorough this time.

Up and down. Side to side. Dipping in and out, in and out, until my pussy isn't so much twitching as fucking *screaming*.

"*More*." I grind his face, reaching for my clit.

Bish is faster.

"Let me." Voice dripping velvet, he shoves aside Dutch's forehead and flattens his fingers against my swollen nub. I guide his wrist to the spot that hitches my breath.

"Yes. Yes. *There~!*"

"So easy to please?" Bish's purr sinks into his fingertips. He rubs slow, maddening strokes. "Little liar. How can you be bad when you behave so good?"

As Jin kisses my nape, Reese dips to lick my nipple, his tongue matching Bishop's lazy pace. Even Dutch falls in sync, moving his tongue side-to-side and rumbling like a plug-in vibrator.

I tear at their arms.

My hips bounce, seeking.

Hot, sweet pressure builds under my shaking abs, rolling down my thighs with every plunge of Dutch's eager tongue. "More. I want more."

"More of what?" Bishop pulls his fingers and licks them clean with the incubus grin that's sexy as hell and irritating as shit.

"I want your fingers." I yank his hand back where it belongs and *grind*, chasing relief for the pressure—the freaking *heat*. "Then I want your knot."

"Done." Bishop curls his fingers, coaxing. "Come for me, Queen. Then show me how a bad girl takes her alpha's cock."

Jin growls, Dutch moans, and Reese tongues my nipple.

"*Come*," Jin commands, teeth grazing my pulse.

Ahhhh.

Yessssssss.

I shudder on Dutch's tongue. He nuzzles deeper, drinking slick and vibrating my inner muscles with a bacon-wrapped moan

The orgasm lights me up for a breathless, perfect second.

Then my empty pussy clenches in protest.

Not enough.

Jin's swelling fly rubs my ass, but the coarse fabric pisses me off.

The audacity of wearing clothes in my nest.

"Take off your pants." I reverse positions in his lap, turning to tear his shirt. He snakes off his belt, then the pack strips and unzips their leader underneath me.

That's fucking teamwork.

Aching to be satisfied, I claw Jin's outlined abs. My body craves his sweat-misted skin. His touch. His attention.

With no more cock-blocking layers, no more shields or lies between us, I rub my slicked heat against his hardness, so wet I glide up and down his electrifying length.

"You want it, Tomcat?" Jin strokes his cock along my entrance until I hit the flaring knot at his base. It won't finish swelling until it's sheathed, locking our bodies, but just a brush of its pulsing hardness leaves me sweating and keening.

My pussy walls work like jaws, hungry to swallow every thick inch

"I want it all." Impatient, I grab his shaft. The hard-hot texture burns my palm like a fireplace poker. I hurry his wide tip inside.

My muscles latch their prize.

Finally trusting my body, I let my instincts rip.

As my pussy welcomes his cock, I grip his shoulders, forcing him deeper.

Jin purrs into my throat, filling me so good my eyes roll.

Almost.

Almost.

My brain fizzles.

So hot.

"Little help?" Always the team player, Reese spreads my ass, parting my thighs to help me impale myself.

There's no pain or resistance.

Just an easy stretch. Held open, I sink smoothly to Jin's base.

Then I stall on his knot

I wiggle, trying to force the wide, hot bump inside.

Jin's ragged purr vibrates my ovaries. Pumping his hips, he helps my greedy inner muscles play tug-of-war.

I pulse around him but can't pull his widest point into the cradle. My body quivers.

Need him so bad I'm shedding brain cells.

"Too much?" Jin pants.

"Not enough." I work my thighs and push against his solid shoulders, but I might as well be fucking a mountain.

The wait leaves room for hormone-fueled doubts.

What if this whole heat is a tease?

What if we weren't really meant to be?

My scent sours.

"You can take me," Jin rasps, kissing my throat. "This knot was made for you."

He drags my hand between us, caressing the slick-soaked bundle that throbs in time with my wild pulse.

"*Mine.*" I rub, teasing him against my entrance.

We're almost one, but my stubborn pussy can't or won't swallow that last gulp.

My belly spasms.

The unfulfilled sting has me screaming, whining, writhing like an animal.

Need it.

Need to be filled.

Neededneedneedneedneed.

"*Shhh* No rush." Reese caresses my thighs. "Just keep rocking on that knot. Nice and gentle. *Ah* Just like that. So fucking pretty, Solly. You're so close."

"Did our boy not stretch you properly?" Bish rubs my stomach, gently indulgent until he turns to snarl at Dutch. "*Redeem yourself.*"

I'm so hot, their touches so tangled, I'm not sure who's touching where until Dutch's massive palms spread my ass.

Then his eager tongue hits from the back.

Surprise lick.

He laps from the stuck edge of Jin's knot to the pucker of my ass

Then he dips inside.

I gasp, spine arching.

"That's it," Reese coaxes, teasing and stretching the edges of my lips as Dutch eats me from behind. "Working so hard for that knot, Solly. Imagine how good it'll feel inside? How full you'll be?"

Yes.

Pleeeeeeeeease.

"You're close," Jin growls.

Unh.

I shudder, no more words.

While Reese spreads me, Bish flicks my clit. Dutch teases my edges, sloppily licking anywhere he can tongue between my ass and Jin's knot.

"Marisol." Hoarse and quaking, Jin kisses my throat. "Let me in."

Maybe it's his words.

Maybe it's his teeth.

Maybe Jin was always magic.

The last barrier between us gives.

"Enh!" Whether a gamma's body is a little different or I'm a stubborn bitch 'til the end, there's no easy pop.

Stretching, stretching, stretching, Jin's cock swelling, his tip pushing so so so so so so deeeeeeeeeeeeeeeeeeeeeeeeeeeeeep—

There's a spiritual *click*, like a battery snapping and hitting the juice.

Then I'm riding the lightning.

Jin's knot swells, hard and blazing hot.

When my ridges hook his widest point, I'm pretty sure my pelvis does that snake-jaw unhooking thing, gaping to swallow him whole.

So full.

I can't breathe, and I don't want to.

My toes curl with the stretch. The raging heat banks to an electric tingle, humming every place we're joined.

Muscles I never knew I had instinctively clock in and go to work.

They milk his knot, dragging his cock deep. Where it belongs.

"Marisol," Jin whispers.

This is the part where the omega submits.

Where I'm supposed to bear my throat and take Jin's bite as I take his knot.

Sounds fun, *buuuut—*

My throat burns hot and dry, and my teeth needle my gums.

I've wanted Jin too long.

"Mine." I snap to claim his throat. When my teeth pierce his ocean-salted skin, his cock jerks, pumping me full.

A wispy mate bond sparkles into being.

I've felt the feathery touch before, but the pearly, welcoming warmth of Jin's soul is nothing like the icky fingers of the past.

My heart cracks open like a walnut, but I don't flinch or think of fighting

I open wide.

Let him see it all.

γ

JIN

"Mine." My tomcat claws me like her personal scratching post.

As she should.

Everything belongs to her.

Marisol's savage possession leaves me shuddering from the darkest corner of my soul.

I want her to engrave all her names in my bones.

My knot pulses like a hammer beating steel. I'm desperate to mark her so deep that even Jericho's ghost knows Marisol Meadows is mine.

But before I can bite, her aura surges, demanding the initiative I'd go to fucking war to steal away from anyone else.

With her?

I relax my throat.

Let my tomcat come to me, any way she's comfortable.

Her sharp, sexy teeth glide under my skin.

The pull of her mouth matches the rhythm of her perfect pussy, sucking the life from my knot.

The instincts that've been raging since she disappeared finally relax, not giving a single fuck who bites first.

Her claim sinks into my spirit, breathing life to a sparkling connection.

The mate bond.

My cock twitches with every draw of her body.

I'm lost in her heat.

Her light.

Bishop, Dutch, and Reese watch over our joining, rubbing her skin, encouraging her in soft whispers.

The thickening bond thrums with Marisol's satisfaction and screams with her need.

She wants me.

My mate wants to claim and own me as deeply and permanently as I've always wanted to claim her.

Fuck.

I pump my hips. "Take it, Tomcat. It's all yours."

She croons at my throat, and as her body strokes my cock, her fluttering vulnerability drives me fucking wild.

"I'm yours." I come shaking, releasing deep in her heat.

But there's no relief.

Locked to her body, my balls tighten.

Have to fill her until her stomach stretches.

Breed.

Rut.

"Jinnie," she gasps, teeth popping free. As I grind into her, she licks the sweet-bleeding bite. "Make it forever."

"Marisol." I kiss her scars, opening my heart as I line up my mark. "It always was."

She yields her throat to my teeth.

Her blood is crisp.

Scalding.

The mate bond crackles as her soul accepts my claim.

Marisol shines sacred and bright. Her inner strength doesn't call me to challenge or even protect—though I'll fucking die to keep her smiling just like now, beaming as she rides my cock.

My breathing breaks as I touch the deepest essence of my mate

Marisol doesn't need a protector.

She calls me to be her *witness.*

I stare into the holy fire and purr.

My mate.

"What's wrong?" A thread of self-consciousness dims her glow.

I drag her hand to my heart.

I don't know if the bond can translate *'I'm fucking honored to be at your side, watching you change the world'* but I send her my savage devotion. "This is the beginning."

Her deep, brown eyes mist.

She flutters, body and soul.

As I fall under the spell of her rawest smile, her pussy clenches, teasingly tugging my cock. "Promise me something?"

"Yes."

"Don't stop fucking me until I can fit two knots at once."

The challenge tightens my spine.

Two knots when she hasn't finished taking mine?

A snarl rips from my throat.

I flip my mate onto her back and drag her ankles to her ears, driving so deep, my molars groan.

Her hair snakes across the sheets like threads of gold. Blood stains her lips, dark and beautiful.

My fierce mate.

Love, trust, and ball-clenching excitement sing through our bond

I press her mound until I feel my cock, buried deep inside. "I'll fuck you until you can take all four."

FIFTY

SOL

JIN RUTS LIKE A CENTAUR. His bed-shaking thrusts rattle the ball at the back of my throat.

Pah, pah, pah!

I come mewling.

Then shaking.

Wordlessly moaning.

Stretched and deeply, *deeply* filled.

He pumps and grinds, not just hammering, but working his hips, biting my nipples and stroking my clit, finding every spot that bows my spine.

But the kiss of death?

The mate bond.

I wasn't ready.

I'll *never* be ready.

My orgasms pulse with the joy of Jin's pleasure.

So freaking pleased with himself.

Every time he fills me, easing the rabid heat, he purrs to stretch my release, melting me into a puddle of lemon cream.

I buck and writhe and scream, savaging his skin and loving how Jin loves when I leave my marks in blood.

I can't stop glowing.

Su-Jin Meadows is *mine.*

And the world is ours as he pumps me to my hundredth keening orgasm. My thighs shake and my pussy tremors, clamping his knot and sucking him to a deep, velvety moan. Dick twitching inside me, Jin falls on my body, purring and licking my sluggish-bleeding throat.

When he's finally spent, Jin curls around me so possessively my heart throbs. He's so strong and lean, I want to scoop him out and wear him like a shell, but I'm on a heat timer.

As soon as Jin's knot starts to ease, my belly clenches, hyper-aware of the unclaimed alphas with pheromones screaming to meet my need.

Reese strokes his cock at the edge of the bed. Bish reclines, arms behind his head, while Dutch has both hands full, double-fisting their cocks.

My pussy quivers.

Next!

Gently, *gratefully* my body releases Jin. I'm so full, it's like popping a cork. But before a drop of slick or seed escapes, Jin palms between my legs.

"Mine." His iron grip curls my toes as hard as the shredded softness of his voice. "Marisol."

Desire strokes our fresh-bitten bond.

He wants my body, my pussy, my heart.

He wants me

The *real* me

Just the way I am.

Jin even wants the dream I didn't dare to keep.

He wants my belly full.

Trembling, I squeeze his palm. "Yours."

Jin's eyes glow in the dark—all soft, swirling fire. Squeezing my mound like he owns it, he drops to kiss my belly button. "Even here?"

Especially there.

My empty walls pinch. "Everywhere."

"Then close your thighs and keep my cum inside." Jin grinds his palm, making me wiggle for more. "I want you to feel me when you claim your pack."

Unh

Yes.

That and more.

I'm claiming *everything* that's mine.

"Dutch," I bark. "On your back."

"Fuck yeah." Dutch rolls across the sheets.

His swollen cock bobs, wagging like a puppy dog tail as he obediently falls into position, holding his thick shaft ready for me to mount. As I swing my leg over his wide hips, Jin moves with us, sealing up his heat.

Starbursts pulse behind my eyes.

Need to be filled.

"Hurry and ride me, Solly." Dutch pulses his ass cheeks, steering his cock toward my entrance. "Rip out my fucking throat."

So eager.

Bet he'll feel like cotton candy when we bond.

I kiss his forehead, his nose, his pancake-soft lips. Starving, Dutch can't wait. He lunges into my mouth, sucking out my air.

But Dutch only attacks to retreat.

He coaxes me between his lips, dragging me to plunder *him* until he's happily moaning into my throat. Maple syrup slows the kiss and the bump of my heart.

On his back, Dutch plays submissive, but his spring-loaded tension rages against my thighs.

My stomach flips.

Not cotton candy.

Dutch is a candy-coated sledgehammer.

DUTCH

Ohfuck-ohfuck-*ohfuuh-uh-uh–uhhh-uhhhhhck*

Don't fucking care if I take or get taken, but it has to be *now.*

I already jerked off enough times to braid the hair on my palms. Now I'm slow-motion exploding.

Solly tastes like cake every-fucking-where.

Glazey, creamy lemon.

I want to fucking *die,* eating her raw.

Reaching between my mate's steamy thighs, I angle my cock toward heaven. "Solly."

Her biting Jin clubbed my last brain cell. The scent of her blood teases my balls, and I can't stop the perma-snarl eking from my bleeding chest.

They're mated.

They're mated *without me.*

And every fucking fraction of a second I'm not part of the pack, I sink deeper in the pit. "Please. Don't leave me behind."

"Dutch Baby." She claws my chest. "You're *mine.*"

My heart squeezes, all my blood surging to my knot.

Solly ordered me to lie down, but my ass shakes from holding back. I taste leather in my throat.

Have to be inside her.

I moan. "I'll be so good. Protect you. Make you come on my tongue"

"I want more than your tongue." Solly rocks on her thighs. Skin flushed. Cheeks pink. Kneeling over my body like the queen of the porn-star angels.

"Look." I rub my swelling cock-balloon, fluffing it out to present to my mate. "I saved this for you."

Solly rakes my chest. *"Good. Boy."*

FUCK.

I spurt pre-cum in a strangled yelp, donut-glazing Jin's gang tattoos. I'd rip his hand off and leave him just a stump, but he's doing the angels' work, making sure our girl gets bred and filled

Now it's my turn.

Please, fucking *Zeus. "Solly."*

Her lemon sharpens. Gasping, abs rolling, she finally takes my dick

Bish and Reese help lift her hips, and Jin holds on until the last fucking second. When his fingers part, Solly drops on my vibrating cock.

The tip of my dick pierces her creamy heat.

SUPERFUCK

My soul pops out.

I knead her ass. Drag her deeper. Burning to make her mine.

I've never fucked anything so perfect.

Actually, I never fucked anything or anyone except my hand and a vacuum cleaner tube that one time we don't talk about.

Lubed with lemony cake batter and Jin's special sauce, Solly takes my cock like a goddess.

Smooth. Warm. So slippery fucking wet, just for me.

Her raging pheromones spur my ass, but I'm *a good fucking boy*

My mate wants to ride me?

Let her take the reins and flay my ass with her spurs.

I moan into the glide as she swallows me. My cock chugs, raging to reach the end of her baby cave. But Solly stalls on my knot.

Thank fuck she's already stretched.

I can't wait.

I already waited.

So long.

So patiently.

No more

Solly pulses, tight with need, calling—no, *begging*—to be eased

Snarling, I palm her ass and *draaaaaag*.

Drop, rock, and lock her on my cock.

Her body slurps my virgin knot.

Walls like fucking *tongues*.

"*Fuck*. This *cunt*." Breaking my damn brain.

"Keep saying it." Reese laughs. "She'll choke you out."

"Promise?" Panting, I drag her hands to my throat.

An alpha can dream.

"Who said I don't like it?" Solly digs my throat apple until my ass cheeks clap.

"My bad. Get that knot, baby." Reese pushes her hips for me.

Thank fucking *fuck*, her pussy-mouth pops open.

"*Unnnnnnh*." I slide home and my knot goes beast mode.

As I pump, Solly clamps.

Our bodies lock.

I want to melt the key and stay forever.

Squatters' rights

I live here now.

"Holy—" Her silky body tightens.

I freeze. "It hurts?"

"No. *No*. Just... Give me a second."

Take my whole fucking life.

As she settles, her pussy makes kissy flutters. My mate's skin glows like liquid honey. Her soft thighs and belly wiggle, and her juicy tits bounce.

Every part of her is eat-able.

Nipples tipped in strawberries

Ass meat like angel food.

And her throat...

Jin's mark glitters.

My teeth go all vampire, desperate to drink her blood and sink my mark while my asshole pulses, going O-o-O-o-O-o-O.

Need her to fill me.

Need her to stay with me, inside me, camping out with the pack and making me whole.

Heart derby-racing, I rabbit-pump my hips. Easy and shallow. Just pre-heating her Dutch oven for my baby batter. "*Mate*."

Her lashes flutter, her pussy quivers, and her soft, sneaky smile is the same one my little cutie always beamed when I stuck lollipops in her pockets. "Dutch. I missed you. So much."

We never should've been apart.

My instincts know we fucked up.

Instead of raging to bite and claim, they roll over.

Submissive and slutty, I offer my throat. "I want it, Solly."

Solly crushes her tits to my chest, licking my jugular with a snarl that strums power cords on my spine.

Fiiiiiiiiiiiiiiiiiiiiiiiiiiiiiiiiiiiiiiiiiiiiiiiiiinally.

My mate takes my throat.

Her teeth punch in, dripping zest and fairy dust.

I slam my hips, my hands, driving deep, craving every part of her.

The mate bond fireworks, weaving our souls and fucking chakras, and the sweetest, brightest, lemon-yellow sunflower blooms in my chest cavity.

I come roaring, pumping a load fat enough to fill my girl with fucking octuplets.

Solly's body demands more.

She moans into my blood, claiming me with teeth and nails and her sucking cunt.

Her happiness slides over me. Liquid sunshine.

She's light.

She's air.

Solly is my everything and she needs me fucking *bad.*

"Mate." My voice cracks. "Let me bite. Give you what you need."

Solly releases her teeth. After a last, soothing lick, she pulls out.

Emotions volley our halfway-there bond. Handing me the keys to the fucking castle in the clouds, Solly tilts the scarred side of her throat. "Here."

She trusts me.

I lick her like she's made of spun sugar.

So fragile.

Have to take such good care of her.

When I accidentally-on-purpose tease Jin's bite, his smugness punches my lungs.

But he's mine.

She's mine.

They're all gonna be fucking mine.

Even Bish won't be able to hide his real, gooey-ass feelings anymore

All because of Solly.

I lick my spot, warming her skin while I trace the freckle-path behind her ear. "My mate. My love."

I'll never be alone again.

FIFTY-ONE

SOL

DUTCH'S COCK hits deep enough to maple-glaze my ribs. But as the mate bond mashes our atoms, I'm not just gasping on his body

Dutch is spiritual buckshot.

He pumps me everywhere, his suffocating adoration lighting me high, while his bottomless thirst for love drags me into a chasm.

Even my nose quivers.

He's so, *so* much.

How can I be what he needs? "I…"

"Group project." Jin rubs my sides. "We take care of him together."

I breathe, overwhelmed until a whiff of nut-buttery cocoa cuts the fog

"Easy, baby. Jinnie? Help me switch them up?" Reese pulls a stack of pillows into the game, working with Jin to flip our position

Together, they ease me onto my back, hauling Dutch on top. Still knotted, he hits deep and heavy, flattening us both into the pillows. My hips strain around his linebacker thickness, but before I can adjust, Reese throws another curve.

"Teach you a trick?" Reese takes my hand. "He's the easiest to handle"

With a wink, Reese guides my reach to Dutch's ass.

I can't see, but I can *feel*.

Not just the sensations on my skin, but Dutch's delicious response

Reese soaks my finger in hot slick, then guides the tip to Dutch's pucker.

"Soll—*uhhh*," Dutch bellows.

His cheeks clench with a ragged thrust that drives me into the mattress. The blissed-out rush of his release whites out the fleeting worry, dragging me back into my body with a pussy-pulsing orgasm.

"See? He has a pause button." Reese stretches me, guiding me to the magic spot that melts my alpha's muscles. "Curl your finger. Right...*there*."

When I tease the secret button, Dutch saws his hips, freaking yodeling and painting my insides. The bond crackles and pops.

When Reese twists out my finger, Dutch and I both moan.

Feels like he's teasing my ass, too.

"Show me more," I croak, obsessed with the shared sensation.

"What kind of show?" Reese purrs. "You want me to help you finish him?"

"Yes."

Absolutely, *that*.

"What about you?" Reese strokes behind Dutch's thighs, making the bigger alpha quiver.

"*Nnn*. Together. Fuck our mate."

Their rumbles sync.

My abs shudder.

"I need—ah. Perfect." He takes the condom Bishop already has ready and offers it to Dutch's teeth. "Bite for me."

Dutch tears into the foil. The bond fireworks, his cock twitches, and I tremble in anticipation.

Teamwork really does make the dream work.

Reese rolls the condom over his shaft and lubes himself in my free-flowing slick. Even wrapped in latex, his cock makes my mouth water.

Reese has eight perfect abs and a V-line like a freaking tortilla chip. He's shaved, not veiny, with a cockhead like a mushroom cap and a slightly oblong knot that promises to slide in smooth and stay for extra innings.

Perfect proportions.

He'd be a killer nude model, but unless one of my guys is secretly drawing smutty webtoons, no one else gets to enjoy the hardware

That body is mine.

"Ass like an omega." Smirking, Reese rubs my slick into Dutch's yielding hole. "I'll show you how to peg him, but next time you're in the middle."

"Don't fucking tease." Dutch shudders.

"I don't tease, Dutch Baby. I deliver." Reese drives into Dutch's ass, sheathing to his knot in one powerful thrust that fills me so full, Dutch shoots pancake batter into my lungs.

"Mate. *Pack*" With his adoration sparkling through the bond, Dutch nips my shoulder. His weight grinds my clit, his sweat slicks my nipples, and his grunting moans drive me wild as shit-flinging monkeys.

Reese snaps his hips like he's swinging for a grand slam. Every time he hits that sweet, sweet spot, Dutch's cock jumps and my pussy greedily swallows his heat.

My alphas' scents meld.

Brown butter and hazelnut.

"Reese," I moan. "Take us home."

"Not me. Tell him." Reese pumps a perfect metronome.

In-and-out-and-in-and-out-and-in-and-out-and —

My pussy spasms around Dutch's jerking cock. "Together. Now. Come—*nnh*!"

Dutch snaps.

Possessed, he drives into me, then see-saws, furiously fucking me, then fucking himself on Reese.

"There you go, Dutch Baby." Reese grabs his shoulders. "Such a good boy for our mate. You like it, Solly? You keeping that pussy slick for me?"

Their combined rhythm liquifies my insides.

"MATE," Dutch roars, coming and coming and coming. I lose control of my legs. Then my arms. Even my nose twitches with the rolling release.

I scream, clawing Dutch, Reese, any alpha close enough to mark

But the more I'm filled, the more I crave.

Holy shit.

How much more can I take?

As Dutch starts to soften, he kisses my lashes. "Let me lick you clean"

"Later." Reese pulls out, making Dutch spurt one last searing load that rolls back my eyes.

He pats Dutch's ass, then hauls him off me, bowling the bigger alpha across the bed to Bish and Jin.

Kneeling over me, Reese strips off the condom. Hard and ready for ten more rounds, his raw cock slingshots to his abs. "My turn"

Yeah, it is.

I stroke his knot—*soft as powdered satin.* "Tell me where you want me"

"Elbows and knees." Reese grins, half Little League champ and half sex god, all dirty and sweet and everything I dreamed. "I'll take you on a ride."

REESE

My cock could pierce drywall, but I've never been more focused

Almost losing Sol twisted my head on straight.

Now she drops to her elbows, tilting that round ass high in the air just because I asked.

And isn't that the fucking thing?

Solly doesn't submit. She follows my lead because she *wants to*, and her trust is a hell of a fucking drug.

Can't disappoint my girl.

I smooth her thighs, rubbing her fluttering lips in slick and cum until she's squirming for me.

That skin is art. Flushed with heat, red with bites and handprints

Makes me wanna add my own tag.

"Open wider, baby." I rub her lower back, guiding her to the perfect angle. "I want you arched for me. Nice and relaxed."

She kicks out her thighs and leans. That glossy, pink pussy pops wider, calling me home.

"Look at you, beautiful. So fucking lucky you're mine." My chest rattles as I pet between her lips. "You ready to take my knot? Make it official?"

"Reese."

"Love it when you call my name." Voice hoarse, cock jumping, I lever her thighs to eat her from behind.

The first taste numbs my scalp.

It's sweeter than cake.

Fresh, lemon donuts, drizzled in hot glaze. I plunge inside, grip dimpling her shaky thighs. *"Mmmm. Fuck."*

"Reese. *Reese.*" Solly rocks on my tongue, drenching my beard, but her panting desperation kills my plans to stop for a drink.

This fucking heat.

I kiss her pussy *goodbye-for-now*, then kneel behind her. Gliding my cock between her thighs, I lube my shaft. Her slick sucks the blood to my knot. I grip her hips, balls tightening. "Got what you need right here. You want it?"

"Need it." Her elbows tremble.

Fuck, it feels good to be wanted.

Can't keep my girl waiting.

I plunge into her needy heat, then hiss as her walls suck me off. "Fucking made for me, Solly."

"Knot."

"Right here." I drag out of her, then circle her entrance, easing back through the contracting ridges of muscle. Feels so. Fucking. *Good* "Can you swallow this cock for me? Take it all the way down. Then I'll feed you this knot and claim your throat."

She rocks into my thrust.

"Just like that. *Fuck* It's so soft. You're taking it so good, Solly Baby"

"So are you," she sighs.

Tingling with her praise, I clench my abs and rock.

My knot pops home. We're sealed.

She gloves my cock until sparks shoot from my tailbone. "Feels good? You comfortable?"

"*Yessss*." Sol melts into the sheets.

I'm dying to sink my bite, to rail her limp and brainless, but I'm even more into coaching her orgasms.

As I smooth her ribs, I catch Bish's eye.

His gel-job is wrecked, hair every-fucking-where, and his vibe hits extra wild when he's bare-ass naked instead of hiding behind five layers of color-coordinated bullshit.

I jerk my chin.

Totally off his game, he slides across the sheets, letting me summon him without a quip.

Even without the bond, Sol must sense the weird. She glances over her shoulder, giving my cock a questioning half-squeeze *what's up?*

Girl can communicate vaginally.

Fucking love having her on my team.

"Lift up on your hands?" I strum her spine, rubbing out her shoulders as she rises on shaking forearms.

No questions, only trust.

"Careful on your wrist." I help ease her weight off the cast.

"Me? What about you?"

"What about me?"

"You were shot?"

I chuckle, knot-deep in dripping heaven. "No such thing as

pain."

"Right?" She shudders around my cock.

My purr ratchets. "Show Bish how good you take care of your alphas"

She double-scrunches my dick; *aye-aye, Captain!*

Woulda thought I'd want my moment alone with Sol, but I don't need to be the superstar—that's all her.

As she sizes up Bish's package, I'm all good.

I belong here.

Don't have to chase or fight or prove shit.

"Kiss the head," I rasp through my epiphany.

She licks Bishop's tip, teasing his weeping eye with the sweep of her tongue.

"Queen," Bish groans, dangerously close to begging. He fists her loose hair. "Don't tease unless you want to be teased."

His cockhead's so purple, I have to take pity.

I nudge Solly forward with my hips. "This your first time?"

"Not my first time thinking about it." She licks her lips.

Bish and I shudder.

Hot as fuck.

I rub her ass. "Who'd you think about?"

"You." Smirking, she squeezes my knot. "All of you."

"Visualization is power." Dutch strokes behind her ear. "Manifest that dick, Solly."

Sol laughs, tickling my cock, and of all alphas, she beams her spotlight smile on *me*. "What next, Coach Reese?"

"Work your lips over his head," I rasp.

She *hums* and opens her mouth. Bish strains his seams, wobbling

Sol needs zero help exploring, licking under, then around his head. But she's out of time for *slow*. Her walls roll, begging me as a soft whine builds from her belly.

"Heat." My knot pulses, desperate to end that sound. "I have to fuck you onto him, okay? We'll go easy."

Her pussy squeezes the *okay*.

I rock into her, purring and caressing her back. "So fucking sexy. Relax your throat for him. Yeah. There you go. Take him down slow."

Moving with her breaths, stomping the urge to rage and rut, I bump her deeper on Bish's cock.

He's the one who chokes. His fingers twist, going fucking wild

As I fuck into her, Dutch reaches under her stomach, sliding toward her clit. Jin makes his spot at her side, one hand gripping her throat, the other teasing the rim of her ass.

It's fucking *magic* how we come together to serve our girl.

Got all the family I ever needed, right here.

But we can't drag this out much longer.

Solly's walls bite 'til my ass cramps and my teeth want to whine

Gotta take her throat.

She's almost kissing Bishop's knot when I have to call the game, guiding her hips and easing back her lips. "Don't finish him yet."

Bish glares like I forgot to iron his slacks, but he'll fucking thank me later. This pussy is *insatiable.*

Glaze-eyed, Solly grabs his thigh. "Touch me."

"Yes." Bish combs her hair away from her throat, baring her skin for me.

Surprisingly gentle for a guy nursing a brass pipe between his thighs

With the pack stroking and purring her, Sol softens.

I curl around her like we're cuddled in the sleeping bag we used to share. Only, Sol doesn't need me to keep her warm.

She's superheated.

Dutch and Jin overlapped their bites. The two linked rings bleed over the older scars.

Not to hide the marks; I wouldn't erase her scars any more than I'd erase mine.

We've all been through some shit.

We earned those stripes.

Important thing is, we made it back to each other.

Now we build from the ash, together, starting with a four-leaf clover on our girl's throat. I kiss her pulse, nosing toward my spot.

My bites are gonna look hot as fuck in her skin, even if she never gets to wear my jersey. Ass tight, I thrust. "From now on, I'll be wherever you are."

"Then be in my throat, or I'm biting you first." Solly's pussy chokes my shaft. Demanding. Claiming.

My heart near fucking explodes.

Roaring from my balls, I buck into her.

My teeth rip that sweet throat.

Then a new fucking universe rips open in my soul.

I feel her.

I expected her need, her heat.

But her satisfaction?

With *me?*

Fucking hell.

The bond glitters and grows, vibrating her happiness. I hug her tight, tangling our limbs.

She purrs like a kitten nestled in her favorite blanket.

I'm her favorite blanket?

Don't know what I did to deserve this girl.

Maybe saved a fucking planet in my last life.

I rise to meet her. Anything she needs. "Call my name."

"Reese," she calls. "Reese. Reese. My Ree—*unh. Reese!"*

"Solomon. Marisol. Solly Baby." I call her everything to cover my bases.

Doesn't matter which name.

She's mine in every form.

Bucking, fucking wild, I clamp her stomach.

Finally

I'm home

FIFTY-TWO

SOL

THE BOND SCREAMS what I already know.

Reese is bittersweet.

Smooth and gentle on the outside. Strong inside. But so hurt, all his craving, hidden under that chocolate shell.

I don't need the trembling mate bond or even my pheromones to dig out his deepest fear; we've always shared the same nightmare

It's not being abandoned, but what comes *after*.

When the people who're supposed to love you the most wash their hands and say *no thanks* Then you have to survive on your own, knowing no one gives a fuck.

"Reese," I call his name.

Just that and he glows, warming me from the inside. "Call me. Tell me where I belong."

"*Reese*" I'll call him forever. Again and again, until he knows he's part of me. As long as I exist, so does he. "Give me your throat."

"I want to see you." He slows his thrust

My pussy pulses in protest, but I let him shift us. The guys help rotate me on Reese's knot

The spin grinds him against my walls.

I fall over his hips, panting.

Reese swallows hard.

His scars aren't as obvious as mine, but with no body fat to cushion the lines and his blood rushing with pheromones, every old mark rises high and red.

I caress his old and new bullet holes, smoothing up his arm to the faded surgical incisions.

Then I kiss his scars.

As Reese's soul wavers, I snake my hips, kissing up his shoulder to the spot on his throat where his scent pulses strongest.

I lick his jugular.

Tastes like chocolate croissant.

"Reese." I rub circles on his knot, squeezing and drawing him out, pleasing myself on the body that eases my heat so good. "Feel how much I need you?"

"I feel it." His gooey center wobbles.

I stroke the bond as I pull at his cock. Then I pierce his throat and make him *mine*, every way I can.

"Sol," Reese gasps. "*Sol.*"

The bite completes our circuit.

He fucks me slow.

He fucks me *deep*.

We're all a little jagged in this pack, but Reese and I share the same damage. Connected, we rock together, passing back and forth the pieces we need.

There's no explosive climax.

I just come and never stop, like roaring down a river, the whole world sprayed in white-water.

I fade in and out with my teeth in his throat.

When the haze parts, Reese hugs me with our foreheads pressed. His beard scrapes my swollen lips. "You're heating up again"

I groan

I'm still speared on Reese, but his knot is as soft as my spent muscles

A cramp pinches. I grip his shoulders, trying to ride it out, not wanting to leave the comfort of his cock.

"Give her to me," someone says raggedly.

The hitch in his voice jolts me alert.

Three complete bonds plaster the holes in my heart, but I'm missing the finishing touch—the champagne toast to complete our mating

Bitter peach hits my throat.

"Bish." I claw into his waiting arms, my heat battery at one percent until I plug myself onto his cock. I work to fill the charge, but Bish stops my hips before I can latch his knot.

"Patience, Queen," his playful smoothness doesn't match the wild fizz of his pheromones. In the dimness of the nest, his eyes gleam black instead of hazel.

No suit. No tie. Just pale skin, burning hot as mine.

I rise and fall as his chest moves. Every breath is scary even.

Four seconds in. Four seconds out.

He's counting breaths.

Clinging to his last silk shred of sanity.

My muscles ripple.

Being filled keeps the itch from spreading, but I can't last long when I'm one bite away from locking down the pack of my fantasies

Neither can he

Bishop's suppressed strain stings sharper than my desperation

I finger-comb his messy hair. "You don't have to hold back. Not with me"

"Humor me." Bish lifts me off the bed and carries me to the kitchenette, edging me on his knot. Clawing his back, I wrap my thighs around his hips, but his grip stops me from stealing his thickest inches.

Without the other three-fourths of my pack shooting love and reassurance through our bond, I'd already be whining like a freaking tea kettle.

Bish sets me on the cold counter.

His pheromones sting more like thousand-proof peach moonshine than his usual champagne. But Bish moves detached. Like his raging scent and the cock twitching inside me have nothing to do with him.

He cracks open a bottle of water and lifts it to my mouth. "Drink"

Ice-cold condensation drips onto my chapped lips.

Suddenly thirsty as hell, I gulp what he's offering.

Bish smooths my hair behind my ears.

Then his smirk clenches my pussy.

Without his knot sealing the gate, I puddle slick and alpha-scented cum all over the chilly countertop.

I shudder, sloshing water down my chin.

Bish *tsks*. "Messy."

He moves like he's standing on his yacht. As if our thighs aren't knocking together with tremors and the pulse in his neck doesn't tease me like a flickering cat toy.

Bish dampens a washcloth and pats my face. He eases the tears crusted around my eyes, wipes dried blood, and cools the sticky sweat. I don't know how he knows exactly what to do, but he cleans my arms and chest without touching my bites or the slope of my belly, where the guys rubbed their scents into my skin

Bish spends the most time on my casted hand, polishing like my finger bones are made of crystal.

So gentle

I'd melt from the softness of his care if his rabid pheromones weren't sawing my throat. I buck against his throbbing knot. "Bish. Enough."

"Finish your water." He stops my hip-thrust and hands me the bottle again

I snatch it and chug.

Hurry.

Hurry

"Are bad girls always so obedient?" He thumbs a stray drop from my chin and smugly licks it clean.

Gasping, I toss the empty bottle.

Bish vibrates under his skin.

I'm not obedient. I just don't know how to reach him.

He'd rather shatter than give up his facade.

Guess that's the answer.

We break together.

"Bish." I grab his chin. "No more lies."

He sucks a breath that ruins his rehearsed rhythm. His voice drops, hoarse and halfway to broken. "What else is there?"

"I don't know." I stroke his jaw. "Let's find out together."

γ

BISHOP

If I have to hang by a thread, it better be spun from vicuna wool.

Fiber by fiber, I'm unspooling.

No buttons to stroke. No comb or cufflinks to distract from the ripping and tearing.

Only one thing slows the fray, and she's the same reason I'm falling apart

Marisol Meadows.

She's too precious to mate on potato sack sheets, but here we fucking are, bonding in a medical setting instead of my finest mating suite

In full-bloom, Sol's pheromones coat my tongue in lemon gâteau

Rich.

Silky.

Exquisite.

My knot pulses, tapping out curses in Morse code and begging to join my cock in the lushness of her sheathe.

Always knew she'd unravel me.

I can't stop the inevitable—wouldn't if I could—but I have to be a stubborn, controlling fuck until the bitter end.

It's the Barrington way.

Her honeyed lemon cunt nibbles at my shaft until I'm dragging my heels on dingy hospital tile, keeping one last measure of control.

Sol wraps hot hands around my throat. "It's me. You don't have to pretend."

"I know." I'd never undress for her, never let her near my boys if she weren't the one. The exception to every one of my rules. "But Marisol."

"Hmm?"

Her stroking hum coaxes out my roughest purr. "I can't be the only one who's ruined."

I pin her thighs and slow-drag my cock.

"*Enh~*"

She makes inarticulate noises, bucking her hips to urge me faster, but I want to savor our first joining. Ignoring my scalding throat and the numbness in my toes, I tease her, hitting every surface on the way out until my swollen crown nestles between her quivering lips.

"Bish," she groans.

"Watch." I stroke into her slickness, slow and hard. Her walls stimulate my shaft, coating me in sultry lemon cream. I strain to control the pace, near popping a blood vessel, deliberately thrusting until my knot knocks her entrance.

Her hips bounce, and pressure pinches from my balls to the base of my spine. I pull out again.

Long and slow as a stretched Cadillac.

"I'm watching. I see you, Bishop."

"I know."

No one looks at me like her.

Like I'm human.

Not an accessory. Not a chip to be played, or a tool to be tossed at the first sign of failure.

Those brown eyes make me fucking *weak*.

That's why I'm taking my time.

Three alphas deep and my mate's still speaking words.

Unacceptable.

My queen deserves the best.

"I won't ever leave you wanting." I kiss her flushed forehead. Her trembling sighs soften.

"The—*enh*!"

I thrust.

In.

Out.

Grinding into her until my glutes shake.

I thrust.

In.

Out.

Marisol mewls. "Bi… Bis… I—*nnh*."

Don't lose it. Not yet.

I thrust.

In.

Out.

Trapping her on the edge of desperation as I train her body to expect a sweeter payoff.

"Hold the counter," I grit. "Don't move your hips."

She has to hold on because *I can't.*

Not with this body

This scent.

In.

Ou–*oh fuck*.

She clamps my shaft.

White-knuckling the counter, thighs quivering, she innocently tips back her throat. "I didn't move my hips."

Her pussy fits like it's bespoke. I rock into her lush slickness, testing her grip as my neck spasms.

Refusing to let her control the pace, I stroke.

Back in. Hitting slow. Hitting deep.

Withholding my knot.

Her sucking tightness begs me to bury myself—knot, cock, and teeth.

I smooth my queen's flushed cheeks.

In no makeup but her natural coloring, her golden hair swinging wild and free, she's Marisol unleashed.

I'm going to drip her in name brands, but nothing's more luxurious than her bare skin. Her open throat. Those wide, unguarded eyes.

Her body shakes as hard as mine.

Vibrating on the edge.

Fearless, she bares her scars.

"I see you, Bishop." Marisol hugs me in raw softness. "Can you see me?"

"I see you," I sigh, my last thread snapping.

I'll fucking admit it.

I broke first.

γ

SOL

Bish wavers like the sheet of ice left behind after rolling down the window on a wintertime Rolls-Royce. Held up by nothing but air and stubbornness, he quavers between my thighs.

I see through him.

Feel him shake.

But he doesn't collapse.

Not Bishop Barrington-Meadows.

Bishop has a thousand ways to smirk, but I've never seen him grin so dark that shadows lace between his teeth.

He cracks *beautifully*.

Madness bleeding from his eyes, Bishop finally lets go.

Not just unbuttoning his tie.

Unzipping his ribs.

Unleashing a snarl like the demon who drinks champagne while he heralds the apocalypse.

Please.

End it all.

I'm dying

Boiling

I'm so cock-hungry my pussy's going to cannibalize him into a cocktail wiener if he doesn't feed me that fucking knot. "Give. Me. *Everything*"

"Yes, my queen."

I almost murder him when drags out his cock.

Then he plunges deep.

No more teasing, dragging, crazy-making strokes.

He drives my ass into the counter. The surface groans, Bishop growls, and I scream in tongues as his knot hits the spot.

And keeps hitting it.

He pump, pump, *pumps,* hammering until my eyes bulge.

Oh—

Holy—!

Unh

I can't.

My brain oozes.

Thighs quaking.

Toes curling to my heels.

Barbarian Bish ruts hard enough to snap my spine.

Let him break me all he wants. The emergency room is right downstairs

I slam into him, clawing his shoulders and meeting him pound for pound.

Can't get enough

"Mate," Bishop grunts.

His elegance is gone, puddled somewhere on the floor with his shirt.

My throat throbs.

The mate bond flickers.

One more alpha.

I tip my throat, showing him my scars and my whole heart.

No makeup

No mask

No scent but my own.

Just me, watching him crumble as I crumble for him.

"Teeth. Bishop. Your bite. *Now. Ah—!*"

His knot and teeth punch.

Filled, taken, I break apart.

Bishop's emotions fizz as he savages my throat.

Wild love.

Rough and possessive.

My pussy quakes, my heart keens, and my teeth sear until my lips steam.

Take him.

Claim your pack.

I rip away from Bish.

There's no pain. Only euphoria and the shivering bond, begging to be completed.

Snarling victory, I take Bishop's throat.

His blood hits like peach syrup.

As Bishop snaps his hips, the mate bond sparkles.

Four bright stars swirl around my heart.

My mates are wild, ecstatic, rabid, elated, awed, and so jackrabbit freaking horny, I come all over Bish's pulsing knot.

Then four sets of hands haul me back to bed, all lips and teeth and a full-pack purr that buzzes my gamma bones.

Beast mode Bish fucks me through a never-ending orgasm.

Dutch steals kisses.

Reese sucks my nipples.

And Jin is everywhere, giving me exactly what I need, whether a rub at my clit, a lick at my throat, or a hoarse, melting reminder of who I am. "Marisol."

This is so much better than my vision board.

When Bish's is finally spent, he lingers on top of me, tonguing and tending my pack's overlapping bites.

I puddle on the sheets like gas station spaghetti.

Jin chuckles. "You warmed up?"

"Can't you hear this pussy purring?" Bishop licks up my throat, dragging his teeth to my ear. "I did that."

I shiver, cramp, and groan.

Do I want a month-long nap?

Or fifty more rounds of god-tier dicking down?

"Heat's no joke." Raspy with thirst, Reese rubs past my belly button, working down to my slicked mound. "We're gonna have to double team."

"Double. Triple. Whatever." Dutch wiggles between our tangled bodies. "Just lose all these legs. I can't reach my lemon cake."

He shoves under Bish and Jin, a bloodhound seeking my inner thigh

Gleeful need tingles through the bond.

My pussy perks.

Definitely fifty more rounds.

I work my thighs around Dutch's shoulders and snag an armful of Jin. "I want five years of make-up orgasms."

"Only five?" Jin purrs.

"To start."

He licks his teeth. "Let's begin."

Adored by their tongues and hands and bodies, I melt into the sheets

For once, I wish there were cameras watching.

Then I could show everyone.

See?

This is me.

These are my alphas.

And this is my pack.

Bitten, fucked, and bound with blood.

They were always meant to be mine.

FIFTY-THREE
SOL

SIX WEEKS LATER...

MY ALARM CLOCK PURRS.

I'd hit snooze, only the sound vibrates from my cervix.

Dutch and Reese aren't just *up*.

They're rising and freaking shining, serving a morning cup of double-penetration that jolts my pussy and jitters our mate bond harder than black espresso.

"Holy—"

It's alllll coming back now.

I remember falling asleep on Dutch's knot after Bish fucked us into the mattress.

Reese was there. I just don't remember him being buried knot-deep in my ass.

He is now.

"Breakfast sandwich?" Reese nips my ear from behind, scraping my throat with his beard.

My sleepy morning groan morphs to a gasp.

I lie pillowed on Dutch in the dimness of our cozy, new nest, deep underneath the Wyvern Compound. Also *deeply* pierced by their cocks.

Reese mounts my ass, smashing me between choco-nutty and maple-bacon muscles like the lemon cream filling melting out of their full-body panini press.

My alphas know what I like.

And they have standing permission to wake me any way they want—as long as they don't expect me to do cardio.

"Make it spicy." I shudder.

"What else is there?" Chuckling, Reese eases back on his thighs. "Relax for me. I'll fuck you both so good."

I follow his lead—another thing I like doing—breathing and lifting my head enough to finally see Dutch's face.

"*Sllleee. Sllleeee*." He beams happiness through his big, blue eyes and the tingly warmth of our bond, but he can't get out my name

He's gagged.

Mouth overflowing with Bishop's red, silk tie.

Riiiiight.

Last night was the best.

So is right now.

"Good morning, Your Highness." Bish claps a hand over Dutch's mouth to silence his grunts, then kisses me like we're all alone

As if I'm not already stretched and speared between two alphas

As if Reese isn't starting to stroke, slow-motion grinding his shaft until it hits Dutch's full-blown knot, taking my ass, clit, and puss prisoner to his melting rhythm.

Bishop's kiss steals what little air I can gasp between my alphas' jerking bodies. His cocky satisfaction smirks along our bond

As if Bishop is whispering, tongue teasing my ear:

Why would you need air when I'm here?

"Don't look at them. Look at me," Bishop commands, not with his dominance, but with the *zzzzzzzzt* of the palm-sized vibrator he pulls from the pocket of his luxe robe. The deep maroon fabric sets off his pale skin and evil smile. He drags the toy down the column of my throat. "Do you want to come?"

My stomach clenches, already halfway there. Reese rocking

me, Dutch stroking my insides with his purr and pulsing knot. "I don't need your permission."

"I know." Bish circles my bite-scars with the vibe. "But you *want* it. Don't you, good girl?"

The vibrations don't just tickle my throat. Bishop's touch feathers the mate bond, leaving the three of us messy, moaning, and desperate for more.

Shit, he's good.

That's the fun thing about Bish.

None of us *have to* obey the alpha with the weakest sway in the pack

But it's always the right choice to play along.

"Tell me when, King Bish." I open my throat to him.

Bishop's eyes lighten, almost green when he smiles for real. Then his gaze drops to Dutch, and those hazel eyes flash so dark my pussy writhes. "You ruined my tie."

Dutch is the easiest to pick from the chaos of alpha emotion. All quick flashes, honest and breath-catchingly pure.

I don't need a bond to read his rumbling indignation: *You're the asshole who stuffed my mouth!*

"Reese." Bish adjusts his belt. "Drag him to the edge of the bed'

Reese presses my back, hugging around me to grab Dutch. "Can you squeeze him for me, Solly? Real tight with those pretty thighs and that hungry pussy. Yeah? Oh, *shit.*" His abs ripple when I give him what he asked for, clenching hard around both cocks. "Squeezing me too? Feels so fucking good. Hold on. *Yeah* Like that. Ah, *Fuuuck* I'm sliding you, okay, Solly Baby?"

He says *slide,* but as Reese knees us across the sheets, it feels more like being pumped. Bishop doesn't help, watching Reese thrust, thrust, thrust our joined bodies to the foot of our massive pack bed

Every inch forward rocks me up and down two thick shafts. Dutch's knot and Reese's cock knock all my nooks and crannies.

Dutch twitches so deep inside me, he's tickling my belly button, but Bishop didn't bother telling *him* to wait.

Dutch knows better than to finish without permission.

When Reese reaches the edge, Dutch's head tips off the bed. He lets his skull relax against the mattress, baring the bite-scarred column of his neck and opening his throat in a *looooong* line of invitation

"Don't slack." Bishop rips the balled-up tie from Dutch's mouth. "Our mate isn't allowed to come until you please me."

He drives the tip of his cock between my alpha's ready lips.

Dutch swallows what he's given, shaking me on his knot.

I moan. "We're going to be late for training. *Again.*"

"Impossible." Bishop drives deeper into Dutch's willing throat.

Reese's laugh tickles my ear. "Right? Long as our Solly's not there, the Wyverns are just early."

Dutch bobs and hums to agree.

Or maybe he's just gulping Bish's cock.

I cup his throat. His thick neck is always delicious. But when Dutch works his jaw to swallow Bishop's shaft, all those beautiful throat muscles roll. I rub the silvery bite-scars while he deepthroats Bish so eagerly that his emotions bounce in time with his ass cheeks.

Moving Meadows Pack to the Wyvern Compound was such the right decision.

Our nest has *mirrors*.

They slope from the domed ceiling, giving me a three-hundred-and-sixty-degree view. Reese's tight ass and rippling back, Dutch's curled, twitching toes, and Bishop's knees, secretly shaking beneath his robe.

Between their hot breaths, hypnotizing pheromones, and the hyper-excited, *love-you-want-you-need-you-so-fucking-much* sensations pumping back and forth through the bond, my clitoris weeps with need

I squeeze Dutch's throat, fighting for control.

Hold your shit together for the four-way orgasm.

It's fun using my muscle-clenching skills for sex instead of survival.

At the SAS, I'd already be sizzling for being thirty seconds behind schedule.

At Wyvern House?

Lilah was already going to opt my mates out of the grueling lifetime merc-work contract they were on the hook to sign.

Then I showed Wyvern Pack my gamma ability, and they begged me to work for them instead.

Now, I'm Wyvern House's highest-paid agent. I get to pick my missions, and I have nights and weekends free to hang with my alphas and my best friend. Plus, I promised Lilah I'd coach the omega softball team whenever the OCC finally reopens.

Meadows Pack signed sweetheart deals all around.

We agreed to come under the Wyvern umbrella as equal partners. Dany and Lisa have a safe home on the compound, and the guys' assets are protected from vultures while the underworld reshuffles

While Bish and Jin work their administrative magic, Dutch, Reese, and I are training for missions with Wyvern House's A-Team, featuring Lilah's big, scary alphas—Atlas, Hunter, Finn, and JJ Wyvern.

We're always late.

Every. Freaking. Morning.

And I don't give a finger-licking shit.

Who the hell could punish me now?

"Focus, Queen." Bish pinches my chin.

Oh, right.

Bish can punish me.

But only because he has a sixth-sense for what I love and stops —no questions asked—when he unknowingly brushes one of my leftover lines

Like binding my wrists.

That's a no.

Dutch is happy for any touch, whether he's bound, gagged, or face-fucked. With his throat filled, he beams total blissed-out sunshine. He milks Bishop's shaft until he's lovingly tonguing the half-blown knot that won't squeeze past his teeth, no matter how expertly he sucks.

"Are you pleased yet?" My walls flutter. Dutch's knot-pulse teases me so close to the edge, I taste sparks.

"Could I answer if I were?" Bishop pumps his hips.

His pupils are wider than normal, but his breath is too steady.

I can be late for work.

But I can't wait *hours* to freaking come.

Reese's purr strokes my spinal cord, teasing his knot against my stretched hole. "Remind him who's in control."

"Give me the vibrator," I growl but don't command.

Don't have to.

Bish takes my requests *very* seriously.

"Your scepter." He curls my fingers around the switched-off toy, bracing on Dutch's shoulders as he brings his face to mine. "And my reward?"

I kiss his evil lips. "You'll get yours when I get mine."

"I wouldn't have it any other way." Bish tucks my hair behind my ear with shaking fingers. With Dutch grunting, and Reese and I breathing like we're sprinting, no one else can hear the whisper he rasps direct to my eardrum. "Break me, Queen."

The vulnerable rawness that softens his eyes brushes the bond like peacock feathers. I'm the only one who can see Bishop's expression, but I'm *not* the only one whose breath catches.

Dutch's moan vibrates four connected bodies.

"*Fuuuck*," Reese groans. "What kinda stamina you think I have?"

"The best." I squeeze my ass, encouraging. "Match my pace?"

"Always with you, Solly Baby." Reese nuzzles my throat.

"Then hold on." I flash Bish the smirk I learned from him—the one that whispers *you'll thank me for the torture.*

Then I click on the vibrator.

It's pink silicone, high-powered and oblong. Last night, the guys showed me alllll its functions.

This morning, I'm sharing the love.

As I rock to show Reese the pace I want, he grips my hips and pumps helpfully from behind. Not too slow, not too fast. His stroke works my walls between his thick shaft and Dutch's ultra-wide knot. When Reese *draaaaags* out of my ass, I drag the vibe down Dutch's neck.

Up and down.

Reese thrusts while I trace the twitching cords of Dutch's well-filled throat. He short-circuits.

Neededneedneedneed-lovelovelovelove-moreMoreMoReMORE!

Bish gasps.

His shallow throat-thrusts stutter.

Dutch's displaced muscles bunch in the shape of Bishop's cock

Relentless, I follow his shaft.

Thank fucking shit for the mate bond, otherwise I'd think Dutch's gurgles meant he was dying. They're *happy* choking slurps that bounce his hips and stir me on his knot, begging me to drag Bishop over the edge with us.

I rock and rock and rock. Reese's thrusts grind me deep on Dutch's knot and rub my clit on Dutch's pelvis. Three perfect purrs vibrate me all over.

I'm so close.

So, *so freaking close*, but—

"*Marisol.*" The husky growl lightning-strikes my spine, rolling down my belly until it liquifies my little toes.

Jin grips my throat and kisses my temple. I can feel him checking me for anything that's wrong.

Checking my mates.

Checking our pack.

Our packleader would fix our problems if we had any left.

But Meadows Pack is all aces.

Stuck swirling on a *fuckyessss* feedback loop that ignites with

Jin's touch. Pleasure, joy, peach, tingles, lightning, syrup, love, cocoa butter, and *holy fucking shit—!*

Jin possessively scrapes my scars.

My pussy spasms.

Chuckling, Jin curls the same hard grip around Bishop's straining throat.

Then my pussy doesn't just spasm.

It overflows.

Desperate.

Chasing.

My thighs shake the mattress. I retract my claws before I really choke Dutch.

Not that he'd mind.

Sight fading to white sparkles, I gasp, "Jinnie."

"*Come*," he commands.

I could fight the seduction of Jin's dark dominance.

But my alphas have to *obey*.

"Ah!" My body rolls.

Dutch pumps me with liquid heat and tooth-aching sweetness. Hugging my back, Reese bites my shoulder and fills my ass so full I taste hot cocoa.

Bishop shoots his release halfway to Dutch's stomach, and his broken gasps shatter me again. With every greedy swallow, Dutch milks out Bishop's exquisite purr and stirs his knot to stretch my orgasm.

All the while, my Jinnie strokes my throat.

Thunder and lightning crackle.

My hips and toes pop with fireworks.

My alphas fill me with love, reassurance and deep, *deep* belonging

Everything's so perfect I get a little choked up.

Or maybe I'm struggling to breathe because I'm overflowing with Dutch's special syrup.

At least eight hours worth. Plus, whatever was left after my alphas took turns filling me and palming my pussy shut

If I can get pregnant outside my heat, then I should be carrying a few hundred Meadows babies by now.

A fucked-up, family-starved gamma girl can hope.

"Good morning," Jin says softly.

Bishop shrugs from Jin's hold and Dutch's throat, straightening his robe. He kisses the corner of my eye. "I'll find you for our shower."

With his mouth finally free, Dutch doesn't waste time breathing. He sparkles through the rasp of his recently fucked throat. "Morning, Solly."

"Good morning." I kiss Dutch's ultra-swollen lips, then moan.

Peach-stuffed pancakes

My stomach rumbles.

Meadows Pack keeps me ravenous.

"Really good fucking morning." Reese scrapes his teeth down the four-leaf-clover of my connected mating scars, teasingly circling his hips as he pulls from my pulsing ass.

"Ohff~!" I orgasm again, clamping Dutch's receding knot

My alphas take turns kissing their bites and easing out of my body. With no more cocks to hold me up, I slide boneless into Jin's arms

Jin knows what I like in the morning, too.

Bare-chested, he flaunts my marks. His obvious pride in my nail-tracks, hickeys, and slowly scarring bites comforts the possessive, gamma goblin who needs everyone to know.

Su-Jin Meadows is owned.

In tight-fitted athletic pants, he drags me between his thighs. While I lean into his heartbeat, he rubs my belly.

His palm is so warm.

Bishop sneaks off to clean himself, and Reese drags Dutch down the hall when he tries to hover.

I close my eyes, wishing I could doze, but the pack's concern buzzes with the same voice that warns our perfect morning is coming to a close.

My heat mostly stopped my need to cover my scars. Now my

alphas have seen every part of my body at angles I didn't know existed

And after mating the only pack I could ever want, most of the nasty, hidden instincts are purged from my system. I can breathe —and control my pheromones—without feeling like I'm fighting for survival.

Jin caresses me, watching slick and seed seep from my still-twitching pussy to soak our pack-scented sheets. His rumbling satisfaction would kill any lingering doubts about much he wants me, even if I couldn't feel him mirroring my possessiveness.

Our obsession is so arrow-stabbingly mutual, my vision board can burn. All I have to do to live my dreams is open my eyes.

And *yet…*

"Do you want to tell me about it?" Jin circles my belly button.

I sigh. "You already know."

"Tell me again."

I don't know what face to make, or how I'm supposed to act or feel, but I don't hide my fear—or my terrifying greed—from my packleader.

My alpha.

My Jinnie.

He never flinches when I drop my mask.

Pressing his hand to my stomach, I unlock the anxiety gnawing at my heart and let him feel my shudder. "What if I can't get pregnant?"

"We have a lot of heats in our future, Tomcat." Jin pulls me onto his lap so he can hug my whole body. "I'm always going to be right here."

I tilt my head to reach the mating bite glimmering on his throat. Purring, I lick the silvery shadow of my teeth.

"You don't have to take the test today. You don't have to do anything you don't want." Jin smooths my hair. "And there's no rush. Wyvern House took so many SAS prisoners, we can start our own research if that's what it takes to get answers."

"I know." This time, my world isn't the only one being rocked.

After the Wyverns sieged the SAS, they dropped one last bomb to weasel themselves out of trouble with the government.

They outed the super-secret gamma program.

Now everyone knows gammas exist.

The officials who write the budgets are pissed that tax dollars were being funneled into unethical research. They're even *more* pissed that the public knows the truth, because they can't stuff the secret back in the bag and use the gammas for themselves

Pack Fissure and Brandon's leftover lab staff are rotting in the compound's prison while JJ Wyvern and his associates *encourage* them to share their research.

Bridget and Elyse survived like sugar-dusted cockroaches, but Wyvern House was pressured into returning the world's last two gammas to government custody.

Telekinetic Dara died in the attack.

And Marisol Darling died five years ago.

On the night I awakened, the SAS declared me dead, erasing me in the same fire they used to erase Orlov Pack.

Now I don't exist.

But since Serafina Redfang vanished with a backpack full of prescription painkillers, I'm borrowing my sister's identity while I keep her inheritance warm.

I don't want the Redfang assets—not even the diamond mines.

Okay. Maybe *one* diamond mine.

The Redfangs are so stupid rich, Serafina won't notice.

If she ever resurfaces.

The Wyverns are looking, but as long as my sister stays in the mist, I'm safe from being clawed back by the government.

Now Bridget and Elyse are the guinea pigs, chained behind very well-ventilated bars.

It turns out?

When gammas can warp brains, nobody sane gives a flip about the scent of their perfume.

Wyvern Pack makes sure I'm the first to hear any new gamma

info dredged from our prisoners, but the drip is slow and more general than specific to me.

I'm going to have to visit the cells to get the answers I need.

For now, I inhale Jin, charging my bravery battery on rain, salt, and packleader reassurance. When my shit is sewn back together, I climb out of his arms, wincing at the maple oozing between my thighs

I never bled after my heat.

But we had a pack meeting after the hormones faded.

I never thought I could have Meadows Pack, and they never wanted to risk dangling a mate in front of Kairo.

Now that we're together, I want to follow in my father's fertile footsteps, only instead of birthing my own syndicate, I'm desperate to build the big, loving family none of us ever had.

The pack enthusiastically agrees.

I leave a snail trail as I slide off our bed. "Wait for me?"

"Forever." He kisses my knuckles, then follows me into the bathroom.

I shut myself in the toilet compartment while he waits outside the door.

Every morning, I take three pregnancy tests.

Alpha, beta, and omega—because who even knows with this body?

After I stop dripping long enough to pee on the sticks, I rejoin Jin. He lifts me onto the counter, pressing between my thighs and kissing me while the timer runs.

Expecting the result, I'm ready for the hit.

I text Lilah before she messages to ask.

Negative

Her bubble pops up fast because she and her mates actually go to work. She sends a string of hearts and the answer that always makes me smile.

LILAH

Ice cream for dinner?

Again?

Every day until we have answers

See you then

Jin doesn't need to ask the result when he can feel me spiraling. He nuzzles until I have to throw my arms around his shoulders. "Let me feed you breakfast."

"You can make me breakfast. But I'm feeding it to you."

"I might eat you instead." Jin pulls me onto his hips.

I nip his throat.

We're running embarrassingly late, and the Wyverns know exactly what we've been doing instead of the morning run.

Who cares?

Everyone needs to know.

Meadows Pack is mine.

I'm not just fucking their brains out. I'll choke anyone who fucks with them.

FIFTY-FOUR

SOL

AFTER JIN GRILLS me a stack of goozey breakfast sandwiches, I hand-feed him and Reese until they're eating off my fingers. Dutch would be eating more than just my hands, but he and Lisa have a meeting at Dany's new school.

My cute little sister begged us not to drag the whole pack and make a scene.

Fair.

Bish whisks me to his bathroom to continue our morning routine. Adjusting the shower temp, he *tsks* "You're covered in blood, cheese, and cum again."

"Is there a better way to start the day?"

"Like this." He kisses me dizzy, then pulls me under the spray.

Systematic but meltingly gentle, Bish cleans me from my ears to the toes that he buffs with a pumice stone. He exfoliates my skin with a weird mitten and massages my scalp until I moan.

The more I melt, the more he softens.

By the time he sits me at the vanity in our shared closet, Bish wears a peach fuzz smile as soft as his unstyled hair.

No one else sees him like this.

Naked. Humming softly as he lotions my skin.

My happy purr edges toward a growl.

I have to protect him.

All of them.

Catching me staring even harder than usual, Bish hugs me

from behind. Resting his chin on my shoulder, he grins through the mirror. "Ready to dress for battle?"

I rub his cheek, swapping my lemon for his addictive peach. "Who are we fighting?"

"Everyone else."

My heart squeezes. "Then we better dress to win."

"Always."

I pour Bish into a tailored, scarlet suit that sets off my scratches on his throat.

He picks me athletic clothes that are perfect for training. Then he brushes my hair into the low ponytail I've been favoring now that I don't have to pretend to be anyone but myself.

I tie his tie and button his cuffs.

He laces my sneakers and tops my outfit with one of Reese's chocolate-soaked hats.

Our shared grooming is so peaceful, I never want it to end, but eventually Jin comes to collect. "I can be late, but you have a board meeting with the Wyvern dads."

"They can't start without me." Bish passes for civilized, even smirking like a demon.

Jin looks *wild* in his black suit.

Maybe it's the button popped to bare his savaged throat. Maybe it's the ink that flashes when he adjusts his cuffs.

Or maybe it's the thunder and lightning that crackle in his eyes when I wrap around him like a starving cobra. "Who are you meeting today?"

"A few groups and their managers." Jin tilts his throat. "Mark me. I want to show off your teeth."

"Good answer." I nip his Adam's apple.

I like that my pack is taking charge of its businesses.

What I *don't like* is my CEO alpha rocking up to the entertainment company he clawed from the Triad, flaunting his fine ass to a bunch of freakishly attractive bubblegum-pop idols.

I mark Jin and Bishop a few more times on our walk to the parking garage

Then I kiss them a few more times, because I'm not going to see them for *hours*.

When they finally drive away, Reese ropes me into his arms. "Ready to kick some Wyvern ass?"

"If you're back in ass-kicking shape, then—"

"Solly Baby." Reese lifts the brim of my hat, shutting me down with a toe-curling kiss. "I just wanna be where you are."

I let Reese drag me into the elevator, but when the door shuts, I slam *him* against the wall. "I don't need to be protected."

"Don't I fucking know it." Reese hauls me close, grinding me on the holsters and straps that crisscross his Wyvern-issued training uniform.

Reese looks *good* in black-ops gear.

But I want to see him in his jersey. "What about your dream?"

"Got a new one." Breathing heavy, Reese kisses up my jaw. "You. Me. Two skybox tickets. Couple beers. Couple ballpark dogs. I'll eat you out during the seventh-inning stretch, then carry you home and make the pack watch me fuck you to sleep in our nest. You free Friday night?"

"Reese."

He bites his mating mark on my throat. "What's my name again?"

"Reese Meadows." My throat ripples from his teeth and the satisfied glow of our bond.

"That's the one."

"Alpha Reese Meadows." I snag his chin, forcing him to look me in the eyes.

"Even better." He rubs me with his beard.

"If you really want to quit baseball, I'll stop asking. *But*—" I thumb his lip until he purrs. "If I find out you stopped playing for me, I'll wax your face. You know the guys will help hold you down."

"I do need to shave."

"Absolutely not."

"Why? You like the beard? Where? On your lips? Or your *other* lips? Dragging up those pretty thighs. Scraping that sweet cunt. All drenched in lemon fucking glaze."

My *sweet cunt* loves when Reese calls her by name.

She answers with a flood of slick. I squeeze my thighs and kiss his filthy mouth shut. "You're not allowed to talk."

I'd already be riding his hips if we didn't live so close to work.

The elevator takes us from the garage to the surface, passing Lilah's floor, then Dany and Lisa's.

The compound's residential area is attached to Wyvern House's training centers and offices, plus Wyvern Academy, which offers the finest non-affiliated military training for students ages pre-school to university.

We cross the grounds, dripping inappropriate pheromones.

I could kill my perfume and hide the scent.

But I won't.

Reese burns so happy, he toasts my heart golden brown, but I know him too well to miss his shadows. We're the same. Always starving for more. "I'm buying you a baseball team."

"Solly. You can't make me some kind of nepo-tizzy sugar baby"

"Why?" The Redfang blood money is basically mine.

Might as well spend it on something good.

Reese drags me to a stop in the middle of the lawn. "Which team?"

"Which one has your favorite mascot?"

"*Fuck* Always taking care of me so good." Reese tackles me to the grass, cradling my head.

He kisses deep.

Eating my air.

I lift my hips and part my lips, putting on a show for the Wyvern trainees jogging past. "You don't have to give up anything else."

None of us do.

"I'm not," Reese rumbles. "Ball could've been my ticket somewhere better, but I don't wanna be stuck playing some doubleheader in the heartland when my pack needs me home. Besides. I'm made for merc shit, and Wyvern House has a beer league team. You gonna be in the stands when they name me MVP?"

My heart squeezes at the image. A beaming future Reese, finally lifting his trophy. Only, I won't be in the stands. "I'll rush the field."

Reese purrs my spine liquid. "See? Already getting everything I wanted'

"Same." But I'm still buying him a team.

Then Reese can play, manage, or take me on dates in the owner's box. Anything he wants, as long as he's happy.

We kiss under the blue sky, breathing sunshine and sharing the same heartbeat. By the time we near the training arena, we're grass-stained, rumpled, and late enough to stop for lunch.

But I veto the canteen when a weird jangle jolts our bond.

Dutch is waiting.

No.

Not just waiting.

Something else.

Finn *fucking* Wyvern.

"Shit." Reese sprints to catch up with me.

I beat him to the training arena, zinging past security toward the source of the unhappy hum.

The arena is packed with obstacle courses and built-to-scale buildings. We've been running scenarios with paintball guns, practicing formations with our new teammates.

Hair and pheromones loose, I leap a mud pit, leaving a class of trainees gasping. My control reached a whole new level after I was sprung free. Now I stun and keep running, in no danger of hurting anyone but the red-headed bastard who needs a fresh lesson

I find Dutch pinned between fake two-story buildings. He crouches behind a mailbox spattered in red paint. The shooter on the roof across the street machine-gun fires, even though Dutch is already dripping fake blood.

Racing for the stairs, I snarl at Reese. "Find Hunter."

We're going to need an adult.

"On it." Reese disappears.

The buildings are bare concrete with no furnishings and nothing to muffle the slap of my sneakers.

I want him to hear me coming.

Heaving as I hit the roof, I flex my scent and wait for the gunfire to die.

When it's silent, I stalk to Finn.

My perfume freezes him on his stomach, finger on the trigger of a mounted gun. The reservoir that holds thousands of paintball pellets is running empty.

What a team.

I kick him onto his back. Finn doesn't cough or choke, even though I'm pumping enough toxin to make another alpha cry.

Meeting his gaze tips me into an icy, black tunnel. *Like falling down an abandoned well.*

Finn isn't living his nightmare.

He *is* the nightmare.

"Solly!" Dutch's bellow echoes from the ground. I've got a few seconds before he scales the stairs.

Without my alphas, I have no reason to smile.

Alone with Finn, I have no reason to pretend.

I meet him dead-eyed stare for dead-eyed stare. "I told you to stop screwing with Dutch."

Finn doesn't answer.

He can't.

Crouching, I reel back my scent and drop my wrist, ready to knock him out if he twitches.

"Dutch Baby—"

I pulse perfume. "You don't get to call him that."

"It's my name."

"Not anymore"

"Then give me something better to play with," Finn says, all sing-song grim reaper. A pulse of recognition scritches my spine.

Lilah is surrounded by freaks.

At least *I* know how to pretend I'm normal.

Since Finn is impossible to threaten, and I can't kill him without hurting my friend, I can only point his chaos somewhere productive. "I'll give you names. Everyone who hurt Lilah."

"My Star told me their names."

"*All* of them? I bet Lilah held back half." I dangle the carrot.

He bites with a black-eyed *snap*. "Now you're speaking Finnglish."

"Give me your phone." When my scent relaxes, Finn cooperates. I punch my number into his contacts. "Text me your number, and I'll send you Lilah's list. If you're that bored, you can help with my list, too."

I've banked a lot of names over the years.

I'm finally free to start crossing them off.

There's one I can't avoid any longer.

He's waiting for me underground.

"I like you." Finn grins.

I return a plastic smile, just as fake as his. "Hurt my pack or my friend one more time, and you won't even know how you died."

A spark flickers in his empty eyes. "I like you a lot, Starfriend."

"Can you acknowledge my threat?" I toss back his phone.

"Nah. I'd kill myself faster." He drags the phone across his throat.

"Great plan."

Dutch's snarl saves me from continuing the heart-to-heart.

My teddy bear alpha roars onto the roof like a pissed grizzly, pumping three paintballs into Finn's chest before snatching me into his arms. "Don't talk to him. He'll fuck up your chakras."

Pancaked, I let myself be dragged away. "He wouldn't know how."

While Dutch purrs, I strip off his paint-splattered body armor. His emotions ping-pong, melty warm when he looks at me, then wary as a bear watching hornets swarm when he tracks Finn over my shoulder.

My throat stops pinching when Finn finally gets bored and ducks off the roof.

Reese pings me before I can check where he went.

ALL-STAR

Hunter wants me to teach Finn a lesson on teamwork. You and Dutch have the afternoon off.

"Solly." Dutch deflates. "I'm supposed to protect you, not—"

"You're *mine*. If a Wyvern breathes on you, I'm putting him in his place." I scrape his throat until his moan melts my vocal cords. "Is that okay?"

"*Fuck*." His knees shake. "Yeah. Super fucking okay."

"Good." I lean into his warmth, stealing a little sunshine. "Want to come somewhere with me?"

"Everywhere."

I squeeze his fingers.

Asking no questions, Dutch follows where I lead.

γ

I'VE ALWAYS HAD permission to visit the Wyvern House prison.

I was just hoping Doctor Brandon would die in captivity, and I'd never have to see, smell, or let him know I'm thinking of him, ever again.

Now, I need to know what he *already knows* about my body. Not about gamma fertility in general, but mine, specifically.

Then I can cut his last hold on me and finally move on.

We pass multiple security checkpoints to reach his dank, underground cell. Helpful Wyvern agents hang the withered alpha's wrists from a hook so he and I can catch up.

Just like home.

Dutch molds to my back while I peer through his tiny cell window, watching Brandon dangle.

I vibrate, ready and so *not ready* to claw answers from his flesh. "What if—"

"What if I shatter his fucking jaw?" Dutch rumbles. "Good idea. You're so smart, Solly."

I laugh

His unconditional warmth soothes the tension buzzing from my glands.

I'm not afraid of Dutch seeing me work.

I'm not even afraid of learning more hard truths.

I'm afraid of losing my shit in front of the *real* monster.

He doesn't deserve to see me crack.

And I'm starting to realize I don't have to take the risk.

I have *people*.

I have a pack.

Opening our bond until my heart quavers, I show everything to Dutch—the pain from the past and my hope for our future.

His sunshine fades, eclipsed by the deep, deep darkness that drops his voice so low it opens a sinkhole beneath my toes. "My turn to protect you. Okay?"

"Okay." Could I force Brandon to answer faster if I used my perfume?

Obviously.

Instead, I pass my list of pregnancy questions to Dutch.

Then I set him loose.

Brandon always loved watching me hurt.

It's my turn to enjoy the show.

With no blades and no weird torture tools, Dutch kicks the shit out of the bad guy the old-fashioned way.

Bare-knuckled.

Every punch knocks Brandon swinging like a pendulum. Cracking bone. Spraying blood. Straining his wrists against his shackles

My sweetest mate burns with the darkest fury.

Violent.

Beautiful.

Mine forever.

It takes a long time for Dutch to force out the answers I need.

But I'm patient, and I don't look away.

Not even once.

Brandon never notices me peeking from the shadows, and I don't catch one whiff of his woodsy scent.

When Dutch bounces out of the cell, freckled in blood, he beams so bright, a tail-wag thumps my bones. "Solly! Pee tests don't work for gammas. Something about a delay for a protective mechanism. We have to test your glee—or glyco—I don't know. Can't say it, but I wrote it down. We have to test your blood."

Dutch scoops me up, already running. Painting my throat with kisses, glowing with love and justice, he carries me back above ground

I can walk and fight my own battles just fine.

But *why?*

I only pull apart from him to reach my phone and text Lilah.

How soon can you schedule a blood test?

LILAH

For what?

Gamma pregnancy marker

Um. NOW???

Meet me at the clinic

I'd text my pack, but I don't have to.

I feel them.

They're already on their way.

γ

WITHIN TEN MINUTES, I'm sitting on a crinkly exam table, surrounded by my alphas and Wyvern House's entire medical team. Bishop, Reese, Dutch, and Jin crowd so close, the doctor can barely draw my blood.

Lilah squeezes my ankle while Orion squeezes her, and their alphas bark at the army of doctors, techs, and researchers flurrying to test the gamma hormone no one—including me—has ever heard of before.

Lisa and Dany hover bright-eyed, trying not to get in the way, and Wyvern Pack's older generation—Lilah's mercenary fathers-in-law—hover behind them for reasons I don't care to guess.

I feel like a lab rat, a guinea pig, and a fish in a bowl.

When I reach to rub my throat, Jin grips it with a touch that steadies my pulse. "You're not alone."

"Never again." Dutch leans over the back of my exam table, rubbing his chin on my scalp.

Bishop *hums*, busy sterilizing my elbow bend like the needle-prick is a fatal wound.

Reese rocks my other arm, twining our fingers and stroking my hand against his beard. "Doesn't matter what the white coats say."

"It doesn't matter?" I repeat.

Reese nips my knuckle. "You know what I mean. We're a team, Solly Baby."

"How long is this going to take?" When Lilah snags the lead doctor, her pack backs up her scowl.

"Please be patient." The doctor stiffens, her gaze flicking to me for help. "We're breaking new scientific ground."

What else is new?

I wave the woman back to work. "Take your time. I don't want to know anything until you're sure."

From the depths of her alpha-sized hoodie, Lilah puffs up like an irritated cat. "Keep playing calm. I need to know if I'm going to be an auntie."

"I'm not playing." Surrounded by so much love and care, I find myself smiling through the nervous flutter. "And I'm not calm."

I can't imagine what expression I make while the staff tests samples, trades heated whispers, and dances around the clinic, reading out numbers that mean nothing and everything.

I'm just…here

Feeling it all with my pack.

Our bond tangles.

Hope, worry, fear, excitement.

I don't know which is mine and which is theirs. It's all *ours*, and I don't bother trying to hide my share of the swirl.

Finally, the doctor huddles with her team.

One last double-check that stops my breath.

She scurries over, beaming too bright to keep us in suspense. "We tested five times. Five out five results were positive for pregnancy."

A smile I've never felt before blooms from my soul—big, breathless, and totally unstoppable.

I'm kissed and purred and passed around, the bond as chaotic as my pulse.

Holy shit.

Is this really real?

"Solly!" Dutch rubs my belly through the tangle of bodies. "We're gonna have a baby gamma! A whole army of baby gammas!"

"No." I cover his well-meaning hand. "I'm the army."

My kids aren't going to fight.

I don't want them bearing any of my bullshit.

Somewhere between kisses, I lock teary eyes with Lilah.

She nods.

She's the army, too.

Dutch bawls, Reese opens his phone to search for tiny sneakers, and Bish starts harassing the doctors over prenatal supplements. Jin holds me tight, murmuring my name over and over. "Marisol. Marisol Meadows."

Now the world knows that gammas exist.

If there are more of us, I'll find them and fight to keep them free

I'm going to be all the things I never believed I'd get to be.

Most of all, I'm going to be happy.

And I'm going to raise our kids so they know:

Before you existed, you were loved.

Just be yourself.

And do whatever the hell you want.

ALSO BY LOLA ROCK

Pack Darling Part One

Pack Darling Part Two

Pack Darling Extended Ending

(Rock Shop exclusive)

Redfang Royal

FIND PRE-ORDERS AND SIGNED BOOKS IN LOLA'S SHOP:

thelolarock.com/shop

Join Lola's Facebook pack for updates:

http://www.facebook.com/groups/lolarockstars/